Tape

SHORT STORIES FROM THE ASIAN PACIFIC RIM

D1306495

REFLECTIONS IN FICTION

EDITED BY SHARON JEROSKI

Nelson Canada

Published in Canada by
Nelson Canada,
A Division of Thomson Canada Limited
1120 Birchmount Road
Scarborough, Ontario
M1K 5G4

ISBN 0-17-603098-0
Teacher's Guide 0-17-603859-0

Co-ordinating Editor: Jean Stinson
Project Manager/Editor: Lana Kong
Copy Editor: Sandra Manley
Art Director: Lorraine Tuson
Designer: Tracy Walker
Cover Design: Tracy Walker
Cover Illustration: Tomio Nitto
Typesetting: Nelson Canada/Trigraph Inc.

Printed and bound in Canada
by The Alger Press Limited

234567890 / AP / 0987654321

This book is printed on acid-free paper. Nelson Canada is committed to using, within the publishing process, the available resources, technology, and suppliers that are as environmentally friendly as possible.

Canadian Cataloguing in Publication Data

Main entry under title:

Tapestries: short stories from the Asian Pacific rim

ISBN 0-17-603098-0

1. Short stories, East Asian–Translations into
English. 2. Short stories, East Asian (English).
3. Short stories, Southeast Asian–Translations
into English. 4. Short stories, Southeast Asian
(English). 5. Short stories, English–Translations
from foreign languages. 6. English fiction–20th
century. I. Jeroski, Sharon, date.

PL494.T36   1991   895   C91-093534-3

CONTENTS

ONE GOOD TURN

FORCED OUT

THE SILENT TRADERS

Introduction

Tapestries *is a collection of contemporary short stories from the Asia Pacific. These stories (some in translation, some written in English) are drawn from an incredible diversity of peoples, languages, cultures, and religions. While I chose specific selections for their appeal to young adults and their exploration of several key themes that emerged from my reading, I also tried to reflect some of the diversity of the region.*

The short story is a relatively recent genre in most Asian countries, but it quickly has become one of the most popular literary forms. Some of the authors in this collection have established international reputations—for example, the work of the Japanese writers Ryunosuke and Shiga is widely available in English translations. Others, like Srinawk of Thailand and Notosusanto of Indonesia, are known mostly within their own countries.

Stories develop from the experiences, images, and ideas of a writer and are set in a particular place and time. However, authors do not write stories to impart factual information about a culture, a setting, or an event. Rather, their stories invite us to revisit and extend our own experiences through our encounters with their characters and the events and emotions that touch their lives. Readers experience stories by making connections to their own lives. Those who come to know and enjoy fiction from many cultures are rewarded by a deepened understanding of the beliefs and values taken for granted in their own culture and an expanded awareness of the multicultural world that surrounds them.

I like the stories in Tapestries. *I feel a special sympathy for those writers, like Toer of Indonesia and many writers living in the People's Republic of China, who, for political reasons, may have difficulty reaching an audience in their own countries.*

Not all stories met my initial expectations—formed from my experiences with Western literature—about how stories "should" be developed or how characters "should" behave. Reading them has expanded my appreciation of the wonderful variations literature can take. I am grateful for the efforts of the translators, editors, and publishers who make the world's literature available beyond the cultures and languages in which it originates.

Sharon Jeroski

A Note on Pronunciation

In *Tapestries*, the system used to romanize non-English words varies from story to story. As so many different languages are represented, no attempt has been made to impose a single standard. In many cases, the words and names are spelled more or less phonetically according to English pronunciation, often with every vowel sounded. (For example, the name of Japanese author Ryunosuke can be pronounced "Ri-u-no-su-kay.") For other names and words, an approximate pronunciation is provided in square brackets directly after the word appears in the text. Note especially the following vowel sounds.

"a" is pronounced "ah" or "au" as in *automatic*
"ae" or "eh" is pronounced as a short e sound, as in *bet*
"ai" is pronounced as a long i sound, as in *Thailand* and *Taiwan*
"ao" is pronounced "ow" as in *how* or *Chairman Mao*
"i" is pronounced as a long e sound, as in *machine*
"u" or "oo" is often pronounced as in *put* or *foot*
"ui" or "uy" is pronounced somewhat like "oi" but with
    more of an "oo" sound

Consultants and Reviewers

The publishers would like to thank the following people who contributed their valuable expertise during the development of this book:

Dr. Shiu L. Kong, former President of the Ontario Advisory Council on
    Multiculturalism and Citizenship, Toronto, Ont.
Cindy Lam, Intercultural Communications Consultant, Toronto, Ont.
Ken Annandale, Sir Winston Churchill Secondary School, Vancouver, B.C.
Patti Buchanan, McGee Secondary School, Vancouver, B.C.
Julie Davis, Claremont Secondary School, Victoria (Saanich), B.C.
David Fisher, Faculty of Education, Simon Fraser University, Burnaby, B.C.
Peter Johnson, Prince of Wales Mini-school, Vancouver, B.C.
Catherine Mar, Steveston Senior Secondary School, Richmond, B.C.
Nick Mitchell, Leaside High School, Toronto (East York), Ont.
Douglas Payne, Wainwright Public High School, Wainwright, Alta.
Maeve Shrieves, Steveston Senior Secondary School, Richmond, B.C.
Charles Shergold, Arbutus Junior Secondary School, Victoria, B.C.

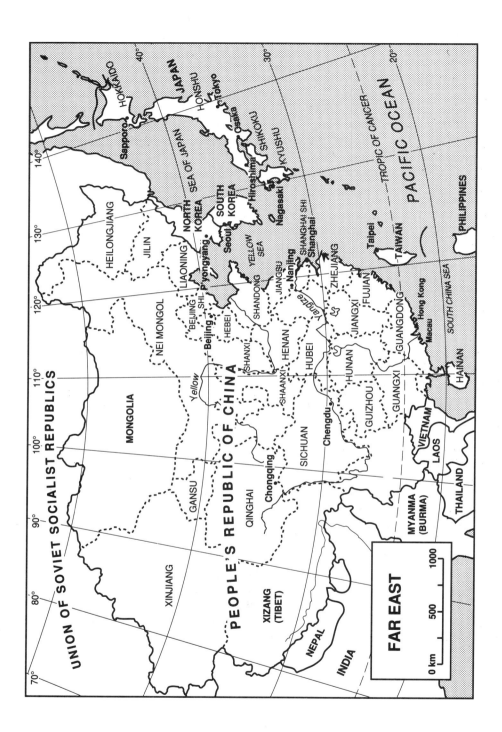

FAR EAST

0 km   500   1000

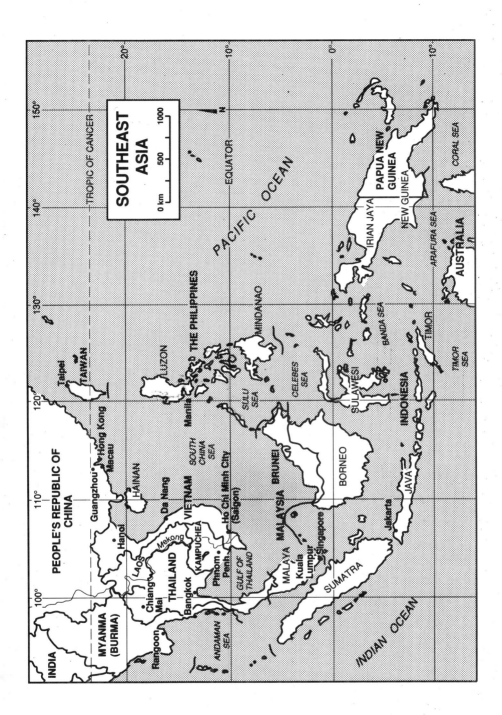

SOUTHEAST ASIA

0 km 500 1000

TROPIC OF CANCER

PEOPLE'S REPUBLIC OF CHINA

INDIA

MYANMA (BURMA)

Rangoon

Chiang Mai

THAILAND

Bangkok

Hanoi

LAOS

Mekong

KAMPUCHEA

Phnom Penh

GULF OF THAILAND

ANDAMAN SEA

VIETNAM

Da Nang

HAINAN

Ho Chi Minh City (Saigon)

SOUTH CHINA SEA

Guangzhou

Hong Kong

Macau

TAIWAN

Taipei

LUZON

Manila

THE PHILIPPINES

MINDANAO

SULU SEA

CELEBES SEA

MALAYSIA

BRUNEI

MALAYA

Kuala Lumpur

Singapore

SUMATRA

BORNEO

SULAWESI

INDONESIA

JAVA

Jakarta

INDIAN OCEAN

PACIFIC OCEAN

EQUATOR

BANDA SEA

TIMOR

TIMOR SEA

IRIAN JAYA

NEW GUINEA

PAPUA NEW GUINEA

CORAL SEA

ARAFURA SEA

AUSTRALIA

20°

10°

0°

10°

150°

140°

130°

120°

110°

100°

9

ONE GOOD TURN

"THE SOUL SO REVEALED . . ."

A market street in Manila,
The Philippines.

The Jade Pendant

BY CATHERINE LIM

Catherine LIM, a native of Singapore and a graduate of the University of Malaya, writes in English and lists Jane Austen, James Thurber, and Alan Paton among the authors she most enjoys.

Her stories frequently deal with the increasingly materialistic society of Singapore which has brought economic and social discrimination to the elderly and the poor. Although she avoids direct moralizing, her sympathies obviously lie with the less fortunate, whom she portrays as often able to overcome wealth and snobbery with cunning. She presents her characters in realistic situations, using natural dialogue, often the variety of English known as "ESM"—the English of Singapore and Malaysia. Her first collection of stories was published in 1978.

"The Jade Pendant" is set in contemporary Singapore, an independent city-state of 2.6 million people.

The Jade Pendant[1] had gathered round it a number of myths, some of which were quite absurd, such as the one that it was worth half-a-million dollars, but the reality was astonishing enough to raise gasps of admiration and envy. The jewel, as big as the palm of a child's hand, consisted of a thick, circular piece of intricately carved jade of the most brilliant and lucid green, surrounded by innumerable diamonds arranged in floral designs. It was to be worn on a chain round the neck, but the sheer weight of the jewel, not to mention the extreme folly of risking loss or theft, had caused it to be little disturbed in its place in the bank vaults. Mrs. Khoo had worn it only twice— once at a banquet given by a sultan—the jewel had been specially flown, under strict security, to the royal town where it made quite a stir, even at a function that glittered with fabulous jewels—and again at the wedding of her nephew. Since then, it had lain safely in the bank vaults, for the myriad weddings and other functions that Mrs. Khoo had subsequently attended were considered too insignificant to justify the presence of this jewel, the like of which nobody had ever seen. But its absence on the broad perfumed bosom of Mrs. Khoo was as likely to provoke comments as its presence: "Ah, you're not wearing the Jade Pendant! That's a disappointment to me, for I had hoped to see it. I've heard so much about it."

To make up for the loss of pleasure that would have been afforded by the sight of the Jade Pendant, Mrs. Khoo would talk about its history—how it had come down to her from her mother who had got it from her own mother, and if its origin was traced far enough, it could be ascertained that the first possessor was a concubine of a Vietnamese emperor of the seventeenth century. Its continuing connections with royalty must be something predestined, for, confided Mrs. Khoo, her mother had once told her that the wife of a sultan who had seen it had actually sent emissaries to begin the task of negotiation and purchase. It was an extremely difficult thing to do, but the persistent royal lady was at last turned down.

The engrossing question had been: to whom would Mrs. Khoo leave the jewel when she died—her daughter-in-law or her daughter? Mrs. Khoo had actually long settled the matter in favour of her daughter. There was nothing she would not do for Lian Kim, her favourite child. Moreover, she would not wait for her death to hand over the jewel—when Lian Kim got married, the gift would be made. The bride would wear the Jade Pendant at the wedding dinner, for every one of the guests to see.

When Lian Kim was home for the holidays with her fiancé, she had insisted on her mother taking the jewel out of the bank for him to see. He was an Art student whom she had met in London, and the wonder on his face and the long whistle of admiration and incredulity as he looked at the Jade Pendant that Lian Kim had laughingly placed on his artist's begrimed sweater, was a small but definite step towards the mollification of his future mother-in-law whose chagrin, when her daughter wrote to her of being engaged to a foreigner, was great indeed. How vexing, she had thought to herself and later said to her husband, although she would not have dared to say the same to her daughter. How vexing to have a daughter married to a foreigner, and a poor one at that. But there was nothing to be done, once the young people of today made up their minds.

Her vexation was increased that day by a very humiliating incident. She had just shown the Jade Pendant to Lian Kim and Ron, and was getting ready to put it back in its case of red velvet, when she heard Ah Soh sweeping outside the room. Upon impulse, she called Ah Soh into the room to view the jewel, thinking afterwards, in the generosity of her heart, that even a humble widowed relative who made cakes and puddings for sale in the streets, could be given the pleasure of looking at the jewel. Ah Soh was all gratitude. She left her broom outside, tiptoed in with a great show of respect and awe, and raised her hands in shrill wonderment even before the box was opened to reveal its treasure. She exclaimed, she praised, she was breathless with the effort of pleasing a rich relative who allowed her and her daughter to live in a room at the back of the great house, to eat the food left on the great table, to benefit by the sale of old clothes, beer bottles, and newspapers.

Unfortunately, Ah Soh's daughter, a simple-minded girl of Lian Kim's age, had ambled in then, looking for her mother; and on seeing the jewel had crowed with childish delight, and actually snatched it up and pranced round the room, shrilly parading it on her chest. The terror of her mother, who had quickly glanced up to see the look of violent disgust and displeasure on the face of Mrs. Khoo, was itself terrifying to behold. She shrieked at the girl, snatched the jewel back, laid it reverently back in its case, and began scolding her erring daughter as vehemently as she could. The insulted pride of the lady, whose countenance had taken on a look of extreme hauteur, was to be mollified by no less than a severe thrashing of the offender, which Ah Soh immediately executed, secret anger against her rich relative lending great strength to her thin scrawny arms. The girl, who looked no more than a child though she was over twenty, whimpered and would have been thrashed sick had not Mrs. Khoo intervened by saying stiffly, "That will do, Ah Soh. Do you want to kill the child?"

"Better for her to be killed than to insult you in this way!" sobbed Ah Soh.

Mrs. Khoo, who found the incident too disgusting to be mentioned to her husband or daughter, soon forgot it. She spent the three weeks of her daughter's vacation home in pleasing the young couple as much as she could. She got the servants to cook all kinds of delicacies, and Ah Soh, anxious to pacify her further, helped as much as she could, endlessly. Whenever she could spare the time from her mah-jong[2], Mrs. Khoo entertained them, not sparing any expense. Mr. Khoo, who doted on his youngest daughter, was even willing to take time off from his gambling and his racehorses to take the couple round and introduce them proudly to his wide circle of friends. Lian Kim and Ron were to be married by the end of the year. "A sad occasion for the mother, ha! ha! Do you know why?" Mr. Khoo would laugh heartily, his round florid face wreathed in smiles. "Because the Jade Pendant will be made over from mother to daughter. Ah, these women and their jewels—" he would then whisper conspiratorially into the ears of his friend, revelling in the look of amazement on the face of the listener.

It would never have occurred to any of their friends to ask Mr. or Mrs. Khoo whether they were thinking of selling the Jade Pendant—it would have been an insult too great to be borne. Yet the possibility had occurred to Mrs. Khoo; and the realization, after some time, that it *would* have to be sold brought a spasm of terror to the lady as she paced about in her room, thinking what a sad state of affairs the family was in financially. The money and the property that had come down to them from their parents and grandparents—

almost all dissipated! Mr. Khoo and his gambling and his horses and entertaining, the expensive education of her two sons and her daughter abroad—they were forever writing home for more money.

The immediate worry was the expense of Lian Kim's wedding. It could not, must not, be on a scale less than the wedding of her elder brother two years ago, or the wedding of the nephew, for that would be a severe loss of family face. Mrs. Khoo made a quick calculation of the cost of the wedding dress and trousseau, specially ordered from a French house of fashion, the furnishings for the new flat in London to be rented by the couple after their marriage, the wedding dinner for at least five hundred people in the Imperial Hotel—where was she to get the money from? She uttered little cries of agitation and wrung her hands in vexation, as she walked about in her room. She had on one occasion represented the difficulties to her husband, but he had only laughed, pinched her cheek, and said, "Now, now, you are always worrying. We are okay, okay, and you go and get whatever you like, old girl." She had not dared to speak of her difficulties to Lian Kim—she could not bear to spoil the happiness of her beloved child.

Once she was tempted to approach Ah Soh to borrow some money—she had heard whispers of the immense sum of money that Ah Soh had slowly accumulated over forty years, money she had saved from her sale of cakes and puddings, and from extreme frugality: Ah Soh made her own cigarettes by rolling the tobacco salvaged from thrown-away cigarette ends in little square pieces of paper, and her simple-minded daughter wore only the cast-off clothes of Lian Kim and other relatives. But Mrs. Khoo had quickly rejected the idea. What, degrade herself by seeking help from a relative who was no better than a servant? Mrs. Khoo's inherent dislike of Ah Soh was increased by her suspicion that behind all that effusive humility and deference was a shrewdness and alertness that saw everything that was going on, and she even fancied that the little frightened-looking eyes in the thin pallid face sometimes laughed at her. After Lian Kim's wedding I shall no longer tolerate her in the house, thought Mrs. Khoo resentfully. She and that imbecile daughter she dotes on so much can pack up and leave.

The thought of the wedding which should have given so much pleasure to her fond mother's heart distressed her, for again and again she wondered where the money was to come from. Their two houses were already mortgaged; the shares would fetch but little. No matter how hard she tried to avoid it, the conclusion she inevitably reached was: the Jade Pendant had to go. The impact of so awesome a decision caused Mrs. Khoo to have a violent headache. The only consolation she could find in so dismal a situation was the thought that nobody need know that the Jade Pendant had been sold, as she could always give some explanation or other for its not being worn at the wedding, whereas if the wedding celebration were to be scaled down, how dreadful a loss of face that would be!

She then went into urgent and secret family consultation in which her husband finally assented to the sale, stressing that they get as good a price for such a jewel as they possibly could. It was not so easy to win her daughter round—Lian Kim fretted excessively about the loss of something she had been promised, and it was only after a great deal of sulking that she would consent to the sale. The prospect of a modest wedding celebration was even more appalling than that of having to do without the Jade Pendant; and of the numerous excuses thought up to account for its absence, she at last settled on this one: that the huge old-fashioned jewel would not go nicely with her Dior gown.

The secrecy with which the sale of the Jade Pendant was to be effected became a matter of first importance. Following the very discreet inquiries about potential buyers, an offer came and with conditions that could not but please Mrs. Khoo—the interested party was a very wealthy lady who made her home in another country, she wanted absolute secrecy in the entire proceeding, she would send round a third person to collect the item. Her offer, moreover, was generous. Insist on cash, said Mr. Khoo. You never know about these so-called rich foreigners. Cash it was, and the Jade Pendant left its place in the bank vaults forever.

With the matter settled, Mrs. Khoo was happy again, and bustled about with the wedding preparations. "My daughter has decided not to wear the Jade Pendant," she told her friends. "Oh, these young people nowadays, they do not appreciate the beautiful things left them by their ancestors, and they are so intolerant of our old ways!" Mrs. Khoo, caught up happily in the whirl of invitations and other preparations, did not, however, forget to tell Ah Soh, but in a kindly voice, "There will be so many guests all dressed grandly and with their jewels, that it is better for you to dress well too. I hope you have bought new clothes for the occasion?" Ah Soh humbly and gratefully assured her that she had.

The wedding dinner and celebration were on a scale as to merit talk for at least the next three days. At least one Minister and three Members of the Parliament, together with numerous business tycoons, were present. Mrs. Khoo moved briskly among the guests, and even in the flutters of maternal anxiety and happiness, had the time to hope that Ah Soh's simple-minded daughter would not do anything to mar the splendour of the occasion. She had wanted, tactfully, to tell Ah Soh not to bring her along, but had decided to be generous and charitable for such an occasion as this—the wedding of her youngest and favourite child.

Her gaze swept briefly over the heads in that large, resplendent, chandeliered room, and rested on a spot in the far corner, where she could easily pick out Ah Soh, decently dressed for once, sitting with her daughter and some relatives. Mrs. Khoo wondered why the gaze, not only of those at that table, but of those from the neighbouring tables, were fixed on the imbecile child—people were positively staring at her, and not only staring, but whispering loudly, urgently, among themselves. The whispering and the staring spread outwards in widening ripples of mounting excitement and tension. Mrs. Khoo made her way towards this focus of tremulous attention, and she too stared—not at the idiot, child-like face but at the jewel that rested awkwardly on the flat, child-like chest. The Jade Pendant! The idiot girl crowed with pleasure, and her mother, who sat very near to her holding her hand affectionately, was nodding to the faces crowding in upon them, the frightened look gone forever from her eyes.

Oh, where is Mr. Khoo? Please do something! shrieked Mrs. Khoo, moving about distractedly, wringing her hands. Oh, what shall we do? How shall we bear it? Lian Kim, she mustn't know, it will kill her to know! And I will kill her for having done this to me! How could she do such a thing to me!

NOTES

[1]Jade symbolizes a pure and benevolent spirit. Among the Chinese, a gift of jade is considered the deepest expression of love and devotion; it is often used as an engagement present.

[2]mah-jong: a game involving both chance and strategy, played by four people who draw and discard tiles of various design, until one player wins with a hand containing four sets of three matching tiles and one set of two

A *Ge*-ware Incense Burner

BY NI KUANG

TRANSLATED BY DON J. COHN

NI Kuang [Nee Kwan] was born in China and, as an idealistic 16-year-old, joined the People's Liberation Army. He was soon branded a "counterrevolutionary" for speaking out about the excesses he saw, and was exiled to a remote area of Mongolia. In 1957 he escaped and made his way to Hong Kong, where his family had settled after fleeing Communist China.

Ni has written so many novels that he says he has lost count. Over half-a-million copies of his books are sold each year, and his newspaper columns are syndicated throughout Asia.

"A Ge-ware Incense Burner" is one of seven stories Ni wrote about "Antiques Alley," a Hong Kong street market where "everything is slightly damaged or incomplete in some way." Connoisseurs haunt the market, hoping to find a priceless antique at bargain prices.

"With a good eye and a bit of luck, you can buy priceless treasures for next to nothing at the most unlikely places in Antiques Alley."

Myths of this nature are fairly common, and there are also a lot of true stories to back them up.

Though there are several hundred stands and shops in Antiques Alley, they are not organized in any way, so there is no reason to suspect that all the proprietors spread such tantalizing rumours. Nonetheless, such rumours have enticed numerous people to test their eye and try their luck in Antiques Alley. Doubtless the idea of acquiring a valuable antique for a song has an almost irresistible appeal.

In the alley there is one rather unique stand that specializes in small ceramics. Instead of laying its wares out on the ground like the other stands, here they are displayed in a glass cabinet, which is something of an antique in its own right, since its framework is made entirely of wood. Ever since aluminum cabinets came into vogue, wooden cabinets like this have become extinct.

The proprietor of this stand is something of a character. He sits on a wooden bench behind his cabinet in exactly the same posture all day long, hardly moving at all, and is exceedingly fond of picking the wax from his ears. As he sits there, keeping watch over his inventory, he works on his ears non-stop, using for the purpose a bamboo ear spoon which is stained a dark maroon from years of handling. First he cleans his left ear, then his right, after which he goes back to his left ear, and so on.

Because of this habit, he never holds his head straight up, and when he tilts it to one side and half-closes his eyes, it's hard to tell if his joy is derived from ear-picking, or from the novelty of watching the world go by at such an odd angle.

Most of the stands in Antiques Alley operate on a self-service basis: customers are free to pick up and examine whatever objects strike their fancy. But because this particular stand is equipped with a glass cabinet, it is impossible to get to the items on display in the front of the cabinet; so if customers wish to examine anything they have to ask the proprietor sitting on his wooden bench to take it out for them. But because the proprietor always seems to be preoccupied with his ears, most customers—unless they are especially eager to buy something—resign themselves to examining the objects through the glass. The proprietor himself never does much in the way of trying to stir up business.

This afternoon, the three of them came once again. I say "again" since they have been coming to this stand for three days running; this was their fourth visit. The proprietor could recall what had taken place the first day. A middle-aged man, who bore all the marks of a connoisseur, had come alone that time. As he passed by the glass cabinet, he stopped dead in his tracks, a strange glimmer in his eyes. Pointing with two fleshy fingers at an item in the case, he said, "I'd like to look at that incense burner with the 'flying' handles."

"Flying" handles is the term used to describe tall, vertical handles on ceramic incense burners. There wasn't a wide selection of items in the cabinet, so the proprietor reached in with one hand and took out the incense burner, which was about the size of his fist, and handed it to the middle-aged man who began to examine it with great care.

While the proprietor gave his ears a workout, the middle-aged man remarked somewhat ironically, "This is a very strange incense burner. It has six feet."

The proprietor responded with a "humph". The middle-aged man said, "What do you call it?"

The proprietor switched his ear spoon from one ear to the other, and said, "It's a Ge-ware[1] incense burner with six feet in a crackling *fenqing*[2] [*fin cheen*] glaze."

The middle-aged man laughed out loud, which instantly drew a small crowd of curiosity seekers around them. Still laughing, the middle-aged man said, "*Ge*-ware? Ha ha! There isn't a dealer on this street who wouldn't make the same claim!"

People who run antiques stands in Antiques Alley generally have a bit more patience than the average person, so the proprietor good-naturedly laughed along with the man. But he never for a moment ceased picking his ears, and it was obvious that his smile and laughter were merely skin-deep.

Though the middle-aged man had made fun of the proprietor, he continued to examine the incense burner quite intensely. "How much do you want for this?" he asked.

For a moment, it seemed, the proprietor actually held his head erect. "Three thousand dollars.[3] No bargaining."

The middle-aged man laughed again, put the incense burner down, and left.

The next day he returned, this time with another man, and together they spent a long time examining the incense burner. Though the middle-aged man had asked this person along to give him advice, everything he said was pure rubbish!

"If it's authentic Ge-ware in *fenqing*, then three thousand dollars is too cheap. Three hundred thousand would be more like it. If it's a fake, though, three thousand is an absurd price; I wouldn't give you three bucks for it."

On the third day, the middle-aged man brought a third person along, whose judgements were somewhat more reasonable. His comment was: "It's only three thousand dollars; if it's a fake, so what? You might as well buy it."

The middle-aged man was hesitant. "I'm not worried about the three thousand dollars," he said. "It's just...you know, if it's a fake, it can be a bit embarrassing. How will I ever live it down?"

He was evidently a noted authority on antiques; otherwise why would he worry so much about damaging his reputation by making a bad purchase?

As usual, the proprietor remained a passive spectator, allowing his customers to make up their minds for themselves. The price had been set at three thousand dollars—no more, no less—regardless of whether the incense burner was real or fake; everything hinged on the price.

Let them take their time, the proprietor thought.

And then today they came for a fourth visit. When the proprietor noticed them approaching, he removed the ceramic incense burner from the cabinet and placed it on the counter.

The middle-aged man picked it up and begain to examine it, as usual. The three of them used a great deal of technical jargon, such as "spur marks" and "dripped glaze." They sounded like real experts.

But when it comes down to distinguishing the genuine from the fake, the greatest expert is in the same boat as the rank amateur.

Ten minutes passed. Then the middle-aged man said, "Please be frank with me. Is this real or is it fake?"

The proprietor replied with a laugh, "You expect a little hole in the wall like this to give you a certificate of authenticity? My friend, you ought to know by now that what counts in buying second-hand goods is a good eye. Look, if you're not sure about it, don't buy it, because if you don't, somebody else will."

These words had the effect of setting the middle-aged man's pants on fire, and he reached into his pocket and took out the three thousand dollars that had been burning a hole there for the past three days. "If you say three thousand, then three thousand it is. I'll take it."

In an unprecedented gesture, the proprietor put down his ear spoon and started to count the three piles of bills the man had handed to him. Before he had finished, however, the middle-aged man interrupted him: "There's a dirty spot here I don't seem to be able to rub off..."

Very casually, the proprietor said, "Don't worry about it. I'll give you another one ...."

For a split second, they all froze, like a freeze shot in a movie.

━━━━━━━━━━

NOTES

[1]*Ge*-ware: ceramic ware

[2]*fenqing*: a pastel green colour characteristic of early Chinese pottery

[3]The Hong Kong dollar is worth about one-fifth of the Canadian dollar.

Bus Ride

BY LIGAYA VICTORIO FRUTO

Ligaya Victorio FRUTO, born in Rizal Province in the Philippines, has been writing short stories in English since 1932. "Ligaya" means "happiness," and her friends believe the name suits her, as she is an innately happy person whose writing, even about the bleakest events, reflects an optimistic outlook.

"Bus Ride" appeared in 1969 in a collection called Yesterday and Other Stories, *where Fruto reminisces about the past, often with an underlying sense of disaster. Her introduction states: "These stories belong to yesterday—the yesterday which was a state of mind and a way of life, filled with a simple idealism that tried to shape a tomorrow."*

"Bus Ride" is set in Manila during the early 1940s.

Lyda [*Lĩda*] watched the blue shining nose of the bus in fascination. Then she poked a finger at the pert tip of her own pretty nose. It isn't powdered, she thought stupidly. Noses shouldn't be shiny. Never allow your nose to get shiny, said a beauty article, if you intend to hold your man. My nose is seldom shiny, she thought in self-pity, and yet here I am losing my man. Hope that girl in his car will sport a shiny nose some time today.

Lyda stamped one foot impatiently. I am beginning to dodder, she thought in a sort of dull rage. Here I am thinking foolish thoughts while a female pirate steals my man away. But perhaps she is just a cousin, or a hitherto undiscovered sister-in-law. Even an aunt. She certainly looked old enough to be his mother.

She saw the bus toot smaller buses out of the way and slide to a stop. She looked at the quivering nose and dusty side. Then quickly, almost without thought, she moved close to the bus, her mind made up. I'll take it, she thought with subdued savagery. I won't wait for his car to pick me up. I'll take this bus and rush home and have a really good mad fit. Let him look for me till the balls of his eyes pop out. I won't give him the satisfaction of lying to me. Not just yet.

She waited with impatience while several passengers fought to get into the bus. Cattle, she thought with disdain. Creatures of instinct. They won't even file in order. How much time they would save if they spent a little more thought on boarding buses.

Once in the bus, she held herself apart from the perspiring crowd. She stood in a small pool of daintiness which the slightly awed passengers conceded her. She looked aloofly towards a desirable seat by a window, and as though her glance had pulled him up, the blue-shirted man with a bundle who occupied it rose and gave it to her. She moved slowly towards the seat and murmured her thanks. She glanced once at the hard seat in doubt, then stepped by the trouser leg withdrawn to let her pass and sank upon the cool wood. Once settled in her seat, she looked out of the window, dismissing the bus crowd.

The city is different, she decided, from a bus seat. Somehow it looks dirtier, more crowded, more impossible to live in. Through a car window, one could regard it with impersonal disdain; one could hold oneself apart from it, secure from its smells and its sounds and its dirty humanity. She was beginning to regret having boarded the bus. Quite an experience, but she could have done without it.

A car—gleaming, magnificent—flowed by, and she turned her face sharply away from the street. There he was, alone this time, an anxious look framed by the windshield. He would never think of glancing up at the bus window, but she kept her face averted just the same. The hurt she had suffered moments before intensified in a fresh pain. You have done it. You have done it to me. How many more times will you do it before—and after—we get married? She recalled the pleasure on his face as he drove beside the laughing girl. The ghost of a girl's gay laughter was like a clean thrust of sound in the bus's stifling air. She would not stand for it, neither now nor later. And she sat rigidly upon her seat, dumb and proud with pain, doubt like an imp gnawing at her breast. And oddly mixed with her exquisite torture was a streak of annoyance because life could go on about her—active, noisy life borne upon bus wheels.

Behind her someone coughed. She sat straight up with disgust. What right had a man with a cough like that to ride in a public conveyance? The cough was repeated, more rackingly this time, and Lyda's irritation expressed itself in a glance of censure flung over her shoulder. He was sick, and not even her glance could summon enough blood to his face to proclaim his embarrassment.

"This cough is so bothersome," he was impelled to explain to the man who sat beside him. "The office doctor says. . ." Here an interrupting cough. "But I cannot rest now. Wife's having a baby this month."

Lyda was shocked speechless. The things people said in buses. There should be a law.

"Same thing happened to a cousin of mine," another voice took up the subject in heavy sympathy. "My cousin took sick when his seventh child was about to be born. Poor fellow. He died two days before the birth of the child."

"Life is so difficult," the first voice sighed, and there was silence for a while.

Other voices, other sounds drifted to Lyda on the heels of his sigh. It was as though the cough had banished a spell which centred her senses solely on herself. She found her consciousness intruded upon with unwelcome frequency. Across the aisle, a group of labourers discussed the war.[1] Their ignorance was like a needle pricking their earnestness, destroying for Lyda the balloons of thought which they flew with such assurance. Lyda was bored. What did she care about war? Her only resentment was that now her veil must come from New York instead of direct from Paris, as had been originally planned.

Two seats ahead of her, a man was talking to another about unions. What unions, she wondered in irritation. Weddings?

"I told you long ago that you were crazy not to join the union." The voice was raised to defeat the heavy purrings of the motor. "The union is the worker's friend, and a friend in need indeed. In companies like ours," the voice was raised further to drown out the tentative response from another, "the union is your life-saver. You need not worry about another job if you had joined when I told you. Let's take your case now. You were kicked out. There would have been investigations. . ."

"There was no good reason." The other voice was sullen. "The cousin of the foreman had gotten married and needed my job."

"That's what I mean. . ."

Lyda played deaf with an effort. I won't listen to soap-box orators, she thought firmly. I won't. Why don't people leave their miseries at home? Tie them to a post like dogs. Feed them, fondle them once they are home. Why carry them about in places where they will merely annoy people who have troubles enough of their own?

And at that thought a fresh flood of self-pity swept over her. She had not known real misery until she had glimpsed that laughing face and heard that airy sound as his car swept by. Perhaps they had driven out to the hills where he and she had gone so often. They had loved the clean fingers of wind which parted their hair as they drove past green slopes and quiet, blossom-bordered lanes. They had known what it was to laugh in the glare of the sun. And those pools of shade by the roadside where they had paused for lovely moments of talk and silence. The snowy tops of flowering weeds that they had passed again and again. Perhaps he had shown *her* those.

Pain sharpened within her and she stirred in her seat. A suffocating smell of gasoline mingled with the human odours which circulated within the hot interior of the bus. Lyda moved closer to the window and exposed her face further to the dust-laden breeze that brushed her cheeks. She looked at the houses which they now passed, filled with wonder that people could live in them. She glimpsed mats and blankets which obviously served as walls, and shuddered at the black dirt which for so many houses was a littered floor. Across the front of one rusty tin hut, faded strips of bunting still clung, a hangover from a forgotten fiesta, like confetti on the face of dilapidation.

The bus gave a sudden jolt, and Lyda heard someone's head bump loudly against the sloping ceiling of the rear end. There was a child's sharp, short scream, and an equally sharp feminine voice which shushed this scream to a whimper. The man who had coughed behind Lyda rose from his seat and proffered his better place to the woman and her child. The woman looked at his pallid face uncertainly, then with a murmur of gratitude transferred herself and her child to the proffered seat.

Lyda looked up the thin length of the man who had offered the seat. He had refused the back seat and stood up to reach for the low beam of the bus ceiling. Lyda thought she saw his slight frame quiver as he sought to steady himself, then he swayed gently to the rhythm of the motor. Oh, well, she dismissed him scornfully, if he must be gallant. . . .

There was a sudden lurch, and Lyda grasped the wood bars of the window to keep from sliding off her seat. She directed an angry glance towards the driver. The fellow had no sense. Why, oh why did she take the bus? What spirit of folly had prompted her to take the bus when she could have ridden in comfort and safety in a taxi? The long ride home was a monotony of discomfort, thanks to her crazy impulsiveness. She looked about her, thoroughly irritated, and somehow the queer sick look of the man who swayed close to her heightened this irritation. Served him right, she thought unfeelingly, as she took in the intent unseeing look upon the almost bloodless face of the man. What on earth could have made him take this evil bus? She hoped savagely that he would not choose this moment to cough. That would be just a little too much.

She looked out of the window once more, noting without pleasure the crowded look of the road. Soon they would be on the provincial road, and there would be less noise and dust. She was a fool not to have waited for his car. She could have hailed him as he passed. By this time she would have been safely home and in the bath, while he smoked cigarette after cigarette on the porch and wondered about her icy remoteness. What could she gain with such tomfoolery as this bus ride? Funny into what discomfort love for a man could goad a woman. She imagined punishments for him while she was punishing herself.

She saw a small bus struggling through a tight space between their bus and a large truck, watching its imprudence without taking in its significance. Then she felt, rather than heard, the sharp grinding of brakes, and a man's weight flung sharply against her. Weak hands strove vainly to cling to something that would hold him away from the dirty floor of the bus. She moved closer to the corner of her seat, her face pale with nausea and horror, as she gingerly tried to lift the thin body off her knees.

"Somebody," she gasped faintly, "somebody, help."

The world was all movement and sound. There were the loud angry words of the driver, the squeals of the women, the indignant voices of the men who had rushed down to examine the trouble. She did not notice when the quarrelling voices lost their edge and softened to shocked pity. She was too stupidly intent on setting her frock to rights and freeing her frame of disgusted shivers. She looked about, pale and helpless, but even the women were not looking at her. They were too intent on a long burden that lately had sprawled against her knee.

There were sounds—too many sounds that made no sense to her. This would happen, this would happen to her. So many other women in the bus and this would happen to her. She felt the last vestiges of her control going. She thought of him and of the girl and of the love like a wounded bird within her. She thought of her beautiful home and her cool garden several minutes away from here.

And then she saw her shoes. With a mounting horror she stared at her once immaculate shoes, only just now beginning to feel the sticky warmth which streaked clear across her feet. She thought, I'm going to be sick. I mustn't be. Not here. I can't bear it here. But the muscles of her eyes refused to move, and she could not turn her gaze away from those horribly smeared shoes. She felt a fine dam loosening within her and the tears long pent were running down her cheeks. There is no one, she sobbed bitterly, no one at all, more miserable than I.

NOTE

[1]During the Second World War, Manila was devastated by the Japanese invasion in 1941 and the Battle of Manila (when Americans liberated the city in 1945).

Man with a Camera

BY ESTRELLA D. ALFON

Estrella D. ALFON (1917–1983) worked as a journalist in Manila. Most of her stories are based on her observations of her own life and of the people she saw around her in Manila.

Alfon's work has a spiritual quality and often deals with the "dark night of the soul." Exploitation is a recurring theme—the loss of innocence experienced by both the exploiter and the exploited. Francisco Arcellano, a leading Filipino writer, described Alfon's stories as compelling, saying, "They make you think of the ancient mariner."

"Man with a Camera" was first published in 1960.

Of all the pictures he had taken of the old beggar, it was the one he had stolen that gave him what he sought. He took the enlarged print out of the solution and looked at it, and a deep surge of pride possessed him over his own work.

Yes, it was all here. The eyes rheumy and bloodshot. The lips curling with disdain. The straggly, unkempt moustache on the upper lip like deeper etchings on a face lined with many wrinkles.

He had posed that beggar in the courtyard of the church. He had tried to entice many expressions from that face. Yet none of the other pictures had come out with the revelations in this one. This one picture he had stolen, before the beggar had noticed him and had seen that he was trying to get a picture. Later, when for a fee, the beggar posed in a corner of the churchyard, attended by all other mendicants and hangers-on that assembled at that particular church, he had tried to beguile the old actor into the poses that are tokens of the beggar trade: the hang-dog look, the outstretched palm. But it was this one picture that showed the beggar for what he was.

If the eyes were indeed the windows to a man's soul, here one shuddered to look into these eyes and see there the soul so revealed. Here was evil reflected in a face.

There were other pictures in his studio. Prints of the beautiful things that his eyes had seen, that his camera had recorded for him. There were details of beauty that his enamoured eyes had tried to show with his camera's help, the beautiful things that made him feel beautiful just to look at them. Skies showing clouds and variations of light in the different aspects of one person's day. The airy branches of lonely trees limned against immense skies. He had sought to express with his pictures the things in his soul, the little moments of quiet and peace and ecstasy he had himself known. How did one without words say the things one wanted to say? He had tried by depicting the veins of a leaf, the dew on a petal, the fleeting remembrance of a heaven left behind seen in a baby's smile. What delight there had been in trying to catch beauty's fleeting moment!

But how different from the feeling of pride that surged through him as he looked at the wet picture he now held up for his own perusal! All the things of beauty I have pictured, he said to himself, were things perhaps only I could see. No one perhaps could really see what I saw, nor react to it the way I reacted. I and my camera tried to depict it, tried to catch it. But this man here, in this portrait of evil, is still in that churchyard, where neither atmosphere of worship, nor propinquity with candle or hyssop, nor hymn, nor prayer can ever change what he has become, here on his face shown like a recorded story: the evil he has known and done, the hate he diffuses against man, the utter lack of regret or resolution.

He hung up the picture with two clips, and then paused to look around at the other pictures on his studio wall. What a hypocrite he had been, when even as he took those other pictures of beauty and loveliness and sweetness and sunshine, he had all the while really been looking for the look of evil, the ugliness in the face of the beggar he had portrayed. He had haunted churchyards and street corners in his search for the look on the face of this beggar.

It had started when he had covered that assignment about the beggar situation with Luisa. She would write, he was to take the pictures. He had not been working for the paper very long, and it was his first assignment with Luisa. She was a name on the paper, a big name. He had noticed the way she worked, the familiarity she affected with stranger or friend, the intense way she searched out facts and figures, and then the whirlwind way she flew at her typewriter, seeming to be actually angry with the typewriter because it couldn't type fast enough for her.

They went, in the course of the assignment, to the social welfare office, had ferreted through the files, and had found several facts that made them laugh because as far as he was concerned it was a confirmation of the things he had suspected. Beggars were a loutish lot, playing on the sympathies of weak persons, unwilling to work, and preferring the easy way: to live by begging.

They had a schedule of hand-out days. On Mondays, they went to the *Hospicio*[1] near the big bridge; on Tuesdays, they were guests of the San Antonio parish in Sampaloc; Wednesday, of course, was the day they went to Baclaran; Thursdays, they could be found early at the Archbishop's Palace; Friday was the day they visited Quiapo; Saturdays were for the Lourdes church in Quezon City and the ladies' associations doles[2] in Paco; Sundays, you'd think they would rest, but that was the day they went to Santo Domingo.[3]

There were other churches, other patios, and, of course, the easy stands at street corners and in restaurants; in a pinch, they went to the social welfare office on San Rafael and bamboozled the investigators with tales of woe and sickness and starvation. But, according to the SWA[4], they refused to go into institutions, or to be employed. Once, when they were rounded up in a campaign to rid the city of beggars, they were taken before a woman judge who lectured the law officers for not having pity. And they ended up getting money from her too.

In the course of their assignment, he and Luisa had sat down at a little pub on a busy street; it was a hot day and they were trying to enjoy a coke. And, inevitably, a beggar approached their table and held out his hand. He was an oldish man, but not thin at all; the arms that stuck out of the white coat he wore with its sleeves cut off were sinewy and firm with flesh. They looked at his palm, then up at his face. Under a dirty, old-fashioned flat straw hat, his face looked lethargic, as though he did not really know too much of what was going on. He had on rubber shoes that looked surprisingly clean. He stood there patiently, holding out his palm to them, without saying anything.

Luisa looked down at his palm again, and then just when the beggar was about to move away, she took a ten-centavo[5] bill from her blouse pocket and gave it to the man, putting it flat on his dirty palm. He looked at the small bill, bowed slightly to Luisa, put away the money, then held out his palm to the man with the camera. The young man's reaction, quick and spontaneous, was to lift his arm as though to brush the beggar away; and the beggar raised his eyebrows at him, shrugged his shoulders, and shuffled away.

"Just you wait now," the cameraman said. "They'll come in droves—the cousins, the wives, the children of that one beggar!"

Indeed, a steady flow of them came, and the cameraman cocked his eyebrows at Luisa and grimaced. They had to escape finally in a taxi.

In a flat voice, he quoted, by rote: "Some of them are professionals who refuse offers to work and do not wish to be committed to welfare associations for the destitute. Investigation reveals that they sometimes make as much as P6 on an ordinary day, and P11[6] on holidays. Some of them own houses; some lend money at interest to other beggars; some are procurers for beggar girls and other prostitutes; most of them steal when there is an opportunity."

"Shut up!" Luisa hissed.

When she did write the article, illustrated with his pictures, they received congratulations from the social welfare office and other charities. The article had ended with a warning to the citizen that to drop a coin or a bill into a beggar's hand was to abet a practice that was an eye-sore to the city, a disgrace to the country, and encouragement to parasites. His pictures had shown several lines of beggars in churchyards identifiable by the spires. Some faces in some lines were identifiable as the same faces in other lines in other churchyards. There were other pictures he had not used—of a blind man and a blind woman with their children. His mind had been filled with the obscene as he took that picture. Blind, yet they had children. And the children begged on the streets, and their conversations with their parents—he had overheard them—had filled his mind with angry shame.

There were other pictures, too, of children with sly faces, trained to whine, trained to pander, silent at their begging trade except for the expertly piteous wail; but when they talked, off guard as it were, the things they said had made his flesh crawl.

And yet Luisa would not stop that special habit she had of giving pennies to beggars. The few times they had been thrown together, how ready she was to reach in her bag and dole out her coins to any outstretched palm. "Look," he said to her, "if and when you and I should ever need coins, can you imagine us holding out our palms and begging?"

"Of course not!"

"Sure, we have to work at it. Sweat at it. Then why are you so soft with them?"

"Look," she had pointed out to him, "it is my coin, isn't it? You keep your coin if you want, and let me dole out my coins if I want. Agreed?"

But he had seen too much of what he couldn't talk to her about. He tried to tell her about it, but she just turned from him, saying, "I've been around too, kid. Don't tell me."

"Then why cater to them?" he said. "What makes you such a sucker for every begging hand?"

"Let's put it this way," she said. "Maybe I am happy that they are begging from me, that I am not the one begging from them. Will you accept that?"

You could not, in the end, argue with a woman who seemed to know more than you did, yet did foolish things because she liked to.

The picture was for her. He'd show it to her.

She stood it on her desk after she had unwrapped it. She looked long and quietly.

"There's your beggar," he said. "Look at that face. Look at the history of evil on that face! If he would tell me his life story, he would tell me he has done everything, broken every one of God's commandments. Look! You've probably given him your share of pennies. With those pennies he has probably enticed some young beggar girl to an assignation. Maybe he has been able to buy some bread with which he has lured some other beggar into adding to her own sins, somewhere, in one of the churchyards they are always defiling!"

Luisa looked up at him. She stopped his hysterical tirade to ask, "You know this man?"

"Me? No!"

"Then why do you hate him so?"

When the photo exhibition was announced, he knew he would win the portrait group with his beggar picture. No one could resist the impact of that look; that recognizable tracing of a man's life lived every wrong way. It was only Luisa who had ever kept quiet in front of that picture. All the others saw in it what he saw, and praised him for capturing a soul in deshabille.

The prize for winning was a cheque for P500. As soon as he received it, he gave it with some ceremony, recorded by cameras for tomorrow's papers, to his wife. A funny little thing happened to him as he handed her the cheque. His wife was big with child. The cameras, for a change, were trained on him, and they were asked to hold that pose, he giving his cheque to his wife, and she opening her palm to receive it. There it was recorded, the flash bulbs had flared. Then a little thought came to him. There was a reminiscent air to the act of his handing over the cheque, his wife's opening her palm to receive it. And he thought to himself: Luisa. Then the moment was over; his wife left him to enjoy the drink on which he and a host of other photographers hoped to get drunk that night.

And then, disturbed that he should be thinking of Luisa, he had stood at the door of the studio where the exhibition was being held, and he had seen a beggar looking at the huge blown-up photograph of his which had won the prize. He tapped the old man on the shoulder: "Do you like yourself?"

The old man looked at him. How long had he been standing there? Had he seen how he looked? Had he himself been appalled by the look of evil there on his portrait, for all the world to see, for all the world to read?

The beggar had thrown a single expletive at him. The beggar said: "Thief!"

What had he stolen? But the word made him think even more strongly of Luisa.

What had Luisa said? "Do you know him? Why do you hate him?"

The other photographers came out; they recognized the beggar and they laughed at him and made him angry; and the angrier he got, the more he looked like his portrait. But he was not violently angry, just shaken inside him, just disturbed. You could see that by the way he did not speak. Then after a while one of them noticed he was crying.

"Look," they said, "he is crying." They thought it was another trick, that he was just putting on a new act. So they started a collection of what money they could spare, and they put it in a paper bag. They gave it to the beggar and they praised him for being handy with his tears, and they left him on the sidewalk, clutching his paper bag.

The photographer himself felt good. He was only twenty-nine, he had just won a prize, and he felt he was going places. Except for a disturbing thought about Luisa that he didn't want to pursue, he felt he was not such a bad fellow and was entitled to get drunk.

Drunk, he looked out again and saw, as in a haze, the same beggar looking at himself—still ludicrously clutching his paper bag. How old was that beggar? He should ask. But he was too drunk to ask; besides, what the hell, the old scrounger seemed such a kill-joy. How queer. That beggar—oh! that beggar!—was looking at himself, and crying!

NOTES

[1]A *Hospicio* is a place of refuge kept by a religious order. Religion plays an important part in the daily life of the Philippines, the only Christian nation in Asia. Over 80% of Filipinos are Catholic, largely a result of 300 years under Spanish rule.

[2]doles: hand-outs or charitable gifts

[3]The places named are districts and parishes in Metro Manila, including the suburb of Quezon City.

[4]SWA: Social Welfare Association

[5]A centavo is worth one-hundredth of a peso.

[6]P6, P11: one Filipino peso is worth about Canadian $0.04

One Good Turn

BY PENSRI KIENGSIRI

TRANSLATED BY JENNIFER DRASKAU

Pensri KIENGSIRI, who also writes under the pen name of Narawadee, is a popular Thai author who has written film scripts, television serials, novels, and magazine serials. Her stories are often based on memories of her childhood in southern Thailand. She is noted for her matter-of-fact humour and close attention to detail.

"One Good Turn" is set in Bangkok, the capital of Thailand, which the Thais call "the City of Angels." It is home to over six million people.

It should have been the end of the rains. Still the sky lay sullen and soggy over Bangkok, bruised black and blue and full of moisture like a rotting fruit. The wet days were not yet over.

Greyness wrapped the city in a shroud of slumber. At Chakravat, on the banks of the Menam, the ships were ready at the pier; there was nothing to stop them loading the rattan and the tins of pig lard. Back and forth, from truck to ship, coolies trudged. The rain had not seeped into the dry tinder of their uncomplicated spirits. Most of them were grinning at nothing in particular.

Chalong, like most Thais, was as happy-go-lucky as the next man. By eleven o'clock, he decided that he had worked quite enough for one day. It didn't do to overdo things. With forty baht[1] in his pocket, he felt he had earned a rest and a brief look at the rest of the world and its ways. One hand in his pocket, rubbing the twenty-baht notes against each other, he strolled along Chakravat Road whistling the latest hit tune. Forty baht...some two American dollars...endless possibilities opened before him.

He would start his spree by treating himself to a cup of coffee and a couple of penny buns at the first rarn cafair[2] he came to. The thought of the hot coffee was warming. He did not even notice that his blue shorts were sopping and the rough shirt was sticking to his shoulders. In any case, his big muscular carcass had stood up to a sight heavier rain than this—for twenty-eight seasons, man and boy. It had never given the least sign of playing him up. No reason why it should begin to do so now.

At the sight of the coffee shop a grin sliced his brown face like a melon. He started across the street toward it.

The squeal of brakes made him jump.

"May the plague eat you! Is it deaf you are, or blind?"

The voice was hot with anger, cold with scorn. Chalong, the blood rushing to his face, glared at the dapper figure at the wheel of the expensive lime-green car. Just as high-class Thais prided themselves on their courtesy and elegance of speech, Chalong the coolie delighted in his quick temper and sharp tongue. He swore volubly.

"May lightning strike you! Think because you own a car you own the whole road? Think that in the pouring rain a man without cover should stand back and let a man sitting in comfort pass by first? Think you can go about—"

The car door slammed. The driver stood in the road glaring up at Chalong. He was in his early thirties, well-dressed, short, but powerful for a man who was rich and did not need a coolie's muscles. The two men faced each other with clenched fists. A gaggle of urchins abandoned the puddles and water spouts of the rain-driven street for the more exciting prospect of a fight. They closed in a ring. They hoped the coolie would give the rich motorist a proper thrashing.

"Go on—you were about to say?" said the motorist with calculated irritation. He could afford to sneer, with a name like Nicomb Surasak, a name that breathed wealth and respect in the neighbourhood; it made him shiver with rage that there could be any living creature within range of his prosperity that did not recognize his consequence. Not to mention so mean a thing as this scarecrow from the docks.

Chalong had a certain talent for exasperating people. At the moment he was exploiting it for all it was worth.

"Can't be bothered," he said.

"What the devil d'you mean, you can't be bothered?" screamed Nicomb. His face went through a bewildering spectrum of every permutation from brown to scarlet.

"Can't be bothered to belt a little runt like you," said Chalong.

Nicomb's face changed from scarlet to purple. His rage made him oblivious to everything around him. He was holding up the traffic; from the honking queue, drivers began to wander up to see what had happened. Every second he stood haranguing a coolie in a public street, the gold was being chipped from Nicomb's halo of respectability. Already the urchins had set up a gleeful clapping, hoping to see him make a display of himself. Nicomb obliged. He lunged out, aiming wildly at Chalong's chin. The coolie ducked, nimble as an ape, and leapt on him like a wildcat. The children set up a hullabaloo. One of them ran into the nearest shop and grabbed a kerosene can. He set up a deafening drumming. Others yelled "*Ow-Kao-Pai! Ow-Kao-Pai!* Go on! Go on!"

The policeman who stopped the fun found Chalong with a bloody mouth and Nicomb with a black eye. But the policeman bowed low to Nicomb, whom he recognized. Nicomb drove away, the hurt from his wounded face and dignity somewhat allayed. The policeman, with a nice sense of propriety, had asked him not to take any further action against the Silly Monkey.

Chalong knew the policeman too. They had often smiled at each other, but there had never been any need to speak before. Chalong, when he spoke now, was peevish.

"What did you want to call me a silly monkey for?" he grumbled. "His fault, just as much as mine. Ought to have taken our names and given us a summons to court, done things a bit proper."

"Come off it," said the policeman cheerfully. "You know Nicomb's got influence—and a younger brother a captain in Chakravat Court. Besides, it's time for me to go off duty—and I'm hungry." He tapped Chalong's shoulder and grinned to show there were no ill feelings.

"Doesn't mean he was in the right of it," said Chalong. "You should call him a name too."

The policeman threw both arms in the air.

"What shall I call him?" he asked.

One of the children, who felt cheated at the fight's abrupt close just when he had settled down on a boulder to enjoy it, shouted "Call him a Stupid Ape!"

"All right," said the policeman affably, "he's a Stupid Ape. Satisfied?"

Chalong was staring sullenly at the steam rising from his coffee cup. He would have to wait for the sting of his burst lip to wear off before he ventured a sip. Tired of watching the steam and the stodgy buns, he let his eyes roam the shop in search of distraction. They stopped travelling sideways and swooped up and down when they reached the figure of a young woman. She had a little girl in her arms. Round the child's huddled back she was stretching out an empty milk tin for the charitable to drop coins in.

All right, so she was a beggar—but did she really need to drag the kid along in this downpour? It only looked about a year old, poor little scrap—it looked like a rag doll.

"Get the hell out of here! I'm sick to death of you beggars." The shopkeeper's voice was harsh. Chalong, with surprise, felt a twitch of pain in his chest as though his heart had moved.

He could just hear the beggar girl's voice. It was shaking. "Please help me. My baby's sick. It's not had milk or rice for two days."

"You got plenty of milk for it under your blouse, by the look of things," leered one of the shop's patrons. The other customers sniggered.

The girl dropped her chin and walked away. The baby began to whimper. Chalong rose to his feet and stood in their way.

"Come and have a bite to eat," he said.

She looked up at him. There were tears in her eyes. If she had not had that beaten look, like a thrashed puppy, she would have been a beauty, he saw to his own amazement. He swallowed hard.

"Come on, then," he said.

"I'm not going back in there," she said.

"They won't say anything now—come on, before your kid passes out with cold and hunger," said Chalong.

"If she dies, I'll die with her. Perhaps it would be better if I did—if we both did," she said. A tear splashed on the baby's hand.

Chalong sat for twenty minutes watching the girl stuff the baby with soft noodles. Every so often she gulped a spoonful herself. When he could bear it no longer he ordered another portion for himself. When she could eat no more, she put her folded hands to the level of her nose and bowed her head to him in thanks. "How can I thank you?" she said. "It is not true that the rich are kinder than the poor."

Chalong's thoughts were directed to practical matters. "Where's your husband?" he asked.

"Oh, him!" she said. "I don't want to talk about him."

"Where do you live?"

"Nowhere and everywhere. I ask shelter in the temples. The monks treat me kindly."

Chalong looked at her through narrowed eyes. "You're not a Bangkok girl," he said. Her dark eyes widened in surprise. "How do you know that?"

Suddenly he liked her very much. She had become more than an act of pride and charity, because a rich man had bested him. Spending his cash had given him his stature back. Now his protégée had become a person instead of a symbol.

"It is always Northern girls who are deceived by Bangkok men," she said. Her voice was small.

"You must be from Chiang Mai, where all the prettiest girls come from," he said. He would not press her further about the husband. He did not like her eyes with that look in them.

"Yes, I'm from Chiang Mai." She stood up. "We must go. You have been very kind." Chalong could not bear her going—but had no idea how to stop her. Awkwardly he fished out his forty baht and pushed it into her hand.

"I can't take it. You aren't rich. You can't afford to give me money!"

"If the kid wasn't sick I might only drop a couple of baht in your milk tin. But that kid needs a doctor if you ask me."

She took the money. Through her tears, her dark Northern eyes were smiling as she turned away.

Chalong returned to the contemplation of his coffee. It had long stopped steaming but he made no move to drink it. He was beaming. His eyes stared at the shop wall without seeing it. He did not focus them even when the harsh-voiced shopkeeper came between him and the wall.

"Eight baht altogether," said the shopkeeper.

"I'll sign for it," said Chalong.

"Sign for it? That's a good one!" bawled the shopkeeper. "You?"

"Yes, me," said the coolie, rising to his full height.

"You can bet you're not signing for anything—not on your life!" said the shopkeeper. He appealed to the multitude. "Comes in here—I don't know his face from a monkey's—wants to sign for things! Cash on the nail—and look sharp!"

"If you let me sign for it, I shall," said Chalong with dignity, "be a constant patron of your esteemed establishment."

"Throws all his money around treating beggar women and now he wants to owe *me*!" said the shopkeeper. "Expects me to trust him for eight baht!"

"Then I *won't* sign for it. But you'll still have to trust me. I'll go back down the pier and earn a bit more—I'll come back and pay you later."

"You'll pay me now, you will—and you won't go down the pier before I've seen the colour of your money!"

Chalong took a deep breath. His chest blew up like a stone fish. He began to roll up his sleeves.

"Come and get it, then," he said casually over his shoulder.

The little shopkeeper sighed. His bald head glistened dispiritedly.

He trotted to a drawer and brought back a corner of paper and a leaky biro. "Go on then, sign for it," he said hoarsely.

Chalong scratched the earth with his toe. "No good bringing me a pen," he said softly.

"What do you want, then?" said the shopkeeper in exasperation.

"A stamp-pad. I'll have to give you my thumbprint."

The little man gasped. "Well, would you believe it!" he said. "The clod doesn't even know how to write his own name!"

True to his word, Chalong the coolie became a constant patron of the esteemed establishment of Mr. Sang, the coffee-shop owner. Before two weeks had passed he had also become a friend. Sang was no fool. He had at an early stage in their friendship made Chalong promise never again to dish out his savings for the sake of a pair of pretty eyes—no matter what hard-luck story might be hidden in their lustrous depths. Chalong, whose heart was as capacious as his cash was modest, had extracted from the flinty Sang a solemn oath that never again would a beggar be insulted or turned away from the doors of the Esteemed Establishment. Failing this, Chalong had promised that he would personally call his friend Sang the dirtiest names that the moment suggested to his fertile and inventive brain.

But even after two weeks, Chalong was still mooning about the dark-eyed Northern girl and the baby. He knew, of course, that there were scores of unsophisticated Northern girls who were an easy prey for lusty young businessmen from the capital. In shoals these pathetic—and often pregnant—innocents invaded the capital in vain hopes of finding their men.

"If I ever met her again, and if she's willing, damn me if I don't go and marry her," said Chalong, sipping his black coffee.

"More fool you!" hissed Sang. Chalong sat up and rubbed his eyes. As if in answer to his thoughts, the beggar walked in. But she was clean, appetizing, even coquettish in her long green *pa-sin*[3], and a white lacy blouse. Her feet were shod in white sandals—he drew in a sharp whistling breath at the daintiness of them—and her hair had been washed and coiled in a rich bun. In her ears rings jingled.

"Khun Chalong!" she said.

"She remembers my name," he thought. His heart contracted with pain. Her new situation had spirited her out of his reach for ever.

"Khun Chalong," she repeated the name with the honourable title before it as a sign of respect.

"My husband and I want to thank you," she said. "We are so grateful. I feel sure your kindness saved the baby's life. If you had not helped us she would have died. Now I am with my husband. He is very affectionate to us both. Our happiness is due to you."

"Well—that's nice to know." His voice was thin and shaky. He could hardly recognize it. Pain had diluted it.

"My husband was on his way to Chiang Mai to collect us many times, but his business was pressing—and then his mother died."

"Yes, yes—you must forgive him—he must be an important man," said Chalong. "What is his name?"

The girl laughed. He had never heard her laugh before, but he had seen her blush—the way she was blushing now. Like a chumpoo[4] fruit ripening. "You will know in a second—he is coming to see you. He wants to thank you in person."

"Where is he now?"

"Looking for a place to park. Parking spaces are so hard to find even for men with influence."

"How did you know I'd be here?" said Chalong. He was trying not to look too hard at her lovely face. He was staring at her neck. That was almost as bad. With an effort he turned his eyes away and looked at the doorway.

"I didn't know. I just hoped," she said. "This is the fifth time my husband and I have been here to find you."

"Sang never told me."

"We asked him not to."

"Why?"

"Because we were afraid you might not want to see us."

Chalong was about to protest. But he knew she was right. He stood up.

"Well, I think I'll be getting along. I wish you and yours all the best."

She put a hand out to him. "Please don't go yet. Look—this is a cheque from my husband. Please don't be angry—we didn't know any other way of showing you how grateful we are."

Chalong swept his eyes along the paper she held out. Before he pushed it back at her his heart leapt treacherously when he saw the figure ten thousand.

"No!" he cried. "I've got to be getting along now—"

"Oh, please—please take it." She had those tears in her eyes again. "Please don't be angry—you gave us your last baht—you, just a coolie! Imagine how ashamed my husband will be if he hears you wouldn't accept! The reward is perhaps too small?"

"I don't want any reward!" shouted Chalong. Suddenly he was bellowing. Behind the counter, Sang clicked his teeth disapprovingly.

"Oh, I used the wrong word again!" she said. The tears began again, and there were tears in his heart, inside, at the sight of them. He brushed past her. At the door he bumped into a man, and stood aside, with the custom of generations, to let the other pass.

The man gaped up at him. "Here comes my husband! Please don't go without talking to him!" She was dabbing at her eyes with a very ornamental but ineffectual handkerchief. Chalong stared down into the face, now neither scarlet nor purple but a more moderate hue of golden tan, of the Stupid Ape. "You!" Chalong's voice was almost a shriek.

Nicomb was humble. He was very humble. He almost grovelled. He knew, of course, they all knew. There were certain debts that cannot be repaid even between friends. While between enemies...Nicomb's palms met in the respectful *wai*[5] greeting. He presented the coolie with a humble view of the top of his bowed head.

Between the two thunderstruck men the pretty, prattling girl stepped. With a bird-like, questing delicate thumb, a mere graceful twitch, she slipped the ten-thousand-baht cheque into Chalong's shirt pocket. Nicomb's cheque. A wave of pleasure washed over him. He made no move to pluck the cheque forth, to brandish or renounce or return it. With tenderness he studied the girl's face, with a sweetness of expression he turned his eyes to Nicomb. Damn him, the fellow was starting to turn purple again! He must have bad circulation like all the idle rich!

"Whoopee!" said Chalong. "I won't have to work for a year!"

NOTES

[1] The baht is a Thai unit of currency.

[2] rarn cafair: a coffee-shop, usually consisting of a few wooden benches or tin chairs around a table

[3] pa-sin: a sarong-like lower garment worn by Thai women

[4] chumpoo: a flowering tree of the rose-apple family

[5] *wai*: a Thai greeting where the palms are pressed together and lifted to the base of the nose, the forehead, etc., to show varying degrees of respect or reverence for the person addressed

FORCED OUT

"THEY FELT NO BITTERNESS . . ."

Temple dancers of Bali, Indonesia.

Friends

BY WANG ANYI

TRANSLATED BY NANCY LEE

WANG Anyi [Wong An-yi] was born in 1954. At age 16, her education was interrupted during the Cultural Revolution (1966–1976), a highly repressive period when most intellectuals, students, and artists were persecuted and sent to the countryside to labour as a form of "re-education." Wang was assigned to a performing arts troupe on a rural commune in the poverty-stricken northern province of Jiangsu. Eight years later, she was allowed to rejoin her family in Shanghai and work as the editor of a children's magazine.

In her stories and novels, Wang tries to explore the difficulties women face in life, and concludes: "Women are born to suffer and to be lonely, patient, and humble. Glory always belongs to men; magnanimity is a male attribute. Would you believe me if I told you that through their endurance of loneliness and hardships, women may have long surpassed men in terms of human nature?"

"Friends" is set in a large city in the Republic of China.

1

Qiaoqiao [*Jiow-jiow*] was all alone at home, playing house with her rag dolls; but after a while she was bored. She read a children's book and soon finished it. She leaned against the window sill and looked around. Today was so wonderful. Early in the morning a big truck came and drove right into the garden and stopped at her window. Pretty soon, two strong ropes were hung from the windows on the third floor. A long sofa went up first, then a big bookcase—Qiaoqiao's little head busily inclined upward and bent downward. She wished she could go out and take a look. However, Aunt Ah Bao would not even let her go downstairs. She explained that a new family had just moved into the third floor, and with so much stuff being pushed around she might get hit. Qiaoqiao could only kneel on the chair and lean against the window. All at once her eyes brightened. Toot toot. . . The truck was here again. A few people stepped out; so did a little boy.

This was the new tenant on the third floor.

2

As Qiaoqiao leaned against the window looking out, she suddenly saw that beyond the iron gate in the garden there was a little figure running fast which then darted inside. Hey, wasn't that the little boy who had just moved in? Qiaoqiao quickly climbed down from the chair and left the room. The door was opened a crack. Sure enough, that little boy ran panting upstairs, turning his head often as if someone were chasing him. But when he came to the landing he stopped.

"Hi, who are you?" he asked in a hoarse voice.

"Who are you?" Qiaoqiao asked quietly and timidly.

"I'm Gu Pan [*Goo Bun*]."

"I'm Qiaoqiao."

"What are you doing?"

"What are you doing?"

"I was playing in nursery school. It was no fun, so I came home."

"They'll come to get you." Qiaoqiao was rather worried.

"I'm not scared." He really did not care.

"I've been to nursery school too. I didn't like it either. But I wouldn't dare to run away. I'm afraid."

"You're a baby," Gu Pan said contemptuously. "You come to play at our house."

"Aunt Ah Bao won't let me go out."

"Who's Aunt Ah Bao?"

"She belongs to our family. She cooks and washes the clothes and takes care of me."

"Is she mean?"

"Not really," Qiaoqiao replied, after thinking a moment.

"Then let me come to play at your house," he suddenly decided; and without Qiaoqiao's consent, he pushed the door open.

3

"Little boss, what are you doing in my house?" Aunt Ah Bao clapped her hands and stood up. She thrust out her two arms to shove Gu Pan away.

"I've come to play with Qiaoqiao." Gu Pan calmly sneaked in under her elbow.

"You don't go to nursery school; instead, you come here to give us trouble."

"None of your business," Gu Pan replied.

Qiaoqiao, who really worshipped Gu Pan now, also said, "None of your business."

"I'm going to tell your granny." Aunt Ah Bao wiped her hands on her apron and went out.

Gu Pan stared at her back. "I don't care even if you call the People's Police," he answered.

"I'm not afraid either," said Qiaoqiao.

Gu Pan glanced about the room: "Let's play train."

"Fine," Qiaoqiao said obediently, although she did not know how to play train.

"Bring chairs," ordered Gu Pan.

"Bring chairs," Qiaoqiao repeated.

A long line of chairs was set up. Gu Pan straddled the front one and said, "Get on board."

"I'll bring my dolly to the train too, all right?"

"Fine, you'll be mommy."

"Who is daddy?"

"Might as well be me," Gu Pan said impatiently. Straightening his body he yelled, "Ooooooo..."

The "Ooooooo" sound had not yet stopped when Aunt Ah Bao and an old lady with small feet darted into the room and charged toward Gu Pan. Gu Pan's grandmother grabbed his arm:

"Darn little devil, how did you get here? Did you cross the street by yourself? Go back right away!"

"I won't go. Don't feel like going back."

"Go back! There's nobody to take care of you at home. Nobody will feed you."

"I don't care. I won't eat. I am not going back." Gu Pan struggled in her grasp.

"No way. Auntie, help me get him."

Aunt Ah Bao had been waiting for this. She came forward and grabbed Gu Pan's other arm.

"I won't go. Just won't go," Gu Pan shouted, his body slumping; however, he had already been dragged outside the door. He stamped his feet, kicked wildly, and then cried loudly. Whether Qiaoqiao was frightened by his courage and stubbornness or moved, she suddenly sobbed and moaned. While Granny and Aunt Ah Bao were stunned by all the commotion, Gu Pan struggled free, went back to the "train," raised his hoarse voice, and cried with gusto.

4

"This kind of make-believe cooking is no fun," Gu Pan said, scornfully pushing away the pan and spilling all the little twigs inside. Qiaoqiao was not angry. She picked them up one by one and carefully stir-fried them with a spatula.

"How about cooking the real thing?" Gu Pan suddenly had an idea.

"Real cooking?" Qiaoqiao did not quite understand.

Now Gu Pan was excited by his own idea. He busily put all the kitchen utensils in a basket and handed it to Qiaoqiao. "You wait for me in the garden. I'm going to steal some rice." Then he swiftly darted out. Since the day he had run away from nursery school, Gu Pan and Qiaoqiao had been playing together with the consent of the mothers. He was happy, Qiaoqiao was happy; only Aunt Ah Bao was not pleased. She always called Gu Pan "little boss." This time when she saw Qiaoqiao sneaking downstairs she scolded, "Don't be tricked by a crook."

Qiaoqiao rolled her eyes and grunted, "Never you mind." She went downstairs anyway. Then Gu Pan came. From his pocket he fetched out a handful of rice, some vegetables, and a box of matches.

"Let's cook a rice-vegetable casserole," he said.

They began busily—washing rice, pouring water, cleaning and cutting vegetables. The most difficult thing was lighting a fire. A spark of fire was ignited in the portable stove but it went out right away. Half the box of matches was soon used up. Gu Pan lay flat on the ground with his face close to the stove.

"Gone again," Qiaoqiao said, discouraged.

"If it's gone, we'll light it again. We'll do it right." Gu Pan's voice sounded as if it came from the underground, but one could still sense his confidence when he said, "You'd better bring some paper over."

After a while, then even a while longer, all the wastepaper in the yard was picked up. Gu Pan said, "You go upstairs to get some more paper."

"I won't." Qiaoqiao hesitated. "Aunt Ah Bao won't let me come down."

"Oh, you baby!" Gu Pan was really contemptuous. He got up, opened the lid of the pan, put in a finger as a test, and said, "Hot. Ready to eat."

Qiaoqiao was very happy. She busily dished out the rice into two small bowls; then the two sat down facing each other and ate.

But it was raw! The water hadn't boiled; the rice was raw and so were the vegetables. Qiaoqiao felt like spitting the stuff out, but she didn't dare. She chewed hard with tears swelling in her eyes. Gu Pan also thought the food awful; he couldn't even distinguish the taste. However, they both smiled and said, "Pretty good, pretty good."

"Hee, hee," suddenly someone laughed.

Qiaoqiao and Gu Pan were scared for a moment. Turning around they saw an eight- or nine-year-old kid climbing on top of the fence. "Some wild little bum from the next alley," Qiaoqiao told Gu Pan quietly.

"Are you two living a married life?"

"Let's go inside." Qiaoqiao timidly shoved Gu Pan.

"None of your business, you little bum," Gu Pan, unyielding, replied.

"Wild little bum, you get away. I'm going to hit your head," said Aunt Ah Bao, flourishing a bamboo stick from the second floor window. The child slid down from the fence.

"What is 'married'?" Qiaoqiao asked Gu Pan.

"Married? That means love." Gu Pan was one year older. He had seen some real movies, so naturally he understood more.

"What is 'love'?" Qiaoqiao kept on with her questions.

"Love? That means two people really feel nice about each other." He thought for a moment. "Are you willing to love me?"

Qiaqiao nodded.

"Same here," Gu Pan said.

"We will always feel nice about each other?"

"Of course!" Gu Pan answered firmly. They both felt very happy, very contented.

5

Gu Pan and Qiaoqiao played every day. They played house, sat in the "train," fought battles, read children's books, and told stories; but just playing began to bore Gu Pan. He suddenly did not want to play anything: "No fun. Our nursery school has big blocks you can build with on the floor. Once Diandian and I built a whole battleship." Qiaoqiao opened her eyes wide and stared at Gu Pan. He continued, "There was also Guo Bin. He can do a somersault very well. Once we did it together; that was really fun."

"Uhm."

"We took naps. Everybody slept on the floor. Real neat. Wang Chuchu [Wong Juju] put his feet into my blanket and made me laugh. Nursery school is really fun."

"Then why did you run away?" Qiaoqiao asked.

Gu Pan gave a start. After thinking for a minute he answered, "Teachers always pick on me. They say I make too much trouble."

"You aren't afraid of the teachers, are you?" Qiaoqiao asked.

"Of course not. I'm going to nursery school this afternoon. I'm going to tell Granny." Gu Pan was leaving as he talked. At the door he waited for a moment, hoping Qiaoqiao would say, "Don't go."

But Qiaoqiao replied stubbornly, "You go ahead. It's none of my business."

When Gu Pan left, they both felt sorry. After the nap in the afternoon Gu Pan came again. The moment he entered the door he said, "My granny said I would be in elementary school in six months, so I'm not going to nursery school."

Qiaoqiao was happy to see him. She had already forgotten about the unpleasantness of the morning.

Gu Pan took two cents from his pocket. "Granny gave me these," he said. "Let's buy some goodies."

"Buy some goodies?" Qiaoqiao was excited too. She had never gone outside to buy anything.

Gu Pan peeked into the little room. "Aunt Ah Bao is sleeping," he said. "Let's go."

The two tiptoed to the garden and went out to the alley. Qiaoqiao's heart beat fast. She was happy, excited, and afraid. Though the grownups always took her out, nothing had ever been so fresh and interesting as this day. She held Gu Pan's hand. Gu Pan frequently turned around, smiling at her, and said, "Baby."

They came to a small general store. Gu Pan took out his money. "Comrade," he called, "comrade, I want to buy, buy, buy two cents worth of goodies."

A deep voice asked, "What kind of goodies?"

"Something delicious," Qiaoqiao answered boldly.

"Lots of it," Gu Pan said.

A thin hand full of bulging veins took the two cents and passed them a small package of salted golden dates. When they opened it, both took a piece and stuffed it into their mouths...the taste was delicious, as if they had never tasted anything like it before.

They started for home. There were several boys playing "cock fight" in the alley. Each, grasping one leg, hopped with the other and attacked one of the bunch. Gu Pan opened his eyes wide and stopped.

"Let's go." Qiaoqiao was rather frightened.

"Wait for a while." Gu Pan was mesmerized by the boys as they attacked, retreated, fell down, got up, and attacked again.

"You go home by yourself," Gu Pan said, without turning his head.

"I want to go home with you." Qiaoqiao was really crying.

"Okay, okay. We'll go." Gu Pan took a step and slowly looked back. He said irritably, "You're a real bother! Look how much fun they have. Can you do that? All you do is play house, play kiddy house!"

Wiping her tears, Qiaoqiao did not answer.

Both felt very disappointed, very dejected.

6

One day in August, Gu Pan ran to Qiaoqiao's house like a gust of wind. "I'm going, going to school!" he yelled.

"Really?" Qiaoqiao blinked her eyes with admiration.

"Oh, our school is so, so big and nice, it's great. Teacher asked me, 'What can you do?' I said I could recite Tang poems. Then I recited 'I see the moonlight shining on my couch.'[1] My mother taught me..."

After several days, Gu Pan came with a treasure. "This is my new book bag," he said. "There are a lot of pockets. This is the pencil case, the pencil, and the pencil sharpener." Qiaoqiao stretched out a finger to touch the elephant-shaped sharpener but was pushed away. "Don't touch! There's a knife inside that will cut your finger, then you'll cry again. This is the eraser, the ruler..."

After another few days Gu Pan brought back a piece of paper. "This is a notice. I am accepted. You see, this is my name—Gu Pan. This is our school—Second Central Elementary School. I am a grade-school student now." He folded the notice solemnly and put it in his hip pocket. Afterwards, Qiaoqiao looked at his hip often, though there was nothing to be seen.

Gu Pan was going to go to school and Qiaoqiao was very unhappy. Aunt Ah Bao, on the other hand, was very much pleased. She said, "Thank heaven, thank heaven!"

Finally, Gu Pan's enrolment day came. He carried the book bag and walked downstairs solemnly. He proudly held up his head without stopping for one step, not even at the second floor though he knew that a pair of bright eyes was looking at him. However, he came to see Qiaoqiao right after school, too excited even to catch his breath. He could no longer restrain himself: "There are many, many kids in our class. I got to know two friends. One is called Fei Xiongxiong [*Fay Sioong-sioong*], another Liang Wei. Fei Xiong-xiong has ridden in a train, a real train. Liang Wei's father is a soldier in the People's Liberation Army. He has carried a real gun, a bayonet gun."

Qiaoqiao was interested in what he said. She laughed with him and really admired everything.

From then on, every day when Gu Pan came home from school, he talked about school business and about his friends: Fei Xiongxiong, Liang Wei, and someone who sounded like string bean and another one like little horse—they seemed to be interesting people. According to Gu Pan, they were all more interesting than Qiaoqiao. When Qiaoqiao heard this, she really had a strange feeling—it might be anger or a sense of neglect, or it might be—anyway, she felt like crying, yet she couldn't do so.

After a while, Gu Pan did not come, not for several days. When Qiaoqiao called him, he answered, "I have to do homework," or "I have to play at my friend's house." He was always busy. Qiaoqiao returned to her old habit of watching from her window all day.

One day she saw Gu Pan coming with two boys, one plump and the other tall. The three of them were digging in the garden. Qiaoqiao took a close look. Oh! That was the very spot where they had built a park not long ago. They had used little pebbles to form a circle and had decorated it with grass and flowers. They had even built a slide. But now they were destroying it, everything was destroyed! Qiaoqiao wanted to stop them but she did not dare.

Just then, Grandpa Professor Shang who lived downstairs came out and asked, "What are you doing?"

"Digging a well," Gu Pan answered loudly. "Teacher said that if you kept on digging, you'd find water."

"Crazy, crazy!" Grandpa Professor shook his head and went inside.

They worked until dark, digging a ditch. The two friends went home. Gu Pan came upstairs all by himself. He swayed to and fro, humming a song that vaguely sounded like "grow, grow." When he came to the corner of the second floor he couldn't help stopping. He saw a pair of serious eyes. He looked at her and wanted to say a few words, but he did not know what to say. Gosh, what can you talk about with a little girl? No fun, no fun! He had grown up. He was a boy, a boy! There were many interesting boys who were his friends now. What could he say to her? He turned around and went upstairs.

The bright eyes became dim and vague. A big tear slipped down.

NOTE

[1]This line is from *Quiet Night* by Li Bo (701–762), a famous poet of the Tang Dynasty. This poem can be recited by most children in China and Japan.

Seibei's Gourds

BY SHIGA NAOYA

TRANSLATED BY IVAN MORRIS

SHIGA Naoya [Sheega No-i-ya] (1883–1971), one of Japan's most famous short story writers, enjoyed a long and distinguished career. His writing is strongly autobiographical, his personal experiences forming the basis for many of his stories.

Shiga aimed for simplicity, sensitivity, and a minimum of sentimentality in his writing. His stories often deal with an individual's attempts to attain harmony; at the same time, his hatred of injustice and betrayal are clear.

"Seibei's Gourds" was published in 1913 and reflects the school and home life experienced by children of that time. Many Japanese collect and preserve gourds. Gourd bottles—which can be very expensive and very old—are bought and sold in curio shops.

$\overline{\qquad}$ $\mathbf{T}$his is the story of a young boy called Seibei [*Say-bay*], and of his gourds. Later on Seibei gave up gourds, but he soon found something to take their place: he started painting pictures. It was not long before Seibei was as absorbed in his paintings as he once had been in his gourds.

Seibei's parents knew that he often went out to buy himself gourds. He got them for a few sen[1] and soon had a sizeable collection. When he came home, he would first bore a neat hole in the top of the gourd and extract the seeds. Next he applied tea leaves to get rid of the unpleasant gourd smell. He then fetched the saké[2] which he had saved up from the dregs in his father's cup and carefully polished the surface.

Seibei was passionately interested in gourds. One day as he was strolling along the beach, absorbed in his favourite subject, he was startled by an unusual sight: he caught a glimpse of the bald, elongated head of an old man hurrying out of one of the huts by the beach. "What a splendid gourd!" thought Seibei. The old man disappeared from sight, wagging his bald pink pate. Only then did Seibei realize his mistake and he stood there laughing loudly to himself. He laughed all the way home.

Whenever he passed a grocery, a curio shop, a confectioner's, or in fact any place that sold gourds, he stood for minutes on end, his eyes glued to the window, appraising the precious fruit.

Seibei was twelve years old and still at primary school. After class, instead of playing with the other children, he usually wandered about the town looking for gourds. Then in the evening he would sit cross-legged in the corner of the living room, working on his newly acquired fruit. When he had finished treating it, he poured in a little saké, inserted a cork stopper which he had fashioned himself, wrapped it in a towel, put this in a tin especially kept for the purpose, and initially placed the whole thing on the charcoal footwarmer. Then he went to bed.

As soon as he woke the next morning, he would open the tin and examine the gourd. The skin would be thoroughly damp from the overnight treatment. Seibei would gaze adoringly at his treasure before tying a string round the middle and hanging it in the sun to dry. Then he set out for school.

Seibei lived in a harbour town. Although it was officially a city, one could walk from one end to the other in a matter of twenty minutes. Seibei was always wandering about the streets and had soon come to know every place that sold gourds and to recognize almost every gourd on the market.

He did not care much about the old, gnarled, peculiarly formed gourds usually favoured by collectors. The type that appealed to Seibei was even and symmetrical.

"That youngster of yours only seems to like the ordinary-looking ones," said a friend of his father's who had come to call. He pointed at the boy, who was sitting in the corner busily polishing a plain, round gourd.

"Fancy a lad spending his time playing around like that with gourds!" said his father, giving Seibei a disgusted look.

"See here, Seibei, my lad," said the friend, "there's no use just collecting lots of those things. It's not the quantity that counts, you know. What you want to do is to find one or two really unusual ones."

"I prefer this kind," said Seibei, and let the matter drop.

Seibei's father and his friend started talking about gourds.

"Remember that Bakin gourd they had at the agricultural show last spring?" said his father. "It was a real beauty, wasn't it?"

"Yes, I remember. That big, long one...."

As Seibei listened to their conversation, he was laughing inwardly. The Bakin gourd had made quite a stir at the time, but when he had gone to see it (having no idea, of course, who the great poet Bakin[3] might be) he had found it rather a stupid-looking object and had walked out of the show.

"I didn't think so much of it," interrupted Seibei. "It's just a clumsy great thing."

His father opened his eyes wide in surprise and anger.

"What's that?" he shouted. "When you don't know what you're talking about, you'd better shut up!"

Seibei did not say another word.

One day when he was walking along an unfamiliar back street he came upon an old woman with a fruit stall. She was selling dried persimmons and oranges; on the shutters of the house behind the stall she had hung a large cluster of gourds.

"Can I have a look?" said Seibei, and immediately ran behind the stall and began examining the gourds. Suddenly he caught sight of one which was about thirteen centimetres long and at first sight looked quite commonplace. Something about it made Seibei's heart beat faster.

"How much is this one?" he asked, panting out the words.

"Well," said the old woman, "since you're just a lad, I'll let you have it for ten sen."

"In that case," said Seibei urgently, "please hold it for me, won't you? I'll be right back with the money."

He dashed home and in no time at all was back at the stall. He bought the gourd and took it home.

From that time on, he was never separated from his new gourd. He even took it along to school and used to polish it under his desk during class time. It was not long before he was caught at this by one of the teachers, who was particularly incensed because it happened to take place in an ethics class.

This teacher came from another part of Japan and found it most offensive that children should indulge in such effeminate pastimes as collecting gourds. He was forever expounding the classical code of the samurai[4], and when Kumoemon, the famous *Naniwabushi*[5] performer, came on tour and recited brave deeds of ancient times, he would attend every single performance, though normally he would not deign to set foot in the disreputable amusement area. He never minded having his students sing *Naniwabushi* ballads, however raucously. Now, when he found Seibei silently polishing his gourd, his voice trembled with fury.

"You're an idiot!" he shouted. "There's absolutely no future for a boy like you." Then and there he confiscated the gourd on which Seibei had spent so many long hours of work. Seibei stared straight ahead and did not cry.

When he got home, Seibei's face was pale. Without a word, he put his feet on the warmer and sat looking blankly at the wall.

After a while the teacher arrived. As Seibei's father was not yet home from the carpenter's shop where he worked, the teacher directed his attack at Seibei's mother.

"This sort of thing is the responsibility of the family," he said in a stern voice. "It is the duty of you parents to see that such things don't happen." In an agony of embarrassment, Seibei's mother muttered some apology.

Meanwhile, Seibei was trying to make himself as inconspicuous as possible in the corner. Terrified, he glanced up at his vindictive teacher and at the wall directly behind where a whole row of fully prepared gourds was hanging. What would happen if the teacher caught sight of them?

Trembling inside, he awaited the worst, but at length the man exhausted his rhetoric and stamped angrily out of the house. Seibei heaved a sigh of relief.

Seibei's mother was sobbing softly. In a querulous whine she began to scold him, and in the midst of this, Seibei's father returned from his shop. As soon as he heard what had happened, he grabbed his son by the collar and gave him a sound beating. "You're no good!" he bawled at him. "You'll never get anywhere in the world the way you're carrying on. I've a good mind to throw you out into the street where you belong!" The gourds on the wall caught his attention. Without a word, he fetched his hammer and systematically smashed them to pieces one after another. Seibei turned pale but said nothing.

The next day the teacher gave Seibei's confiscated gourd to an old porter who worked in the school. "Here, take this," he said, as if handing over some unclean object. The porter took the gourd home with him and hung it on the wall of his small, sooty room.

About two months later the porter, finding himself even more hard-pressed for money than usual, decided to take the gourd to a local curio shop to see if he could get a few coppers for it. The curio dealer examined the gourd carefully; then, assuming an uninterested tone, he handed it back to the porter, saying, "I might give you five yen for it."

The porter was astounded, but being quite an astute old man, he replied coolly, "I certainly wouldn't part with it for that." The dealer immediately raised his offer to ten yen, but the porter was still adamant.

In the end the curio dealer had to pay fifty yen for the gourd. The porter left the shop, delighted at his luck. It wasn't often that the teachers gave one a free gift equivalent to a year's wages! He was so clever as not to mention the matter to anyone, and neither Seibei nor the teacher ever heard what had happened to the gourd. Yes, the porter was clever, but he was not clever enough: little did he imagine that this same gourd would be passed on by the curio dealer to a wealthy collector in the district for six hundred yen.

Seibei is now engrossed in his pictures. He no longer feels any bitterness either toward the teacher, or toward his father who smashed all his precious gourds to pieces.

Yet gradually his father has begun to scold him for painting pictures.

<hr/>

NOTES

[1]sen: a Japanese unit of currency. There are one hundred sen in a yen.

[2]saké: a Japanese rice wine

[3]Bakin (1767–1848) was the pen name of Takizawa Toku, a writer of the Edo period, renowned for his historical fiction.

[4]The samurai were warriors who formed the military aristocracy of feudal Japan.

[5]*Naniwabushi*: a professional reciter of stories

Forced Out

BY HSIAO YEH

TRANSLATED BY MARK FRIEDMAN

HSIAO Yeh [Shiow Ye-eh] (1951–   ) is the pen name of Li Yuan. Like many Taiwanese authors, Hsiao is a refugee from mainland China, born in Fujian province in southern China. He is a member of the young generation of Taiwanese authors who write about the problems of ordinary people—especially young people—struggling against cultural and economic pressures.

"Forced Out" is told through an interior monologue and a series of flashbacks during a Little League game. Baseball—especially Little League—is an extremely popular sport in Taiwan. Taiwanese teams frequently win the Little League World Series which is held each year in the United States.

After several weeks of drought the ball field was dried and cracked, the grass scorched and withered. The wisps of dust gave people the impression that fumes were rising out of the baked earth.

Ah Ts'ai[1] dragged himself somewhat unsteadily towards the batter's box. The bat in his hand seemed to have changed into one of the beam-weights his family used for weighing piglets. He was taller than other boys his age, but against the vast baseball field he seemed to shrink to the size of a spotted green caterpillar.

The sweating fans started standing up in the bleachers, as if their behinds had been roasted by the scorching sun. And the announcer blared out frenetically:

"Bottom half of the last inning, with Chu Chin-ts'ai [*Ju Chin-chī*] up to bat for the Divine Eagles. It's three to two in favour of the Red Barbarians.

Two outs. One man on third. If the clean-up batter, Chu Chin-ts'ai, can smash one out there, they could turn the tables on the Red Barbarians. If he doesn't. . . ."

"Show us what you can do, Ah Ts'ai!"

"Hit a homer!"

"Kill 'em, Ah Ts'ai!"

"Chu Chin-ts'ai is carrying a real load on his shoulders. He's walking up to the batter's box with confidence. The coach can't stop worrying. He's following him out to give him some instructions."

Ah Ts'ai settled himself in the batter's box and drew in a deep breath of hot air. The scorching sun burned fiercely, intensifying the crowd's excitement. The pitcher intently watched the catcher's hand signals. He nodded but then indecisively glanced at the runner on third, who was itching to take wing. The runner on third moved away from the base with a lot of noisy chatter trying to break the pitcher's concentration.

"I've got to hit a long drive." All of Ah Ts'ai's energy was concentrated on the pitcher's bent arm concealed behind his body. "I've got to belt one out there and give them a homer. I could be a national player with this hit. Winning this game is my only chance to go to America. Except for Father, everyone in the family would cluck at me in admiration. It's no joking matter. Cousin Ah Kuo [*Ah Gwah*] is in America studying for a Ph.D. and earning American dollars. It's certainly not a joking matter. America!"

A hit to settle the game. A hit to reach America. He limbered up his neck and flexed his wrists, striking up a spirited hit-out-to-America pose.

"There's the first pitch. Chu Chin-ts'ai swings. . . ."

Crack—that familiar, crisp, exciting sound.

"A high fly to left field. It's flying high, high. . . ."

The spectators were yelling, seething like boiling water.

"Ah—too bad. A long foul to left field."

The crowd ah-ed, some in disappointment, some in relief.

Like a movie being run backwards, Ah Ts'ai was pulled back to his original position. He wiped off his sweaty hands on his pants and picked up his bat.

He relaxed for a bit, when the pitcher shouted to his infielders. Unexpectedly, there was a strange sensation of a heavy burden being lifted. Lucky it wasn't a safe hit. Father is the only one who doesn't hope that I'll get a safe hit. He bet 200,000 yuan[2] with another man on the Red Barbarians. If that hit had been a home run, Father's 200,000 yuan would have flown like the baseball and disappeared into another man's pocket.

"Give us a homer, Ah Ts'ai!"

"Hit a home run!"

The excited cheers enveloped Ah Ts'ai like the ever-present swarm of flies around the pigsties at home.

Throw the game. Just don't swing. Three strikes and you're out. We really can't afford to lose 200,000 yuan. Father has already sold most of the piglets.

But, can I lose? Can I steel my heart to look at the disappointed faces of the team captain, the coach, my teammates, my family, neighbours, and elders?

Before the game, the baseball team had moved into a decrepit nunnery to save hotel expenses. Every day at dawn and dusk, along with the bells in the morning and drums in the evening[3], the team captain and the coach took turns giving pep talks.

"We've worked out so hard for so long and the village elders have so much hope for us. Under the scorching sun, rapping them out, ball by ball, bang, bang, bang, bang. Why did we discipline, ball by ball? Because if we don't take the championship, I swear we won't go back home!"

Yes, ball after ball we practised, and we were punished for every error we committed. After that kind of rigorous training it just wouldn't be worth it to lose.

Several days ago there was a businessman calling himself Hung who searched us out at the nunnery and sent a large basket of seedless watermelons. He said that he's bet 500,000 yuan on the Divine Eagles and that if we really did win, he would take out 100,000 yuan for us to buy some new equipment and also souvenirs in America.

"You all are poor enough," he said, gesturing expansively. "So poor you can't even afford to stay in a hotel. But, young friends, it doesn't matter! All you have to do is win the game and all your problems will be solved!"

When he got as far as the word "solved," he slashed down with his right hand as if cutting a watermelon.

That's right. Win. All we have to do is win the game. But will that really solve things? Is it as easy as cutting a watermelon?

The second pitch was about to come. Ah Ts'ai's arms felt a little stiff. He had just wiped his palms dry. How come they were all sweaty again?

There it was—a white sphere right in front of him, spinning larger and larger like a whirlpool of blazing white.

"The swing—missed! Two strikes, no balls, two outs."

The members of the Red Barbarians team whooped it up in the centre of the field. One more strike and this game would be theirs. The runner on third yanked off his cap and stamped his feet. Things didn't look good. Ah Ts'ai had swung too impulsively, which caused him to stagger. He brought his bat back around and straightened his helmet. The sun dazzled and confused him! Was it as torturingly hot in America? Perhaps what we need is a good rain.

Last month, Ah Kuo's letter home to Uncle's family had this to say: "No matter how smoothly their work or studies are going, the overseas Chinese here always feel a kind of intangible gloom deep in their hearts. We're hoping the team from our homeland will beat these barbarians so badly they won't be able to fight back. I hope Ah Ts'ai can also come here and have a taste of glory. That time last year was really great. I don't care if I have to drive two days and two nights or risk flunking an exam, I'll be there to root at this game for sure."

When Mother heard Uncle read her this part of the letter she laughed, chattering incessantly: "Our Ah Kuo studied over ten years, until he got nearsighted and hunchbacked from reading, before he got to go to America! All Ah Ts'ai has to do to go is play a good game of baseball."

Mother didn't know a thing about Father's 200,000 yuan bet.

That night, their dog started barking and someone shook Ah Ts'ai out of his sleep. His father's breath reeked of wine and his face was contorted like a pig approaching the knife. He dragged Ah Ts'ai over by the door. The door had not been latched and a heavy gust of cold night wind whirled in and poured into Ah Ts'ai's flimsy T-shirt.

His father said thickly, "The fellow betting with me is a stranger that Pai Mao [Bǐ Mao] introduced to me. He doesn't know that old 'Ceremonial Pig's'[4] son is the best player on the Divine Eagles team. Just listen to your father. In the decisive point of the game, play off-form, let yourself be forced out or tagged out, and your father will win the biggest part of that 200,000 yuan. I've had enough bad luck lately. I lost 100,000 yuan to Pai Mao and I don't have the money to pay him. Pai Mao gave me this idea—ha! ha! Ah Ts'ai, your father picked this name for you just so that you could bring in wealth and riches.[5] People like me, we just don't have any luck. I've never even won 100 yuan in the National Lottery. Damn it—Ah Ts'ai, don't let your father down this time."

Ah Ts'ai absolutely hated it when people called his father "Ceremonial Pig." If Father was a Ceremonial Pig, then weren't all of his children piglets?

If Father didn't gamble, sister Ah Chin wouldn't have been given to that vile Pai Mao. And she wouldn't have suffered such a tragic death under the wheels of a train, either. She was only eleven years old that year.

"Ladies and gentlemen, this is a tense moment. Chu Chin-ts'ai is straining at the bat. The pitcher is starting his wind-up. There's the pitch!"

Ah Ts'ai stared at the ball blankly, like a lifeless scarecrow planted on top of a ridge in a rice field, yet without any resemblance to Sadaharu Oh's stance of raising one leg.[6] Several scattered sparrows buzzed past his helmet as though they were flying over a quiet field. The scarecrow didn't budge.

"Too low and on the inside. A ball! The pitcher is stringing him on. Two strikes, one ball, two outs. . . ."

If she hadn't been given to Pai Mao, Ah Chin wouldn't have died. Mother had cried and wailed by the side of that small, crushed corpse, and berated Father.

"It's divine retribution. Poor Ah Chin! We should have raised our own child ourselves. You'll roast in hell, Ceremonial Pig! If you go on like this, you'll have to sell your wife and sons to pay off your gambling debts."

Everyone said Pai Mao specialized in this kind of dirty business. Who knew how many girls he had gotten into his clutches because people couldn't pay back their gambling debts. And as soon as the girls grew a little older he would send them to those filthy places.

Maybe it was better that Ah Chin had died and didn't have to suffer that kind of bodily insult. Someday Ah Ts'ai would grow up big and strong and slaughter Pai Mao like a piglet. What he'd spit out then wouldn't be red betel[7] juice but the bright, hot blood that a piglet, pierced to its heart, spurts out!

Hit a home run! Let Father go and lose 200,000 yuan and do away with bad luck. Let them try to laugh that one off!

The blood pounded through his body. He gripped the bat and looked savagely at the pitcher. Damn—I'll give you something to look at. . . .

The ball came floating over again at a very slow speed. It kept spinning until he was dazzled. A curve ball floating in a little low and on the outside.

Smash it out. A home run. Kill 'em!

"Oh—a curve ball. Too much English on it. Too far out to the right. It's a ball! That was really dangerous, really dangerous. Chu Chin-ts'ai had already twisted around to swing and then checked his swing at the last instant. He's getting a little edgy."

The pitcher suddenly whipped the ball over to third base. The runner scrambled back and stepped on the base. This comical action caused some laughter, but it quickly died out.

A flock of pigeons flew over the ball field. The sun blazed straight down. Not too many people looked up. Maybe we really should have some rain. The coach brayed something from the sidelines. Ah Ts'ai looked back but he couldn't make out what the coach had said. He seemed to be hearing what Pai Mao had said when he came to the house to collect his gambling debt. He was chewing a mouthful of red betel nut. His voice was filled with arrogance.

"Where's that damned Ceremonial Pig? He isn't trying to welsh on me, is he?"

Ah Chin wouldn't have died if it hadn't been for Pai Mao.

One evening, about a year after she died, the whole family was still up. Father was the only one not there. He was out gambling again. He'd said he wanted to win some money to pay for the children's school fees. Suddenly, there was a loud thud against the door and Father staggered in. He grabbed a half-full bottle of rice wine and started pouring it down his throat. His face flushed pale and then red. His eyeballs rolled upwards and the whites bulged out like the meat of a *lung-yen*[8]. His purplish lips opened and closed mechanically with a regular smacking sound.

He was being shaken by a gigantic, demon-like force, trembling from head to toe. His words were barely audible: "Ah Chin, don't hurt me! Ah Chin, don't hurt me!"

His eyelids blinked open and shut as though they were being manipulated by a puppet string. Mother calmly said that Father was possessed by a demon. She told Ah Ts'ai and his brother to move the tea table to the yard and put an incense burner on it. The three of them combined their strength to drag Father in front of the tea table, and asked him to kneel down and kowtow.

Mother put several stacks of spirit money into the wash basin and burned them. Then she lit several sticks of incense and made repeated obeisances, mumbling a chant.

"Ah Chin, we're burning some money for you to buy some new clothes and some good things to eat. Please, let Father go. . . ."

The chill wind carried off the ashes of the spirit money in the basin and filled the air with them. The unextinguished embers twinkled eerily in the night. The dog shrank into a corner and whined, intensifying the desolate gloom of that dark, sleepless night.

By the time all of the black ashes had floated back down, the sky had gradually started to lighten. Father, completely exhausted, began to come back to life and said that he'd definitely seen Ah Chin sobbing, sitting in the same place at the railroad crossing where her corpse had been. He said she blamed him for giving her away.

Could it really have been the ghost of poor little Ah Chin?

After the ball team moved into the nunnery in preparation for this campaign, Ah Ts'ai would often walk back and forth by the side of the dark crematorium crypt. His evenings were haunted by those horrible memories. The shadows of the nuns passing soundlessly with bowed heads were projected onto the paper windows, and he trembled through the night thinking each one was Ah Chin.

Having seen Father's desperate state that time left him with a deep disquietude. Poor Father. Unable to give up gambling, he had become Pai Mao's slave.

Forget about hitting. For Father, for our 200,000 yuan. Just one grounder in front of the pitcher will do it. Let them force me out at first base. It's as easy as that.

"Ladies and gentlemen, we'll soon know who's going to win. Three to two in favour of the Red Barbarians. . . ."

He could imagine Father squeezing his way into some corner of the ball field and yelling like a lunatic. He would be standing there, with his filthy hair dishevelled, his jet-black eye balls protruding like *lung-yen* pits, and an outstretched, trembling fat hand, craving to grasp that 200,000 yuan. Be a filial son for once! All you have to do is strike out or make a short hit, and Father can caper around embracing a stack of bank notes. It's been such a long time since I've seen that miserable face break into a smile.

Ah Ts'ai's hands grew weak and the bat dropped. . . .

The pitcher was playing with the baseball in his glove, his eyes darting around constantly.

Thick layers of clouds drifted across the sky. The enormous clouds hovered lower and lower, oppressing the entire ball field. They cast their shadows on the people and their faces. Perhaps it was a propitious sign of a heavy rain. It was time for a rain.

All those anxious, longing faces flashed through his mind with the speed of a charcoal sketch: the coach, the team captain, his teammates, Mother, Ah Kuo, and his neighbours. All, one by one, opening their mouths and crying out. . . .

You have to beat 'em! If you don't win, don't come home!

Under the oppressing shadow of the clouds he felt dizzy and empty.

Come on, Ah Ts'ai! Come on, Ah Ts'ai! Hit a home run! A home run to go proudly to America. Are there weeks of drought in America, too? I do want to go to America. I'll bring back some American clothes for Mother and a talking doll for Sister. I'll give Fa—Father something that he's never tasted before—champagne. Mr. Hung said all we have to do is win, and all our problems will be solved as neatly as cutting a watermelon.

The bat slowly rose in his sweating hands, up above his head.

The pitcher threw the third ball. It was too low and crashed into the ground. The catcher stuck his chest out to block the runaway pellet which, like an unexploded hand grenade, just raised circles of dust.

"Two strikes and three balls. This is the last pitch! The deciding pitch! Ladies and gentlemen—ladies and gentlemen—"

The broadcaster's voice was not up to conveying the tense atmosphere he wished to create. It seemed that the first person to faint from over-excitement would be he himself.

At this moment, the sun poked through the layers of clouds and the sky looked like it had just been given a coat of shining wax. Dust wafted fitfully through the dry hot air. The myriad heads in the bleachers and along the grassy slope outside the field had been in agitated motion for quite some time. Suddenly, everything became extraordinarily still.

The completeness of the silence was overwhelming. A flock of pigeons, as if they were previously familiar with it all, flew flapping across the sky. A flapping that was unwilling to accept the quietness. Flap. Flap. Flap.

The batter and pitcher's unblinking eyes were fastened on each other. Ferocity was frozen in their stares.

Ah Ts'ai's mind was a blank. The only thought he had was to control his breathing—his heart had already risen up into his throat.

The pitcher went into his wind-up and the ball paused an instant above his head.

Everyone was waiting. With the exception of the pitcher's very exaggerated raising of his left leg, there was an extraordinary stillness.

In the blink of an eye, a ramrod-straight, white snake left the pitcher's hand with lightning speed and, swiftly lengthening, flew towards the batter.

Ah Ts'ai viciously bit down on his lower lip and swung without mercy. Crack—!

It was a hit and the ball flew out toward left field.

The emotions of all the spectators in the ball park were submerged in their own roars. The ball soared out and hit the fence, and there was an outbreak of wild pandemonium. Everyone's mouth was open so wide that you could have chucked a baseball in.

Ah Ts'ai threw the bat down like a hot potato and took off wildly for first base.

Fa–Father. Father's 200,000 yuan! Let me fall down and be forced out at first base!

Run—run—the whole park shouted thunderously.

We've got to win. We must win. I can't be tagged out. . . .

After he'd flown through first base, he sped on towards second without stopping.

"It's a beautiful hit. The ball hit the fence and took a long bounce. Placement is extremely good. The runner on third is home. Three to three. Chu Chin-ts'ai is on second. . . ."

Father, I'm very, very sorry. I can't be tagged out. I want to win, I must win. Run, run, run, run madly without stopping. . . .

"Oh no! He shouldn't have left second. It's too risky. This is really unusual. He's running on towards third like a runaway car. The left fielder has the ball, and is making a long throw to third—"

Far-away America. Ah Kuo, you're going to see Ah Ts'ai battle in that strange place and make us Chinese feel proud. I'm going to whip them all!

Oh! Father, poor Father. 200,000 yuan! You can't afford to lose that. Oh—let me be forced out at third! Father, don't blame me. I'll be a good filial son. . . .

"Ladies and gentlemen, Chu Chin-ts'ai is throwing it away by running to third. It's a disastrous mistake. Oh—the third baseman has fumbled the ball. Fumbled. Ah Ts'ai is running madly on for home plate."

The sound of the crazed mob's screams shattered the packed bleachers into little pieces. The clouds of dust Ah Ts'ai raised in his mad run settled slowly to the ground.

Go—go, Ah Ts'ai!

The coach, team captain, and teammates all took off their caps and waved them violently. Everyone's veins stood out blue, eyes open wide and teeth bared.

Run! Run!

He rode forward on those waves of sound.

The pitcher was anxiously waiting at home plate, helping the catcher to tag out the batter running home.

"Chu Chin-ts'ai made a mistake by running home. Third base was lucky enough. He's simply gone crazy. He seems to have completely lost control, lost his reason and sense of judgement. Now—"

The third baseman pounced, retrieved the fumbled ball, and hurriedly threw it towards home plate.

Father, Father. In the end I'm going to be tagged out at home plate. Father. It's too late. I can't score. Fa—.

In front of his eyes was a boundless blur of grey. The pitcher and catcher were waiting for him at home plate. What was projected onto the pupils of his eyes, soaked and dripping with sweat, looked like the ox-headed and horse-faced demons at the far end of the long hallway in the temple of the city god, baring their fangs, clawing with their paws, and calling home the souls of the dead.

He was gripped with a terror of death, as if looking at Ah Chin's mutilated little corpse. His whole body was numb. He wasn't going to make it.

Run back? Run back!

He briefly entertained the idea of running back but then it was gone—he was just as easily doomed by running back. Everyone was blocking him, closing him off, including the coach, the team captain, and his teammates. Father, save me, Father. Oh...Father....

Ox-headed and horse-faced demons—to bring in wealth and riches—200,000 yuan—to feel proud.

Three, four steps away from the plate, he was compelled to lower his body and, like an egret coming in for a landing, slid towards home plate. During his slide, the catcher caught the third baseman's throw and placed himself in Ah Ts'ai's path. The home plate umpire's hand flew up to signal an out. He mercilessly roared out one word.

"Out!—Ladies and gentlemen, Chu Chin-ts'ai was finally put out at home plate. He shouldn't have pushed his luck so far...."

Ah Ts'ai was lying prostrate on the ground. His twitching cheeks were pressed hard against the icy cold home plate. An enervated hand reached out, wishing to grasp in reality a handful of sand, even a few stalks of green grass. But, in fact, he was as weak as a loach fish abandoned in the mud, flopping and struggling.

The coach and team captain stamped their feet and said to the disappointed team members, "He shouldn't have run home."

Grieved sounds were tossed back and forth where the spectators were sitting. A real shame! What a real shame!

The sun blazed even hotter, seeming to be melting in circular ripples, dazzling the fluffy clouds into reflectors. A dark blue bird flapped its large wings and fled from the ball field to the shade of the covered bleachers. The medics, carrying first-aid kits, hurried towards home plate. All that could be heard was the voice of the broadcaster, trying to sound as loud and excited as before but managing only a wooden listlessness.

"The game will now go on until one side scores. . . ."

There was still no trace of an afternoon breeze but the commotion had begun to quiet down.

Maybe it was really time for a good rain.

NOTES

[1]Ah Ts'ai's full name is Chu Chin-ts'ai. Ah Ts'ai is a familiar form of his name.

[2]yuan: the Taiwanese dollar, worth about Canadian $0.04

[3]Bells and drums are used in Buddhist temples to announce the time and to arouse people to renewed faith.

[4]A "Ceremonial Pig" (*chu kung*) is brought out for display during Taiwanese religious festivities. It is the biggest and fattest pig in the locale.

[5]The word "chin" in Ah Ts'ai's full name means "wealth."

[6]Sadaharu Oh was a Taiwanese-born home-run king on the Tokyo Giants baseball team. He was famous for his one-legged batting stance.

[7]The betel nut is the seed of a tall palm, chewed with dried betel leaves and lime as a stimulant.

[8]*lung-yen*: a fruit; after shelling, the meat is very pale white

Begonia

BY XI XI

TRANSLATED BY HANNAH CHEUNG

Xi Xi [Si Si] is the pen name of Zhang Yan, who moved to Hong Kong from Shanghai with her family in 1950. Her greatest literary influences include fairy tales, European and Japanese films, and Latin American and European writers.

Xi Xi is a cosmopolitan and versatile writer who deals with a variety of themes in a deceptively simple manner. Her stories, set against the cross-cultural environment of Hong Kong, feature conflicts between traditional and contemporary values. Having taught primary school for many years, Xi Xi often writes about characters who view the world with a spontaneous, childlike wonder and enjoyment.

They saw the Dumb Boy's begonia—a wax-leaved begonia. Dozens of densely packed, upright, round leaves with clusters of lotus-red flowers spread among the jade-green and dark brown leaves: the unopened buds looked like seashells all in a row, the blooming flowers resembled peonies, and at the core of every blossom, there were also three or four new rose-like buds emerging over the tops of the overlapping crowded petals. They were surprised: Dumb Boy, so you like flowers too!

On all their desks and on the window sills beside their desks were arranged rich displays of the plants they had grown: delicate but sturdy "living rocks," soft but prickly white-web balls; but most of them were African violets. The mottled leaves, ruffled petals, and curving edges of their leaves were recurrent topics of conversation.

All the time they thought that whatever the dirty-faced Dumb Boy carried in his hand would either be a pail or a mop. But after lunch, they saw that he was actually holding a potted plant with a firm, strong stem and soft, fluffy leaves. The Dumb Boy crossed the lobby and walked all the way to the storeroom and placed that plant under a wooden chair behind the door. So they went over to remove the plant from that dark corner, and put it in a place where there was lots of light. They said: Dumb Boy, plants need light, it's too dark under the chair. The Dumb Boy blinked and said: Ah-ah.

They said: Dumb Boy, this is a pretty begonia, you should take good care of it. Loose soft sandy soil is good for it, so that its roots can breathe easily. This plastic pot doesn't let any air in; you should get an earthenware one. The Dumb Boy just blinked and said: Ah-ah. They said: Dumb Boy, all plants need to be fertilized; you should do it once every ten days or every fortnight. Begonias have flowers, so choose a fertilizer suitable for flowering plants. Begonias need a lot of phosphate too. The Dumb Boy blinked and said: Ah-ah. They said: Dumb Boy, when begonias are flourishing, a lot of small shoots will start growing out from the sides of the main stem; you can make cuttings—just cut under the node, pick off the old leaves, stick them in the soil, and soon you'll have a new begonia. Before long, you will have so many begonias it'll be like a carpet. The Dumb Boy blinked and said: Ah-ah.

Suddenly they saw a tiny white butterfly[1] resting for an instant on a fishtail fern, then it flapped its wings and flew away. The butterfly alighted on the densely blossoming gloxinia, and on the cherry shell which seemed to have long ears like a rabbit. Finally it struck the window with a tiny thud. They did not know how this little creature had flown in, as all the doors and windows were closed. They said: Maybe the white butterfly flew in from the garden across the street. They said: Maybe it came in during the power-cut this morning to visit the hyacinth. So they opened a window and let the butterfly out.

At noon, they had decided to go out and have lunch together. Because of this change in plans, one of them gave the Dumb Boy the lunch box he had ordered by phone. The weather was still warm, and the Dumb Boy had a dish of rice at a stall in a side alley; then, carrying the lunch box, he went inside the cool arcade. Strolling down the long corridor, munching on a hot dog, he sought out a spot where it was not crowded. He met many people coming towards him holding their noses, but the Dumb Boy kept on going. It turned out that there was a flower shop at the end of the long corridor. The Dumb

Boy stood there, at the very spot from which all the people had turned away. And it was at that spot, through the glass pane, that the Dumb Boy saw that his own nose was pointing right at a very good-looking caterpillar. Like himself, the caterpillar was having its lunch silently, on its own. The caterpillar had glittering black and white patches all over its body, which was so soft, with fine hair like velvet, that it looked as if it was wrapped up in a piece of fine embroidery. For a long long time, the Dumb Boy did not move. Only the flower-shop owner moved about, with small steps.

The flower-shop owner asked: What kind of potted plants do you like? Is it for a present or for yourself? Please come in and have a look around. The Dumb Boy blinked. The shop owner said: Do you like begonias? This is a diamond begonia, a new species; it's always in bloom, and it's especially beautiful in the autumn. Begonias are easy to take care of, just give them plenty of water and some sunshine, and they will grow very well. The Dumb Boy blinked. The shop owner said: My shop's badly located, right opposite the toilet. We're going out of business, so we are holding a clearance sale now. Buy two plants and I'll give you a third one free. If you only want one, you can have it at half-price. It's a real bargain. The Dumb Boy blinked. He saw the caterpillar. It was very fat and had chewed a big hole in the middle of a thick leaf. From the reflection in the glass, the Dumb Boy saw that he was also very fat himself, and noticed the big hole in the hot dog he was holding. The shop owner said: There are only three days left. Everything has to go. We'll sell it to you at the lowest possible price. This is really quite a fine begonia. The Dumb Boy blinked.

The Dumb Boy sat down on the stone bench in the shade in the garden. He took the plant out of its vest-shaped plastic bag, tore off the old newspaper wrapped around the pot, turned the pot around slowly, and saw the caterpillar again. The caterpillar had eaten its fill and was taking a walk. The caterpillar had lots of legs, and walked very slowly. Having so many legs and yet walking so slowly, it must be taking a leisurely stroll. Only when the caterpillar moved could the Dumb Boy tell its head from its tail. When the Dumb Boy finished his hot dog, he started to eat the potato chips in the bag. He held out a potato chip to the caterpillar; it panicked, withdrew to the leaf, and froze. It was a long while before it continued its walk. When the caterpillar rolled itself up on the leaf, the Dumb Boy could not tell its head from its tail. When the Dumb Boy finished the potato chips, he picked up the begonia with both hands and took it back to the office. He put the caterpillar under the chair he sat on when he took a break.

The butterfly glided out of the window and disappeared instantly in the strong white sunlight, as if no white butterfly had ever flapped its wings by the window pane; as if the butterfly was just an illusion of their own making. But they still said: Soon this place will be a garden, won't it? The Dumb Boy picked up his pail and went to fill it in preparation for mopping the steps outside the door. They said: The butterfly is really an illusory creature. They also sat down and started working: they typed, they edited things, they looked up words in the dictionary, they took a pile of papers from one wooden drawer and put it in another wooden drawer.

When the Dumb Boy went to draw fresh water, he passed by the flower pot and stopped there quietly, searching carefully for something. The caterpillar had gone to sleep. So caterpillars like to take afternoon naps. The Dumb Boy did not take afternoon naps. They gave him a stack of letters to mail. Soon the Dumb Boy came back with a small cup. He carefully poured the water from the cup onto the soil of the begonia. He watered it carefully, so that water came up as far as the edge of the pot but did not spill onto the caterpillar. The caterpillar wasn't wearing a raincoat anyway. At half past three, they said: It's time for afternoon tea. They suddenly remembered that one of them was supposed to treat everyone to ice cream as a punishment for something he had done, so they wrote down what they wanted and asked the Dumb Boy to go out and get it and bring it back packed in dry ice.

Soon the Dumb Boy returned, bringing with him the ice cream and a bag of "Magic Soil." They each took their ice cream and went off to eat it. The Dumb Boy opened the box of fertilizer and piled the little white balls around the roots of the begonia. The caterpillar should be taking its after-noon tea now, but perhaps it was busy weaving. The Dumb Boy turned the pot round several times, but he could not see the caterpillar. They said: Dumb Boy, your begonia was being attacked by insects. What a horrible caterpillar, it was so fat it would soon have gobbled up the whole plant. The Magic Soil spilled out of the Dumb Boy's hand and rolled all over the floor. They said: There are holes in seven or eight of the leaves. You're lucky we found it early. We were very brave, and got rid of that worm for you. The Dumb Boy eagerly searched through the waste-paper basket. They said: It was such a horrible, fat caterpillar. Don't look for it now, it's all squashed. The Dumb Boy turned around and opened his mouth wide.

NOTE

[1]In Chinese culture, the butterfly is a symbol of joy.

Inem

BY PRAMOEDYA ANANTA TOER

TRANSLATED BY HARRY AVELING

Pramoedya Ananta TOER (1925–   ) is one of the best-known Indonesian writers, although his work has been banned in Indonesia since 1966. Most of his stories and novels were written during the 16 years he spent as a political prisoner, first under Dutch rule during the Indonesian Revolution (1945–1949) and later by order of the Indonesia Army, who suspected him of being a Communist. Although often deprived of pen and paper during his second imprisonment, Toer was able to "write" four historical novels orally, reciting passages to his fellow prisoners each day, so that the material would not be lost even if he were never able to write it down.

Many of Toer's stories are based on his memories of growing up in a poor village in East Java during the 1930s, and reflect his continuing commitment to traditional Javanese culture, although he is clearly repelled by many aspects of this culture. His stories are compelling, simply told, and emotionally intense. "Inem," published in 1952, is such a story, and is told through the eyes of a child.

Note: Many of the practices described in the story no longer occur in Indonesia.

Inem [*Ee-num*] was my friend. She was eight, two years older than I was. She was just like all the other girls, except that she was thought to be rather pretty. People liked her. She was polite, natural, intelligent, and a good worker. Because of this she quickly became well-known in the village and people began to say, "Inem would be a good daughter-in-law to have."

Then one day, as she boiled water in our kitchen, she told me, " 'Muk, I'm getting married."

"Really?" I said.

"Yes. Someone asked for me a week ago. My parents and kin have accepted him."

"Imagine being married!" I shouted.

It was true. Her mother came one day and talked to my mother. Inem had been entrusted to my parents. She helped with the cooking and looked after me and the others when we played.

Inem's mother lived on what she earned making batik[1]. In our village women made batik when they weren't working in the fields. Some made skirt lengths, others made headbands. The poor made headbands because they were easier to make and one got paid more quickly. Inem's mother made headbands. Her boss gave her white cloth and candle-wax and paid her one and a half cents for every two lengths she prepared. One could dye eight to eleven bands a day.

Inem's father was a professional cock-fighter. He gambled each day with his winnings. If he lost, the winner took his rooster and anything from three cents to a dollar. If he won, he played cards with the neighbours for cents.

Sometimes he was away for a month at a time. When he returned it meant that he had money again.

Mother once told me that he robbed people in the teak forest between our Blora and the coastal town of Rembang. In the first grade I heard a lot of stories about robbers, pirates, thieves, and murderers, so I was scared of Inem's father.

Everyone knew that he was a criminal but no one dared report him to the police. No one had any evidence. So the police never arrested him. Besides, most of Inem's uncles on her mother's side were policemen. Some were even first-class detectives. And Inem's father had once been a policeman himself, until he was dismissed for taking bribes.

Mother also told me that he had once been a major criminal. The Dutch enlisted him against his friends. He never broke into anyone's house after that. Even so, most of the people I knew distrusted him.

When Inem's mother came, Inem was boiling water in the kitchen. I met her mother too. Her mother, my mother, and I all sat on the low red couch.

"Madam," Inem's mother said, "I've come to ask for Inem back."

"Why? Isn't she better off here? You don't have to spend money on her and she can learn cooking."

"But, madam, I want to marry her after the harvest is over."

"What!" Mother exclaimed. "Marry her?"

"Yes madam. She's old enough now—eight," Inem's mother replied.

Mother laughed, much to her guest's consternation. "She's only a child."

"We're not upper-class people, madam. I think she's already a year too old. Asih married her girl off two years ago."

Mother tried to dissuade her, but Inem's mother had other reasons. Finally she said, "I'm glad someone's asked for her at last. If we postponed this, perhaps no one would ask for her again. I'd be ashamed of her if she was an old maid. Perhaps she can make things easier for me when I'm old."

Mother would not agree. She turned to me and said, "Go and get the betel nut[2] and the spittoon."

I went and fetched the teak utensils.

"What does your husband think of the idea?"

"He agrees. Especially as Markaban's parents are rich. He is their only child. He has started selling cows—in Rembang, Chepu, Medang, Pati, Ngawan, and in Blora as well."

Mother was cheered by the news although I couldn't understand why. Then she called Inem from the kitchen. Inem came. And Mother asked her, "Inem, do you want to have a husband?"

Inem bowed her head. She respected Mother. I never heard her disagree with her once. Although she was the sort of person who never disagreed with anyone.

Inem looked delighted. She often did. If anyone gave her something which she at all liked, she was delighted. But she could never say "thank you." Villagers found the word strange. They showed their gratitude by their expression.

"Yes madam," she said slowly, almost inaudibly.

Mother and Inem's mother chewed betel. Mother did not like betel nut very much and only took it when she had guests. From time to time she spit the red juice into the spittoon.

"She's too young," Mother said, when Inem returned to the kitchen.

Inem's mother was annoyed, but said nothing. Her eyes too were silent.

"I married at eighteen," Mother said.

The other woman's anger vanished. She still said nothing.

"She's too young," Mother repeated.

The woman was annoyed.

"Her children will be dwarfs."

The anger vanished again. "Yes madam." Then, coldly: "My mother was eight when she married." My mother ignored the comment and continued, "Not just physically. It's not good for her health."

"Yes madam. But our family are famous for living a long time. My mother is still alive and she is over fifty-eight. My grandmother is still alive. She is seventy-six, I think. She's still healthy and can still pound corn."

Again Mother ignored her. "It's worse if the husband is a child too."

"Yes madam. But Markaban is seventeen."

"Seventeen! My husband was thirty when he married me."

Inem's mother fell silent. She rolled the crushed tobacco between her lips, first to the right, then to the left, then round and round, cleaning her charcoal-black teeth.

Mother had no more arguments to use against her guest. She said, "If you really want to marry her—well—I hope she gets a good man who can look after her. I hope he loves her."

Inem's mother returned home, still rolling the tobacco around her mouth.

"I hope nothing happens to the poor child," Mother said.

"Will something happen to her?" I asked.

"No, 'Muk, nothing." Mother turned to something else. "If they are better off, perhaps we won't lose any more hens."

"Do they steal our hens, Mother?" I asked.

"No, 'Muk, no," she said slowly. "So young. Eight. Poor thing. But they need the dowry. It's the only way they can get money."

Then she went to the field at the back of the house to pick some long beans for soup.

Fifteen days later Inem's mother returned for her daughter. She was pleased that Inem did not object. And as Inem left, never to be a member of our household again, she said slowly at the kitchen door very politely, "Goodbye 'Muk, I'm going 'Muk." She went like a small child expecting a gift.

Inem never returned to our house. She was a good friend and I missed her. From that day on one of my foster brothers washed my feet in the bathroom before bed.

From time to time I wanted very much to see her again. As I lay in bed I often thought of her leaving our house hand-in-hand with her mother, for her own house was behind the wooden fence at the back of our yard.

She had been gone a month. I often went to her house to play with her. Mother was always angry when she found out. She always said, "What do you think you can learn there?" I could never find any answer. Mother always had her reasons when she was angry. Her words were thick walls which no excuses could ever pierce. So I thought it best to say nothing. The key to her anger almost certainly lay in the sentence she repeated over and over: "Why play with her? There are lots of other children, aren't there? She is almost a married woman."

But I kept going to her house, secretly. I was often surprised at the prohibition and my need to defy it. The defiance gave me pleasure. Children such as I had many restrictions and prohibitions placed upon us. Everything in the world had been placed there to discipline us and stop us doing what we wanted. Consciously or not, we felt that the world had been created for adults.

The wedding day came.

Inem's family cooked food and delicacies for five days prior to it. I went to their house often.

The day before the wedding Inem was dressed in beautiful clothes. Mother sent me with five kilos of rice and a farthing as our contribution to the feast. In the afternoon we children gathered around and stared at Inem's dressing. The hair on her forehead and in front of her ears, as well as her eyelashes, was trimmed and carefully curled, then set with mascara. The bun of hair behind her head was enlarged with teak bark and ornamented with paper flowers called *sunduk mentul*. Her clothes were of satin. Her skirt was genuine Solo batik. They had hired the lot from a Chinese merchant near the town square—the gold rings and bangles too.

The house was decorated with leaves of banyan[3] and young coconut. Tricoloured flags were placed in crosses on the walls and surrounded with palm branches. The pillars were decorated with tricoloured ribbon.

My mother came and helped. Although not for very long. She seldom did this for any but very close neighbours. She stayed less than an hour. Inem's future husband sent presents of food, a billy goat, rice, a parcel of salt, a sack of husked coconuts, and half a sack of sugar.

The harvest was just over. Rice was cheap. And when rice was cheap everything was. Marriages were celebrated ostentatiously. Inem's family, however, had not been able to hire a puppet show because the puppeteers had prior bookings from other families in other villages. The puppet show was the most popular form of entertainment in our district. There were three types: the classical flat leather puppets which dealt with episodes from the Indian epics *Ramayana*[4] and *Mahabharata*[5]; the flat wooden puppets which dealt with stories from Arabia, Persia, India, China, and medieval Java; and the not very popular wooden dolls.

Because there were no puppeteers, Inem's family decided, after fierce argument, to hire some dancing girls. Inem's mother's family were devoutly religious. But her father refused to give in. The dancing girls came, and the orchestra.

Mother forbade me to watch, but I did.

"Why do you watch those vile creatures? Look at your religious teacher. He is Inem's father's brother-in-law. He won't look at them. You know that."

The teacher's house was to the right of Inem's, also behind ours. Mother later exulted in his refusal to attend. He was a truly pious man. Inem's father was a fiend. Not everyone agreed.

Mother's anger was intensified by something which I didn't understand at the time, their "lack of respect for womanhood" as she bitterly put it.

When it was time for the bride to be joined with the groom, Inem was led away from the mat she sat on to the waiting bridegroom. Little Inem squatted and bowed to her future husband, then washed his feet with rosewater from a teak jar. Then they were bound together and led back to the mat. The guests repeated among themselves, "One child becomes two, one child becomes two, one child becomes two." The women smiled as though that delight was their own.

But I noticed that Inem was crying. The tears made stripes down her face and ruined her rouge. At home I asked why. Mother told me, "If a bride cries it means that she is thinking of her ancestors. Their spirits take part in the ceremony too. And they are pleased that their descendants have been married happily."

I thought no more about it. Later I found out the real reason. Inem wanted to urinate but didn't dare tell anyone.

The celebrations ended joylessly. No other guests came to contribute. The decorations were taken down. And by the time the merchants came to collect their debts, Inem's father had left. Inem and her mother made batik continuously, day and night. They were often found working at three in the morning. The smoke of the candle-wax used for pattern-making billowed up between them. There were regular quarrels too.

Once when I was asleep in Mother's bed, I was wakened by loud shouts: "I won't! I won't!" I heard beating on a door and hollow thumping. It was Inem.

"Mummy, why is Inem crying?" I asked.

"They are fighting. I hope nothing happens to her, poor child," she said, without further explanation.

"Will something happen to her?" I demanded.

Mother refused to say more. And then, when the screaming was over, we went back to sleep. Inem screamed almost every night. Screamed and screamed. Each time I heard her, I asked Mother about it but I was never given a satisfactory answer. Sometimes she sighed, "Poor thing. She's so young."

One day Inem came to our house and went straight to my mother. Her face was pale. She began conversation by crying, politely. Mother spoke first. "Why are you crying, Inem? Have you been fighting?"

"Madam," Inem said, "please," sobbing, "take me back again."

"Are you married, Inem?"

Inem cried again. As she cried she said, "I don't like it, madam."

"Why, Inem? Don't you like your husband?"

"Madam, please. He fights with me every night."

"Can't you say, 'Don't do that, please'?"

"I'm scared. Scared of him. He is so big. He holds me so tightly that I can't breathe. Please take me back."

"I would if you weren't married, Inem. But as you are. . . ." Mother said.

Inem cried. "I don't want to be, madam."

"You may not want to be, Inem, but you are. Perhaps one day your husband will treat you as he should and you'll be happy together then. You wanted to get married before, didn't you?"

"Yes madam. . .but, but. . ."

"Inem, no matter what happens a woman must be loyal to her husband. If she is not, her ancestors will curse her."

Inem cried so much that she could not speak.

"You must promise me, Inem, that you will always have his meals ready when he wants them. If you have been lazy, you must ask God's forgiveness. You must wash his clothes properly and comfort him when he is tired. You must give him proper medicine when he is sick."

Inem said nothing. She continued crying.

"Go home and be a good wife. If he is bad, you must be good. If he is good, you must be better. He is your husband."

Inem did not move. She continued to sit on the floor.

"Stand up and go back to your husband. If you leave him, nothing good will ever happen to you again."

"Yes madam," she said, broken.

She slowly stood up and walked home.

"Poor thing, so young," Mother said.

"Mummy, did Daddy ever fight with you?" I asked.

Mother looked carefully into my eyes. Then her serious expression disappeared and she smiled. "No," she said. "Your father was the gentlest man in the whole world, 'Muk."

She went into the kitchen and took a hoe, and began digging next to me in the garden.

A year passed by, unnoticed. One day Inem came again. She had grown. She was mature, although only nine years old. As usual, she went straight to Mother and sat on the floor with her head bowed.

"Madam, I'm not married now."

"What?"

"I'm not married."

"Has he divorced you?" Mother asked.

"Yes madam."

"Why?"

Inem did not answer.

"Weren't you a good wife?"

"I think so."

"Did you comfort him when he was tired?"

"Yes madam. I did everything you told me."

"Why did he divorce you?"

"He used to hit me."

"Hit you? A child like you?"

"I was a good wife. If he hit me and I hurt, I was being good, wasn't I?" she asked, seeking guidance.

Mother looked at her in silence.

Then she whispered, "He hit you."

"Yes madam, he hit me. Like my parents do."

"Perhaps you weren't a good wife. A man would not hit a woman if she served him properly."

Inem did not reply. Then she shifted the direction of the conversation. "Will you take me back now, madam?"

Mother answered firmly. With great determination she said, "Inem, you are now a divorced woman. I have a number of young men staying in the house. Do you think that would be right?"

"They wouldn't hit me, would they?"

"No, that isn't what I mean. A young divorcee in a house full of men—people would talk."

"Would they talk about me, madam?"

"No, they would talk about decency."

"Decency, madam? Is that why I can't work for you?"

"It is, Inem."

The young divorcee said nothing. She sat on the floor, with no apparent intention of leaving. Mother went to her and caressed her shoulder. "You must go back, Inem—help your parents. I'm very sorry I can't take you."

Two teardrops formed in the young woman's eyes. She stood and walked wearily out of our house. After that she seldom left her parents' house She was a nine-year-old divorcee, a burden on her parents, and anyone who wanted to hit her could: her mother, her younger brother, her uncle, the neighbours, her aunt. She never came back to our house.

Often I heard her calling out in pain. I covered my ears. Mother continued steadfast in her defence of propriety.

NOTES

[1]Batik patterns are produced by dipping fabric into a dye bath over and over again, each time covering portions of the design with wax. Intricate patterns in wax are traced onto the fabric with a small copper tool or applied with a stamp. Some of the most elaborate batiks come from the Solo region in eastern Java.

[2]The betel nut is the seed of a tall palm, chewed with dried betel leaves and lime as a stimulant.

[3]banyan: a fig tree

[4]*Ramayana*: a Sanskrit epic, based on legends, about the hero Rama

[5]*Mahabharata*: a Sanskrit epic from ancient times, telling of a great battle fought by the descendants of King Bharata

Flatcar

BY AKUTAGAWA RYUNOSUKE

TRANSLATED BY RICHARD N. McKINNON

AKUTAGAWA Ryunosuke (1892–1927) was a master storyteller whose stories reflect his belief that people are responsible for their own behaviour. Many of his stories focus on the conflicting and contradictory choices the characters make. Akutagawa had an unhappy childhood and adolescence, and often retreated into the world of literature where he could observe human behaviour without being hurt by it.

He is one of the most widely translated Japanese authors and is known world-wide as the author of "Rashomon," the story which is the basis of director Akira Kurosawa's 1950 film Rashomon, the first internationally acclaimed Japanese motion picture.

"Flatcar," published in 1922, is based on the experiences of an acquaintance.

Ryohei [*Rio-hay*] was eight years old when they started working on the light railway between Odawara and Atami. Ryohei went to the edge of town every day to watch them at work. Actually, the work amounted to nothing more than transporting dirt on flatcars, but he went because he enjoyed watching this operation.

Two labourers would be standing at the back of the flatcar behind a pile of dirt. Since the flatcar came down the mountainside, it would swoop downhill under its own power. The chassis would quiver as if whipped by the wind; the labourers' coattails would flap in the air, and the thin rails would bend under the impact. Watching this sight, Ryohei would wish that he could become a labourer. At times he would also wish he could ride alongside the labourers on the flatcar even if it were only once. When the flatcar reached the edge of town where the ground was level, it would automatically come to a stop. The labourers would hop down from the flatcar, and immediately pour the dirt out at the end of the tracks. They would then start pushing the flatcar back up the hill. It was at times like this that Ryohei wished he could at least push the flatcar up the hill, even if he couldn't get a ride.

One evening in early February, Ryohei went to the edge of town where the flatcars were kept. He took along his little brother, two years younger than he, and a neighbour's child who was the same age as his brother. The mud-caked flatcars were lined up in the half-twilight. He looked around but there were no signs of labourers anywhere. Hesitantly, the three pushed the flatcar which stood last in line. Suddenly, under their combined efforts, the wheels began to roll. The sound of the wheels scared Ryohei, but when he heard them a second time he was no longer afraid. Thump, thump—the flatcar slowly made its way up the tracks under the pressure of three pairs of hands.

When it had travelled some twenty metres the grade got steeper, and although they applied themselves the flatcar wouldn't move any further. In fact, at times, they were almost pushed back down along with the flatcar. Thinking they had come far enough, Ryohei signalled the two younger boys:

"Come on; let's hop on."

They let go together and swung onto the flatcar, which went slowly at first, but gradually gained speed until it was going down the tracks very fast. The scenery ahead rapidly unfolded before Ryohei's eyes and seemed, instantly, to be parted to the sides. The evening breeze grazing his cheeks, the quivering flatcar dancing under his feet—Ryohei was almost delirious with joy.

But in a few minutes the flatcar had come to the end of the line, and to a dead stop.

"Come on; we'll do it again!"

With the two younger boys Ryohei prepared to push the flatcar again. But, suddenly, before the wheels started to roll they heard footsteps behind them, which almost instantly turned into shouts.

"Hey, you there. Who told you you could touch those flatcars?" A tall labourer stood there motionless, wearing an old work jacket and an out-of-season straw hat. But, by the time they had made him out, they were already some twenty metres from where they had been, and were running. Ryohei never again felt like riding flatcars, although he had seen them untended in the work area on his way home from running errands. Ryohei can still vividly recall the way that labourer had looked—the small yellow straw hat flickering in the half-twilight. But even that impression seems to fade with every passing year.

One afternoon, some ten days later, Ryohei again stood alone in the work area watching the flatcars come by. One of them was piled high with dirt; but there was a second one coming up the heavy tracks which were to become the main line. It was loaded with railroad ties. Two younger men were pushing this particular flatcar, and as soon as Ryohei noticed them he felt he could be friends with them. "They won't shout at me," he thought to himself and ran toward them.

"Mister, shall I help push?"

"Why, sure; help us push!"

Just as Ryohei had expected, one of them—the man wearing a striped shirt—replied pleasantly, as he continued to push with his head down. Ryohei got between the two men and started to push with all his strength.

"You're pretty strong there, boy!"

The other man—he had a cigarette behind his ear—praised Ryohei, too.

After a while the grade got easier. Ryohei was terribly worried that, at any moment, they might say, "You don't need to push any more." But the two labourers went on pushing without a word, holding themselves a little more erect now than before. Ryohei could no longer keep his thoughts to himself, and timidly asked:

"Can I just go on pushing?"

"Sure thing," they both replied.

Ryohei thought to himself, "They are real nice." When they had gone some four or five hundred metres, the grade rose sharply again. There were tangerine orchards on both sides of the tracks, and the sunlight shone upon the countless golden fruit.

"I'd much rather climb, 'cause they'll let me keep on pushing," Ryohei was thinking as he put the strength of his whole body into pushing the flatcar.

When they had climbed to the very top of the slope through the tangerine orchards, the roadbed took a sharp turn downward. The man with the striped shirt called to Ryohei, "Hey, hop on." Ryohei scrambled onto the car. As soon as they had all jumped on, the car sped down the tracks, whipping up the fragrant smell from the tangerine orchards. Ryohei's coat was bulging in the breeze.

"It's much more fun to ride than to push." Such obvious thoughts entered his mind. "If one has to push a lot on the way over, there will be many places to ride on the return trip."

When they came to a bamboo grove the car slowly came to a stop. The three of them once again started pushing the heavy flatcar. The bamboo grove, in turn, changed to a thicket. Here and there along the incline there was such an accumulation of dead leaves that they almost completely covered the rusty tracks. When they finally made it to the top, a cool sea opened up before them beyond a high cliff, and, at that instant, Ryohei realized he had come too far.

The three climbed onto the flatcar again. The flatcar ran under the branches of the thicket with the sea on their right. Ryohei, however, could no longer enjoy the ride in the way he had before. He even wished hard that they would turn back. But it was obvious even to him that neither they nor the flatcar could turn back until they got to their destination.

The next time the flatcar came to a stop they were in front of a straw-thatched teahouse, and immediately behind it rose a mountain which had been cut through. The labourers went into the teahouse and leisurely sipped some tea with a woman who carried an infant tied to her back. Left to his own devices, Ryohei became fretful and kept circling the flatcar. The mud which spattered on the wooden side boards on top of the chassis was caked dry.

A few minutes later the man who had had a cigarette behind his ear came out of the teahouse and gave him some candy wrapped in a newspaper. "Thank you," Ryohei said without any feeling. Then he realized immediately how rude he had been and stuck a piece of candy into his mouth as if to make amends. It smelled of kerosene, apparently from the newspaper.

The three trundled the flatcar along a gentle slope. Ryohei had his hands on the flatcar, but his mind was on other things.

When they reached the bottom of the hill on the other side there was another teahouse just like the first one, and when the labourers went in, Ryohei sat on the flatcar, concentrating on the one thought of going home. The light of the setting sun slowly faded from the plum blossoms in front of the teahouse.

"It's almost sundown." When this thought came to him he couldn't just sit there doing nothing. He tried to divert his mind from his worries—he kicked the wheels of the flatcar, and even tried pushing the flatcar with all his might, knowing full well how futile it was.

When the labourers came out they rested their hands on the railroad ties on the flatcar and casually remarked:

"Boy, you better run along. We're spending the night at the other end."

"If you're too late getting home your folks will probably worry."

For an instant Ryohei was completely taken aback. It was already getting dark. He had travelled as far as Iwamura last year, but today he had come fully three or four times that far. He would have to travel that road all alone, and on foot. All these things flashed through his mind. Ryohei was almost in tears, but he thought that nothing was gained by crying, that this was no time for crying. He gave a perfunctory bow to the two young labourers and started running along the tracks.

For a while Ryohei ran along the tracks as if in a daze. Soon he realized that the package of candy was getting in the way. He tossed it away by the roadside, and while he was at it he also kicked off his sandals. The gravel cut into the soles of his stockinged feet but his feet felt much lighter. He ran up the steep hill, feeling the ocean on his left. He screwed up his face as he choked up with tears now and then—he was trying to be brave, but even so he sniffled constantly.

As he rushed past the bamboo grove, the last glow of the setting sun was fading from the sky over the mountain. Ryohei was beside himself with worry. Perhaps it was because he was now travelling in the opposite direction. He felt uneasy about the change in scenery. His clothes were drenched with perspiration. His jacket was a nuisance, and he flung it off. Desperately he kept on running.

By the time he got to the tangerine orchards it was fast growing dark. "If I can only stay alive..." Ryohei told himself as he just kept on running whether he slipped or stumbled.

When in the distant twilight he finally caught sight of the work area at the edge of town, Ryohei was suddenly seized by a desire to cry his heart out. He twisted his face, but kept right on running without crying.

When he entered the town, lights were burning in the houses on both sides of the street. In the light he could see the steam rising from his head. The women who were drawing water at the well and the men who were returning from their farms noticed Ryohei breathing heavily as he ran. "What's the matter?" they called to him. But he said nothing and ran past the variety store, the barbershop, and the brightly-lit houses.

When, at last, he dashed into the front door of his home Ryohei could no longer keep from bursting into tears. His father and mother rushed to his side when they heard him. His mother held him close to her and said something. But Ryohei flailed about with his arms and legs and went on sobbing and crying. Several women in the neighbourhood, probably hearing his loud wails, gathered in the dark doorway. Like his parents they asked him why he was crying. But no matter what they said, Ryohei could only continue to cry. It seemed to him that no amount of crying could fully make up for the sense of loneliness he had experienced when he was running along that long road.

Ryohei was twenty-five when he came out to Tokyo with his wife and children. He is now a proofreader and works on the second floor of a certain publishing house. But every now and then that experience comes back to him for no reason at all. For no reason?—Exhausted from his daily work, even now, as in his earlier years, he sees a narrow road fitfully running through dark groves and hills.

THE SKY'S ESCAPE

"WHEN WILL IT ALL BE OVER?"

Canadian troops in Korea during the 1950s.

The Ox Bell

EXCERPT FROM THE NOVEL *THE YELLOW RIVER FLOWS EAST*

BY LI ZHUN

TRANSLATED BY WANG MINGJIE

LI Zhun [Lee Jun] (1928–   ), labelled a "counterrevolutionary" and sent to labour in the countryside during the Cultural Revolution (1966–1976) when most writers were persecuted, usually writes about Chinese peasants in their struggle for a new and better life.

"The Ox Bell" is taken from his two-volume novel, The Yellow River Flows East, *set near the beginning of World War II when the Japanese invaded China. The Chinese government of the time, the Kuomintang, broke the dikes on the Yellow River, flooding the countryside of central China to stop the advance of the Japanese. According to Li, over ten million people were forced to flee their homes; nearly one million died in the flood. Fourteen years old at the time, Li was one of the refugees who fled west.*

The Yellow River Flows East tells the stories of seven refugee families who fled the floodwaters and of their struggle to survive.

Old Qing's [*Ching*] ox-cart was appropriated by Kuomintang[1] [*Gwah-min-dang*] troops. Under the supervision of a battalion aide-de-camp named Cui [*Chuy*], it was driven to the battalion's temporary headquarters in a primary school in front of the village and loaded with box after box of ammunition. When two bundles of rifles were brought, Old Qing spoke up: "Sir, you can't put any more on it. It's all made of iron. Too heavy!"

"What are you afraid of?" retorted Cui. "Your ox is big and strong."

"Sir, he appears big but he's actually very young," Old Qing explained. "Only a calf, in fact. Please don't add any more."

"Okay, okay!"

Despite this, he had another two huge wicker chests and a large basket put on the cart. The basket was full of cooking utensils, beneath which was a pair of incense burners made of a copper-nickel alloy, probably part of their loot.

Each time an article was loaded on, Old Qing's heart missed a beat. The cart had only been made the previous year from a plane tree he had felled and painted with *tong* oil[2] not long ago. Now, under such a heavy load, it creaked, making the old man's heart ache. He tried to lift the shafts to see how heavy it was. It was over eight hundred catties[3], he reckoned. The battalion leader's wife came out of the gate and climbed on to the cart. Old Qing looked at the plump woman and then at his ox and could not help heaving a soft sigh.

He hitched the harness over the beast's head and patted it on the back, saying as if cajoling a child, "Giddyap! Giddyap!" Suddenly the ox thrust its head forward and the cart began to move. Cui jumped onto it as agilely as a monkey and sat very close to the woman.

An orderly called Xiao Qi [*Siow Chee*] followed the cart but as soon as it was out of the village, he stealthily climbed on and sat at the back.

Cui asked Old Qing, "Old man, why don't you sit on the cart? Come on. Jump on!"

"No," replied Old Qing. "We peasants have a rule: Never sit on a heavily loaded cart."

Cui sniffed and said, "Bumpkin! Too fussy."

Old Qing pretended not to hear him and decided to say nothing. Clouds of dust rose on the loess road, for the Kuomintang's defeated soldiers swarmed along it towards the west. Some carried heavy loads of iron cauldrons, oil containers, their caps stuck on one side of their heads, their rifles pointing downwards. Puttees on some thin legs were already loose over the feet. Officers on horses shouted, urging them on.

Perhaps thinking the soldiers were too slow, officers at the rear fired their pistols abruptly while shouting at the top of their voices, "The Japs are behind us. Hurry up!" "At the double! Quick march, those at the back!" More clouds of dust rose on the road as the soldiers began to run like herds of sheep.

Cui cried out too, "Old man, can't this ox of yours gallop?"

"It can fly," Old Qing said, tongue in cheek, "if you'll give it two wings. Better to draw a heavy load rather than lumps of heavy meat! Don't you see he's already sweating?"

Snubbed, Cui was very put out. A short distance later, he saw a few small willow trees at the roadside. He jumped down and snapped off a branch. When he resumed his seat, he trimmed off all the little twigs and then ferociously whipped the rump of the calf.

The young ox had never been flogged like this. After two slashes, it glared and galloped for all it was worth. Old Qing, lagging behind, shouted while running, "Please stop! Stop!" But Cui kept flailing the beast which, after running for more than ten *li*⁴, was drenched with sweat. Old Qing caught up at last and grasped the rope round the ox's nose. "Sir," he said, "what do you think you're doing? Do you want to whip him to death?"

"You can't hold me up in my official duty! What if the Japs catch up? Will you answer to that?"

"Why didn't you take a car, or better still a plane?"

"I'll teach you a good lesson, you old fool!" Cui brandished his switch and was about to jump off when the battalion leader's wife caught him and said, "Forget it, Cui. Forget it. There are still a couple of days to Xuchang. You mustn't lose your temper on the way." Then she turned to Old Qing, "Let's carry on, old brother. We're all in the same boat now. In a way we're like one family. Surely there's nothing we can't discuss."

When they passed a pool, Old Qing fetched a pail of water and let the ox drink. The ox was so thirsty that it drank it all in one gulp. It had never drunk like this before. Licking its upper lip, it looked at Old Qing as though pleading for more. Old Qing brought another half-pail which it soon emptied.

It was dusk when they reached a small inn called the Five-*li* Inn. Cui found a room for the woman and settled her down. Old Qing prepared to feed his ox. As he unharnessed it, he noticed on its neck a raw patch as large as his palm. The sight of the red flesh with traces of blood made the old man's heart ache. He had no appetite for supper.

He burnt some paper and spread the ashes on the wound. The calf licked his hand as if showing its gratitude. "Have a good rest," said Old Qing. "You'll have to work tomorrow. If only I could replace you."

After two helpings of fodder, the ox knelt beside the shafts. Old Qing, having smoked two bowls of tobacco, felt drowsy. But he couldn't fall asleep despite the whole day's running because the ox hadn't chewed its cud. He always slept only when the ox began to chew its cud. Every night, when it did this, the bell dangling from its neck would strike a rhythmic ding...dong...

ding...dong...sending the old man off to sleep. But tonight, there was no sound of the bell. Old Qing waited restlessly, his bloodshot eyes wide-open.

"Why not chew your cud?" With that, Old Qing stepped over and felt the calf's nose, which was cold and covered with tiny beads of sweat.

"He's bloated!" Old Qing murmured, with pain. But there was nowhere to find any medicine, no herbs, not even a piece of ginger.

It was very late but the ox could not digest its food. It stood and knelt by turns, panting heavily. Old Qing could do nothing but drape his worn-out padded coat over it.

At dawn, Old Qing found out that there was a local vet. He wanted to take the ox to him and entered the house to tell Cui. Reaching his room, he tried to push open the door, but it was bolted from inside. There was a lattice window beside the door. Since the upper part of the window was not secured, he pushed it open a crack. He was about to call out to Cui, when to his surprise he saw two people in the bed. The battalion leader's wife's blue gown was draped over the back of a chair. Terrified, he quickly shut the window.

"Who is it? What is it?" Cui's voice sounded from inside. Old Qing trotted out of the house and went back to his ox. He spat and cursed, "Dammit! Just my bad luck! Those creatures...."

Cui, probably frightened too, was in a very bad mood that morning. He kicked the orderly, Xiao Qi, and flung a stone at a dog in the street. When Old Qing told him that the ox was ill, he bellowed, his arms akimbo, "I don't care a damn about your ox, but I must get to Linying County this afternoon or I'll shoot you!"

Old Qing glared at him, swallowing hard.

When he tried to harness the ox, it refused to go between the shafts. Cui withdrew the iron rod from his rifle to strike it.

Old Qing rushed to stand between Cui and the ox and protested, "Sir, he's a dumb creature. You can't beat him at random." He then untied a towel around his waist and wrapped it round the ox's headband. As though understanding his predicament, the ox sighed and stepped reluctantly in between the shafts.

They continued the journey, but the ox's steps became very unsteady. Seeing a slope ahead, Old Qing pleaded with those on the cart, "Please jump off and walk a few steps. He's unable to pull it up."

Embarrassed, Xiao Qi dismounted. Cui, his head wrapped in a heavy coat, snored in reply.

Old Qing, knowing he was only pretending, ignored him. He tied a thick hemp rope to the cart and pulled it laboriously up the slope. Xiao Qi, shy of pushing the cart, disappeared into the field to pee.

The two on the cart began flirting, pinching, and nipping amid titters and giggles. One of them threw a cucumber on the ground. Old Qing felt disgusted. If only he could give them a good thrashing.

It was about noon, and the road was almost smoking under the scorching sun. Gunfire sounded in the distance behind them. People passing said that some refugees had tried to rob some soldiers of their guns. Hearing this, Cui began to whip the ox again. It galloped off in a frenzy. But after six *li* or so, its forelegs gave way and it collapsed before a small mound.

Old Qing rushed over, cut off the strap beneath the ox's neck, and helped to lift the shafts. But the ox only stared, its legs stretched out. No amount of shouting or kicking would make it rise again.

Old Qing unharnessed it and pushed the cart to the roadside. Fearing the heat, Cui and the woman went to find some food in the village ahead. The orderly took the opportunity to steal a watermelon from a nearby field. He broke it open and offered Old Qing a piece.

"Have a piece of melon, uncle. It's delicious."

Old Qing shook his head and said, "You go ahead." But Xiao Qi insisted, "Have a piece. It's so hot."

The old man took a piece and gave it to the ox. The ox opened its eyes, looked at it and then, after two breaths, closed them again.

The rims of Old Qing's eyes became red. He put his straw hat on the ox's head and, finding himself a twig, fanned away the flies.

Darkness fell. The ox's breathing was laboured and it was unable to stand. Cui had returned twice, but seeing there was no hope went back to the village to find a replacement. Xiao Qi was already sound asleep on the cart.

Old Qing, exhausted by now, slept with his back against a persimmon tree. But late at night, he awoke feeling something soft nestling against him. It was his ox! Goodness knows when it had come and lain beside him. It was dead. Old Qing struck two flints together to make a light and had a close look at it. Its eyes were shut with two big tears at the corners.

Tears streamed down Old Qing's cheeks. He remembered how, when he had first bought it, the little calf had followed him as he went to hoe his field. Sometimes, it would play games with him, brushing against him or taking away the towel round his waist without his knowing it. The first time the calf pulled a plough, it ran like a tiger, and Old Qing found it difficult to control. When it reached the end of the field, it turned round automatically and carried on at exactly the right furrow. . . .

It had brought him excitement and joy. But now he was very miserable. Presently, he caught sight of two dogs lurking nearby staring at the dead ox, their eyes gleaming.

"So it was those two dogs which chased my ox here! They pestered him. That's why he came to me." Fury raged in his heart. He tiptoed to the cart and picked up his whip. Just as the two dogs were approaching the ox, he lashed out and set one dog rolling on the ground. The other fled with its tail between its legs. Old Qing caught up with it and slashed at its leg. The dog, with one leg up, yelped and ran wildly.

Old Qing was known for his skill with a whip. He was able to whip away the burning head of a joss-stick at night or a persimmon from a tree without damaging a leaf. But what was the use of that?

At dawn, Cui returned from the village.

"How's your ox, old man?" he asked in a loud voice. "Is it all right?"

Old Qing ignored him.

Cui looked at the ox and said again, "Oh, is it dead? Too spoilt, I suppose."

The old man still kept silent.

"Better sell it and have it cut up right away. It's fat and young. You'll get a lot of money."

At this, Old Qing said, "Sir, you go ahead and sell it. And you can have all the money. In your eyes, it's only a beast while you are a man. To me, he was a person. Do you know how we peasants feel about it? Don't you know we treat the ox as a human being? When you want grain, we give you grain; when you want money, we give you money; when you want a cart, we provide the cart. But what are *you* doing? When the Japs came, you fled west without firing a shot. Yet you complained that the ox was too slow. Now you've worked him to death! You've got a pistol in your hand, and all I have is my whip. I'm no match for you. But you've no right to bully me! None!"

Old Qing was shaking all over, his eyes bloodshot. Scared, Cui, murmured, "The old man's crazy! He's crazy!"

NOTES

[1]In 1949 the Kuomintang (or Nationalist Chinese) forces, led by Chiang Kai-shek, were defeated by the Communist People's Army and forced to flee to Taiwan.

[2]*tong* oil: derived from the *tong* tree, this oil is valued for its water-repelling properties

[3]catties: one catty is equivalent to 600 grams

[4]*li*: a measure of distance equal to 0.5 km

A Row of Shop-houses in our Village

BY KERIS MAS

TRANSLATED BY HARRY AVELING

Keris MAS is the pen name of Kamaludin Muhammad, a well-known Malay short story writer. He began writing in 1945 at the end of the Japanese occupation of Malaysia. Prior to the occupation, Malaysia had been ruled by the British. When the British returned in 1945, they faced a strong independence movement, and in 1948 proclaimed the Emergency Regulations. The struggle lasted until 1956 when Malaysia gained its independence.

Mas was active in the independence movement and contended that: "Language and literature are instruments for national solidarity. . . [and] for the advancement of popular thought in line with the aspiration for social justice, prosperity, peace, and harmony." His stories are marked by a sense of realism and a passion for social and economic equality.

Malaysia has a highly diverse population—53% Malay, 35% Chinese, 11% East Indian, and 1% aboriginal peoples. "A Row of Shop-houses in Our Village" shows the Malaysian struggle for independence and how this struggle sometimes caused divided loyalties among Malaysians of different ethnic backgrounds.

The row of shop-houses in my village—eight in all—has just been destroyed by fire.

The first light of dawn is over. It is almost day.

One by one, everyone has gone home. The pale glow of the electric street lights reflects blankly on the road. Smoke mingles with the swirling mist. The magpies are silent, their melodious cries stilled by the sadness. And the sobs of the victims of the fire fill the air.

Undisturbed by any wind, the thin trails of smoke rise into the sky from the black pillars as they emerge more starkly against the early light.

We went to the mosque on this occasion. Many turned up for the early morning prayers. Muezzin Seman's[1] call rose, pure and undefiled, to heights beyond the imagination. We all prayed: "O Lord, protect us from all disaster!"

Disaster is all we have known the last few months. Nine of our young men have been taken away by the powers that be. Three of them were Chinese boys, who had been born and raised as one of us. Their parents and grandparents had worked with our parents and grandparents in establishing the village many decades ago.

Some of them had become rich traders. And some of us had become senior government officials. But most of us and most of them—the Malays and Chinese living in the village—shared the same fate: poverty and misery. We got on well with the merchants because we Malays worked hard in their rubber plantations. And the Chinese who rented the eight shop-houses became petty traders, reselling the things they had bought from the shops of the big merchants in town.

And we all, Malays and Chinese alike, looked up to the senior government officials, who came from our own stock, becaue they represented the lawful authorities and maintained the peace in the village.

During the Japanese Occupation, we had become even more united. Not only the poor, but the rich—the traders and government officials—shared the same manner of life, which was one of continuous hardship.

Some of our young men went to the jungle to help in the guerrilla movement against the Japanese. Some of us, all Chinese, were killed by the Japanese because of that.

When the British returned, our young men came home too, with their rifles and machine-guns. All of us, Malay and Chinese, shared a brief sense of relief.

During the Sino-Malay troubles, our village remained peaceful. No one swore "Death to the Infidels," and there were no Chinese making trouble as there were no Malays sharpening their *parangs*[2].

Then came the period of awakening. We—the Malays—began joining political parties. Our youth learnt to march, to sing, and to make speeches. Sometimes the Chinese lads joined in those songs and attended those meetings.

The youth, all of us in fact, had a new slogan, *Merdeka*, Independence! The Chinese boys learnt how to say it, even though the adults did not.

The eight shops went up in a solid sheet of flame. Two of the shops were occupied by Malays. They were the first Malay petty traders we had ever had in our village. One ran a sundry store, the other a coffee shop, selling cakes and cigarettes as well.

Things were peaceful then. But the poverty became more severe. People began worrying about feeding themselves, about their children's education, and about the lack of jobs for the increasing number of young people.

Our government officials did nothing. There were still forty hectares of unused forest land behind the village. Our young people had asked, time and again, if they could have title to the land and work it. Their requests had always been refused.

And our big Chinese traders had forced two of their tenants to get out of their shop-houses because they couldn't pay their rent. All the shopkeepers began to suffer. The villagers did not go to the shops as much as they used to, but instead began turning to the jungle and the river for their food. The two petty traders now took out licenses to farm vegetables on the edge of the forest. One of their boys learnt how to drive a truck and once a month, or even more often, took his father's vegetables into town to sell them. The truck often took our boys to their "independence" meetings too.

As unemployment spread, there were more and more political meetings. In the end the red and white flag was unfurled in our village and the children learnt to shout *Merdeka*!

Our old *Datok Penghulu*, the area headman, asked his assistant, "Why have things changed so much?"

"Our people are suffering too much," replied his assistant. "The big Chinese merchants don't care, and the government officers simply do as their superiors tell them, not considering nor bothering about the villagers' interests."

"And so?"

"So they join political parties. They want to have a voice and they want the authorities to hear their voice, while, on the other hand, those in authority at present only listen to the voice of their white masters."

"Will they fight us?"

"I don't think so. They don't want to fight anyone. They just want their rights."

"Then, what should we do?"

"Just wait and see. We have failed in our first responsibility, which is to look after the general welfare because many of our young people have no work; the government won't let them have the land they need. Our second responsibility is to keep the peace in the village. As long as they don't disturb the peace, I think all we can do is wait and see what happens."

The old *Datok Penghulu* nodded. Not long after, he told his assistant that he thought he was getting too old to deal with these new problems. It was time he retired.

A year later he did retire, and a year after that he passed away. He did not live to see how far the changes of the various forces that were so vigorously shaking up the lives of his young charges would go.

He did not hear the Emergency proclaimed. He did not see the trucks full of armed police passing along the road which ran through the village. He did not hear his neighbours lamenting the loss of their sons, as they were taken away in those police vehicles. And he did not see his young assistant take to the jungle with some of his Chinese and Malay friends.

The village was quiet then. The eight shops opened and closed as their owners felt inclined. Food could no longer be sold freely, and those who wanted to buy resorted more and more to the forests and to the rivers, and less and less to the shops. There was very little money about.

The boy stopped delivering his father's vegetables to town. His father and one of his father's friends—who helped him with the market gardens on the edge of the jungle—were among the nine men taken away by the police. Once they had gone, they never returned.

Finally, the security forces came to our village every day. They cleared the forest behind the village and established a base there. That was the end of any hope our young men might still have had to clear and cultivate new land.

The lifeless row of eight shops is finished—destroyed by fire. No one knows how it began.

Earlier in the morning, before dawn and the start of the fire, we were awakened by the sound of gunfire in the jungle. (Waking up in the middle of the night is something we have recently become accustomed to. The security forces in the jungle near our village often exchange fire, perhaps even with the assistant headman and those of our young men who went into the jungle with him.)

When the shots died away, we all ran outside because someone was shouting, "Fire! Fire!"

The dawn prayers made us feel calmer and more confident. We were briefly freed from the tragedy of the fire.

And then our worries revived as soon as we left the mosque. Anxiety hung over the village, disturbing the early morning's tranquillity. We faced the realities: What was to be done about the victims of the blaze?

Our community spirit was still there—we would share the good and the bad times together, but our energies had long been sapped by unendurable poverty.

Even before the sun had risen, the row of eight shop-houses had caused the villagers to gather and stand around. Bewilderment showed in their faces—and in their hearts.

And then the hand of authority appeared, the hand which has increasingly interfered in our affairs over the past few months, the hand which continues to play the major role in upsetting the calm of the village by day and night.

We are to be shifted. We, our families, our livestock, our rice, our loves, and our hatreds. Everything.

They say we have been helping the terrorists, helping our young men in the jungle. The shops are the pride of our village, yet they accuse us of setting fire to them so that we could distract the security forces from their pursuit of our boys in the jungle last night.

We are as powerless to meet their accusations as a beautiful woman in the hands of a terrible giant. We have lost all that we love best, all that we have lived for.

The early morning wind has started to blow, scattering the smoke from the black stumps of the eight shops which have been destroyed.

NOTES

[1]Muezzin: a Muslim crier who summons the faithful to prayer. Most Malays are Muslim.

[2]*parang*: a short machete

The Rainy Spell

(PART 3)

BY YUN HEUNG-GIL

TRANSLATED BY SUH JI-MOON

YUN Heung-gil [Yoon Hioong-gil] (1942–   ) grew up in extreme poverty during World War II and the Korean War. In his stories, he is concerned with the underprivileged and a social structure he perceives as irrational in modern Korea; however, his characters are not stereotypes—they are simply individuals trying to live in harmony with each other. His stories have been described as "quests into the problem of how life can be lived at all, and how it can be lived meaningfully."

"The Rainy Spell" is set during the Korean War (1950–1953), which occurred after Korea was arbitrarily divided into a Communist North and a non-Communist South at the end of World War II. Although the Thirty-eighth Parallel (of latitude) physically divided the country, people's loyalties were not so easily sorted out and many found themselves on the "wrong" side of the border. Families, friends, and neighbours were drawn into opposing camps, and spying and treachery were common.

In this excerpt from a longer story, a young boy living in a Southern village finds himself inadvertently drawn into the conflict. His uncle, who is clearly working with the North Korean forces, would be viewed as an enemy and a traitor in South Korea, thus bringing suspicion on his family.

A boy who had lately come to live in our village as a refugee from the North came to where we were playing, accompanied by a man wearing a straw hat. The boy, whose face was all scabby, said a few words to the man, pointing at me with his hand that had been scratching his bare, dirt-stained belly. The man gave me an attentive stare from beneath the wide brim of the straw hat which was shading a good part of his face. The boy from the North took what the strange man gave him from out of his pocket and galloped away like a fleeing hare. The tall man with the straw hat walked up to me directly. His dark, tanned skin, his sharp, penetrating eyes, and his unhesitating stride were somehow overpowering to me.

"What a fine boy!"

The stranger's eyes seemed to narrow and, surprisingly, unlike what I expected from my first impression, a friendly smile filled his face. He stroked my head a few times.

"You'd be a really lovely boy if you answered my questions straight."

The man's attitude made me extremely uneasy. I could not look into his eyes, so I opened and closed my hands for no reason, and kept standing there with my head lowered. In my palm was my paternal grandmother's silver hair-slide, which I had rubbed against a stone mortar into a giant nail, and which earned me victory over all the neighbourhood boys in nail fights.

"Your father's name is Kim Soon-ku, isn't it?" The man unbuttoned his white tieless shirt. "Then Kim Soon-chul must be your uncle, isn't he?"

The man took off his straw hat. I had not said a word till then. But he went on ingratiatingly, "That's right. You answer just like the clever boy you are!"

He shook his straw hat as if it were a fan, holding open his tieless shirt to ventilate his body.

"I'm your uncle's friend. We're very close friends, but it's been a long time since we met last. I have something very important to discuss with your uncle. Will you tell me where he is?"

The man, whom I had met for the first time in my life, used the standard Seoul dialect meticulously, like Aunt.

"Oh, isn't it hot! It's very hot in here. Shall we go over there where it's breezy and talk a little?"

He forbade the other children to follow. When we reached the shade of a tree on the hill behind the village where other children couldn't see us, the man halted and fumbled in his pocket.

"I've got a very important message to convey to your uncle. If you tell me where he is, I'll give you these," he said, holding out in his palm five flat pieces of something wrapped in silver paper. He unwrapped one of them and proffered it in front of my nose.

"Have you ever tasted anything like this?"

The dark-brown-coloured thing gave off a delicious fragrance.

"These are chocolates. I'll give you all of them if only you answer my question straight."

I took a great deal of care not to let my eyes rest on the strange treat. But I could not suppress my swallowing.

"There's nothing to be shy about. It's natural for good boys to get rewards. Now, won't you tell me? If only you tell me what I've asked you, I'll be happy because I'll meet my friend, and you'll be happy because you'll eat these delicious chocolates."

I don't know what it was that made me hesitate. Was it because I was undecided about the ethical propriety of accepting such a gift? Or was it because of the shyness of a country boy in front of a stranger, a shyness common to most country boys my age? I don't remember distinctly. But I think I remained standing there unresponsively for quite a while.

"Don't you want them?" the man pressed me. "You're sure you don't want them?" He made an expression of regret. "Well, then, there's no helping it. I did very much want to find you acting like a good boy and give you these delicious things. I myself don't need these sweets. Here, look. I'll just have to throw them away, even though that's not what I want to do with them."

Unbelievably, the man really threw one of them on the ground carelessly. He not only threw it down but stepped on it and crushed it. Casting a glance at me, he threw one more on the ground.

"I thought you were a bright boy. I'm really sorry."

He crushed the third one under his foot. There were only two pieces of the sweet remaining on his palm. It was evident that he was quite capable of crushing the remaining two into the ground. He suddenly chuckled loudly.

"You're crying? Poor boy! Hey, lad, it's not too late now. Think carefully. Hasn't your uncle been to the house? When was it?"

It was at that moment that I felt I was powerless to fend off sophisticated grown-ups' tactics. Then, as I thought that this man might really be a friend of my uncle, my heart felt a good deal lighter.

The first few words were the most difficult to utter. Once I began, however, I related what had happened as smoothly as reeling yarn off a spool.

My paternal aunt, who lived some thirteen kilometres off, came to visit us, walking the entire distance under the broiling July sun. There was no reason for me to attach any special meaning to Aunt's visit, as she had several times come to our house without announcement to stay for a day or two, even in those days of unrest. But things began to look very different when Mother, who had gone into the inner room with Aunt, sprang out of the room with a yellow complexion. Instead of sending me, as was usual, she ran out herself to fetch Father. Father, who had been weeding in the rice paddies, ran directly into the inner room with his muddy clothes and feet, without stopping to wash himself at the well. Mother, who returned hard upon his heels, fastened the twig gate shut even though it was broad daylight. Everybody seemed slightly out of their right senses. In the inner room the whole family, except my maternal grandmother and maternal aunt and me, was gathered and seemed to be discussing something momentous. Around sunset, the three of us who had been left out were given a bowl of cold rice each. As I finished my meal, I saw Father had changed into clean clothes. I looked suspiciously at Father's back as he stepped out of the twig gate into the alley paved with darkness.

"You go to sleep early," Mother told me, as she spread my mattress right beside where Paternal Grandmother was sitting. It seemed that everyone was bent on pushing me into sleep, even though it was still early in the evening.

"Wouldn't it be better to have him sleep in the other room?" Paternal Aunt queried of Mother, pointing her chin at me.

"I think it'll be all right," Paternal Grandmother said. "He sleeps deeply once he falls asleep."

"You must be dead tired from playing all day long. You must sleep like the dead until tomorrow morning, and not open your eyes a bit all through the night. You understand?" Mother instructed me.

I knew that Father had not gone out for a friendly visit. It was obvious that he went out on important business. I wanted to stay wide awake until Father returned. I was determined to find out what that important business of the grown-ups was that I was excluded from. To that end, it was necessary to pretend to obey their orders to go to sleep at once. I listened attentively for the least sound in the room, fighting back the sleep that overwhelmed me as soon as I lay down and closed my eyes. But no one said anything of any significance. And, before the important event of Father's arrival, I had fallen fast asleep.

I was awakened by a dull thud on the floor of the room.

"My God! Isn't that a bomb?"

I heard Paternal Grandmother's frightened voice. The two bulks that were blocking my sight were the seated figures of Father and Mother. Dull lamplight seeped dimly through the opening between the two large bulks.

"Undo your waistband, too," Father said to someone imperiously. The person seemed to hesitate a little, but there came a rustle from beyond

Father's bulk.

"*Two* pistols!"

"My God!" Mother and Grandmother softly exclaimed simultaneously. Sleep had completely deserted me, and a chill slid down my spine like a snake. Even though I knew nobody was paying any attention to me, I realized it was unsafe to let the grown-ups notice my wakefulness, and so I had to take painstaking care in moving my glance little by little. I concentrated all my nerves on what was happening in the small space visible to me.

"Has Dongman gone to sleep without knowing I'm coming?"

As it seemed that Father was about to turn to me, I closed my eyes quickly. The shadow that had been shielding my face moved aside quickly, and lamplight pricked my eyelids.

"We kept him in the dark," Mother said proudly, as if that had been some meritorious deed.

"Don't worry. Once he falls asleep, a team of horses couldn't kick him awake," Grandmother assisted.

There was a short silence in the room. It seemed that nobody dared open his mouth. But my ears were brimming with the thick voice of the man who had sneaked into the house in the dark, carrying pistols and hand grenades. If that man is really my uncle, I thought, news of whom the whole family had been fretting about, his voice has, regrettably, become so rough as to be unrecognizable to me at first. His voice didn't use to be as rough as a clay pot that has been carelessly handled on pebbles, or so heavily gloomy that nothing seemed capable of cheering it up. As far as I could remember, my uncle chuckled heartily at the slightest joke, frown as his elders might on such manners, rarely remaining aloof from disputes, but always trying to involve many people in them. He was easily excited or moved. But, no matter how I reckoned, there was no one but my uncle who could be the owner of that voice I had just heard. I imagined my uncle's face and form, which must have become as rough as the voice. Then, suddenly, I felt an uncontrollable itch in the hollows of my knees. The itch spread instantly over my entire body, as if I had been lying on ant-infested grass, and I had an uncontrollable yearning to scratch such parts as the middle of my back or my armpits or between my toes—places I could not reach with my hand to scratch while lying flat on my back without being noticed by the grown-ups. On top of this, my throat itched with an imminent cough, and my mouth filled with water.

Grandmother seemed most anxious to know what Uncle's life on the mountain was like. She heaped question upon question about how he fared on

the mountain. To all the questions Uncle answered barely a word or two, and seemed irked by the necessity of saying even that much. But Grandmother seemed not to have noticed Uncle's mood, and kept on asking questions without end.

"You say there are many others besides you, but they must all be men. Who cooks rice and soup at each mealtime?"

"We do."

"You make preserves and season vegetables, too?"

"Yes."

"How on earth! If only I could be there beside you, I'd prepare your food with proper seasoning!"

No response.

"Do they taste all right?"

"Yes."

"I know they couldn't, but I can't help asking all the same."

"They're all right."

"Don't you skip meals too often, because you move here and there?"

"No."

"Promise me you won't eat raw rice, however hungry you may get. You'd get diarrhea. If you did, what could you do in the depths of the mountain? You can't call a doctor or concoct medicine. Do pay attention, won't you?"

"Don't worry."

"And since you are in the depths of the mountain, it must be cold as January at night, even in summer like this. Do each of you have a quilt to cover your middle at night?"

"Of course."

"Padded with cotton wool?"

No response.

"Don't stay in the cold too long. And, for frostbite, eggplant stems are the best remedy. You boil the stems and soak your hands and feet in the fluid. That takes out the frostbite at once. If I was beside you..."

"Please don't worry!"

"How can I help it? It tears my heart to see your frostbitten hands and feet. The times are rough, but for you, my darling last-born, to get so frostbitten!"

"Please, Mother, stop!" Uncle sighed with impatience.

"Do, Mother, that's enough," Father chimed in cautiously.

"Do you mean I shouldn't worry, even though my son's hands are frostbitten like that?" Grandmother raised her voice angrily. Such things were to her of the utmost importance. But Father also raised his voice.

"It's going to be daybreak soon, and you keep wasting time with idle questions! How can you worry about preserves and quilts when his life's at stake?"

Grandmother was silenced. Of course she had many more questions, but a certain tone in Father's rebuke silenced her, stubborn as she was.

"What are you going to do from now on?" Father asked, after a pregnant silence. The question was directed at Uncle.

"About what?"

"Are you going to go back to the mountain and stay there?"

When Uncle kept silent, Father asked him if he would consider giving himself up to the police. Father slowly began his persuasion, as if it were something he had carefully considered for a long time. He emphasized again and again the misery of a hunted existence. Citing as an example a certain young man who had delivered himself up to the police and was now living quietly on his own farm, Father recommended urgently that Uncle do the same. He repeated again and again that, otherwise, Uncle would die a dog's death. A dog's death, a dog's death, a dog's death, a dog's death.

"Why do you keep saying it's a dog's death?" Uncle retorted sullenly. He swore that before long the People's Army[1] would win back the South. Vowing that he had only to remain alive until that day, he even recommended that Father should so conduct himself as not to get hurt when the government changed. Listening to his talk, I was struck once again by the great change in my uncle. His talk was fluent. In the old days, my uncle never used to be able to talk so logically. Because he had difficulty getting his points across by logical argument, he often used to resort to the aid of his fists in his sanguine impatience.

Uncle began to collect things, saying that he must go up the mountain before the sunrise. It must have been his pistols and hand grenades that he gathered up. Everybody moved at once.

"I won't let you go, never, now that you're in my house!"

I opened my eyes at last. In that sudden turmoil, nobody paid any attention to me slowly raising my body and sitting up. Uncle's face was covered all over with a bushy beard. Father and Aunt were on either side of him, almost hugging him as he sat leaning against the wall on the warmer part of the floor.

Grandmother snatched Uncle's arm from Aunt and, shaking it to and fro, entreated, "Because your brother told me lies, I thought you were staying comfortably somewhere. I thought you spent your days sitting on a chair in a town office somewhere, doing things like bawling out harsh constables. But now that I know the truth I won't let you go back to such a dreadful place! I'd die first rather than let you go!"

Grandmother wept, stroking Uncle's cheek with her palm.

"I'd let you go if I could go with you and look after you day and night, but since it seems I can't, I'll tie you down in this room and not let you out of my sight, day or night. Why can't you stay at home, farm the land, get married, and let me hold your children before I die?"

Aunt opened her lips for the first time in my hearing that night and talked to Uncle about the joys of married life, while Mother supported her with timely assents. Father talked again persuasively. He explained minutely what the drift of the war was, and tried to make Uncle realize that he was being deceived by the empty promises of the Communists. He said further that, as he knew a couple of people in the police force, there would be ways to get Uncle released without suffering bodily hurt. But Uncle at long last opened his mouth only to say, "Are you, too, trying to trick me into it?" and shook off Father's hand.

"What do you mean, trick you?"

"I've heard all about it." Uncle said that the police slaughtered all of the people who went down the mountain to surrender, decoyed by promises of pardon in printed handbills. He said that promises of unconditional pardon and freedom were scheming lies and tricks.

"And you, too, are trying to push me into the trap?"

"What?" Father's arm shot up in the air and the next moment there was the sound of a sharp slap on Uncle's cheek. Father panted furiously and glared at Uncle, as if he would have liked to tear him apart.

"How dare you strike my poor boy!" Grandmother wept aloud, covering Uncle with her body. Father drew the tobacco box near. His hands shook as he rolled up the green tobacco. Uncle dropped his head.

A cock crowed. At the sound Uncle lifted his head in fright and looked around at the members of the family. The short summer's night was about to end.

"I've killed people," he murmured huskily, like one who had just set down a heavy load he had carried a long, long way. "Many, many people."

Thus began Uncle's wavering toward self-surrender. It was a long persuasion that Father carried out that night, and the patience he showed for it was truly remarkable. At last everything was settled as Father had planned, and it was agreed that Uncle was to remain in hiding for a couple of days until Father obtained assurance from the police for Uncle's safety. Uncle was to go to the dug-out cave in the bamboo grove that Maternal Uncle had used for hiding during Communist occupation.

Everything was settled, and all that remained to be done was for everybody to snatch a wink of sleep before it was broad daylight. But that instant Uncle, who was about to pull off his shirt, suddenly bent forward and pressed his ear to the floor. Grandmother almost jumped from fright.

"What is it?"

"Ssh!"

Uncle put his forefinger on his lips and eyed the door of the room. Everybody's face stiffened, and all listened attentively for noise from outside.

"Someone's there."

My ears caught no sound. There were distant chirps of grass insects, but I could hear nothing like a human sound. But Uncle had his ear still glued to the floor and didn't seem likely to straighten up. For a while I heard only the loud pounding of my heart in that suffocating tension, but I caught a certain sound that Uncle must have spoken of. That sound, which distinctly was not the sound of a heart pounding, was of footsteps treading ground with long intervals in-between. They were so soft and careful that it was hard to tell whether they were approaching or receding.

"Who's that outside?"

Father's voice was low, but the reprimand was severe. Then the sound of movement stopped altogether. Suddenly it occurred to me that it was a familiar tread, of someone I knew very well. I quickly ransacked my brain, trying to work out who it might be. The footsteps began again. They seemed to be moving a little faster this time. Uncle's body shot up erect. Within the blinking of an eye, the dark bulk jumped over my seated form. The back door fell to the ground with a shattering sound, and Uncle's big bulk rushed away in the dark. He had already crossed the bamboo grove. His motion was so swift that nobody had had a second to say a word.

I went out through the frame of the back door that Uncle had knocked to the ground. I ran past the kitchen into the inner yard. I wasn't at all afraid, even though I was alone. I surveyed everything within the twig fence, from the yard and the kitchen garden down to the gates, but I could see nothing. When my eyes fell on the unlighted guest room, however, I caught the half-opened door of that room closing noiselessly, shutting out the dim, whitish glare of the morning. I savoured the discovery with rapture. It was indeed a familiar tread, of someone I knew very well.

"I'd have packed things for him to take if I'd known it would come to this! I didn't feed him a morsel, nor give him one clean garment! If only I'd known! How could I have not fed him one bowl of warm rice! If only I'd known!" Paternal Grandmother wailed, beating her chest. Paternal Aunt grasped my hand tightly and pulled me to one corner. Then she poured her hot breath into my ear.

"You mustn't tell anyone your uncle's been home. Do you understand? If you talk about such things to anybody, all of us must go to jail. Do you hear? Do you hear?"

Village people were surrounding my house, standing in multiple ranks in front of the gate. They were whispering things to each other and trying to look over the gate into the house. The wailing of women that I could hear from as far as the hill behind the village, I now found to be coming from my house. As I approached all eyes turned on me. Villagers exchanged meaning-ful glances among themselves, pointing their chins at me, and whispered again. The palisade of people suddenly parted in two, as if to make way. A strange man walked out ahead, with my father following. One step behind him I could see the man with the straw hat. He was holding coiled around his hand the rope that bound both my father's hands behind his back. On seeing me, he grinned and winked. Father halted in front of me. His eyes seemed yearning to say something to me, but he silently resumed walking. At the gate Mother, Paternal Aunt, and Paternal Grandmother were wailing and crying, repeatedly collapsing and sinking to the ground. Only then did pain begin to rise in me. During the entire day, while I was ransacking the village in search of the boy from the North who had conducted the man with the straw hat to me, the pain assailed me sometimes with a sense of betrayal, or a terrible fury, or an unbearable sorrow that stung my eyes and stabbed my heart. The man with the straw hat had promised me on his oath that he would never tell anybody what I would tell him. It was the first mortal treachery I experienced at the hands of a grown-up.

From that night Maternal Grandmother became my sole protectress and friend. Between us there was the shared secret of sinners. It could have been this secret that gave the two of us the strength to support each other through many persecutions. My Paternal Grandmother was a woman of very strong temper. If she so much as caught sight of me, she started back as if she had stepped on a snake, and she refused not only to talk to me but even to let me have my meals in the inner room with the family.

Father returned home after spending seven full days at the police station. My mother, who had made frequent trips to town to bring in Father's food, sprinkled salt again and again on his head, sniffing and sobbing, as he stepped into the gate. Father's good-looking face had changed a great deal in those seven days. His eyes were sunken, his cheekbones stood out, and his face, which had become pale-bluish like newly bleached cotton, looked indescribably shabby. But what hurt me most of all was the look of pain that appeared on Father's face whenever he moved his right leg with a limping lurch. On the night of his return home, he ate no less than three cakes of raw bean curd which, along with the sprinkling of salt, was believed to be a good preventive against a second trip to the police station. Father had always been of taciturn disposition, but he uttered not a single word that day. From time to time he gazed vacantly at my face and seemed about to say something, but each time he withdrew his gaze silently. I was fully resolved never to run away should Father decide to give me a flogging, even if I were to die under his switch. And there, within his easy reach, were the wooden pillow and the lamp-pole. I felt I could not withdraw from Father's sight without receiving my due punishment. I waited, solemnly kneeling before him. But Father uttered not a word about what had passed. Only he did not forget to lay this command on me before lying down to sleep:

"Dongman, if you ever so much as step an inch out of the gate from tomorrow on, I'll break your legs."

Ah, how happily I would have closed my eyes for good, if Father had wielded his switch like mad that night, leaving these as my last words, "Father, I deserve to die."

NOTE

[1]People's Army: North Korean Communist forces

The Soldier

BY NUGROHO NOTOSUSANTO

TRANSLATED BY HARRY AVELING

Nugroho NOTOSUSANTO (1931–   ), born in Java, teaches history at the University of Indonesia and directs research in Army history. First published as a poet, he has written several volumes of short stories, most often about war. Because of this focus and his direct, terse style, Notosusanto has sometimes been compared to Hemingway.

"The Soldier" is set shortly after the Indonesian Revolution (1945–1949). Indonesian Republican forces fought not only with the Dutch, who had controlled Indonesia as the colony of "Dutch East India" since the 1500s, but also with Communist forces who tried to establish a People's Republic and with ethnic splinter groups such as Daru'l Islam who wanted to form their own independent countries. Although the Dutch were defeated in 1949, fighting among the other groups continued until the mid-1950s, when the Republican (government) Army was victorious. During this time of unrest, fighting was bitter and casualties were high. In some cities, as many as half the adult males were killed.

"The Soldier" was published in 1956, in a book that Notosusanto dedicated to "the soldiers of the Indonesian Army who remain loyal to their vocation (dharma)."

Lance Corporal Tatang wiped the sweat from his face. He shifted his black beret back on his head. He stood holding the left side of the armoured car. Green rice fields spread out in the valleys below. It was very hot. The light blue sky was shredded with white cloud. The sun was almost at its peak. Its rays shone at them from the left, right, and underneath. The sweat poured from his body. The iron plating was hot. The sides were hot, the floor was hot. They had not bothered to fix the canvas roof.

The road wound around and around. Its surface was unpaved. It was very bumpy. The armoured car bounced along like a canoe. The road turned towards a valley angled northeast-southwest.

Tatang had only recently come to West Java. He was a veteran of the Revolution. He remembered how he used to wonder what it was like being in an armoured vehicle as he watched the Dutch convoys pass beneath their ambushes. Now he was in an armoured vehicle. He did not feel as protected as he thought he might. Perhaps because this was the first time. He didn't know. He would have preferred to be hidden behind the large rocks on the hill. He looked up. The steep wall of the valley to their right shut out a third of the sky. He wondered what would happen if a Daru'l-Islam[1] platoon attacked them. If more than one platoon attacked. Intelligence said that they had two water-cooled machine guns in perfect condition. He reckoned their own strength. The armoured car had a 12.7 submachine gun and a bren. Private Onom had a Lee Enfield .303. In the cabin, Lance Corporal Yusuf had a sten-gun; the driver, Private Anwar, had an FN rifle. They were travelling with Captain Arifin's jeep. The jeep had three Thompson sub-machine guns and a Vickers.

Tatang's reckoning was interrupted by Lance Corporal Nanang, who stood on an ammunition case behind the 12.7. "We're almost there." In front of them the jeep threw up a long trail of dust, which washed over the armoured car. In front of the jeep, the road cut through a wall, like an uncovered tunnel.

Nanang cocked the breech block of the 12.7, then allowed it to come forward again. It clicked. He repositioned the belt feed. Then he sat down on the ammunition case again and gripped the trigger guard. He pointed the weapon upwards.

Tatang watched him carefully, then turned frontwards again. The green tunnel was very close. He cocked the bren and pointed its barrel outwards. Onom had not readied his weapon. Tatang could just see his bullet-belt and thought how thrifty a marksman Onom was. The other soldiers in the cabin were silent. They were more composed than those in the back of the car.

It was quiet. Tatang thought of such moments endured during the Revolution and subsequent operations against the Communists in the Merapi-Merbabu mountain complex. His heart beat more rapidly. The silence oppressed him. His feelings were razor-sharp. The sweat poured from under his beret and down his back, washing the dirt deposited by the jeep.

The attack began and ended very quickly. A grenade lobbed into the car in the middle of the cutting. Onom threw it out and it exploded behind them. They exchanged shots. Tatang enjoyed the heavy scream of the 12.7. His own tension had gone as soon as he pressed the trigger, as usual. He felt very safe behind the walls of the armoured car. They were protected from low-flying bullets. He was calm.

Tatang leapt down from Captain Arifin's jeep.

"Thanks for the lift, sir." He saluted.

"Have a good leave!" The jeep vanished around the bend.

The barracks had once been a Chinese shop-house. There were Chinese characters over the front door. Tatang slowed down as he entered the dark corridor. He was suddenly very tired. They had been in the area four months, and on each leave he was more and more appalled by the dirty, stinking accommodation.

The corridor was lined with woven-bamboo walls. There were nearly thirty rooms. Some had electricity, most had only oil lamps. Tatang quickly crossed the space which separated the front and back of the building, passing the bathroom and toilet. He looked into the well for a moment, and then grimaced at the thought of the smell of the latrine as sunset approached. He walked to a door, stopped in front of it, and listened. Light from the oil lamp shone through the crude wall.

" 'Jah," he called softly.

He waited. There was no reply.

" 'Jah!" he called more loudly.

A woman's weak voice answered. A soldier passed, wearing a sentry's armband.

"Just back, 'Tang?" he asked.

Tatang nodded.

"She's been sick again," the sentry said. Tatang said nothing. He opened the noisy door slowly. His eyes were dazzled by the light hung near the door. He looked for his wife in the small room and finally saw her on the small couch to the right of the door. She was wrapped in a white, blue-striped blanket. Green medicinal powder lay thick on her forehead.

"Just back, love?" she asked weakly.

"Yes," he said. He closed the door and placed his bag on the chair next to the table. He stood beside her.

"How long have you been like this, 'Jah?" He felt her forehead.

"Three days."

"Did you tell the doctor?"

"Yes. He came yesterday."

"What did he say?"

"The usual."

Tatang sighed. He was very tired. He looked briefly around the room, and sighed again. It was almost large enough to park a jeep in, he thought.

"How many days have you got?" she asked.

"The usual."

"A week."

"Yes."

The cold night air began to filter in through the walls. The room was on the corner of the block. Hadijah began to shiver. Various sounds of communal living came through the walls.

" 'Tang?"

"Hm?"

"Why can't I go south with you?"

"I've told you before. Only the men can go."

She shivered again. "I'm lonely here."

Tatang took off his beret in silence, then walked to the table. He took the medicine and looked at it.

"Have you had this yet?"

"Yes. I have to have an injection tomorrow."

He returned with a chair.

"A liver injection?"

"Yes."

He sat next to her. They fell silent.

"I'm lonely here, 'Tang," she repeated.

He said nothing. Instead he took out a cigarette and began to smoke.

"Can't you do something so I can be nearer?"

"Don't be difficult."

"But I'm lonely."

"It's a dangerous area. What if something happened to you? I couldn't concentrate if anything happened to you."

"Aren't there any army wives there?"

"No," he replied angrily.

"Honestly?"

"No!" Then, as though regretting his harshness, he said, "You mustn't think about things so much."

"What else is there to do?"

Tatang did not reply. She looked so fragile. Sick. There are no doctors in the south, he thought—what if she were sick there? Even if she could get permission to be there.

"There are no doctors in the south. It would be impossible if you were sick," he said aloud.

Hadijah was silent.

"You're better off here. Only the men can go south."

She looked at the roof without saying anything. A large gecko sat alone in one corner.

"I wish Fatimah was still alive," she said.

Tatang was silent. Fatimah had been as fragile as her mother. She had caught tropical malaria in a camp in Jakarta and died.

"We can have other children," he said.

"When? I'm not strong enough to have children."

Tatang sighed. She was difficult when she was sick.

"I wish we could have a nice house like the one we had in Magelang when we got married," 'Dijah said.

"We can't," Tatang—almost—snapped.

"When will they transfer you to somewhere where there's enough accommodation?" she asked, trying to ignore his annoyance.

"You are bloody difficult."

"No, I'm not. I just want to live decently."

"You know it's impossible, don't you?"

"Why is it? Fatimah wouldn't have died if we hadn't been living in that badly ventilated factory." She was bitter.

" 'Dijah!" Tatang's voice clicked hard and cold like a rifle at night. "You are married to a soldier." He stopped for a moment, trying to make the words sound impressive. "You know what that means, don't you?" The words protected him like the walls of the armoured car.

'Dijah sobbed. "I can't take living in these foul boxes all the time."

He felt as though exposed to superior fire-power. He grabbed her arm. "'Dijah, you knew I was a soldier when you married me. You knew what it meant." She cried. "A soldier, not a mercenary," he said, as though talking to himself. "A regular soldier sacrifices everything he has for his ideals." The words protected him, like armour plating.

"But I thought things would be different after the Revolution," she said. "I had ideals too. I wanted my own house. Or at least large, airy quarters, not like these."

"Don't be selfish."

"I'm being honest."

"I want that too. But there are more important things. National unity, for one."

"I want a house. I want my health. I want to be strong enough to look after you and any children we might have."

"If you get any worse I'll put you in hospital. I promise."

"I can't live in hospital forever."

Tatang could smell the latrines now. "We have to be strong," he said. "The struggle isn't over yet. There are still many dissident elements."

"Why do we have to fight them all the time? Why can't someone else?"

"We have to. I'm a soldier."

"Why is there no end to it? I don't understand."

Tatang reached out and caressed her face.

"You have to understand."

"I want to. But I can't."

"Why are you so stupid?"

"Why can't we fight *and* build houses?"

"The state is poor."

"When will it all be over?"

"I don't know."

'Dijah sighed again. "Perhaps you should get out of the army. Look for another job."

"I don't want another job."

"It would be better than this."

"I can't yet."

"When?"

"I don't know."

"You don't understand either, do you," she said accusingly. "You're stupid too."

"You really are bloody difficult."

"I know. But I can't go on like this."

It began to rain. Cold gusts of wind blew into the room. 'Dijah shivered. So did Tatang.

"You don't like me anymore," Tatang sighed.

"I do. Of course I do. I don't like living like this."

The silence turned stagnant. It was raining hard now. From time to time they could hear the traffic pass.

"I'll put in for a transfer."

"Will you?"

"Yes."

"Where to?"

"Anywhere. As long as it's better than this."

"Bandung and Bogor aren't that far away."

"I'll try. I don't care where we go."

They were quiet again. 'Dijah shivered. "I'm tired," she whispered.

"So am I. Worrying about you."

Hadijah looked at her husband. She looked at his green uniform. The red and black stripes on his sleeves. She couldn't imagine him dressed in anything else. He had always worn a uniform.

"I've never seen you in anything but your uniform," she said.

"I'm a soldier."

She looked at him and whispered: "Yes, you're a soldier. I married a soldier."

The rain seemed determined to wipe the room from the face of the earth.

Tatang sat on the ammunition box. The sun had set behind the hills, and the mountain wind began to brush against his body. The walls of the armoured car began to freeze. His rifle was cold. The streetlights were beginning to come on. The bushes along the road—other than those under the street-lights—were black. The crew was weary. They were only a kilometre from the base. Tatang sighed, thinking of his wife. He wanted the transfer very badly. He had applied through his commanding officer and now had to wait for the decision. The officer seemed to think the idea was reasonable. What if they told him tonight? What if they moved him in the morning? The thought cheered him a little.

The armoured car turned into the base, then left the main road and turned down a lane. They stopped in front of the duty office, which was lit by a kerosene lantern. Tatang stood and straightened his trousers. The duty officer came out.

"The Captain wants to see you."

"Me, Sergeant?"

"You."

Tatang jumped down. The decision? Favourable or not? He began to feel gratitude for the possibility of a new life for his wife. Where to? Bandung? Bogor? Magelang? Out of Java? Impossible. It was impossible to leave a theatre of operations.

Captain Arifin, the battalion commander, returned his salute. He said nothing. In his hand was a piece of paper. Tatang restrained his impatience.

"How long have you been in the army?" the officer finally asked.

Tatang searched for the answer. He had joined during the Dutch First Offensive. That was 1947. It was now 1956. "Nine years, sir."

"Nine years," the captain repeated. "You must have been through a lot. You must have seen a lot of action in nine years."

Tatang said nothing. Then, awkwardly, the officer told him, "You can go to town tomorrow." He gave Tatang the piece of paper. "Your wife died this morning."

Tatang took the piece of paper. He still stood to attention, but unconsciously he was shaking. He felt as though he had been thrown from the armoured car at night and was under heavy fire.

He walked slowly towards his quarters. His mind was as dark as the night around him. The cold mountain wind beat against his body. He shivered again, defensively. He was appalled.

At the edge of the road the armoured car merged with the shadows of the surrounding buildings. He turned instinctively towards it and sat in the back, near the driver's cabin, with his knees folded under his chin. Then he cried like a child in its mother's lap.

NOTE

[1]Daru'l Islam (Home of Islam): a movement that began in West Java in 1949, trying to break away from the Republic of Indonesia to form separate Muslim states. By the mid-fifties, the movement had been brought under control.

The Bird of Passage

BY O YŎNGSU

TRANSLATED BY PETER H. LEE

O Yŏngsu (1914–1978), one of Korea's best-known authors, grew up during the Japanese occupation of Korea (1910–1945) and attended the Tokyo National Arts Academy. Although much of his writing describes the devastation during and after the Korean War (1950–1953), his stories derive a sense of optimism from the humanity and compassion displayed by his characters. He relied on simple plots with few characters, and his stories typically end with a separation.

"The Bird of Passage" is set in Seoul in the aftermath of the Korean War. Millions were left homeless by the war, many of them displaced and orphaned children who lived on the streets as best they could. This story was one of the author's own favourites, and he said of it: "There were I don't know how many young boys like Kuch'ŏl, the shoeshine boy. They were not acknowledged by society, had no parents, were given no education, nor were they received by a church. . . . They were not to blame for the misfortunes visited upon them, but society turned a cold shoulder to them. . . . I should be gratified if people read of the character of Kuch'ŏl and were to look with greater warmth on his kind."

They come with the warm weather and go away when it grows cold. Or they come with the cold and leave when it grows warm.

They always go off in search of food in flocks, and then flock together again when they return.

Such is the behaviour of migratory birds. But there are some that follow a different pattern.

It happened last autumn. The leaves of the city's trees were just beginning to fall, so it must have been mid-October.

Minu was walking down Ŭlchiro Sixth Avenue, heading for his quarters outside the East Gate, when suddenly a shoeshine boy was blocking his way and tugging at his sleeve. Minu was in a sour mood just then, and the sight of that grimy hand grasping the sleeve of his new suit irritated him. "No shine! Hands off!" he shouted. The boy, unabashed, kept tugging at Minu's sleeve.

"But. . . Teacher, don't you recognize me?" he asked.

Then Minu looked at the boy. Indeed it did seem that he had often seen that face before, but for a moment he could not recall where.

"In Pusan. I used to shine your shoes all the time."

Then it came back to Minu clearly. "Oh, now I remember. You're Kuch'iri, that's right. When did you come to Seoul?"

"Last spring."

"You did? You didn't do well in Pusan?"

At these words Kuch'iri released Minu's sleeve; his face fell, a tear struck the tip of his shoe, as he lowered his gaze to the pavement. Though he did not know what had happened, Minu, too, felt sad.

Kuch'iri's turtleneck pullover had tattered elbows and frayed cuffs. His trousers were glossy with dirt. He looked like any other shoeshine boy, except that the army boots he was wearing were absurdly blunt-toed and each one was big enough alone to hold both feet. They were clumsy, even comical.

Minu took out a cigarette. "Did you come alone?"

Instead of answering, Kuch'iri pulled Minu's sleeve: "Please come over here." Minu followed him into a nearby alley. Kuch'iri put down his plain wooden stool by the concrete outer wall of a house and asked Minu to sit. He wanted to shine Minu's shoes before telling his story.

Minu placed one foot on the shoeshine box. "It's been a long time since you shined my shoes. More than a year, isn't it?"

"Aren't these the same shoes you had then?"

The boy's home was in Ch'ungch'ŏng Province, but he could speak the Pusan dialect fluently.

"Yes, they're the same shoes. But why'd you come to Seoul? Didn't it go well at the school?"

Kuch'iri dislodged some dirt from the sole of Minu's shoe with a metal scraper and said, "Please don't ask about the school. I got into trouble."

"Trouble? What kind of trouble?"

"Just a while after you left for Seoul..."

"What happened?"

"Some money disappeared from the office. Seven thousand hwan[1]."

"Really?"

"Yeah, and the Disciplinarian claimed I took it. He took me into the storeroom and gave me an awful beating."

"You mean that Mr. Ch'oe [*Chŏ*]?"

"Yes. And even though I told him I didn't take it..."

"But whose money was it?"

"They said it was the Patriots' Club dues."

"Then what did the Disciplinarian do?"

"He said if I didn't confess by the next day he'd tell the police."

"And then?"

"Please put your other foot up."

"And?"

"The next day he stuck a pencil between my fingers and twisted it hard. I thought I'd die..."

"He did what?"

"So I told him I took the money; he asked how come I didn't confess earlier. And he kept asking me what I'd done with the money."

"So what did you say?"

"I told him I only confessed because of the pain, that I really didn't take the money. He said I made a fool of him and took the leg of a chair and beat me so hard that I..."

"Hey, enough polishing. A quick shine is all I want. So what happened next?"

"I don't know. When I opened my eyes the old janitor was splashing water on my face."

"Hmmm. And then?"

"So the janitor took me home. I was sick for days."

"Just a quick shine, I said."

"But I'll have to get that dirt off. Anyway, I was sick in bed at home, and my friend came and told me Mr. Ch'oe was asking for me. My big sister took me to him. I went limping along."

"What did he say?"

"He said they'd caught the guy who took the money. He said he was sorry, and he gave me two hundred hwan and told me to buy some dog soup with it."

"Who did take the money?"

"He said it was that bastard of an office boy!"

"Did you get some dog soup, then?"

"I was crying so hard. All I did was cry. My big sister was crying, too."

"Really...?"

"I said I didn't want any money, and we went back home. I kept thinking of you, Teacher."

"Is that why you left for Seoul?"

"Since I was sick I couldn't make any money, so my stepmother kept telling me to get out of the house. My father got drunk and gave me a beating. So I got in with a bunch of guys who were going to Seoul, and I came up here with them."

"Hm."

"Look at this, Teacher."

The boy held out his hand. The flesh of the second and third fingers was discoloured, and the joints were swollen. This, he said, was due to the cruel twisting of the pencil that day. Minu gently felt the injured fingers, then released them.

"Does it still hurt?"

Kuch'iri was silent.

"How are the shoes coming?"

"They're all done."

Minu knew the boy would not let him pay, so he thought he would take him for something to eat. When he stood up Kuch'iri stood up too, packed up his shoeshine box, and followed along as if by agreement. When they got to the Kyerim movie theatre, Kuch'iri caught Minu's sleeve again and pointed to the billboard. "Teacher, have you seen that movie?" he asked.

Minu just shook his head.

"Teacher, please go see it. I'll treat you."

For a moment Minu merely gazed dumbfounded at Kuch'iri.

"Teacher! That guy with one eye closed, holding the pistol—see? He's great!"

"Okay, I'll take you in."

"No. I've seen it. You watch it. I can get us in for free. Come on, let's go."

"Kuch'iri, the next time a good movie comes along, I'll take you to see it. I'm pretty busy today."

Kuch'iri seemed to be on the verge of tears. "Please don't go. Come see the movie. Please come with me." he said, tugging harder on Minu's sleeve.

Kuch'iri was not going to give up until Minu agreed to watch the movie. It was an awkward fix, for Minu saw that an abrupt refusal would hurt the boy's feelings. He hesitated a moment and then said, "Okay. Let's go."

Kuch'iri set down his shoeshine box at the side of the theatre and left Minu standing next to it. He went to the entrance and negotiated briefly. Soon he came hurrying back, waving one arm and mincing along in his GI boots. He shouldered the shoeshine box and took the stool in one hand. With the other he led Minu along. "It's all settled," he said. "Come with me. Let's go in now."

Just as Kuch'iri had promised, he and Minu entered the theatre unchallenged. When they got inside, Kuch'iri hurried up to the front, found a seat, and showed Minu to it. He whispered in Minu's ear, "The show's continuous, you know. It'll start from the beginning again soon. You stay here and watch. I'll go shine those people's shoes over there and then I'll come back." With these words he was gone.

The film was a western. Minu's eyes were on the screen, but his own thoughts absorbed all his attention.

Minu had been teaching at W Middle School in Pusan, where he stayed until the recapture of Seoul[2]. They called it a school, but it was a makeshift affair, just a group of tents with no fence or wall. All kinds of peddlers came there, but the shoeshine boys were the worst. Sometimes as many as seven or eight would come in one group. Over forty teachers sat back-to-back in the small office, and even a shoeshine would cause a stir. To Minu, whose responsibility it was to keep the campus in order, fell the futile task of ejecting the shoeshine boys, only to have them reappear once his back was turned. The boys swarmed to the school like flies to carrion, sometimes camping quietly beside the office and playing marbles or batting about a shuttlecock.

One day, Minu was on his way back from the washroom after having ejected that morning's crowd of shoeshine boys. One of the shoeshine boys, who had somehow managed to follow him, held out his stool and said, "Shine, sir?"

"But I just got rid of you guys!"

Minu, half-smiling, half-frowning, took a poke at the boy with his fist, but the boy pulled a tin out of his pocket and held it out, saying, "Teacher, this is the best American polish, you've heard of it, haven't you? I bought it yesterday. Please be my first customer." Minu had no class during the first hour, so he set his foot on the box. The boy threw himself into the job, spitting and shining the first shoe. Then, "Sir!"

"What?"

"There are too many shoeshine boys here, aren't there?"

"They're a headache!"

"I have an idea, Teacher. I'll shine all the teachers' shoes for just twenty hwan, and with the best polish, if you will fix it so that I'm the only one allowed to shine shoes here."

"You're a greedy one!"

"Come on, let me, sir!"

It made sense. If Minu authorized just one boy to shine shoes, the others would not come. Moreover, the teachers would welcome this new price of twenty hwan, instead of the usual thirty.

"I'll talk to the others about it."

"Please, sir!"

That afternoon in the general meeting Minu made the proposal. From the principal and the supervisor on down, all agreed. They decided the chosen boy should wear an armband. The next day Minu made an armband of yellow cloth with a W on it. He called the shoesine boys together and made the announcement: "The boy wearing this armband is the only one who will be allowed to shine shoes here. There's no need for the rest of you to come anymore. You'd better go elsewhere."

However, the boys all protested, some of them pressing home their grievances. "Aren't we all refugees together here?" "That's unfair." "Choose one each day and we'll take turns." "Make it one a week. . . ."

"Maybe you're right," Minu replied. "But it's been decided, so there's nothing I can do about it." Thus Minu managed to quiet the boys. Yet he could not help feeling moved when they said that they were all refugees together, for Minu himself was a refugee school teacher who had left his home in the North.

The boy who received the armband would arrive early each morning and bow smartly to each of the teachers. When the principal arrived, the boy would promptly bring his slippers, exchange them for his shoes, and begin polishing.

In a spare moment one day, Minu had his shoes shined. "How many pairs do you shine every day?"

"Including the students', it comes to about twenty pairs."

"Two times two is four. . .Can you make a profit at four hundred hwan?"

"It's fine."

"Is it better than before?"

"*Better?* Before it was hard to take in even two hundred a day."

"Hmmm. . .What's your name?"

"Yi Kuch'ŏl."

Just then the P.E. teacher came by. He said, "No, it can't be Kuch'ŏl—since you shine shoes you'd better change it to Kuch'iri[3]." And so Kuch'ŏl came to be known as Kuch'iri.

His home was in Ch'ungch'ŏng province, and his father worked down on the docks.

Lunch hour was the busiest time for Kuch'iri. Some of the teachers had their shoes shined while they ate. Working in the small teachers' office, Kuch'iri was sometimes kicked in the seat of his pants or struck on the head with a roll-book. When they were busy, the teachers would ask him to get them lunch or have him do other small tasks in place of the errandboy.

When a new principal was appointed, Minu left the school and went to Seoul. He completely forgot about Kuch'iri.

Ch'oe's misunderstanding and mistreatment of the boy may have been increased by his dislike of Minu. Kuch'iri firmly refused to accept money from Minu, and this was all the more irritating. Once, when Kuch'iri said he had polished Ch'oe's shoes ten times, Ch'oe insisted that he had only done it six or seven times. At last Ch'oe derided Kuch'iri and soundly slapped his face. One day the teachers ordered lunch from the usual chophouse. Kuch'iri brought Minu's lunch first, and Ch'oe plainly showed his irritation. On one occasion Ch'oe and Minu nearly clashed openly.

When the teachers had a party, Ch'oe looked askance at Minu's gathering squid heads or leftover cookie bits and giving them to Kuch'iri; and when relief goods were distributed, Ch'oe was irritated by Minu's giving unwanted items to the boy. It was hard to know whether Ch'oe disliked Minu for taking sides with a boy he hated, or whether it was because he hated Minu that he could not stand Kuch'iri. In either case, Minu had no love for Ch'oe either.

Ch'oe could be quite cruel. For example, he would bring into the office two pupils accused of misbehaving in class. He would stand them face to face and order one to slap the other on the cheek. But eye to eye as they were, the two could only grin sheepishly. However, Ch'oe was standing there beside them, stick in hand. One pupil, seeing no escape, would lightly slap the other on the cheek. Then Ch'oe would tell the pupil who had been hit to return the blow. Helpless, the second pupil would slap back about as hard as he thought he had been slapped. But the other boy, probably thinking this slap a bit harder than the first, would hit back still harder. And his comrade, thinking this slap much harder than the one he had delivered, would hit back hard indeed. By this time no threats from the teacher were necessary; the two would just go on slapping each other with all their strength until their ears and cheeks were red and swollen. Everyone would laugh at the spectacle.

As Minu sketched this portrait of Ch'oe in his mind's eye, he felt sure that Kuch'iri had been beaten all the harder on his account.

"Teacher, you see he's fallen off his horse. But it's a trick. He doesn't get killed. Watch him jump back and get away. He's really great!" Kuch'iri had come back and was sitting beside him explaining the movie.

Kuch'iri waited for Minu by the same corner every day, and each time he wanted to shine Minu's shoes. If Minu said he was busy, the boy would at least give the shoes a quick brushing. Sometimes, when Kuch'iri was busy shining someone else's shoes, Minu just went by in silence. When they met the next day, Kuch'iri would ask why Minu had not gone to work and where he had been, and he would say that he had waited for Minu until dark. One day when Minu was on his way home a little later than usual, he saw Kuch'iri, hands thrust into his pants pockets, whistling and marching along in time with the tune. It was a popular song that went "...though I miss my home..."

"What are you doing here so late?"

"I was waiting for you, Teacher," he replied, shouldering his shoeshine box and walking along after Minu.

"What for?"

"Just because..."

When they got to the East Gate train station, Kuch'iri simply bowed to Minu and said, "Goodbye, Teacher."

Kuch'iri lived in the second-to-last shack in the row along the bank of the stream just outside the station. One time, thinking it odd that Kuch'iri went into the station every evening, Minu had asked him where he lived. Kuch'iri took his sleeve and drew him to the ticket gate, where he pointed out the shack just opposite. He said he lived there with an old lady who raised bean sprouts and sold them in the market.

Minu would leave work as early as possible, knowing that Kuch'iri was waiting for him. Somehow Kuch'iri had found a permanent place in his heart. This was Minu's weakness: if a neighbour's dog wagged its tail at him, he would feel fond of it. Or perhaps it was partly that Minu's youngest nephew was still in the North, where there was no way to get news of him, and whenever Minu saw Kuch'iri it was just like seeing the little nephew who had always tagged after him.

"How long are you going to go on shining shoes?"

"Why?"

"That's a job for little kids, you know."

Kuch'iri was silent.

"How old are you now?"

"On New Year's I'll turn fourteen."

"Wouldn't you like to get a job as a carpenter, or ironworker?" Such were Minu's hopes for the boy, and he had thoughts of sending him to night school. "Well, what do you want to do?"

"I want to make some money so I can open a shoe store."

"Hm? A shoe store?"

"In Pusan, at the head of our alley."

"Why on earth there?"

"So I can show it to that kid."

"What kid?"

"My stepmother's kid."

"But still, he's your brother, isn't he?"

"Him? I can't stand that brat. Because of him I've been beaten enough. And my big sister, too. She's always getting a licking because of him. I really feel sorry for my big sister. If I open a shoe store, she can come live with me."

"It takes a lot of money to open a shoe store. Do you have any saved up?"

Kuch'iri looked up at Minu with a quick grin and rubbed harder with the polishing cloth. "I've saved six thousand hwan since I came to Seoul. Plus nine hundred I gave to the old woman to help her with her bean sprout business."

"How did you get to know her?"

"One time she asked me to open her bean sprout bucket for her. I could tell by her dialect that she was from Ch'ungch'ŏng, too."

"Does she have a family?"

"She says her husband died last year, and her son was killed in the war."

It was two days before Christmas.

Kuch'iri had been shining Minu's shoes once every two or three days but had refused to accept payment. Now Kuch'iri looked so cold that Minu handed him two thousand hwan and said, "Here, buy yourself a shirt. How can you go around in those clothes in the winter?"

Kuch'iri stared at the money and back at Minu, and deftly thrust the bills back into Minu's pocket. "I don't want it. I don't want your money."

Minu pulled the money back out and stuck it under Kuch'iri's nose. "Come on, take it," he said.

"I don't want it!"

"Hurry up and take it."

Kuch'iri did not move.

"Look, how can I accept your favours then?"

Minu dropped the money in front of Kuch'iri and turned away. But Kuch'iri, stumbling in his oversized boots, came from behind and stood in his path. "I don't want money. I don't want it." Wiping his eyes with his fist, he held the money out to Minu. Passersby turned to watch.

"What are you crying for?" Minu said.

"I don't want it. Money. . ."

This was a predicament. "Okay, then, bring your things and come with me."

Again Kuch'iri shoved the money back into Minu's overcoat pocket. He shouldered his stool and box and followed along. The two went into a restaurant and ordered two bowls of dumpling soup.

"Why do you wait for me every day?"

Kuch'iri lowered his gaze.

"Speak up!"

"Because I like you!"

"What do you mean, you like me?"

"I just do."

"Just do? What. . .? Really!"

The waiter brought the soup.

"But look, Kuch'iri." Again Minu got out his money. "Look, you shine my shoes and then I'll buy you a shirt, okay? That's what people do at Christmas. So buy a shirt with this and start wearing it tomorrow, won't you?"

"But I don't want you to give me any money!"

"You're a stubborn little. . .Look, if you don't do what I tell you, I won't come by here and I won't let you shine my shoes anymore. How would you like that?"

Kuch'iri sniffed.

"Your nose is running into your soup."

Kuch'iri snuffled, and with a look of reproach for Minu he took the money.

They left the restaurant and were walking side by side. Minu asked, "Do you want to see a movie? I'll treat you."

"No, thank you. I've got to go home now."

"What for?"

"The old woman can't see too well at night anymore."

"So what do you do?"

"I carry water and sort the bean sprouts for her."

They did not meet the next day, for it was Sunday.

When Kuch'iri saw Minu on Christmas morning, he was beaming as he held out his arms to show off the jacket he had gotten in a second-hand clothes shop. He also showed Minu a can of shoe polish he had bought with the change. Minu was pleased and said, "That's good. But you could use a haircut, too."

They say the peak season for shoeshine boys begins when the forsythia bloom, as people emerge into the fine weather, wanting to look their best after a long winter indoors. For Kuch'iri work was plentiful, and he said that he could earn in one day now what during the winter had taken two days to earn.

While he was polishing Minu's shoes one day, Kuch'iri said, "Teacher, your shoes are all worn out."

"Yes, it's time to buy a new pair."

"Don't buy any. I'll get you some high-quality American ones from a guy I know." He measured Minu's foot with a cord.

A few days later Kuch'iri told him, "Teacher, I asked him to get the shoes. He says he'll get the best. It's okay if they're second-hand, isn't it?"

"What's the price?"

"Let's see...They'll sell them cheap to us, say about four or five thousand hwan."

"That low?"

"Yeah. On the black market a good pair of American shoes'll go for at least ten thousand hwan, even if they're used."

After that, Kuch'iri worried about his offer each time he shined Minu's shoes. "I saw the guy yesterday and he says he'll get them soon," he would say and then mutter something to himself.

On Saturday in early May, Minu left work somewhat earlier than usual. Kuch'iri was nowhere to be seen, though his box and stool lay abandoned on the ground. Thinking that Kuch'iri must have gone to the washroom, Minu sat down on the stool and took out a cigarette.

A clamour like that of quarrelling urchins came from a nearby alleyway. Minu smoked his cigarette and waited, but still Kuch'iri did not return. Thinking Kuch'iri might be watching the fight, Minu stepped into the alley. There from behind he saw a young man, apparently smartly dressed, surrounded by four or five shoeshine boys. The young man was striking somebody. He wore rubber slippers on his feet and held a pair of leather shoes in his hand. Minu moved closer, thinking that the boy being struck resembled Kuch'iri.

"Teacher, go away. Don't come in here. It's nothing." It was Kuch'iri.

Blood dribbled from his nose and smeared his face.

"Kuch'iri! What's going on here?"

Kuch'iri, spitting blood and wiping the side of his mouth, yelled almost desperately, "Teacher, go away. It's nothing. Please go away!"

With that the young man turned and looked angrily at Minu. "Who are you?" he asked.

Minu had no ready answer, but hesitated a moment and then said, "It doesn't matter who I am, but what on earth...?"

Kuch'iri took his chance to escape. He ran down the alley with all his might and was rounding the corner before the surprised young man uttered a curse and ran after him.

Minu thought to himself, "Whatever it's all about, I just hope Kuch'iri doesn't get caught." He asked the shoeshine boys standing there what had happened to Kuch'iri. But as if by agreement they did not say a word and slipped away. At that point, a boy came to pick up Kuch'iri's stool and box. The boy said that he was a friend of Kuch'iri's and that he would take care of Kuch'iri's things. Minu consented and had the boy shine his shoes, hoping to find out more. "Hey, what was that all about?" he asked.

The boy glanced up at him and answered, "He was caught stealing shoes at the restaurant over there."

"Kuch'iri was?"

"Him and another kid, but the other one got away and Kuch'iri got caught."

Minu's head began to swim and his eyesight blurred. He shut his eyes for a moment to calm himself. "It was all because of that promise of his," he muttered. He was angered by this breach of faith, but he felt sorry for Kuch'iri. "If I see him, I'll really teach him a lesson, the little thief." Yet even as he said this, Minu really felt as if he would burst into tears if he met Kuch'iri now.

"Ha, if I'd only caught that bastard I'd have bashed his skull in like a chestnut!" It was the young man with the shoes, coming back out of breath.

"What happened?"

"He got away."

Minu was relieved.

"Look at this. It hasn't been a week since I bought these shoes." He took off the rubber slippers, put on the shoes, and headed off across the trolley line.

From that day on Kuch'iri was nowhere to be found.

On the fourth day Minu went to the shack outside the train station where the old lady who sold bean sprouts lived. The old lady did live there, he was told, but the door was latched; she must have been at the market.

Every day on his way to and from work, Minu stopped at Kuch'iri's old shoeshine spot. About ten days or so later, another boy took over the spot. Setting his foot on the box, Minu asked, "Do you know Kuch'iri, who used to shine shoes here?"

"Yeah, I know him. He's gone to an American army base up near the DMZ[4]."

"Alone?"

"No, he joined a group of guys who were going up there." The boy said that every summer groups of shoeshine boys went to the American army bases to make money. It would be autumn before they returned, the boy said in reply to Minu's query.

A wearisome August passed, and then September drew to a close.

Autumn came late that year.

One day, as leaves were beginning to fall along the street, Minu glanced up at the sky. A flock of geese flew by in a neat V, on their way from somewhere to somewhere else. Minu was deeply moved. "Kuch'iri, too, will be coming back soon," he thought.

———

NOTES

[1]hwan: a former Korean unit of currency

[2]During 1950–51, Seoul was captured by the Communists twice and "liberated" (recaptured) by American and South Korean forces both times.

[3]The "ch'ŏl" of "Kuch'ŏl" has been changed to the similar sounding "ch'iri," which means "polish" in Korean.

[4]DMZ: a demilitarized zone, extending six-and-a-half kilometres, established at the Thirty-eighth Parallel to provide a buffer between North and South Korea at the end of the Korean War

The Sky's Escape

BY YUAN CH'IUNG-CH'IUNG

TRANSLATED BY MICHAEL S. DUKE

YUAN Chi'iung-ch'iung [Yeurn Choong-choong] (1950–   ) was born in Sichuan province in mainland China but grew up and was educated in Taiwan. Besides writing short stories and essays, she writes poetry under the pen name of Chu Ling.

"The Sky's Escape" tells the story of a young Vietnamese refugee who escaped from Saigon (now Ho Chi Minh City) after the Communist takeover in 1975, leaving family and friends behind. During the Vietnam War, the United States supported the South Vietnamese government in its struggle against the North Vietnamese Communists, who were eventually victorious. When the Americans left and the Communists took control, many South Vietnamese were persecuted and imprisoned. Ethnic Chinese, such as the protagonist of this story, were often victims. Refugees made desperate attempts to flee, most often by sea in overcrowded, unsafe boats; they became known as the "boat people."

1

Wang-jih [*Wong ji-eh*] lay flat on the beach with his face pressed tightly against the sand. The sand felt soft, moist, and chilly. Darkness surrounded him like a tightly covered box. And those sounds of footsteps seemed to tap on the box—distant and hollow. Wang-jih felt a kind of dark terror licking up his spine like some creeping insect. His face sank into the putrid odour of the sand. His heart beat fast, the footsteps came nearer across the sand, muffled and relaxed, almost exhausting him. Wang-jih lay flat, as if his whole body were being stretched out tautly on that spot, straight and stiff as a stick. However, in such an utterly stiff position, his body felt somehow strangely paralytic and limp, as if it had become a kind of air-filled toy, inflating and deflating repeatedly, now becoming very large, then suddenly quite small again. Wang-jih was afraid. The footsteps were very firm and unhurried. The night was murky black and everything merged into a confused, tangled mass. Wang-jih yearned for a glass of water so badly. He opened his mouth and took a deep breath—the loudness of that breath was frightening! He did not breathe in life, only dirt. Those footsteps came closer and closer, like a pair of hands slowly peeling open the darkness. Wang-jih was a seed hiding in the dark night, just about to be peeled open and exposed.

He woke up.

Opening his eyes, he felt everything was strangely quiet, almost maddeningly so. Click-clack, click-clack, the train rumbled rhythmically, guilelessly, happily. The fat man in the next seat was sleeping like a still life. The sunlight outside was intense; the curtains were almost all drawn, and the light inside the car was soft and warm. Wang-jih leaned out from his seat and looked around. Most of the people were still sleeping: the men with their shirts unbuttoned and their legs spread apart; the children curled up in the adults' laps like folded blankets; the women with their hair falling across their cheeks, as they slept with their heads rolled over to one side while their bodies were sitting up straight and proper, as if someone had just slapped them and they had wordlessly turned their heads to one side. Half-reclining against the backs of the dark blue seats, pillowed on clean white seat covers, rows of peaceful, relaxed faces were confidently sleeping with complete faith that the train would take them to their destination.

Wang-jih straightened himself in his seat and looked farther off. Although there did not seem to be anyone in the aisle seat near the door, the lightly muffled sound of quiet conversation drifted over. Looking more closely, a small patch of a plaid shirt could be seen; the man had leaned over to the inside seat. Probably becoming aware of Wang-jih's movements, the patch of plaid shirt leaned out, half of a shoulder, above which was the face of a long-haired young man. The girl at his side immediately straightened up also—a young girl with a tiny face and downcast eyes, not really looking at anyone. The young man stared challengingly at Wang-jih, and Wang-jih quickly drew back into his seat.

The fat gentleman slept on with his face turned up. His face made one think of steamed buns: small and large lumps of flesh were like unevenly risen buns, some puffed out, some flat.

Everyone was sleeping. Wang-jih suddenly felt anxious. He could not remember at all the dream he'd just had; he had only a confused feeling that he had been puffing up fantastically, then shrinking down. He remembered that strange black night, hazy yet distinct. Wang-jih knew that he had had a nightmare, but couldn't remember the details. He did not want to sleep any more, so he pulled the curtain open a little and looked out the window.

The train was just then passing some rice fields. Wang-jih had noticed that Taiwan had many rice fields; every time he took the train he always went past patch after patch of them. Bright green paddies separated by pale brown paths. Sometimes the paths were planted with trees, short clumps of deep green, bathed in soft opaque sunlight, while distant mountain ranges blending into the clouds formed a dreamlike background. The afternoon sunlight and scenery often had a special kind of softness, a pure peacefulness, like a baby's sleep, with neither worries nor fears. People and cars passing on the road were also like picture cutouts, strangely maintaining a peaceful stillness in the midst of movement.

When he first returned to Taiwan, Wang-jih had felt almost a kind of anger toward everything he encountered. He had returned through dangers and fears, and Taiwan was too quiet, too peaceful; yet, compared to his recent past, life in Taiwan was too active and noisy. Stimulated by these various incitements, Wang-jih felt that both his body and his mind were gradually being reborn. He was very happy to be angry, very happy that he could once again experience such powerful emotions. For such a long time he had been weak and unable to bear feelings like joy and anger, happiness and grief. Powerful emotions can only be expressed by a very healthy body and mind. Wang-jih knew that he was becoming a human being again.

That time was behind him now, but the scars were cut into his heart and guts, and he would wear them for life. Whether in places where it could be seen or not, the dark past, like dripping water cutting through stone, bore holes everywhere. After the fall of Vietnam, he had stayed on for only two years, but those two years had destroyed every bit of his confidence and sense of security. He was always standing on thin ice watching himself suddenly sink without a sound, all the way to the bottom, with no one seeing him. That sharp penetrating coldness sliced him into little strips. It had already become a habit: often, for no reason at all, his whole body would become cold as ice, his palms breaking out in a cold sweat as if he were holding a mass of sticky, squirming maggots, and a painfully numbing sensation tingling up his spine.

Wang-jih looked out the window. That vast sky, cloudless, heated to a faded blue. Only the sky was a little bit like Saigon. Or maybe not—it had been some time since he had seen the Saigon sky; his deepest impression was of the ground. He seemed to have held his head down during that whole time. The ground was grey and full of holes and ruts; walking over it you felt as if you might suddenly fall. The sun was always a damp misty yellow, and he could not recall seeing the sky; throughout the entire two years he had been like paper soaked in water—limp and lifeless.

The fat gentleman in the next seat stretched himself, coughing as he extended his arms, and bumped Wang-jih with his elbow. As Wang-jih turned around, the fat man was just turning his face away, his head supported by a thick, wrinkled fleshy neck. His head was very large, covered with thickly matted hair, for all the world like some kind of animal. His two hands were interlaced behind his head, making a triangle with his two elbows, and as he worked his arms back and forth like a fan, he gave a great yawn.

The fat gentleman looked at Wang-jih, his dark eyelids giving his eyes an unusually warm expression:

"Why didn't you sleep?"

"I slept, but I woke up."

"*Hai* . . ." the fat man looked all around and yawned again. "That's right, you have to take an air-conditioned car; otherwise how can you sleep? Ah, this weather. . . ." He yawned, his mouth stupidly wide, looking straight ahead.

The fat man was very cordial, but he certainly was fat; the way he sat in his seat made one uncomfortable. Stuffed in, he filled the seat up entirely; however, his movements were still lively. As soon as he boarded the train, he smilingly offered Wang-jih a cigarette. He bent down, pulled out a handkerchief, and began to wipe his neck and chin. Seeing such a fat man on such a hot day made Wang-jih unaccountably restless. The fat man kept on wiping his neck, opening his shirt collar, and looking all around with a smile. His mouth seemingly smiled, but his eyebrows were knitted in a frown, as he spoke to Wang-jih: "It's so hot!" Wang-jih did not want to smoke nor talk, but the fat man was very enthusiastic; the cigarette being refused, he offered some chewing gum. Wang-jih shook his head. The fat man looked sheepishly at the pack of gum and said, "I bought it for the children; they just love it." Maintaining that rather timid smile, he put the package away.

Wang-jih was going the same way the fat man was, to Taitung [*Tīdung*]. The fat man was very happy. "It's so nice to be able to sit together. Let me tell you, Taitung is the place to be; it's hot, all right, but it's simply hot, not stifling like Taipei! It doesn't make you feel full of steam inside and unable to let it all out."

The fat man was about fifty, spoke with a broad rural accent, and dressed very simply. On hearing that Wang-jih was visiting Taitung for the first time, he told him of several places "you've just got to see, really fine, nothing like it any place else." Wang-jih listened to him quite impatiently and was very surprised by his self-confidence. This was the first time he had run into anyone like this on a train.

The fat man had a fruit orchard in Taitung. He drew a picture in the air: over here was the family house, over there were pear trees, and over there were peach trees. He was very proud of himself. "When my peaches reach the market they sell for $40 NT[1] apiece. They're really fine, all the same size, very plump, pale pink with a touch of red, better looking than in the picture posters." He wanted Wang-jih to come and visit his orchard if he had the time.

The fat man looked up ahead, half-opened his mouth, and suddenly laughed out loud. Wang-jih followed his look. A couple of seats away, a little girl had stuck her head out over the back of her seat; under black bangs her eyes were black and unmoving, innocently round. The fat man waved at her, and she quickly drew back. In a little while, a wisp of black hair and a little patch of face appeared up over the seat back; the fat man waved again, and once again she drew back and the sound of a child's shrill excited laughter broke out.

"Just like my daughter," the fat man said. He carried photos with him, four or five of them, all coloured ones. One was rather overexposed; the face was very white, but those lovely eyes were quite startling. From the rest of the pictures, it was apparent that she was a dark child with intense bright eyes and white teeth, obviously with a strain of aborigine blood. She had a crude bowl-shaped haircut that covered her eyebrows, square and stiff; but her face was very pretty, with an already grown-up kind of beauty. She looked calmly into the camera, her slight smile showing her white teeth, completely disassociated from the deep, unruffled pools of her eyes.

The fat man sighed, saying proudly, "She's so pretty, and so sensible." The child was only six years old. Looking at the fat man's features, so completely lacking in beauty, Wang-jih marvelled at the mysterious ways of the Creator.

Wang-jih had come out alone, leaving his parents, brother, sisters, and friends behind in that place. And also Nan-chen. When he left, he did not even let Nan-chen know. There wasn't time; and besides, the fewer people who knew about such things the better.

Actually he and Nan-chen were not really that close, but he always thought of her, especially when he first came out. Every memory of the past only brought him pain. He remembered everything: his elder brother's death, hunger, fear, his parents' faces. These memories entangled his mind day and night, dragging him down into a state of sad and lonely struggling. In his memories, only Nan-chen was beautifully pure and bright. In the midst of his ugly and fearful memories, only Nan-chen stood out, wistfully grieving, yet beautiful.

There had been a possibility of a future for him and Nan-chen. In early spring at the flower market on Nuyen-huei Street, twenty or thirty thousand flower pots were set out in a single night. Petals were strewn on the ground like stars in the sky, their brilliant colours making the street itself glow. The beauties of Saigon, with hair flowing down to their waists, soft-hued long gowns drifting along, silently glided through the flower market like a warm spring breeze. Beautiful flowers and beautiful women. Nan-chen stood in the surging crowd, turning her head, her face softly warm and calm. He had known her all along, as he was a close friend of her elder brother; but it was in the flower market of Nuyen-huei Street that he suddenly discovered her beauty.

It could have been possible, if Saigon had not fallen so suddenly. He had felt the noise and uncertainty during the time before Saigon fell, he knew, yet it had all seemed so confused and unreal. The funny thing was, at that time, they had only been taking long walks together. In the soft darkness of twilight, Saigon's setting sun brilliantly lit up the horizon as if it would never really set. Nan-chen, delicately scented, would walk along lightly beside him, her soft white diaphanous gown fluttering gently about her. They had been together a few times and had never even held hands because they loved that kind of pure, innocent tenderness.

Then Saigon fell.

They lost contact; that delicate, almost unreal, contact. After the fall, a lid seemed to clamp down and covered the city with a heavy quietness, beneath which people's hearts became troubled and fearful. And their relationship also cooled.

Once he just happened to pass by the street where Nan-chen lived. He walked along slowly; the street was deserted and dirty. This huge city had suddenly grown old and decrepit. He had been to Nan-chen's home many times, and now as he slowly walked by, he felt an oppressive sadness. The whole house had suddenly become strange, with an indescribable aura of cruelty and darkness. He discovered that all of the window curtains had been torn down. The empty windows suddenly appeared evil, evil and tragic. He was not used to seeing the inside of the house laid open so completely, with no furniture and not a trace of human life.

It could have been possible. His mother liked Nan-chen and his father liked her family background. But after the fall, family background became a fearful thing; the better one's family background, the more one had to suffer. Like all the beautiful women of Saigon, Nan-chen had beautiful long hair, soft and glossy black. Nan-chen's smile, quiet with downcast eyes; her black hair brushing her cheek, a sharp contrast of black and white—all contributed to an air of pure elegance. Nan-chen's image grew larger and larger, until it became Saigon, the dead and buried Saigon of the past. Nan-chen's beauty was a dead spirit.

The fat man continued to tell Wang-jih about his daughter. He was so pleased that he laughed out loud with every few words he said. Wang-jih listened without interest, keeping a slight smile on his face. Most of the people in the car were awake, a little bemused; some of them were moving around in their seats. On the seat across the aisle sat a rather cold-looking woman. She glanced around sharply, then taking out her compact she began to refresh her make-up. Wang-jih watched her applying her lipstick and thought it rather strange and tiring. No matter where women begin to put on make-up, it always arouses a sense of timelessness. She painted her lips very slowly, stroke by stroke, raising her little finger to lightly rub away the places where she had gone past the natural border of her lips. Her movements were extremely well-practised, meticulous, and careful. They made one feel that there was a kind of rhythmical routine in a woman's application of make-up. There was a sense of security and peace in her movements. Her make-up finished, she stared proudly at Wang-jih, fully confident that she was beautiful and unapproachable.

Wang-jih was amused. He always felt that the people of Taiwan were of two kinds of temperament: extremely self-confident and extremely peaceful, both of which could only develop from living under stable conditions for a long, long time, so that stability becomes a habit and is no longer merely a kind of hope. Some of these people may be unhappy or anxious, lazy or active, but they all have the same smooth faces. Their expressions are only marred by simple troubles and anxieties, not by terror. In Saigon Wang-jih had not really been worried; the people of Saigon had no worries because simple, everyday worries had already become laughably extravagant luxuries, and even terror had become numbed. There was only a kind of vague sinking feeling, waiting for something to happen, something that would hurt or wound. And then just being afraid of that waiting.

Wang-jih now had several friends who were good talkers. They had a lot of criticisms of present conditions, and all the time they would complain loudly about one thing or another. Wang-jih rarely offered any opinions, but listening to these discussions always left him with two contradictory feelings. For one thing, it made him realize ever more strongly his own personal security. Only in this place was it possible to criticize any way he wanted to criticize, or to attack any way he wished to do so. He was truly living in freedom. On the other hand, he also felt deeply troubled and anxious. He was afraid of all the noise and clamour. He had just recently escaped from that other land of noisy clamour. It was under such extreme freedom that Vietnam was lost. Those numberless, many-opinioned, boisterous voices. . .it was they who had eaten up Vietnam. Vietnam had become a very quiet country now, extremely quiet; if it were not quiet it would die.

Suddenly Wang-jih felt uncomfortable. He shifted around in his seat. The fat man asked, "Do you want to take a nap?"

Wang-jih nodded mechanically. He pressed his faced against the window. The window pane was cold from the air-conditioning in the car, but as he pressed tightly against it for a while he seemed able to feel the warmth from outside, slightly, imperceptibly. Wang-jih carefully raised his face and gazed at the sky through that little corner of window. The sky was soft blue, a brilliant void. Wang-jih had an extremely powerful feeling that that was the sky of Vietnam, the sky of Saigon, washed pure and bright in the air of freedom. Oh unfeeling Heaven! The Wang-jih who had escaped from Saigon was just like this sky, having left his past behind. All that remained was but a white void. But at least he had truly escaped. The lofty distant sky, vast and empty, soft and cloudless, was like a face struck dumb by incredible suffering.

2

When Wang-jih got off the train, a middle-aged man was there to meet him. He had been sent by the school and although he was older than Wang-jih, he was very polite and considerate. "It is truly an honour for us to have you come and talk at our school; having come from so far away. . . ."

Wang-jih felt very uncomfortable. "You're much too polite."

The man did not really resemble his father—Wang-jih's father was somewhat shorter and fatter—but men of about that age always made him think of his father.

"I'm really sorry...It's so hot..."

"It's all right, it's all right."

Wang-jih could not see how the heat in Taitung was any stronger than that in Taipei. It was just as hot, perhaps even a little hotter, and a warm breeze licked his face like a fiery tongue. They waited a long time for a cab, most of them having been taken by other people. The man was very apologetic again. "Of all the...in this heat, standing here..."

"It's all right, it's all right."

The two of them stood on the bleached white ground. The sky above was sea-blue, but not one drop of water fell from it.

The man's name was Li. He handed Wang-jih a name card: Li Ho-t'ing [*Lee Ho-teen*]. He had a long nondescript face, very ordinary. He was so diplomatic that he didn't even have a face of his own. He started right in, with studied deliberation, to praise Wang-jih, from "I often see your fine articles in the papers," to "you certainly suffered many things that most ordinary people never suffer."

Wang-jih had little appetite for this kind of meaningless and inconsequential talk, but he did feel appreciative; at least Li was a man of feeling. A little later, Li sighed, "Since what you have experienced was truly at the risk of your life, everyone should come to hear such a valuable lecture. It's just that the timing is bad; the school is in the middle of final examinations...."

Wang-jih was feeling so comfortable in the air-conditioned taxi that Li's words didn't carry any force. Not until he mounted the podium did Wang-jih realize that Mr. Li's warning had been a mild one. After the scattered and very light applause stopped, he began to talk: "Ladies and gentlemen, I feel very honoured today to have been invited to your school to talk about 'Vietnam after the Communist takeover.' "

Below the stage, the faces of the people seated there were like an uneven border of flowers decorating the edges of the empty seats behind. Wang-jih silently kidded himself that he should pretend that the empty seats were also listening to his lecture. Perhaps the empty seats were even more capable of understanding his feelings. Seats with no one in them are incomplete; a person with no memories is also incomplete.

"It has been two years now since Vietnam fell, and the cruel and evil things that the Communists have done are too numerous to mention. In a Communist-ruled area, all news is controlled and twisted, so that there are many things and events that have probably never even been heard about in the free world. . . ."

Wang-jih felt very lonely. He had lectured to many different types of audience on many different occasions, but every time he stood on the stage he still felt that sense of complete loneliness and isolation. Standing on the stage were he and his Vietnam, but he could not even tell for certain whether the audience in front of him really cared or not.

". . . The destruction of Vietnam is the greatest tragedy of this century. Vietnam used the blood and tears of twenty million people to paint a danger sign for the free world in hopes that no other nation will follow the road of Vietnam. . . ."

Those young faces, short-haired, long-haired, intelligent honest faces. . . . "Everyone knows about Vietnam. Her fame rests in the fact that she died so vilely and tragically; not like the glorious end of a country, but like a refugee dragging around a body full of festering sores and dying in a dirty ditch somewhere. What is the Vietnam you have in your minds? It is only ceaseless war, day after day on the front pages of your newspapers. The papers printed Vietnam, many people talked of Vietnam, magazines featured black-and-white photos of those yellow-skinned mothers of Vietnam, woodenly black and white. That Vietnam was lifeless, a degraded empty Vietnam without any feelings. That Vietnam was on sale in the book stalls, day after day—a country struggling on the verge of death, becoming the star performance in the whole world, watched by millions; but none of them cared.

"The mothers of Vietnam cried on the pages of the magazines filled with agonized faces, carrying their children in baskets. A home could be reduced to such simplicity: one shoulder pole and two wicker baskets. In those homely and simple faces, only I can see the terrible fear in those seemingly expressionless eyes. Behind them was their country, like an ebb tide. The tremendous force of the incoming waves surged up high, huge curling billows, then suddenly broke and receded, receding right out of the ranks of history. In one night Vietnam was completely overthrown, while the entire world sat in their homes and read the papers; the death of Vietnam was just so many black words on white paper."

As Wang-jih talked on, he gradually became impassioned again. So what if there were so few people? Even if there was only one person, he'd still have to talk. Wang-jih's every word weighed down like a ton of lead, the weight of pain and suffering. He was Chinese and had returned to his country, but his heart still clung intimately to Saigon; he had grown up there. Seeing a map of

Saigon, he would run his hands over those unfeeling lines, and everywhere his fingers touched bore the traces of the years of his life.

His parents were still there. His mother was Vietnamese, old but still elegant. With those clear soft eyes, she always had the bearing of a young lady from an upper-class family. When he was little, his mother had held his hand as she took him to Da Nang[2] to visit relatives. Along the way, he kept looking around him, quite unconcerned about watching the road because his mother was holding his hand. His love for Vietnam was the love he had for his family, his parents, his brother and sisters, his childhood; the love for the years he had lived there. Then in an instant Vietnam had changed completely and his whole world had simply turned its face away. He had lived in the Communist-occupied area for two years, and those two years had made him forget everything, forget how he had lived before. He was rather fragile and sensitive. For fear of being hurt, he had very quickly armed himself: he always kept his face absolutely expressionless. His elder brother couldn't do it. One day he went to Da Nang and never came back.

On that day, as Wang-jih was passing by the Cloudscape Club, he saw a young man whose hands were trussed up with wire, black wire tying his hands behind him. His very young and handsome face was bloodless. Several rifle-carrying Communist cadres followed a few dozen paces behind him. Wang-jih knew what was happening. After "liberation[3]," those activist college students were complaining again, and this was the price of their complaints. Wang-jih couldn't help following; the young man was just about Wang-jih's own age. The young man limped along unsteadily, lifted his head to look at the sky, then looked back and forth at the houses and the crowd of people around him. Knowing full well that the youth had not actually seen him, Wang-jih suddenly froze with fear. The youth's eyes looked just like his elder brother's. A big bus came from the opposite direction, and the youth suddenly ran forward.

Wang-jih was very close and heard the soft, weak thud of the human body slamming against the metal body of the bus. The bus screeched to a halt, but the man's body had already fallen like an arrow and lay there stiffly on the road. The body of the big bus was flecked with blood like flower petals scattered from a radiant centre, almost a joyous sprinkling of blood.

Wang-jih stood at the side of the street, his feet so wobbly he couldn't move because he was afraid and also grief-stricken. He knew then that his elder brother would not return; his had been the look of one heading for death.

Wang-jih did not have the spirit for seeking death. He wanted to live. He fervently wanted to live. The shock of that incident made him impatient. He was living like he was dead, but it was more troublesome than actually being dead because he still had a body that needed to eat and drink, and a mind that every once in a while would go into action. Such basic human necessities, physical and spiritual, had already become forbidden in that place; they were unobtainable and not permitted to be obtained.

Wang-jih looked at the faces in front of him. Those young faces. Curious faces. Impassive faces. Wang-jih was not really much older than they were. Those self-confident faces full of high hopes, so completely self-confident without really knowing wherein their good fortune lay. Their good fortune was in the years lived under a beautiful sky; the life they had lived was still with them. A childhood spent in the shadow of red brick walls, an adolescence spent on grassy fields, and a youth spent under the stars. Every memory was there. They did not know that homesickness was the most painful emotion.

An enthusiastic applause rose up from the audience. Wang-jih especially appreciated the tall boy in the first row who was clapping very loudly. His large-boned hands were pounding fiercely as if he were trying to crush something to pieces. He had a long face and slightly bucked teeth. After Wang-jih had stepped down from the podium, he was surrounded by the students, who asked him all sorts of questions. But the tall boy remained in his seat, his eyes never leaving Wang-jih. He did not approach, but Wang-jih felt his presence. After everyone else had gone, he still remained seated there. Wang-jih walked toward him. The boy raised his face. His eyes were moist, filled with pain.

He said something in Vietnamese.

Wang-jih's mind exploded. He stood there, stunned, suddenly finding it difficult to move. He waited for the blood that had surged to his head to gradually flow back into his body, before continuing to walk over.

The boy was an overseas student from Vietnam. Except for him, his whole family was still in Vietnam. He was no longer studying; he didn't have any money and didn't have the heart for it either.

Wang-jih stared at him. Another simple, ordinary face; passing him in the street, Wang-jih would not have paid him any special attention. Looking at him now, Wang-jih felt strangely moved, as if in the boy's slightly darkened skin he could see the Saigon sun. Those moist eyes gazed at Wang-jih, sad and fearful. Those were the eyes of a refugee, and Wang-jih knew that he had them too. They had lost everything except their memories of escape. Like spending a long time on a ship and still feeling the sea after coming onto dry land. People who have lost their freedom still cannot believe it when they live in freedom. Wang-jih looked at those eyes, and it was as if he were looking at himself, forever startled, forever touched with fragmented sorrow—the emotions of an escapee. Except for the terror of their escape, they really didn't have any other memories.

3

Wang-jih was eating in a northern-style restaurant. It was the busiest time of day, all of the tables were full, and the waiter was running back and forth shouting orders. Wang-jih enjoyed this ebulliently happy atmosphere; it was so different from his lifelong tastes that it made him just a little uneasy. Paradoxically, this slight uneasiness made him feel all the more peaceful and secure.

A family was seated at the opposite table, a young couple with two children. The little girl, about three or four years old, was concentrating on the soy sauce dish in front of her, putting her finger in it and then licking her finger. The smaller one was still in his mother's arms, and dressed scantily, his plump body bulging here and there. He lay back in his mother's arms, staring lethargically at some point directly ahead of him. The whole family was out for a treat on their day off. The woman was smiling and talking to the man. The man said nothing, just looked nervously down the aisle. Their food had not yet come.

Three young women were seated at another table, all dressed very stylishly. Their chins resting on their palms, they chatted softly with restrained dignity in a cultured manner. It was a very studied pose, as if they had an audience of thousands watching them. The short-haired young woman raised her eyebrows theatrically, opened her eyes wide, and shook her head. Her golden earrings flashed. She was very affected but very lovely.

The waiter shouted, "Coming through, coming through!" as he carried the dishes and cleared the way quite unceremoniously. A middle-aged man seated against the wall with three dishes and a bottle of beer in front of him continued to eat carefully with nothing else on his mind. As the waiter raced by him like the wind, he just kept on eating and drinking. Wang-jih admired his poise.

The family's food arrived. The little girl took her chopsticks and poked around at random in the food, while her mother admonished, "Be a good girl and don't do that." The child replied, "But I want to!" She had a lovely face and was wearing an off-the-shoulder dress showing her full round shoulders and her plump little arms, powdery white and delectable, like something to eat. A healthy child. Seeing such a healthy, plump child made one hungry.

After Saigon fell, food rationing was insufficient and hunger was most obvious in the bodies of children. All of the children began to be malformed, their little heads and faces shrunken and emaciated, like dried nuts. Children are the fruits of a nation, and the fruits of Vietnam were these strange dried things totally lacking in nourishment. If Vietnam's fall had not yet pierced Wang-jih's heart, these children would have done it. He did not really think that much, he could simply pretend not to see any of the children of Vietnam; but he could not let his own progeny become like them. He was the only male child left in his family. His family depended on him to carry on the line, but he wanted healthy descendants, born healthy and then living in health, like that little girl.

His food came, and Wang-jih was eating when he heard the sound of a dish crashing to the floor. It was from that table with the children. The culprit was not the older child, but the baby in his mother's arms who had made little fists and was flailing them around in the air. The mother sort of gasped in disbelief, and the baby smiled sweetly, still waving his small hands around in the air. The father pushed his chair back and stood up: "*Aiya*, what's going on!"

The waiter, a short, sturdy man with an air of experience, came over and calmly surveyed the damage. "It's all right, nothing serious, nothing serious. We'll clean it up in a minute. Don't run around now, little girl. Be careful of the broken pieces." He called for someone to clean up at the same time that he deftly reopened the menu. "How about it? Order something more, it's not much money. What a shame, you hadn't even had a couple of bites. How about ordering a smaller dish this time?"

Swept up into the dust pan, the plate of spilled food was mixed with dust and was no longer fit to eat; but in Vietnam that was just the sort of thing they ate. Wang-jih looked carefully at it and thought it looked just like that: grey dust and black sand mixed together with the dirty, ghastly colour of vegetables.

He never used to be this way, but after he escaped he had an almost religious attitude toward food. He ate very carefully, fearing that he might miss something, whether of colour, aroma, or taste. After all, having a wide variety of different foods to choose from is something special for human beings. He ate with reverence, afraid of wasting anything, and looking very carefully at the rich colours of the food. Some people, after suffering from famine, became gluttonous. Wang-jih had not gone to such an extreme, but he had never before imagined that food could arouse so many emotions, from the most bitter to the most beautiful, from the most base to the most lofty. When Wang-jih first arrived in Taiwan, he had wanted to cry at the sight of food; he could not eat it, but just liked to keep on looking and looking at it. So this world really had such a place where there was plenty of food to eat and clothes to wear without worry! How utterly fortunate! Wang-jih couldn't eat the food because he feared that when he finished there would be no more; but he also wanted to gulp it down hurriedly because he feared that if he did not eat it, it would disappear. Those fearful years...Wang-jih thought of his parents still eating only greens boiled in water, and he cried as he ate every bit of his food.

Now he was a little more distant from those days, but his sufferings in the Communist-occupied area could not easily be forgotten. Over there he had lived like a plant, dependent only on sunlight, air, and water, and feeling that even those things were insufficient.

In terms of eating, Wang-jih had begun to have some confidence, but he still preferred to eat alone. He felt that every kind of food was delicious to him, and he loved to try every sort of strange flavour. There were no foods that he could not eat. Except for those greens they ate in Vietnam. He had a kind of superstition about those greens, feeling that they were bad for the health. In Saigon, day in and day out, they ate those greens, those greens that really had no taste of their own. One had to rely completely on the idea that "this is food" in order to keep swallowing them down. Wang-jih was afraid of that feeling: rotten and grainy, the greens were more like tattered bits of old cloth and rotten wood. Even though he forced himself to swallow them, it did no good; he kept on growing weaker. When he stood up, his legs wobbled and could hardly support his body.

Do you know that sort of feeling?

Wang-jih swept his eyes over all the other customers in the restaurant, over all the food left behind on the tables. What abundance and fullness. Everyone's face displayed the unconcern and indifference of people who are used to being comfortable and who do not overly treasure food or anything else in life. His mind continually bounced back to the bitter feelings of that time in Vietnam.

Wang-jih walked out of the restaurant into the black night. That black night was also the black night that he had escaped in, the black night that had protected him. The others had not been as fortunate as he was. He had heard two others being discovered. The silence of the pitch-black night was suddenly pierced by the desperate cries of those two who were caught. They all knew their fate. He had seen many corpses of those buried alive on the beach.

On that night, as he slipped into the water, he raised his head to look at the sky. It was the last time he would ever see the sky over his homeland. That

compassionate, distant starlight. The moonlight followed him, as if it were sending him off or as if it were also escaping with him.

The entire vault of the sky was tipped over as if it were falling. As he swam in the sea, Wang-jih watched that vast escaping sky. It was always in front of him. Escaping that night were Wang-jih and the Vietnamese sky.

NOTES

[1]The NT (New Taiwan) dollar is worth about Canadian $0.04.

[2]Da Nang was an important military base for South Vietnamese and American forces during the Vietnam War.

[3]The Communists referred to their takeover of South Vietnam as the "liberation."

OUR CORNER

"THE LIGHT IN OUR HEARTS . . ."

A village park in Dali, China.

Cranes

BY HWANG SUNWŎN

TRANSLATED BY PETER H. LEE

HWANG Sunwŏn (1915–   ) is one of Korea's most respected fiction writers. In his short stories and novels, he combines realism with the use of lyrical prose and traditional imagery to create strong images of Korea and the Korean people. Often, his stories portray harsh circumstances with a sense of resignation and intuitive faith.

After the Second World War, Korea was divided into "North" (under the protection of the Soviet Union and China) and "South" (under the protection of the United States) in 1945. The boundary was arbitrarily drawn at the Thirty-eighth Parallel, leaving families and friends divided. Many people in the Communist-dominated North went South to support the anti-Communists; others in the South travelled North to support the Communists. During the Korean war (1950–1953), which began when the North invaded the South, friend often fought against friend.

"Cranes" tells of the wartime meeting of two such friends, one belonging to the North Korean army, the other fighting for South Korea.

The northern village lay snug beneath the high, bright autumn sky, near the border at the Thirty-eighth Parallel.

White gourds lay one against the other on the dirt floor of an empty farmhouse. Any village elders who passed by extinguished their bamboo pipes first, and the children, too, turned back some distance off. Their faces were marked with fear.

As a whole, the village showed little damage from the war, but it still did not seem like the same village Sŏngsam had known as a boy.

At the foot of a chestnut grove on the hill behind the village he stopped and climbed a chestnut tree. Somewhere far back in his mind he heard the old man with a wen shout, "You bad boy, climbing up my chestnut tree again!"

The old man must have passed away, for he was not among the few village elders Sŏngsam had met. Holding on to the trunk of the tree, Sŏngsam gazed up at the blue sky for a time. Some chestnuts fell to the ground as the dry clusters opened of their own accord.

A young man stood, his hands bound, before a farmhouse that had been converted into a Public Peace Police office. He seemed to be a stranger, so Sŏngsam went up for a closer look. He was stunned: this young man was none other than his boyhood playmate, Tŏkchae [*Tok-jeh*].

Sŏngsam asked the police officer who had come with him from Ch'ŏnt'ae for an explanation. The prisoner was the vice-chairman of the Farmers' Communist League and had just been flushed out of hiding in his own house, Sŏngsam learned.

Sŏngsam sat down on the dirt floor and lit a cigarette.

Tŏkchae was to be escorted to Ch'ŏngdan by one of the peace police.

After a time, Sŏngsam lit a new cigarette from the first and stood up. "I'll take him with me."

Tŏkchae averted his face and refused to look at Sŏngsam. The two left the village.

Sŏngsam went on smoking, but the tobacco had no flavour. He just kept drawing the smoke in and blowing it out. Then suddenly he thought that Tŏkchae, too, must want a puff. He thought of the days when they had shared dried gourd leaves behind sheltering walls, hidden from the adults' view. But today, how could he offer a cigarette to a fellow like this?

Once, when they were small, he went with Tŏkchae to steal some chestnuts from the old man with the wen. It was Sŏngsam's turn to climb the tree. Suddenly the old man began shouting. Sŏngsam slipped and fell to the ground. He got chestnut burrs all over his bottom, but he kept on running. Only when the two had reached a safe place where the old man could not overtake them did Sŏngsam turn his bottom to Tŏkchae. The burrs hurt so much as they were plucked out that Sŏngsam could not keep tears from welling up in his eyes. Tŏkchae produced a fistful of chestnuts from his pocket and thrust them into Sŏngsam's. . . . Sŏngsam threw away the cigarette he had just lit, and then made up his mind not to light another while he was escorting Tŏkchae.

They reached the pass at the hill where he and Tŏkchae had cut fodder for the cows until Sŏngsam had to move to a spot near Ch'ŏnt'ae, south of the Thirty-eighth Parallel, two years before the liberation[1].

Sŏngsam felt a sudden a surge of anger in spite of himself and shouted, "So how many have you killed?"

For the first time, Tŏkchae cast a quick glance at him and then looked away.

"You! How many have you killed?" Sŏngsam asked again.

Tŏkchae looked at him again and glared. The glare grew intense, and his mouth twitched.

"So you managed to kill quite a few, eh?" Sŏngsam felt his mind becoming clear of itself, as if some obstruction had been removed. "If you were vice-chairman of the Communist League, why didn't you run? You must have been lying low with a secret mission."

Tŏkchae did not reply.

"Speak up. What was your mission?"

Tŏkchae kept walking. Tŏkchae was hiding something, Sŏngsam thought. He wanted to take a good look at him, but Tŏkchae kept his face averted.

Fingering the revolver at his side, Sŏngsam went on: "There's no need to make excuses. You're going to be shot anyway. Why don't you tell the truth here and now?"

"I'm not going to make any excuses. They made me vice-chairman of the League because I was a hardworking farmer, and one of the poorest. If that's a capital offence, so be it. I'm still what I used to be—the only thing I'm good at is tilling the soil." After a short pause, Tŏkchae added, "My old man is bedridden at home. He's been ill almost half a year." His father was a widower, a poor, hardworking farmer who lived only for his son. Seven years before, his back had given out, and he had contracted a skin disease.

"Are you married?"

"Yes," Tŏkchae replied after a time.

"To whom?"

"Shorty."

"To Shorty?" How interesting! A woman so small and plump that she knew the earth's vastness, but not the sky's height. Such a cold fish! He and Tŏkchae had teased her and made her cry. And Tŏkchae had married her!

"How many kids?"

"The first is arriving this fall, she says."

Sŏngsam had difficulty swallowing a laugh that he was about to let burst forth in spite of himself. Although he had asked how many children Tŏkchae had, he could not help wanting to break out laughing at the thought of the wife sitting there with her huge stomach, one span around. But he realized that this was no time for joking.

"Anyway, it's strange you didn't run away."

"I tried to escape. They said that once the South invaded, not a man would be spared. So all of us between seventeen and forty were taken to the North. I thought of evacuating, even if I had to carry my father on my back. But Father said no. How could we farmers leave the land behind when the crops were ready for harvesting? He grew old on that farm, depending on me as the prop and the mainstay of the family. I wanted to be with him in his last moments so I could close his eyes with my own hand. Besides, where can farmers like us go, when all we know how to do is live on the land?"

Sŏngsam had had to flee the previous June. At night he had broken the news privately to his father. But his father had said the same thing: Where could a farmer go, leaving all the chores behind? So Sŏngsam had left alone. Roaming about the strange streets and villages in the South, he had been haunted by thoughts of his old parents and the young children, who had been left with all the chores. Fortunately, his family had been safe then, as it was now.

They had crossed over a hill. This time Sŏngsam walked with his face averted. The autumn sun was hot on his forehead. This was an ideal day for the harvest, he thought.

When they reached the foot of the hill, Sŏngsam gradually came to a halt. In the middle of a field he espied a group of cranes[2] that resembled men in white, all bent over. This had been the demilitarized zone along the Thirty-eighth Parallel. The cranes were still living here, as before, though the people were all gone.

Once, when Sŏngsam and Tŏkchae were about twelve, they had set a trap here, unbeknown to the adults, and caught a crane, a Tanjong crane. They had tied the crane up, even binding its wings, and paid it daily visits, patting its neck and riding on its back. Then one day they overheard the neighbours whispering: someone had come from Seoul with a permit from the governor general's office to catch cranes as some kind of specimens. Then and there the two boys had dashed off to the field. That they would be found out and punished had no longer mattered; all they cared about was the fate of their crane. Without a moment's delay, still out of breath from running, they untied the crane's feet and wings, but the bird could hardly walk. It must have been weak from having been bound.

The two held the crane up. Then, suddenly, they heard a gunshot. The crane fluttered its wings once or twice and then sank back to the ground.

The boys thought their crane had been shot. But the next moment, as another crane from a nearby bush fluttered its wings, the boys' crane stretched its long neck, gave out a whoop, and disappeared into the sky. For a long while the two boys could not tear their eyes away from the blue sky up into which their crane had soared.

"Hey, why don't we stop here for a crane hunt?" Sŏngsam said suddenly.

Tŏkchae was dumbfounded.

"I'll make a trap with this rope; you flush a crane over here."

Sŏngsam had untied Tŏkchae's hands and was already crawling through the weeds.

Tŏkchae's face whitened. "You're sure to be shot anyway"—these words flashed through his mind. Any instant a bullet would come flying from Sŏngsam's direction, Tŏkchae thought.

Some paces away, Sŏngsam quickly turned toward him.

"Hey, how come you're standing there like a dummy? Go flush a crane!"

Only then did Tŏkchae understand. He began crawling through the weeds.

A pair of Tanjong cranes soared high into the clear blue autumn sky, flapping their huge wings.

———

NOTES

[1]Korea was liberated from Japanese occupation at the end of World War II.

[2]In many Asian cultures, the crane is a symbol of longevity.

Our Corner

BY JIN SHUI

TRANSLATED BY KUANG WENDONG

JIN Shui [Jin Suy] (1951–   ) is the pen name of Shi Tiesheng, a native of Beijing. As a young man, he was sent to the countryside for "re-education" during the Cultural Revolution (1966–1976). While living there, he was involved in an accident that left him paralyzed.

After his accident, Jin joined a neighbourhood cooperative factory, similar to the one described in "Our Corner." In such factories, much of the work—particularly decoration—is done by hand.

Our corner used to be different with its blotched walls under the low, cobwebbed ceiling. We liked that corner, because it was on the lee side, as Tiezi [*Ti-eh-zi*] put it, and Kejian [*Kuh-jian*] said it was cosy. And me? I just wanted to keep away from the window, from which you could see a college, the gate of a song-and-dance troupe, and the chimneys of some regular factories. We liked this corner. It was the technicians' corner, to which our whole neighbourhood production team attached the greatest importance. There Tiezi designed graceful ladies of old, which the women workers in the team copied painstakingly on furniture modelled after antiques. But only Kejian and I could give the finishing touches—give the ladies features expressing tenderness and love. The women were loud in their praise: "You're young fellows after all!" "Our team couldn't do without you."

Pleased with himself, Kejian began to whistle while Tiezi contentedly lit a cigarette.

"But what about free medical care?" I grumbled. "And our pay is still only eighty cents a day!"

"How you do grouse!" remarked one of the women. "There'd be no problem if we had any say. We all have children...." She choked with tears.

We started humming *The Bodhi Tree* without looking at each other.

> Before the gate a bodhi tree[1]
> Is standing by the well,
> And in its green shade I have had
> More dreams than I can tell.

We found the plaintive melody comforting. Tiezi and Kejian must be like me, I thought, recalling my dreamlike childhood and our life in the countryside of Shaan-xi province, the northeast, and Inner Mongolia....

But what had become of us?

In the morning, at noon, or in the evening you could see us walking together along the quiet alley. What we dreaded most was running into innocent, artless children.

"Look, mama!"

We all hung our heads.

"Those guys have been hurt, there's something wrong with their legs, so...."

Tiezi would speed up his wheelchair while Kejian and I tried to go a little faster.

"Are they cripples?" the child asked.

The mother's slap seemed a blow on our hearts.

What could we do about an innocent child and a kind-hearted mother? If it had been anyone else, we would have stopped to fight. What had we to lose? The cadres in the school vocational office tried to console us; factory recruiters eyed us superciliously—we didn't pass muster. And we were a worry to our parents, a burden to our brothers and sisters....

An elderly woman, wiping her eyes, had urged me, "Don't take things too hard. Your little sister will take care of you. She won't neglect you...." I can't imagine what I looked like then when she took me in her trembling arms and kept calling my name. So, that was all my life was worth. God! But our paintings were neither fewer nor less skilled than those done by regular workers. Enduring the pain, we worked extra hard to be independent, like normal people, to change our status as cripples.

"Forget it," Tiezi said. "Do you think we'll be so thick-skinned as to live on after our parents kick the bucket?"

"Get a pack of dynamite and we'll blow ourselves up with the next swine who sneers at us!" Kejian pounded his crutches so hard that he nearly fell down.

It is lucky that people can die. We seemed to have nothing to fear and in the quiet alley we sang:

> Today, as in the past,
> I roam till late at night,
> Wandering in the dark,
> My eyes closed tight...

She came in the season when the spring wind began to turn the willows green.

"I'm Wang Xue [*Wong Shoe*]. Can I sit here?" She came into our corner.

"Sure."

"If you like."

"Why not?"

Each of us gave a cold reply. Then Kejian whispered to me, "Disgusting, nauseous." Tiezi's frosty eyes glinted behind his spectacles, then he lowered his head with a grunt. Taking the offensive was a defensive tactic. But what were we on our guard against?

She was quite a pretty girl.

"Have you come back too because of illness?" I asked.

She shook her head. "No, my parents need my help. Are you waiting for jobs too?"

None of us uttered a word. Waiting for jobs? Heaven knows how many more years we would have to wait!

"I'll sit here and watch how you work first." She smiled at me, probably finding me less difficult to get on with.

The radio music for exercises from the college broke the silence of our corner.

Her head was close to Tiezi's and her eyebrows almost touched Kejian's shoulder. They were like schoolchildren holding their breath in fear, the fools! Where was their haughtiness of a moment ago? It was all I could do not to laugh. Neither of them had ever intruded into the heart of a girl. Only I... but that was all past.

Kejian made several faulty strokes in succession and the hair of the lady Tiezi was painting looked like old wool unravelled from a sweater. Many past events flashed through my mind. What were they? It was that letter again. . . .

Suddenly she burst out laughing.

We all raised our heads in bewilderment.

She kept on laughing.

An angry look appeared on Tiezi's face.

"I can see my own nose!" she exclaimed. "I was watching you painting and suddenly saw my own nose. I didn't realize it was possible!" She tilted her head slightly to squint down at her nose, chuckling.

We couldn't help laughing too. A gentle breeze blew a touch of warmth into our corner.

A flash of lightning through the fine spring drizzle aroused three atrophied hearts.

From morning till night our corner echoed with songs: *The Bodhi Tree, The Marmot, Fate, The Boundless Grasslands.* . . . We started with a soft humming, then sang in low voices. Tiezi tried hard not to open his mouth too wide while Kejian, in order to sing the bass, pressed his chin as low as he could. I stole a glance at Wang Xue, and noticed that they were peeping at her too. Her head was swaying gently in time with the music, her plaits dangling over her shoulders. Our singing gained in volume.

> Ol' man river, dat ol' man river!
> He must know something'
> But don't say nothin'. . .

"Why sing all these dismal songs?" she suddenly asked.

"What would you like to hear then?" Kejian flushed.

"*Making Hay.* I love to hear Hu Songhua[2] sing that." She cleared her throat and sang:

> With pitch and prong the whole day long,
> We both were making hay,
> And there she was and there I was,
> And we were worlds away. . .

I thought of that letter again. It had been written by a well-meaning fellow to my sweetheart. Forget it! That's over and done with.

Wang Xue was still singing softly, her plaits swinging with the lively rhythm.

The three of us just stopped work and stared blankly at her. The defences in our hearts had been dismantled. In our mind's eye a vast expanse

of spring water glimmering with patches of sunlight like gems, gently lapping at the solitary embankment, appeared. How beautiful she was! But unlike certain actresses, she didn't make eyes at the audience or put on airs to please them. No, she was her natural self. And her thoughts were written on her face: she didn't look down on us.

All of a sudden Tiezi's voice rang out:

> I wish I were a little lamb,
> To follow by her side.
> I wish she'd take a little whip
> To flick my woolly hide.

Wang Xue doubled up with laughter, nearly choking. "What sort of rubbishy song is that! Who wants to be whipped? You must have made it up yourself." She casually took hold of Tiezi's arm and shook it.

She seemed more like a little girl than someone in her twenties.

Just like in the song, we worked together all day long. We would paint while singing *Making Hay, Auld Lang Syne, Aiyo Mama,* and other lively songs. Our output increased with each passing day, surprising the rest of the team. Wang Xue was eager to learn, and we vied to teach her all our special skills. Soon we were all talking to her in an avuncular way:

"Wang Xue, you ought to take more exercise."

"Wang Xue, you should learn a foreign language. It's not too difficult. Where there's a will there's a way."

"Or learn to play the violin. There's nothing you can't do, if you put your mind to it."

"You must make something of your life, Wang Xue. You're not like us...."

And Wang Xue? Such advice delighted her. She would fish some sweets from her pocket and quietly put them in front of us, or pour us each a cup of fragrant tea.

"Is this a reward, little girl?"

"No!" She was delightfully naive. "It's a punishment."

"A punishment?"

"Yes. Why should you expect so much from me, but not from yourselves?"

We fell silent again. Sweets taste sweet but we felt bitter.

"I...I haven't offended you, have I?" She glanced at us, then lowering her eyes, added, "What I mean is, you should live like that too. Am I right?"

Quite right, Wang Xue, but wait, we have to think things over carefully....

After that, she came half an hour earlier than usual to tidy up the workshop and our corner. She was always cheerful, conscientious about everything, and thoroughly enjoyed life. Amidst her singing, the dust in our corner vanished. A beautiful calendar was hung on the shabby wall. Gradually we three, who had formerly limped into our corner only when the bell sounded, also came earlier and earlier, each trying to arrive before the others. I was not at first aware of what was happening. Only when I sensed a certain constraint among the three of us did I realize that it was due to unconscious jealousy. Every one of us hoped to stay a little longer with Wang Xue. Eight hours a day was too little. What was the meaning of this jealousy?

After that I gave up going to work too early. I was by no means the kind of noble lover you read about in novels who makes way for his rival. It was precisely because I loved Wang Xue so deeply that I quite naturally rebuilt the defence in my heart. It was a trench, a deep scar inscribed with the glaring warning: "Impossible!" Besides, there was that letter! That letter.... Ah, just as my heart was seeking a little happiness in life, it underwent bitter pain. All I could do was stifle that pain in my heart, turning it into an apathetic smile to conceal what my heart sought.

Later, Tiezi and Kejian stopped coming earlier too. I daresay it was for the same reason!

Wang Xue really was like a little girl. She failed to see these subtle changes. One summer evening she begged us to accompany her to a film to be shown in a nearby park. Holding up four tickets she declared, "*To Make Life Sweeter*, a good film. Come along!"

Tiezi shook his head and Kejian said, "I won't go either. What sweeter life?"

"Won't you go with me?" She turned to me. "It's very dark on the way back after the film."

"Are you afraid?" we all asked together.

"Mm." She knitted her eyebrows, nodding sheepishly.

Then we all agreed to go with her. I felt rather proud because we could protect her. No doubt so did Tiezi and Kejian.

In the park the gentle evening breeze carried the faint scent of flowers. How many years now? Five! Ever since I'd had to use crutches, I'd never come here. Why should I? It would only remind me of the past. This was my childhood playground. I seemed to have sung and laughed here only yesterday. Here I felt the hopes of my boyhood. However, I could not recognize the poplars I had planted. On that lawn there had gathered many youngsters ready to settle down in the countryside, who used their simple, heartfelt verses to express their magnificent ideals. But what had happened later?

It was not yet dark. There were only a few children sitting there quietly, looking up at the blank screen. Tiezi and Kejian were also silent.

Suddenly Wang Xue laughed.

In the grove young lovers were strolling arm in arm, kissing.

"What's so funny? You'll be doing that yourself some day." I blurted out.

"What nonsense! I won't!" she stammered, red in the face.

Well, better not think of such things.

However, Tiezi burst out, "Doesn't it give you the creeps being with us, Wang Xue?"

"Why should it?" She jumped up to pick two leaves and mischievously stuffed them into Kejian's collar.

"Aren't you afraid?" I asked.

"Of what?"

I was tongue-tied. That letter! It read, "Don't be too friendly with him. Better keep your distance. Otherwise he will probably fall in love with you and you can only make him suffer...."

"What's there to be afraid of, eh?" She gave me a punch, holding a ladybird in her other hand. Oh, if only she could stay like a little girl for ever!

"Well, I mean, are you scared of the dark?"

"Don't be silly!" She blushed. "Are we going to see the film or not?"

Humming a song, we turned back along the small path. Still holding the ladybird she chattered away, keeping Tiezi and Kejian in fits of laughter. All at once I felt that the world was beautiful and sweet, and that we had become three happy elder brothers keeping their lovable sister company.

She was really like a little sister. As soon as the film started she began to giggle, clutching at my crutches. Her laughter made it hard to hear what the actors were saying. I wished time would stand still so that she would remain a little sister and we her happy brothers, forgetting the past, the present, and the future, and everything on earth....In fact, I so far forgot myself that I bent down, without the support of my crutches, to pick up a ball of knitting wool she had dropped. I fell flat on my face and cut my arm.... But I would gladly have fallen ten more times, because when she was on the verge of tears the casual way I passed it off made her laugh again.

One day Wang Xue was suddenly depressed, staring blankly and sighing without a word. When asked what was wrong, she hummed and hawed, glancing at us with embarrassment.

"Tell us what's up," said Tiezi anxiously. "Who's bullied you?"

"Who's tired of living? Tell me who?" Kejian clenched his fists.

"No, nobody's bullied me," she stuttered. "It's my mother. She wants me to meet that man. . . ."

There was dead silence in our corner.

"A university student. Introduced by my second aunt. . . ."

We heard the whistling of the wind along the electric wires.

That was something to be expected and I had already built up my defences, yet I seemed to feel my heart rolling down a dry well. I was not clear what went through my mind at that instant. It seemed that I was only thinking about how to get through the coming day. I longed for a cigarette. Tiezi and Kejian had already lit theirs and handed the lighter to me. My heart hit the bottom of the pitch-dark well. I wished I could stay there for ever, forgetting the world and forgotten by the world.

However, fixing expectant eyes on us, Wang Xue asked timidly, "Should I go to meet him?"

A girl like Wang Xue really deserved more happiness than other people. Just because she was too simple-minded to shun us, how could we undermine her happiness? Must she sacrifice it to prove her fine qualities?

"I don't want to meet him. What's the point. . .?"

She was expecting our help; she needed our help. A moment ago I had really been too selfish!

"You should go." Tiezi was the first to return to his senses.

"Love is something that can make you happy," I said. "Then you'll work and study harder. Even the world will become more beautiful. . . ."

"That's right!" chimed in Kejian.

We held forth on love, and Wang Xue listened trustingly and raptly. We could see from her shining eyes that she admired us and thought highly of us. We were prompted by a sense of pride to give our "little sister" good advice without any thought of ourselves. . . .

Still, when we left by the small alley that evening, we once again sang the song that had been banished from our minds all through the summer.

Today, as in the past,
I roam till late at night,
Wandering in the dark,
My eyes closed tight.
It seems the leaves are calling without cease:
Come back to me, friend, to find peace.

The following day in our corner there were indications that Wang Xue wanted to talk with the three of us alone. But better not, Wang Xue. I felt somewhat anxious. She smiled at us, looking so relaxed that my heart felt as if gripped by an icy hand. I kept reminding myself: You are glad of your sister's happiness, right?

"Sing a song, Tiezi," I suggested.

"Yes, let's sing, Kejian," Tiezi responded.

But we were in no mood to sing.

At the break Wang Xue finally found a chance and told us hastily, "Hey, I met that man last night and broke off with him."

We made neither head nor tail of this at first, looking at each other tensely. The next moment Tiezi started to splutter with laughter. "You silly girl! You talk of breaking off, as if you'd known him for ages."

"It's true, I'm not kidding you." She sounded anxious.

"That means she didn't agree to see any more of him. Is that right?" Kejian turned to ask me cheerfully.

The icy hand on my heart had loosened its grip. It was no good, really, gloating over someone else's misfortune.

"Why didn't you agree?" I asked her.

"He kept a straight face like a big cadre, and lectured me all the time as if he didn't even know how to smile. He said I was naive. Not just rather naive, but *extremely* naive. Dear me! My head started buzzing. Oh, spare me, I'm not short of tutors." She rattled this off, her nose twitching, then dashed out, calling over her shoulder, "I'm going to find a newspaper and see if there's a film show in the park tonight!"

I found I had started humming a tune already. Why? Because I was happy? What if she were my real sister? Even so I'd never agree to her marrying such a man.

We went to the small park again. That summer we spent many a sweet evening together in that small park. Wang Xue told me many things about herself. I can't remember now what film we saw. What remains in my memory is the setting sun, the evening wind, the moon, the stars, and little Wang Xue who loved us as if we were her own brothers. And we began to love everything around us just as she did.

As I recall them now, those memories are as precious as gold. . . .

University? Oh, yes. Wang Xue was admitted to a university later. It was in the autumn of that year when she and her mother were at loggerheads over that university student that the news spread apace: students must be enrolled through an entrance examination.[3]

The day we heard that, Tiezi sat there lost in thought. I knew what he was thinking about. He had been one of the best students in a well-known middle school.

"Forget it, Tiezi," I said. "Just ignore the whole business."

"You can only deceive yourself," he countered, with a wry smile.

The street lamps swayed in the wind. Tiezi and I sat face to face at the door of his house without a word. The autumn cicadas would go on chirping till midnight.

"Wang Xue!" Teizi exclaimed as if he were dreaming.

"Where?" I looked round.

"I mean Wang Xue can go to university now."

"Sure! But can she pass the exam?"

"She told me she did quite well in it the year Zhang Tiesheng[4] [*Jang Ti-eh-shung*] was enrolled."

"Right!" My eyes sparkled. "You can help her with maths and physics."

"And you with Chinese, mainly composition."

"Exactly!"

From then on every evening the light in our corner was on while crickets chirped away outside.

Bending over the table Tiezi and Wang Xue were engrossed in points, lines, logarithms, sines, drawing, and ciphering. As for me, I taught her grammar and classical prose, and wrote classical essays for her to imitate. Only Kejian sat silently outside the door boiling water for us, occasionally poking his head in with an envious grin when he heard us laughing. The kettle sang merrily over the blue-tongued flames. There was a look of depression in his bright eyes, for he could not understand what we were talking about. In fact, he had not even finished primary school.

Using my crutches, I walked over to him and patted him on the shoulder. "Perhaps you have some useful books at home?"

He didn't answer. He was feeling upset because he could not give Wang Xue a hand. Poor Kejian!

The next day he limped over with a book entitled *The Absolute Discrimination of Sound*, which he gave to Wang Xue, not knowing what it was about. It turned out to be a foreign novel. Pretending to be overjoyed, the kind-hearted girl said she loved to read such books.

The lamplight was serene and soft. I'd seen that kind of lamplight when I was a boy and my mother came home from work and kissed me on the neck. Why can't we spread such a light over all darkness around?

The light was still on when the crickets stopped chirping.

The light was still on when the leaves fell.

The light was still on when the north wind grew colder and colder.

One evening we sang *Lamplight*:

> A young girl
> Sees a soldier off to the war.
> They bid farewell in the dark.
> Those steps before...

Wang Xue's voice suddenly broke, tears filled her eyes. "If I'm admitted to a university far away from here, we won't be able to be together again."

A shooting star swiftly disappeared on the horizon.

None of us spoke, as if aware of this problem. To be frank, we were worried about her, prayed for her every day, and felt comforted when we imagined her sitting in a lecture room. . . .

"You'll write to me, won't you?"

There was only the rustling of fallen leaves on the pavement in the small, dark alley.

"Anyway, I'll write to you whenever I have time."

The wheelchair creaked, crutches thumped.

"Promise me just one thing, please. . . ." She sounded choked.

"What?"

She halted and all of a sudden burst out sobbing.

"Yes, we will, Wang Xue," we chorused. "We will write to you!" We were only too pleased to say this.

"Just one thing." She stopped crying with a great effort. " Never talk about death again; never talk about dynamite packs. . . ."

She knew everything. She had never brought that up before but she knew everything! She probably hadn't mentioned it because she hated to talk like that "big cadre with a straight face." However, she told us all that was in her heart. She liked to hear us singing cheerful songs. She liked us to go to films with her and to tell us amusing "news." All this had converged into a warm stream that thawed out our frozen hearts. Thank you, little girl! No, you weren't a little girl and we shouldn't thank you. We shouldn't let your painstaking efforts come to nothing.

"Do you promise me? OK?"

That reminded me of a fairy tale: A mother sheep told her three lambs before she went out, "Wolves have long snouts and pointed ears. Don't open the door for them. Promise me?" So we were like three little lambs Wang Xue worried about.

"OK, Wang Xue, we do!" we promised her.

A street lamp flashed past, lighting up her anxious face. We had not set her mind at ease. We passed another light. Putting on an air of cheerfulness she said, "I may not pass the exam!"

Well, well, she was the first to comfort us again.

I felt something rending my heart as I said, "Don't worry, Wang Xue! We'll bite that wolf to death!"

"Wolf?" She faced me, her eyes glistening with tears. Oh, little girl, you still didn't understand!

I began to talk excitedly about Jack London's novel *Love of Life* and Lenin's comments on it. How the hero fought with a wolf; how he overcame hunger, piercing cold, and weakness; how steadfast he was and how strong his will to live. As I went on Wang Xue's eyes shone; so did Tiezi's and Kejian's. The three of us struck up a tune and then Wang Xue joined in. Our spirited, stirring singing made the quiet alley ring. . . .

That winter, just as she had predicted, Wang Xue was admitted to a medical college in another province. She had always wondered why our legs could not be cured now that there were so many hospitals in our country. Clinging to the window of the southward bound train, she said earnestly, "Just wait and be patient. I'm taking your medical records with me." We waved goodbye to her as we had as boys when we saw our brothers and sisters off to school. She didn't seem to be leaving us for a remote city in the south but for somewhere so close that she could come back at any time.

Look, here is our corner. The beautiful calendar is the one Wang Xue hung there. There's not a speck of dust on it, I can assure you! We no longer sing those melancholy songs. Whenever dusk falls in that little alley, we seem to hear Wang Xue's voice and call to mind the story about the wolf. Here in this world, at this moment, a kind and beautiful girl is concerned about us. She has kindled the light in our hearts. We should be her brave fighters. As to the future. . .friends, no need to remind us. We've thought of everything. We wish Wang Xue a happy life. And the warm stream in our hearts will never run dry nor grow cold. What if I could pour a warm stream into all other icy hearts as Wang Xue has done? Then, wouldn't the world in which we live turn into a better place?

NOTES

[1]The bodhi tree (also called "bo tree" or "peepul"), a type of fig tree, is considered sacred by Buddhists. Buddha was sitting under the bodhi tree when he received enlightenment; hence, it is known as the "tree of wisdom."

[2]Hu Songhua: a famous folk singer

[3]Between 1966 and 1972, at the height of the Cultural Revolution, colleges and universities were closed; when they reopened, students were selected according to their political beliefs. In 1977, entrance examinations were reinstated.

[4]Zhang Tiesheng was a student who handed in a blank examination paper, claiming to have been too busy working to study for the exam.

Another Country

BY SHIRLEY LIM

Shirley Goek-Lin [Giok-Lin] LIM grew up in Malaysia and has been publishing stories and poetry in southeast Asia, Australia, and the United States since 1967. She has a Ph.D. in English and American literature, and teaches in New York. In 1980, she won the Commonwealth Poetry Prize for her book of poems, Crossing the Peninsula.

Realistic and unsentimental, Lim's stories often feature young female characters who experience change and displacement. The stories also have a strong quality of reminiscence—of remembering other places and other times.

"Another Country" is set in urban, contemporary Malaysia, and reflects the multi-ethnic, multi-linguistic nature of Malaysian society.

When Su Weng regained consciousness, she was alone. Her head was helmeted in a swath of bandages, her right arm and hand disappeared into a roll of white cotton, and her left leg was raised by a pulley above the bed, the foot encased in a large wrap. Her bed was screened on two sides, and at the foot of the bed was only a blank white wall. A fat plaster sat on her right cheek partially blocking her vision.

"I say, you look like Pharaoh's mummy! I think you surely die when they bring you in. You look really terrible, *lah*[1]!"

Su Weng painfully adjusted her aching neck towards the left from where the cheerful voice was coming. Dimly she was aware of a shapeless figure in a loose white gown, half-hidden by the screen.

"What's your name, eh?" The white shape approached her bed.

"Mrs. Hashim. Mrs. Hashim! What are you doing here? You're not allowed in this room. The doctor is coming, and he will be angry if he sees you here."

At the sound of this brisk voice coming from somewhere out of sight, the shape turned and vanished. Su Weng kept her neck strained, waiting for someone else to appear, the nurse or doctor or some more familiar visitor. But no one came and soon she was drifting off into dark emptiness. At one point she woke at hearing voices and saw a group of men and women standing around the bed, then she must have slept again. When she woke up, it was three days after the car her father had been driving had gone off the road and crashed into a telephone pole and she, the sole passenger, was thrown a hundred metres onto the five-foot way[2].

"So, you finally woke up," the neat little nurse said, pushing before her a white, enamelled cart loaded with vials, bottles, rolls of cotton wool and gauze, metal cups, sponges, trays of syringes, scissors, knives, and other gleaming steel utensils. "We're going to clean you up today. Your bandages need a changing." Out came a large pair of scissors. Snipping deftly, she dropped masses of gauze into a plastic pail. The gauze was clean, then stained with yellow ointment, then brown with dried blood. The last layers were stuck to the body and whenever the nurse peeled a piece, it left the wound freshly raw and bleeding. It took an hour to peel the dried gauze off and Su Weng, exhausted, had stopped screaming by then. It was apparent there wasn't much whole skin left on her. The nurse was sweating and trembling as she washed Su Weng with a cool liquid and reapplied the ointment; this time, only a light gauze was taped.

"Eh, can hear you ten kilometres away. People think you're being murdered, *lah*! You got a lot of pain?"

The dim grey shape shifted, focused, and coalesced. Su Weng stared numbly at the woman who was surveying her, it seemed, in close-up.

"You're in Ward 4B. My name is Fadzillah Hashim, I been in 4B for one month already, so, you wanna know anything, just ask me. Must have fun in this place, you know. Otherwise, can die, *lah*!" She giggled and hopped on one foot. Su Weng became aware that the giddy motion of Mrs. Hashim's shape was not because of her own dizziness but because Mrs. Hashim was constantly fidgeting. She was in a continuous dance, and the white hospital gown swayed and bobbed as her head and shoulders weaved and her arms swung. "You come and see me in room 10. I know everybody in 4B. Can introduce you to some nice boys. You're not so bad. Cannot see your face anyway, so doesn't matter if you're not pretty, eh?"

"Mrs. Hashim, Mrs. Hashim, visitors for you," the call came from somewhere. She ducked around the screen and Su Weng found herself alone and finally wide awake.

Loud, confident voices were walking along the corridor outside her room. Concealed by the screen, a patient groaned to the right. A nurse came and removed the left screen; the bed on the left which was by the door was empty. Su Weng gazed eagerly out through the open door.

Her mother and brother came. He sat on the metal folding chair next to the bed and said nothing. Her mother stood by the side and explained that her father had not been hurt in the crash, but he would not be able to visit because hospital sights and smells upset him. Su Weng's eyes filled with tears. She was her father's pet, and she knew he must be distressed by the accident.

A clatter and heavy smell of boiled vegetables and rice reminded them it was dinner time. Her mother waited to see the kind of food served to Su Weng: watery potato soup, a bowl of rice, a plate of pale cabbage, and a saucer of stringy beef. "I will bring liver and spinach tomorrow. Hospital food isn't nutritious. You must promise not to eat anything with soy sauce in it. Soy sauce will scar and blacken your wounds." Su Weng thought of the numerous stitches on her face, arms, legs, and back, and of the white and pink flesh that the nurse had stripped, and she nodded.

She was studying dismally the rejected tray of food which her mother had left on the chair when Mrs. Hashim appeared at the door. "Visitors gone? Nuisance, eh? Always make you feel bad. Never mind, I'll get a nicer visitor for you." She disappeared and returned a few minutes later pulling a young man along behind her. "This is my friend, Chun Hong. He's a very bright boy, in university in Australia. But cannot take the pressure, eh, Chun Hong? Come back home because got stomach ache all the time."

"Actually, I have ulcers," he said.

"Really, cute, eh? Like elephant nose," Mrs. Hashim said, waving her hand at the thin plastic tube which was clipped into his right nostril and which dangled down his pajama shirt.

"I can't eat solids. This tube drips liquids into my system." His face was sallow and melancholy; thick black hair sprang, uncombed, straight up from his forehead. His expression of reluctance and embarrassment changed to curiosity. "I heard you had concussion. Do you remember anything about the accident?"

Su Weng shook her head.

"Nothing about coming to the hospital? Perhaps you're better off not remembering. Mrs. Hashim has been telling me all sorts of things about you. You're on your way to the university in Kuala Lumpur."

Su Weng nodded and began to cry. She was supposed to leave for the campus in a week when the car went off the road. Now she wouldn't be there in time for the beginning of the first term.

"Hey, hey, no crying allowed here!" Mrs. Hashim said with a wild jump. She did a little dance. "Tomorrow you ask the nurse if you can get up and we'll have a party. Chun Hong and I must visit other people now." She grabbed his hand and pulled him out of the room. He smiled and winked as he left.

Su Weng stopped crying immediately. Her left foot was hot and throbbing; she tried to sleep, but the pain flashed every few seconds like the beam of a lighthouse sweeping through a dark ocean swell. When the nurse came to give her medication, she swallowed a sleeping pill and slept fitfully. Now and again she woke and listened to the woman in the next bed moaning. The fluorescent lights outside cast a pale glow in the room. Half-asleep through the night, she heard the nurses' murmurs as they passed each other and their footsteps hurrying up and down the long corridor.

The next morning, as the nurse changed her bandages, she gripped her pillow hard and didn't scream. The gauze came off more easily this time, and, besides, she knew that somewhere, Mrs. Hashim was listening. "No, you can't get out of bed," the nurse said as she turned her over and slipped a fresh sheet under. "You can't put your foot down yet. The doctor thinks you may have blood poisoning." The cut on the left foot had left the white bone showing, the nurse explained, and even with twenty-two stitches, if the infection got out of control, she might lose the foot. After the nurse had tucked the grey blanket in and bundled the soiled linen out of the room, Su Weng sat up in bed and reached over and touched her bandaged foot. It had ballooned to twice its normal size.

"Must stay in bed, eh? Never mind. Your foot won't drop off," Mrs. Hashim said. Su Weng blinked back her tears. "You know how to play poker? I got cards here." Mrs. Hashim waved a pack of worn pink-backed cards. "No money involved. Cannot gamble, you know, but just for fun, eh. We pass the time like good friends." She perched on the bed and dangled her slippers with her toes. Swiftly she dealt and laid the cards on the uncrumpled sheet. Su Weng picked them up painfully; her right hand was taped up and only her fingers were free to manoeuvre. They played for a while, Su Weng silent and Mrs. Hashim laughing and calling out in excitement. "*Ada nasib*!"[3] she exclaimed as she won a hand. "Oh, oh, dangerous, *lah*! Must watch out for you."

"Mrs. Hashim, Mrs. Hashim, where are you?"

"Sshhh." She put her finger to her lips.

"Mrs. Hashim," the nurse said, standing at the door with her hands on her hips. "You know you're not supposed to be out of bed. Doctor's orders. CRIB, remember!" Mrs. Hashim picked up her cards and waved them unpenitently. "You must stop disturbing the patients."

"She wasn't disturbing me," Su Weng protested, waving back with her left hand.

"She's probably got you overexcited, your temperature's gone up," the nurse said, putting her hand to Su Weng's forehead. "Lie back and go to sleep."

"What is CRIB?"

"Doctor's orders for Mrs. Hashim. Complete Rest in Bed. She's not supposed to get out of bed at all. The same for you." She frowned down and left.

Mrs. Hashim was back many times and the nurses' cries of "Mrs. Hashim, CRIB!" became commonplace to Su Weng. In a week her foot had healed enough for her to hobble to the bathroom down the corridor. "Eh, you," Mrs. Hashim said as Su Weng emerged, damp and flushed from a tortured shower. "Come and meet Uncle Tan." She took Su Weng's towel and dripping soapbox in one hand and supported her at the elbow with the other. Dancing and hobbling, they walked down the length of the dormitory-style second-class area. It was a section for patients undergoing surgery. In some beds men and women slept like grey stones; in others, they were reading or gazing ahead of them or sitting by the sides of the beds bent over. Mrs. Hashim stopped by a bed; a heavy man in his fifties was sitting up in it, propped on his pillow and reading *The Straits Times.* He was wearing the usual hospital pajamas for men, grey-and-white-striped shirt and trousers, and he had his legs stretched out with the ankles crossed. From his neck downwards he appeared massive and inert, but when he looked up, his brown face flashed with life and intelligence. His smile lifted his eyebrows and crinkled the skin around his eyes.

"Aha, Mrs. Hashim! Have you come to cheer me up?"

"Oh, Uncle Tan, you are the one with the good jokes. This is my friend, Su Weng. Under the bandages she is a pretty woman." They laughed while Su Weng smiled bitterly. "Uncle Tan is a very smart man," Mrs. Hashim said, taking Su Weng by the hand and guiding her to the bedside. "He's a philosopher, you know, a lover of wisdom. Uncle Tan's been married, eh?"

"Two wives," he replied. "Two big mistakes."

"Don't say that," Mrs. Hashim exclaimed. "Mrs. Tan will be very sad to hear that."

"In the first marriage, my wife was the mistake, but now, I am the mistake," he responded.

"Come, come, uncle, a clever man like you! You are a big prize for any woman."

"Ah, yes, an expensive prize, and Mrs. Tan is a poor woman. So, have you come to wish me good luck?"

"*Nasib*, you're asking me for *nasib*? Cannot, *lah*, uncle, I got too little. What you want good luck for?"

"I'm going for the operation on Wednesday. You think I will come out all right?"

"Very hard to kill a big man like you. You come out of the operation with less, but don't worry, your wife won't miss what the doctor take away."

Mr. Tan suddenly looked sad. "I don't know..." he sighed as if he were tired.

Mrs. Hashim rose up quickly from the bed. "Must leave you, eh. You need rest for the big day. Cheer up, uncle." She was bobbing down the long room before Su Weng could gather her towel and soapbox to leave.

Mr. Tan had closed his eyes; his face was now a grey mass of wrinkles and unhappy droops, and Su Weng limped away without saying goodbye.

Su Weng had few visitors; her friends had left already for the start of the term in the university. The patches of flesh from where the skin had been torn were healing slowly. By the second week, only her mother came to visit regularly. Every evening she brought a triple tiffin carrier, the lowest dish filled with rice, the second with fried liver, and the top dish with watercress soup. The blood lost, she said, was best replaced by eating the freshest pork liver, and the shock to Su Weng's spirit which was causing her to droop her head and cry each evening was best treated through a potion of bitter bark and ginger steeped in rice wine and masked by sprigs of watercress. She would get up to leave only after Su Weng had eaten a satisfactory meal. Su Weng thought the tears which involuntarily rolled down her cheeks every evening were caused actually by her strong distaste for the slices of grey liver and the pungent soup, but she concentrated on her mother's hope for her recovery and swallowed each spoonful silently.

One evening, her mother had to attend a relative's funeral and Su Weng was alone during the dinner hour. Rejecting the hospital meal, she decided to see what Mrs. Hashim was eating on her Muslim diet. As she approached Mrs. Hashim's first-class room, she heard a loud chatter of many voices. Around Mrs. Hashim's bed were clustered a number of women dressed in bright *baju kurongs*[4]; on the bed with her, children were lying, some clinging to her arms and some sprawled by her feet. By the window sat an old woman with a baby on her lap. A handsome man stood by the head of her bed, observing the activities with a broad smile.

"Eh, my friend, Su Weng. *Mari-lah*[5], and meet my family."

Su Weng stood shyly by the door, conscious of the coarse faded gown in which she felt like an abandoned orphan. Mrs. Hashim was also dressed in a similar gown, but, surrounded by children, she appeared like a mother goddess robed in flowing white.

"These are my children, Ibrahim, Ahmad, Norina, Nazir." She tapped them gently on their heads as she named them, and they each adoringly tried to capture her swiftly moving hand. "And there is my youngest, Fatimah," she said, gesturing towards the elderly woman by the window. "And my mother-in-law."

"*Masok*[6], *lah*," the woman smiled, showing her toothless gums, and the baby stared at Su Weng with round, solemn eyes.

"My sisters and sisters-in-law," Mrs. Hashim continued, motioning towards the women who (with the same solemn gaze as the baby's) had all stepped back to observe Su Weng. "And my husband, Abdul Hashim."

The man shook her hand courteously, said in an indifferent tone, "How do you do?" and turned back to his wife. The women began chattering again, the children tugged at Mrs. Hashim possessively with cries for attention. Su Weng waved good-bye to the mother-in-law who was still smiling sweetly at her, and walked away; there was clearly no room for her in there.

"Do you know Mrs. Hashim has five children?" Su Weng asked Chun Hong. They were standing by an open window along the corridor watching the cars and vans drive up the hill on which their building was situated. When they tired of visiting each other's rooms or playing cards or reading, they would stroll down the corridor and lean over the windows to look enviously down on the traffic and pedestrians hurrying below, seemingly full of purpose and health. Chun Hong no longer carried tubes attached to his body, and he would be leaving in a week if his ulcers healed by then.

"Why are you surprised?"

"Well, I never thought of her having a family outside."

"Don't you have a family outside?"

"What do you mean?" Su Weng was offended.

"You're angry," he replied calmly. "Do you think I have a family?"

"I don't know. I suppose so. Everyone has a family somewhere."

"Most people do. It depends on what you think is a family. I used to think I didn't have a family. I read too many western books. When I went to Adelaide, I discovered what family was. Actually, the reason I got so sick there was that I was depressed for a long time. I was lonely in Australia. The moment I got home, I felt better. I'm not close to my parents, you know. They're Chinese-educated, have a bicycle shop in Tampin, but with a family, you take what you have. I don't ask to be different from them any more." Chun Hong spoke slowly. There was a suggestion of sadness in his voice. "But you haven't decided what you want to be yet. You are still in conflict." He held her hand diffidently. Su Weng felt sorry for him.

Mrs. Hashim found them playing cards that afternoon. "Sshh," she whispered. "I'm CRIB. Come, I've found a secret place." They walked through the ward in which every bed seemed inhabited by a prone figure suspended between lunch and tea-time. They passed the first-class section, through a heavy fire-door, into a large room with windows on three sides, cushioned rattan chairs, lounges, and low book cases. "This is the doctors' rest room," Mrs. Hashim said with a throaty laugh. "But no doctors come, *lah*. So far, always empty. We can talk here till tea-time."

"How did you meet your husband?" Su Weng asked. His broad handsome face and good eyes still intrigued her.

"Ah, another woman interested in Mr. Abdul Hashim!" Mrs. Hashim replied in a sarcastic manner. "We met in college. He was a *kampung*[7] boy, never dated until he met me. I was an Arts Freshie, he was a senior in Engineering. We got married the next year because he was going to Manchester to study."

Su Weng was confused. "You went to England?"

"Oh, yes. What's so wonderful about England? Just another country." Mrs. Hashim's voice softened. "Three years in Manchester. No children yet, no mother-in-law, no sisters-in-law. Abdul has a heart. We went to London a lot, lots of trips, parties." She began to bounce lightly in her seat. "That was a long time ago. Now Abdul is head of the Municipal Waterworks, very important job." She began to speak in pidgin, tripping the words like a simple melody. "Life funny, eh? Now I'm Mrs. Hashim. Yah, the doctor say I stay two more weeks here. Must watch my blood count."

"I'll visit you," Chun Hong said.

"Oh, you visit your girlfriend, eh, Su Weng?"

But Su Weng had taken a *Reader's Digest* Condensed Books volume from the shelf and pretended not to hear.

It was Friday, eleven a.m., a time when orderlies, nurses, and doctors had completed their morning duties, and the men and women in Ward 4B, bandaged, medicated, and tranquillized, were left alone amid the sharp ammonia scent of mopped floors to contemplate time passing before the clatter of lunch carts and the smells of food, like the smells of wet cloths steaming before a fire, announced that time had, indeed, passed. Mrs. Hashim took Su Weng to visit Mr. Tan who had an emergency operation that morning, two days after surgery for a hernia. His bed was screened all around and in the shadowed quiet of the small enclosed womb, Mr. Tan was lying motionless. They stood silently, observing him sleep. His face was drawn and quite peaceful. Then he opened his eyes and looked at Mrs. Hashim. For a moment, a recognition flickered in his eyes.

"Uncle, *ada baik*[8]?" Mrs. Hashim leaned over and spoke softly with her face close to his. "We missed you, eh. Where you been?"

Mr. Tan said distinctly in a hoarse whisper, "In another country." He moved his hand as if to reach for her and closed his eyes.

Mrs. Hashim leaned by his side for another moment while his eyes remained closed. Then she walked away without her usual dancing motions and went to her room to lie down.

Chun Hong visited Su Weng on Monday morning to say goodbye. Dressed in a white shirt and khaki pants he looked ordinary and dull. Only the pallor of his complexion and his long uncut hair indicated that he had been ill for some time. "I'll ring you when you come for the holidays," he said as he shook her hand.

"Aren't you coming back to visit Mrs. Hashim?"

"No, there's no point."

"No point? I don't understand." Su Weng felt a shock of anger. Her face was sullen as she stepped back and sat on her bed.

"You like Mrs. Hashim," he responded, his thin face unmoved and still friendly.

"Yes, she's the happiest person in the ward."

He shook his head. "If being crazy is happy, she's happy."

"She isn't crazy!" Su Weng said violently. "She just can't stay still."

"She's a manic-depressive." He began to walk up and down by her bed, turning occasionally to give her a quick look. "Besides, she's never going to get well. She has leukemia."

Su Weng pressed her fingers into her palms. Her eyes were pricking with tears and she stared at him hatefully. She didn't want to hear what Chun Hong was saying.

"You don't know what these words mean, do you?" he asked.

Su Weng could only repeat, "She's not crazy."

He stopped pacing and took her tightly fisted hand. "We're all crazy. I'm crazy; I'm depressed all the time. Mr. Tan is crazy; he's dying and doesn't know where he is. You're crazy also, but you don't know it." He said all this calmly as if he were instructing her.

She remained silent and allowed her hand to remain in his.

"It's different here. Things are normal here that are crazy outside. When you return home, you'll find that you've changed. You won't be normal any more."

Su Weng didn't believe him, but she didn't wish to argue. "All right." She pulled her hand gently away from his grip. "I hope you'll be okay in the future."

He suddenly appeared embarrassed, mumbled some words, and left abruptly.

She stayed in her room the rest of the day, reading and waiting for her mother's visit. Mrs. Hashim didn't appear. On Tuesday, she went to look for Mrs. Hashim and found that she had been moved to the isolation room at the end of the ward and wasn't permitted any visitors except for her family. Su Weng was leaving the ward the next day; she had already missed two weeks of study in the university.

Before she changed out of the hospital gown into the dress that her mother had brought, Su Weng sneaked into the isolation room to say goodbye. Mrs. Hashim was sitting up in bed, reading a Penguin paperback on art in the Muslim world. She had grown perceptibly thinner in the last few days, but she gave a gleeful grin when Su Weng slipped through the door. "Getting lonely, eh? What to do! Nurses make sure I stay in bed all the time."

"I'm leaving today, Mrs. Hashim," Su Weng said, drawing nearer.

Mrs. Hashim's eyes were full of grieving. "So soon going away? Good luck, eh. You looking beautiful today."

Su Weng felt her mouth dry up; she thought she had never loved a friend like Mrs. Hashim, but she didn't know what to say. "I hope you'll be all right," she whispered.

"Oh, fine, fine, I'm doing fine. The doctors say, maybe two more weeks, then I can go home also." Mrs. Hashim had dropped her book and was waving her hands elaborately. She jiggled up and down as if impatient, and the metal bars on the bed creaked.

"Oh, Mrs. Hashim," Su Weng exclaimed, alarmed, "Complete rest in bed, remember! Please don't get excited. Goodbye!" and she left hastily, vigorously waving goodbye.

Walking down the hill with her mother, Su Weng turned back and looked up towards the windows of Ward 4B. She wondered which was the window that Chun Hong and she had leaned over these past weeks, envying the people walking below. Someone was leaning out of a window on the fourth floor, and, for a moment, she thought she recognized Mrs. Hashim's face, but, of course, it was too far for her to be sure. Briefly she pondered on the misery in Mrs. Hashim's eyes earlier, then she looked up at the trees which lined the hospital road and at the great green stars springing from the branches, and she felt a tremendous happiness at being alive.

NOTES

[1]"*Lah*" in ESM (the English of Singapore and Malaysia) is a suffix that implies friendliness without commitment.

[2]A five-foot way is a covered pavement or arcade which runs along in front of a row of shop-houses.

[3]*Ada nasib*: "I've good luck." All the non-English expressions in this story are Malay.

[4]A *baju kurong* is a dress worn by a female Malay.

[5]*Mari*: "Come"

[6]*Masok*: "Come in"

[7]*kampung*: village

[8]*ada baik*: "Are you well?"

Three Years of Carefree Happiness

BY HOU CHEN

TRANSLATED BY DAVID STEELMAN

HOU Chen [Ho Chin] was born in the southern province of Guangdong in mainland China, but now lives in Taiwan on an airbase near Taipei. "Three Years of Carefree Happiness," published in 1978, is one of her first published stories.

The title "Three Years of Carefree Happiness" refers to the Chinese traditional belief that old age is a time of carefree life and happiness when the elderly are looked after by their children. However, as Taiwan has moved from being a rural society to a highly industrialized one, the traditional family where several generations live together with the older members in control, has begun to change. Today, many group homes for the elderly have been established, especially in Taipei.

When I woke up my old bones told me the weather was going to be good, a nice day for a trip. I didn't eat much for breakfast. I guess it was because I had too much on my mind. Fortunately my son and his wife didn't notice. After they went to work and my grandsons went off to school, I packed a few things in a bag, left a note on the table, and brought to end three years of "carefree happiness" to start a new life at seventy-three.

Three years ago, just after my seventieth birthday, my wife suddenly fell sick and passed away. I couldn't face the loneliness in that house where there were so many tender memories of our years together, so I accepted my son's offer and moved to live with him and his wife and children in this apartment.

My son went to a lot of trouble to get me to move in with him. He fixed up a room for me and made it really cosy, too; a desk by the window, a big bookcase against the wall, a bed, and a rocking chair alongside the desk. He even hung some paintings and calligraphy up for me. And there was a big closet to keep all my stuff in. It looked like a pretty big closet, but to try and fit into it twenty years of my life was no mean trick. My son kept telling me to keep only what I could use and get rid of the rest, and his wife thought that the only things worth keeping were some imitation antique vases. She even wanted me to get rid of the old quilt that was a part of my wife's dowry. I agreed to put a new cover on it, but I couldn't part with the quilt we'd slept under for so many years.

In spite of what they said, I brought enough stuff to fill that closet to the brim. The rest of the things I gave to the neighbours. My son's wife said if I had gotten somebody in to buy the whole lot, I could probably have gotten quite a few dollars out of it even if it was just a lot of old junk. But how could she know how I felt. That was all stuff that my wife had cherished while she was alive. I'm sure she'd be glad to know that if I couldn't keep her things any longer, at least they were with her old neighbours who had been close to her. And as for the house which I was entitled to occupy for as long as I lived, I abided by the standing rules and turned it over to one of my former colleagues. And so with envy and happiness for me, the neighbours saw me bring to an end the twenty years my wife and I had shared in this house since we came to Taiwan. It's hard for someone to change his way of life, especially for old people, and especially for someone like me who had become so dependent on his wife for so many years.

They say you never stop learning. Well, I had a lot to learn after I moved in with my son. One of the first things I had to learn was when to go to the bathroom. After twenty years, I'd gotten in the habit of going to the bathroom every morning at six. This had to be changed. There was only one bathroom at my son's and at six in the morning there was a mad rush for it. Since I was the only one who didn't have to go to work or school, there was really no reason for me to try to get in when it was so busy, so I started going to the bathroom at five. One day my son said to me, "Dad, why do you have to get up and go to the bathroom so early? You wake everybody up when you flush the toilet." I'd never thought about that. Well, if I couldn't go before the morning rush, it looked like I'd just have to hold my horses until afterwards. By eight everyone was gone and I could use the bathroom in peace.

One Sunday morning my ten-year-old grandson said to me, "Grandpa, I just about suffocated in the toilet. Would you please not smoke in there anymore?" That was something else I'd never thought about. There wasn't any window in the bathroom and when I closed the door there wasn't a bit of circulation. Normally I'd leave the door open after I finished and it would clear out eventually, but with the heavy Sunday traffic that day, it just never got a chance. No wonder the child couldn't stand it. After retirement, I'd gotten into the habit of making a leisurely trip to the bathroom every morning with the newspaper and a cigarette. The bathroom was in the back of the house with plenty of ventilation, and there was nobody else around but my wife, so I could take my sweet time. That hour in the early morning had always been such a refreshing time, but it looked like my old habit would have to be changed.

Taking a bath here was another art. At home I used to have a big round tub. My wife used to heat the water for me and get it just the right temperature, and I'd sit in the middle on a squat bamboo stool and wash away in comfort. But I didn't know how to handle this new-fangled bathtub. They had a little plastic stool but it always gave me the feeling that if I sat down on it I'd never get back up again. The first time I took a bath here, I filled the tub with water, put the little stool in the tub, and, hanging onto the wall, tried to sit down very carefully. The stool floated in the water and I missed it. I had to take a rest before I could start my bath. Being a little on the heavy side I find it difficult to move in the water, and with this tub there just wasn't any room to move, so it wasn't a very enjoyable bath.

Ever since my wife died I've had trouble getting around. It feels like I have a half-kilogram weight on me every time I try to move an arm or a leg. And with this bathtub being as difficult as it was to get into, I started thinking: with the bathroom door closed, I was shut off from the rest of the world. Who would help me if I slipped in the tub? I started getting scared. That really made me wonder about myself, an army veteran in his old age being afraid of a door. And then I got to thinking about what it was like taking a bath at home. I'd be able to hear her in the kitchen, cooking while I washed, and every once in a while she'd peek in and ask me if I wanted any more hot water.

Humans are one of the most adaptable creatures in the world, and gradually I found myself getting used to a new routine. After eight o'clock there wasn't anybody home but me so I spent the morning reading the papers. My son subscribed to the *China Times* but he also put in a subscription for the *Central Daily News* because he knew I'd always liked to read it. He also took an evening paper. So that two dailies kept me busy in the morning. At noon my daughter-in-law would come home from the neighbourhood school where she taught and fix me some noodles for lunch. She said she didn't normally come home at lunchtime, she just did it for me. Fortunately the school was close by. Part of the reason my son picked the apartment was so his wife would be close to where she taught and his children would be close to school. Then after lunch I'd take a nap and then start waiting for the evening paper. Usually by the time the paper got here, the children would be back from school. You'd think that would liven up the place a bit but not so. When they got back they'd give me a polite greeting, head for the refrigerator to get something to eat, and then start on their homework. They'd keep one eye on the clock the whole time, and when it was time, off they'd go with their violins to music lessons.

It was not for nothing that my daughter-in-law was a teacher. She had brought the two boys up to be very polite and obedient. "Mom said we can't watch cartoons if we don't have our homework done." After that nobody had to worry about them getting their homework done.

Once a day the family would get together over the dinner table. My son would usually be home on time if he didn't have business obligations. The children would set the table, bring out the dinner, and help me to my seat. I didn't really need to be helped, but it was the only chance I got to hold their little hands. There was always plenty of food, but the atmosphere was a little too stiff. Nobody talked. Once in a while the youngest grandson would remember something funny that happened at school and start talking and laughing about it. Then his mother would say, "How can you be so boisterous in front of your grandfather?" Actually I enjoyed hearing them talk while they ate and listening to what had happened to them during the day. I always felt like asking my grandson to finish his story but I didn't want to undo all their mother's good training so I'd just silently eat my dinner. Of course I'd start thinking about what dinners used to be like at home with my wife. After we got a TV set my wife became addicted to watching it. We'd even have to have our dinner in front of it, so we'd always eat slowly and do a lot of talking as we watched the programs. When the cat knocked over a plate in the kitchen, my wife would jump up, run into the kitchen, rush back, and before she had even sat down, she would ask me what she'd missed. But the new generations are different. Growing up in different times, with a different way of education, the way of thinking is different. The way they live is different. I don't know which is right and which is wrong.

After dinner, my daughter-in-law would brew two cups of tea, one for me and one for my son. There we'd sit together, father and son, with so much to be said, so much to ask, but my son would just bury his head in a pile of newspapers. So I just sat there with my eyes on the TV, blowing on my tea to cool it. After the news my son would stand up and say, "Well, it's getting late, Dad. Why don't you try to get some sleep?" My son had already told me good night, how could I do otherwise? The children had already changed into their pajamas and said good night to us. They'd fall asleep as soon as they lay down. But me? I remembered when my wife was alive she would putter around till midnight even if she didn't have anything to do, and I wouldn't be able to sleep until she did.

The best thing to do when you can't sleep is to read, but I'd been reading the paper all day and I didn't feel like reading anything more. Well, at least there was the rocking chair, so I tried that out.

The tea was keeping me awake and it made me want to go to the bathroom. So I opened the door real quietly, and tiptoed out. The lights were down low in the living room, and my son and his wife were watching TV. No matter how careful I was they'd always look up at me. After several trips I got to feeling self-conscious about it myself. I was thinking about getting a chamber pot but then I wasn't sure if you could use them in these new apartments. From the fact that such a small thing could bother me, one can see how humans are indeed creatures of worry.

So this quiet life passed by in increasing quietness. One afternoon, after I'd just gotten up from my nap some old neighbours dropped by for a visit. We were really happy to see each other after so long. They looked enviously at the room my son had fixed up for me and said it was really a far cry from the dependants' village.

"How's your luck been at mah-jong[1] lately?"

"Oh, I haven't played for ages."

"With a table like this you mean to tell us you don't play?"

"Oh, that's my son's. He and his friends play."

"Don't you play with them?"

"No, they play with all these new-fangled rules I don't understand."

"Well, we'll just stay and play a few hands with you. Same stakes, OK?"

"Fine, that'd be just great."

So we seventy-year-olds forgot our dignity and started playing like a bunch of children, and it wasn't until the grandsons came home from school that we began to act a little more like the senior generation.

My daughter-in-law made tea for us when she came home and I followed her back to the kitchen and asked her, "I'd like to ask them to stay for dinner. Do you have anything in the house you can fix up?"

"Yes, I'll get started now."

My daughter-in-law whipped up a really nice dinner. I peeked in the liquor cabinet and saw half a bottle of imported liquor left over from a party my son had had a few days earlier.

"Old Ding, would you like a glass with dinner?"

He must have noticed something strange in the way I asked. "No thanks, we'll have to be getting back pretty soon."

Old Ding was really a good drinker and we had always been pretty close. If friends stopped by his house he'd ask me over to join them for a glass or two. If my wife fixed anything special we'd have him over to join us for a glass. I didn't know if my son had heard us mention having a drink. He didn't say anything so I did not bring it up again. It was a shame not to have something to drink with such a nice dinner. My son didn't say anything at the table and everyone was acting very formal. We had a lot of food but not much of it was eaten. I kept hoping my son wouldn't act so restrained. It would have been so much better if he'd acted like he did when his own friends were over. But I never joined them when his friends came. He always asked his wife to fix dinner for me first so I wouldn't have to wait. I didn't want to sit in the living room after I'd finished since there was only the liquor cabinet separating it from the dining room. I might have put a damper on their party mood, so I just went back to my room.

"Why doesn't your father join us?"

"At his age he needs quiet. He's already had dinner and is reading in his room." So whenever my son had guests I spent most of the time in my room. And then sometimes I'd go out for a walk. Back in our village a walk would be very interesting for I knew all the people around and could talk and laugh with them. Around here there were only cars. No wonder my son worried about me when I went out for a walk. "Dad, don't you think it would be better if you just practise your shadow boxing in the apartment? What if you got hit by a car while you were taking a walk?"

Well, it was really fun that day. We'd played from sometime in the afternoon till ten o'clock that night. I really felt sort of tired. The next morning while I was reading the paper my son said to me, "Dad, Shu-chuan [*Shoe-chwan*] works all day and also has a lot of housework to do. When people come over without you telling her beforehand, it really tires her out. I hope you don't let it happen again."

Don't let it happen again, don't let it happen again. Those words bothered me all day. I just couldn't get them out of my mind. I couldn't even swallow the noodles my daughter-in-law fixed for me that noon.

My wife had been right. Now I understood why she wouldn't move in with my son and his wife. The year I retired, my son had tried to get us to move in with them.

"You don't have to go to work any more, Dad. If you move in with us it will be easier for us to take better care of you."

"If you really want to look after us, then move back here."

"But this house is too..."

"You lived here when you first got married, didn't you? Chungerh [*Jung-er*] was born here, wasn't he?"

"It's not the same now and there's not room enough."

"There's plenty of room in the backyard. The Chens next door put on an addition and now they've got plenty of room."

"You'd have some appreciation in property value if it were your own house but here in the dependants' village you could never sell the place. You couldn't even get out of it what you put into it."

"What's this nonsense about property values? After we retake the mainland nobody'll want their houses. You think somebody's going to stay here just to buy your house?"

And so mother and son argued. I didn't care. It didn't make any difference to me where we lived.

"He's got a point," I said. "He's already got a place ready to move into. If he moves over here, then we've got a lot of work to do."

"You're really getting old. You don't even know what your son is up to. If they move in here I'm still the mistress of the house, but if we move in there we would just have to do what they want us to do."

"We haven't got that many more years to live. Why worry about things like this. Wouldn't it be nice to have somebody else do the cooking and the housework? You've worked hard all these years. Why not take it easy for a few years and enjoy life!"

"You know, there are a lot of things I don't even feel like wasting my breath talking to you about. I know my own son. You go playing your mah-jong or start a game of chess."

I never would have thought that I, who had travelled all over China and earned money to support a family, would be less far-sighted than an old woman who'd never been out the front door. She was right. If they moved in with us she'd still be the boss. If we moved in with them everything would be up to them.

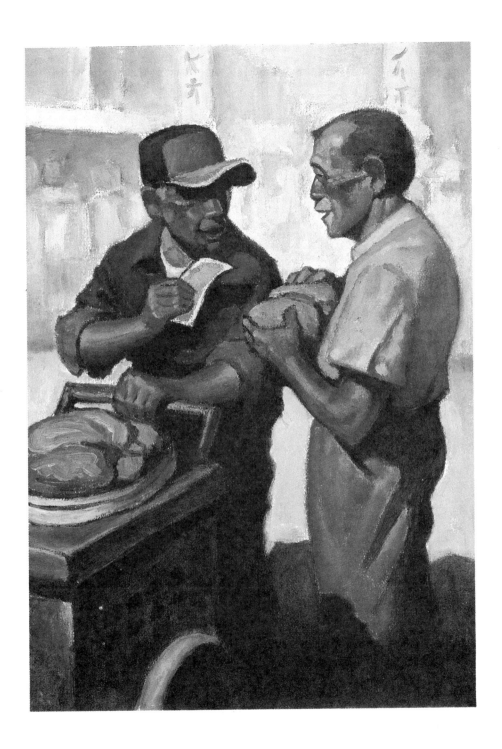

"If something really happens to me, get Mrs. Chen next door to hire a woman to come in and do the cooking." Even up until she died, she never had said a thing about me moving in with my son. It looked like I'd made the wrong choice.

"Don't let it happen again." All right I won't. Anyway, I didn't care as much about playing mah-jong as I used to. Why get all upset about something my son said to me? Enjoy my carefree life, I thought as I picked up the paper.

Seems like I was always hungry these days. Must be because I didn't have anything to do. I'd have plenty for breakfast and by ten o'clock I'd be hungry again. The same thing happened after lunch, but it was worst in the evening after dinner. I'd feel I was so hungry that I'd never get to sleep. There was that big refrigerator but there wasn't anything in it I could grab for a snack. Just when I was really feeling bad, I heard the *mantou*[2] [*mantō*] vendor go by. Every morning I'd buy three *mantous* from the old vendor, who was even from my own province, and made three snacks out of them. After that I didn't have to go hungry anymore and I could sleep peacefully. Another good thing about the *mantou* vendor going by was that I could chat with him. Otherwise I wouldn't have had a chance to use my vocal chords at all. My son didn't like to talk, his wife liked to even less, and the children never had time. It seemed like the only time I ever opened my mouth was when the grandchildren said goodbye in the morning or good night in the evening.

One day the *mantou* vendor didn't have enough change for my hundred-dollar bill. I told him it didn't make any difference if he was short ten dollars. He could pay me tomorrow. Anyway I saw him every day. When my daughter-in-law came home from work that afternoon, she gave me ten dollars, saying the *mantou* vendor had told her he owed it to me. So the old man came twice a day. I hadn't wanted anybody to know I was buying *mantous*. "If you want anything to eat, just let me know and I'll buy it for you. If people saw you go out to buy *mantous* and did not know any better, they'd think we didn't take good care of you."

"I just buy one or two for a late snack in case I get hungry and can't sleep. I don't like cookies or any sweet things."

"Well, then, I'll stop by the bakery after work and get some rolls for you." What more could I ask of such a daughter-in-law? In my mind's eye I gave my wife a challenging look.

A few days later my son had something to say. "The doctors say you shouldn't eat before going to bed. It causes stomach trouble. Older people especially are supposed to be careful." His mother had said just the opposite: "If you don't eat something before going to bed, the tapeworms will gnaw at your intestines." I didn't feel like arguing with him so I just pretended I didn't hear him.

In a wink two years went by. The younger grandson had started middle school and his schedule became even tighter. Now besides violin lessons he had painting lessons, English lessons, choral practice at school, and even Sundays were scheduled full. It was really rough on the boy. But what could I say as I saw him losing weight? I'd thought I'd have two grandchildren to keep me company in my old age. I'd gotten a lot of stories together to tell them, but in two years I hadn't told a single one.

My wife had wanted one of the grandchildren to live with us, but my daughter-in-law wouldn't permit it. My wife had grumbled about it for a long time. "Since when can't grandchildren stay with their grandmother? When we left the mainland and mother didn't want to leave, didn't we leave Da-bao [Da-bow] with her? Otherwise..." Every time she thought of the son we had left on the mainland she would grieve. Now, seeing the hopes my daughter-in-law had for her children and how much pain she took with their education, she knew that they would not be allowed to stay with us.

I guess having too much time on one's hands isn't good for a person. Whenever I tried to read the papers or a book I always felt restless. I was sure my mother on the mainland had passed away, and I had no idea what had happened to the son we'd left with her. Even my wife was gone. Only I was left to enjoy my "carefree life." I suppose I should be content; what more could I ask for? But there are some basic conditions for being able to enjoy one's blessings. And lately I just hadn't been feeling well. Something wasn't right. I felt thirsty all the time and had to go to the bathroom often. I felt just plain worn-out. I guess my son noticed something wrong at dinner one night. "Dad, you're going to have another bowl of rice? You just had three."

"I just can't seem to get full lately. Have you noticed how I'm losing weight? I've tightened my belt three notches. Something must be wrong with me."

"Well, if you can eat and sleep it can't be anything serious. However, since you are covered by your government health insurance, it is very convenient for you to go to the hospital. Why don't you go in for a check-up?"

The next day I went to the hospital right after they left, but it was already too late to register. I ran into one of my old neighbours who was there to see the doctor. "You have to come at six and get in line to register, otherwise you'll be too late. Some people come in at four or five," he said. So I'd made a trip for nothing. The next morning, bright and early, I took a cab to the hospital. That time, fortunately, I got registered. After I told the doctor what was wrong and he examined me, he scheduled me for a blood test before breakfast the next morning. He also transferred me to the metabolism section. The next day I followed instructions and went in for my test. The doctor diagnosed it as diabetes. He gave me a booklet which said, "Diabetes is not serious. Your body functions normally. All you have to do is follow the instructions in this booklet and have an examination each month. The most important thing is to take your medicine regularly, keep in good spirits, and you'll enjoy a long life." They gave me a whole bunch of medicines to take home so from then on, besides waiting for the paper, I'd have to watch the time to take my medicine. That would keep me busy.

My daughter-in-law was very concerned about me. "How did the tests turn out? What's the matter?"

"The doctor said it is diabetes."

"Diabetes! What exactly is that? Is it contagious?" She's an educated woman. How could she ask such an infantile question? I guess she was just too nervous to think straight.

"I don't think so. The doctor just said for me to watch my diet and I'd be OK."

That evening when my son got back he had to give me his opinion on the subject. "I knew you were going to get sick. We don't eat as much as you and we have to go to work every day. Everybody knows it's not good for you to eat too much rice. The older generation doesn't like to listen to other people's advice. Well, now you'll know better." So what if I know better. People still get sick anyway.

That medicine really worked. After a few days I started perking up and didn't feel as thirsty or as hungry as before. I told the *mantou* vendor all about it. I couldn't stand that western bread and milk they kept around for me. I asked him to bring me a few *mantous* every day and not to let anyone know about it. I stashed them away in my room in case I got hungry.

After my trip to the hospital the days passed by just as quietly as before, but I couldn't get my thoughts to quiet down. Something kept bothering me. I kept thinking of all kinds of things, even remembering the time when my grandson got sick. That day he came home from school complaining about not feeling well. When his mother got back and saw he was sick, she called her husband and he rushed home and they took the boy to see the doctor. When they got home they said it was the flu. He'd been given a shot and was taking some medicine but they still weren't satisfied. The next day they took him to the hospital to have him examined. It was still the flu. Well, this finally satisfied them, but they'd really been worried for a couple of days. Why did I think about these little things? Could I possibly be jealous of the attention they gave him when he was sick? To compare myself with my grandson was truly idiotic. They often say we all have a second childhood, but it seemed that I was regressing more every day. But it is indeed true that all troubles grow in one's mind. And the more I tried not to think of certain things, the more I thought about them. The doctor had told me there was absolutely nothing to worry about, but I just couldn't seem to get it off my mind.

One day I happened to remember old Pan, and from then on I couldn't get him out of my mind. We hadn't seen each other for almost three years, from the time when my wife passed away. When he heard about her death he came up from Tainan and stayed with me for a few days after the funeral. We were from the same province and he'd graduated a year before me. After we came to Taiwan he'd never remarried. He loved my wife's old hometown cooking, so whenever a holiday came up we had him over. After his retirement we'd asked him to move in with us, but he picked the place he's in now. It was good of him to come and keep me company, sharing my grief at losing my mate in my old age. We talked a lot during those days.

"How are things where you are? Tell me what it's like." I was thinking about trying to get him to move in with me.

"Oh, it's real nice; nice surroundings with modern buildings. And most of the people there are about the same as I am. And if you want to do your own cooking we have kitchen privileges. They also have a cafeteria if you don't want to be bothered, but I've eaten in cafeterias for so long I thought I'd try to learn a few dishes myself. It's really sort of interesting to be learning to cook at this age."

"I hear old Chen lives there too."

"Right. And Chang Nien also. There are a few of us that get along real well together. We cook together. In the morning we walk over and do our grocery shopping and exchange cooking secrets. If we can make a foursome we usually play a few hands of mah-jong, or else play chess. In the evenings we go into the reading room and watch TV. They've got colour and black-and-white. Everybody takes his own tea and finds his favourite chair. If we don't feel like watching TV we just get together and talk. And then we have a doctor that comes in regularly to give us physical checkups. It would seem like we didn't have anything to do, but we lead very regular lives. The only thing bad about it is once in a while an old friend passes away before you, but then at our age that has to be expected. Nobody can stay around forever."

"Could I move in there?"

"Of course, just as long as there's a room available. But you're not in the same boat as I am. You've got a family. Your wife's gone but you've still got your son. He was just telling me yesterday to try to get you to move in with him to give him a chance to be a filial son. After all, we raise our sons to take care of us in our old age. You should move in with him. And you have two grandchildren and a nice daughter-in-law. That's where you should enjoy the happiness of old age."

Enjoy happiness! Enjoy happiness! If I hadn't gotten sick I'd probably be there "enjoying" to the end of my days. "Take your medicine regularly, keep in good spirits, and you'll enjoy a long life." Take my medicine so I can live a long life...live a long life so I can take my medicine? No, I'm going to make one more change in my life. I've enjoyed three years of "carefree happiness" already and that's enough. I'm going to go find my old friends. The government has set up an old people's park for us, I'll go there and enjoy my "happiness." If they don't have a room I'll just wait. I've still got enough money to stay in a hotel.

I went to the train station and bought a ticket down south. The train came and I walked once again into the crowd.

NOTES

[1]mah-jong: a game involving both chance and strategy, played by four people who draw and discard tiles of various design, until one player wins with a hand containing four sets of three matching tiles and one set of two

[2]*mantou*: a steamed bread bun

Spring Storm

BY MORI YOKO

TRANSLATED BY MAKOTO UEDA

MORI Yoko is a self-professed fan of "everything Western" and her writing contains frequent allusions to Western films, personalities, and books. Her stories are urban and contemporary, with themes that often probe the relationships between men and women.

"Spring Storm," published in 1986, is set in a large city in contemporary Japan.

The small orange light on the lobby wall showed the elevator was still at the seventh floor. Natsuo's eyes were fixed on it.

From time to time her heart pounded furiously, so furiously that it seemed to begin skipping beats. For some time now she had been wild with excitement.

Intense joy is somewhat like pain, she thought. Or like a dizzy spell. Strangely, it was not unlike grief. The suffocating feeling in her chest was almost unbearable.

The elevator still had not moved from the seventh floor.

The emergency stairway was located alongside the outer walls of the building, completely exposed to the elements. Unfortunately for Natsuo, it was raining outside. There was a wind, too.

A spring storm. The words, perhaps romantic, well described the heavy, slanting rain, driven by a wind that had retained the rawness of winter. If Natsuo were to climb the stairs to the sixth floor, she would be soaked to the skin.

She took a cigarette from her handbag and lit it.

This is unusual for me, she thought. She had never smoked while waiting for the elevator. Indeed, she had not smoked anywhere while standing up.

Exhaling the smoke from the depths of her throat, she fell to thinking. I'll be experiencing all kinds of new things from now on, I've just come a big step up the ladder. No, not just one, I've jumped as many as ten steps in one leap. There were thirty-four rivals, and I beat them all.

All thirty-four people were well-experienced performers. There was a dancer with considerably more skill than she. Physically also, the odds were against her: there were a sizeable number of women with long, stylish legs and tight, shapely waists. One Eurasian woman had such alluring looks that everyone admired her. There were professional actresses currently active on the stage, too.

In spite of everything, Natsuo was the one selected for the role.

When the agency called to tell her the news, she at first thought she was being teased.

"You must be kidding me," she said, a little irritated. She had indeed taken it for a bad joke. "You can't trick me like this. I don't believe you."

"Let me ask you a question, then," responded the man who had been acting as her manager. In a teasing voice, he continued, "Were you just kidding when you auditioned for that musical?"

"Of course not!" she retorted. She had been quite serious and, although she would not admit it, she had wanted the role desperately. At the audition, she had done her very best.

"But I'm sure I didn't make it," she said to her manager. "At the interview, I blushed terribly."

Whenever she tried to express herself in front of other people, blood would rush to her face, turning it scarlet.

"You're a bashful person, aren't you?" one of her examiners had commented to her at the interview. His tone carried an objective observation rather than sympathetic inquiry.

"Do you think you're an introvert?" another examiner asked.

"I'm probably on the shy side," Natsuo answered, painfully aware that her earlobes had turned embarrassingly red and her palms were moist.

"The heroine of this drama," added the third examiner, "is a spirited woman with strong willpower. Do you know that?"

Natsuo had sensed the skepticism that was running through the panel of examiners. Without doubt she was going to fail the test, unless she did something right now. She looked up.

"It's true that I'm not yet very good at expressing myself, or speaking up for myself, in front of other people. But playing a dramatic role is something different. It's very different." She was getting desperate. "I'm very bashful about myself. But I'm perfectly all right when I play someone else."

If I am to express someone else's emotion, I have no reason to be shy, she confirmed to herself. I can calmly go about doing the job.

"Well, then, would you please play someone else?" the chief examiner said, with a nod toward the stage.

Natsuo retired to the wings of the stage and tried to calm herself. When she trotted out onto the stage and confidently faced them, she was no longer a timid, blushing woman.

It was impossible to guess, though, how the examiners appraised her performance. They showed little, if any, emotion. When the test was over there was a chorus of murmured "Thank yous." That was all.

Her manager was still speaking on the phone. "I don't know about the third-raters. But I can tell you that most good actors and actresses are introverted, naive, and always feeling nervous inside."

He then added, "If you don't believe me, why don't you go to the office of that production company and find out for yourself?"

Natsuo decided to do just that.

At the end of a dimly lit hallway, a small group of men and women were looking at a large blackboard. Most of the board was powdered with half-obliterated previous scribblings, but at the top was written the cast of the new musical, with the names of the actors and actresses selected for the roles.

Natsuo's name was second from the top. It was scrawled in a large, carefree hand. The name at the top was her co-star, a well-known actor in musicals.

Natsuo stood immobile for ten seconds or so, staring at her name on the blackboard. It was her own name, but she felt as if it belonged to someone else. Her eyes still fixed on the name, she moved a few steps backwards. Then she turned and hurried out of the building. It never occurred to her to stop by the office and thank the staff.

Sheer joy hit her a little later.

It was raining, and there was wind, too. She had an umbrella with her, but she walked without opening it. Finally realizing the fact, she stopped to unfold the umbrella.

"I did it!" she cried aloud. That was the moment. An incomparable joy began to rise up inside her, like the bubbles crowding to exit from a champagne bottle; and not just joy, pain as well, accompanied by the flow and ebb of some new irritation. That was how she experienced her moment of victory.

When she came to, she found herself standing in the lobby of her apartment building. The first person she wanted to tell the news to was, naturally, her husband, Yusuke.

The elevator seemed to be out of order. It was not moving at all. How long had she been waiting there? Ten minutes? A couple of minutes? Natsuo had no idea. Her senses had been numbed. A round clock on the wall showed 9:25. Natsuo gave up and walked away.

The emergency stairway that zigzagged upwards was quite steep and barely wide enough for one person, so Natsuo could not open her umbrella. She climbed up the stairs at a dash.

By the time she reached the sixth floor, her hair was dripping wet and, with no raincoat on, her dress, too, was heavy with rain.

But Natsuo was smiling. Drenched and panting, she was still beaming with an excess of happiness when she pushed the intercom buzzer of their apartment.

"Why are you grinning? You make me nervous," Yusuke said as he let her in. "You're soaking wet, too."

"The elevator never came."

"Who would have considered using the emergency stairs in this rain!"

"This apartment is no good, with a stairway like that," Natsuo said with a grin. "Let's move to a better place."

"You talk as if that were something very simple." Yusuke laughed wryly and tossed a terry robe to her.

"But it is simple."

"Where would we find the money?"

"Just be patient. We'll get the money very soon," Natsuo said cheerfully, taking off her wet clothes.

"You passed the audition, didn't you?" Yusuke asked, staring intently at her face. "Didn't you?"

Natsuo stared back at him. He looked nervous, holding his breath and waiting for her answer.

"Natsuo, did you pass the audition?" As he asked again, his face collapsed, his shoulders fell. He looked utterly forlorn.

"How. . ." she answered impulsively, "how could I have passed? I was just kidding."

Yusuke frowned. "You failed?"

"I was competing with professionals, you know—actresses with real stage experience. How could I have beaten them?" Natsuo named several contending actresses.

"You didn't pass?" Yusuke repeated, his frown deepening. "Answer me clearly, please. You still haven't told me whether you passed."

"What a mean person you are!" Natsuo stuttered. "You must have guessed by now, but you're forcing me to spell it out." Her eyes met his for a moment. "I didn't make it," she said, averting her eyes. "I failed with flying colours."

There was silence. Wiping her wet hair with a towel, Natsuo was aghast and mystified at her lie.

"No kidding?" said Yusuke, starting to walk toward the kitchen. "I was in a state of shock for a minute, really."

"How come? Were you so sure I wouldn't make it?" Natsuo spoke to him from behind, her tone a test of his sincerity.

"You were competing with professionals." There was not a trace of consolation in his voice. "It couldn't be helped. You'll have another chance."

Although Yusuke was showing sympathy, happiness hung in the air about him.

"You sound as if you were pleased to see me fail and lose my chance."

Combing her hair, Natsuo inspected her facial expression in the small mirror on the wall. You're a liar, she told her image. How are you going to unravel this mess you've got yourself into?

"How could I be happy to see you fail?" Yusuke responded, placing a kettle on the gas range. His words carried with them the tarnish of guilt. "But, you know, it's not that great for you to get chosen for a major role all of a sudden."

"Why not?"

"Because you'd be a star. A big new star."

"You are being a bit too dramatic." Natsuo's voice sank low.

"When that happens, your husband would become like a Mr. Judy Garland. Asai Yusuke would disappear completely, and in his place there would be just the husband of Midori Natsuo. I wouldn't like that."

"You're inventing problems for yourself," she said, "You are what you are. You are a script writer named Asai Yusuke."

"A script writer who might soon be forced to write a musical."

"But hasn't that been your dream, to write a musical?" Natsuo's voice was tender. "Suppose, just suppose, that I make a successful debut as an actress in a musical. As soon as I become influential enough and people begin to listen to what I say, I'll let you write a script for a musical."

"Let you write, huh?" Yusuke picked on Natsuo's phrasing. "If you talk like that even when you're making it up, I wonder how it'd be for real."

The kettle began to erupt steam. Yusuke flicked off the flame, dropped instant coffee into two cups, and splashed in the hot water.

"Did you hear that story about Ingrid Bergman?" Yusuke asked, his eyes looking into the distance. "Her third husband was a famous theatrical producer. A talented producer, too." Passing one of the cups to Natsuo, he continued. "One day Bergman asked her producer-husband, 'Why don't you ever try to get me a good play to act in?' He answered, 'Because you're a goose that lays golden eggs. Any play that features you is going to be a success. It will be a sellout for sure. For me, that's too easy.'" Yusuke sipped the coffee slowly. Then, across the rising steam, he added, "I perfectly understand how he felt."

"Does this mean that I'll have to be a minor actress all my life?" Natsuo mused.

"Who knows? I may become famous one of these days," Yusuke sighed. "Or maybe you first."

"And what would you do in the latter case?"

"Well," Yusuke stared at the coffee. "If that happens, we'll get a divorce. That will be the best solution. Then, neither of us will be bothered by all the petty problems."

Natsuo walked toward the window. "Are you serious?" she asked.

"Yes." Yusuke came and stood next to her. "That's the only way to handle the situation. That way, I'll be able to feel happy for you from the bottom of my heart."

"Can't a husband be happy for his wife's success?"

"Ingrid Bergman's second husband was Roberto Rosselini. Do you know the last words he said to her? He said, 'I'm tired of living as Mr. Ingrid Bergman.' Even Rosselini felt that way."

"You are not a Rosselini, nor I a Bergman."

"Our situation would be even worse."

From time to time, gusts of rain slapped at the window.

"When this spring storm is over, I expect the cherry blossoms will suddenly be bursting out," Yusuke whispered.

"There'll be another storm in no time. The blossoms will be gone, and summer will be here." Brushing back her still-moist hair with her fingers, Natsuo turned and looked over the apartment she knew so well.

"You've been standing all this time. Aren't you getting tired?" her husband asked in a gentle voice. She shook her head.

"You're looking over the apartment as though it were for the first time," Yusuke said, gazing at his wife's profile. "Or, is it for the last time?"

Startled by his last words, Natsuo impulsively reached into her handbag for a cigarette and put it in her mouth. Yusuke produced a lighter from his pocket and lit it for her.

"Aren't you going to continue with your work this evening?" she asked.

"No. No more work tonight."

"What's the matter?"

"I can't concentrate when someone else is in the apartment. You know that, don't you?"

Natsuo nodded.

"Won't you sit down?" Yusuke said.

"Why?"

"I have an uneasy feeling when you stand there and smoke like that."

Natsuo cast her eyes on the cigarette held between her fingers. "This is the second time today I've been smoking without sitting down." The words seemed to flow from her mouth at their own volition. His back towards her, Yusuke was collecting some sheets of writing paper scattered on his desk.

"You passed the audition. Right?" he said. His voice was so low that the last word was almost inaudible.

"How did you know?"

"I knew it from the beginning."

"From the beginning?"

"From the moment you came in. You were shouting with your whole body—'I've made it, I'm the winner!' You were trembling like a drenched cat, but your face was lit up like a Christmas tree."

Natsuo did not respond.

"The clearest evidence is the way you're smoking right now."

"Did you notice it?"

"Yes."

"Me, too. It first happened when I was waiting for the elevator down in the lobby. I was so impatient, I smoked a cigarette while standing. I've got the strangest feeling about myself."

"You feel like a celebrity?"

"I feel I've outreached myself."

"But the way you look now, it's not you."

"No, it's not me."

"You'd better not smoke standing up."

"Right. I won't do it again."

There was silence.

"You don't at all feel like congratulating me?" Natsuo asked.

Yusuke did not answer.

"Somehow I knew it might be like this," Yusuke continued. "I knew this moment was coming."

Now she knew why her joy had felt like pain, a pain almost indistinguishable from grief. Now she knew the source of the suffocating presence in her chest.

"That Rosselini, you know..." Yusuke began again.

"Can't we drop the topic?"

"Please listen to me, dear. Rosselini was a jealous person and didn't want to see his wife working for any director other than himself. He would say to her, 'Don't get yourself involved in that play. It'll be a disaster.' One time, Bergman ignored the warning and took a part in a play. It was a big success. Rosselini was watching the stage from the wings. At the curtain call, Bergman glanced at him while bowing to the audience. Their eyes met. That instant, they both knew their love was over, with the thundering applause of the audience ringing in their ears...." Yusuke paused, and then added, "I'll go and see your musical on the opening day."

Natsuo contemplated her husband's face from the wings of the room. He looked across.

Their eyes met.

⌒

THE SILENT TRADERS

''BARGAINS FOR SURVIVAL''

Tokyo, Japan.

The Tiger

BY S. RAJARATNAM

S. (Sinnathamby) RAJARATNAM (1915–   ), a journalist and politician, began publishing stories in the 1940s. From 1959 to his retirement in 1989, he held a number of positions in the governments of Singapore and Malaysia, including 15 years as Minister for Foreign Affairs. He writes in English, one of the four official languages of Singapore and Malaysia (the others are Malay, Chinese, and Tamil). He was influenced by a number of western writers, including Katherine Mansfield and Somerset Maugham.

"The Tiger" is set in a Malay village on the edge of a jungle.

Fatima felt the cool yellow waters of the river—a sheet of burnished gold in the dying sunglow—flow sluggishly around her. She clung to the bank and moved further along until she stood waist-deep in a shallower part of the river. The wet sarong clung to her plump, brown figure, and accentuated the full breasts and womb of a pregnant woman. The round, high-cheekboned face, so typical of the Malays, had been drained of its dark sensuality, and instead an ethereal melancholy in the black oblique eyes gave her the expression of one brooding over some pulsating vision within herself.

With a quick toss of her head she unloosed her black, glossy hair, and let the wind whisper gently through it. From where she stood she could neither hear nor see the village obscured by the creepers and trees at the bend of the river. In front of her stretched an unbroken expanse of lalang grass[1], tall trees, and a bewildering luxuriance of foliage. The languid stillness of the evening was occasionally disturbed by the cry of a lonely waterfowl, or the sinister flap, flap of night birds stirring from their sleep. Now and then a rat dived with a gentle splash into the river, whilst timid, nervous animals rustled their way through the tall grass and creepers. The air was full of the scent of wild flowers and mud and grass. A feeling of loneliness and desolation came over her, as though she had stumbled into a world still in the dawn of creation, when the earth was an oozing swamp in which wallowed a host of hideous monsters.

Hence when she heard the low, vibrant growl of the tiger it only heightened the illusion, until the tiger broke into a dull angry roar and convinced her that it was not a creature of her imagination.

Framed by the lalang and low to the ground were the massive head and shoulders of the tiger, not more than twenty metres from her. The sun imparted a wicked glint to its staring, yellow eyes and its ears drawn back warningly. It turned its head and snarled, revealing its red tongue and yellow fangs that looked like tree stumps.

Fatima was hypnotized into a helpless fear by the glaring eyes of the tiger, and the sudden stillness that fell around her numbed her mind. She dared not move or take her eyes away from the watching animal, which too was still as if it had been rendered motionless by the unexpected meeting with a human being.

Fatima and the animal watched one another, she frightened and it suspicious. Except for occasional growls, which became less menacing each time, the tiger showed no signs of really wanting to attack her. Instead, after a while the animal took a diminishing interest in her. Its huge paws, stretched out in front, now and then dug its claws into the damp grass. Except when she moved the animal's attention seemed to be nowhere in particular. The glare of its eyes had changed into a sullen and frequently bored expression, so that Fatima noticed the surprising changes of mood in the animal's eyes.

Meanwhile the dusk which had crept from over the hills had obliterated the colourful scene of a moment ago, and replaced it with grey shadows which drifted imperceptibly into darkness. A faint mist had risen from the river, and had spread itself over the land. The shrill scream of a cicada and the distant hoot of an owl signalled transition of the day into night.

Now that she had only a quiet fear of the tiger, she felt exhaustion creep over her. She shivered with the cold, and as the tiger showed no signs of going away she grew desperate. Her hands wandered over her stomach, and the realization that she was a being of two lives engendered in her a fierce determination to escape. She could still discern the shadowy form of the tiger by the failing light. Fatima had studied the animal very carefully and could sense when it would turn its eyes away from her. She waited, her body tense in the water and radiating a feeling of fearful strength. Then with a desperate movement she dived under water so that she scraped the riverbed as she swam. Fatima made for the opposite bank and in the direction of the village, coming to the surface only when she felt that her lungs would burst for air. She felt bewildered and lost in the middle of the river, but when she heard the far-away growl, a fear which she had not felt even in the presence of the tiger seized her.

She swam frantically towards the shore until she saw the twinkling oil-lamps of the village.

The village was in a panic by the time Fatima's mother had spread an exaggerated version of the story her daughter had told her. The women, clucking like hens at the sight of a wheeling hawk, gathered the children into their arms, and having bolted their flimsy doors called out to the men to do something about the marauding tiger. The men rushed around anxious about their cattle and goats, while the old men munched betel nut[2] and demanded what the fuss was all about.

Fatima lay exhausted on a straw mat when the village headman and a crowd came to question her as to the whereabouts of the tiger. Fatima's mother proceeded to give a graphic and noisy tale of her daughter's encounter with the "hairy one" until the headman with an impatient gesture commanded the old lady to hold her peace for a while. He then turned to question Fatima. There was impatience in her voice as she answered his questions. For some reason, unlike the anxious villagers around her, she was averse to having the tiger hunted and killed. The headman frowned.

"Allah!" exclaimed the old lady, wishing to be the centre of interest once more. "It was the providence of Allah which snatched my daughter away from the jaws of the 'hairy one.'"

She threw up her skinny brown hands in a gesture of thanks to Allah. The headman shrugged his shoulders.

"Perhaps it was," he said, "but the next time Allah will not be as merciful. A tiger, perhaps by now drunk with the scent of human flesh, is not a pleasant thing to have roving near our village. For the peace and safety of the women and children, the beast must be hunted down and destroyed without delay."

He scanned the faces of the men, silent and nervous. They were fully alive to the dangers of tracking down a tiger at night, especially when the dense, shadowy lalang afforded it an advantageous position from which to strike quickly and silently.

"Well!" said the headman.

The men regarded the floor in silence. The headman's face twitched and he was about to upbraid them for their cowardice, when Mamood, his youthful face afire with excitement, came in with a gun slung across his shoulders.

"What is this I hear?" he asked eagerly. "The women told me that a tiger has attacked our Fatima. Is it true?"

While the headman told him the facts, briefly and accurately, Mamood fingered his new, double-barrelled gun with all the impatience of one whose hunting spirit had been aroused. He was all for hunting the tiger at once, simply because he loved hunting. The fact that his quarry was a tiger made him all the more eager.

"That's true," said Mamood, when the headman had finished. "We have to think of the women and children. The poor creatures will never move an inch out of their houses until they know that the tiger is dead. It is the duty of the menfolk to protect them. Now who will come with Mamood and help him slay the tiger? As surely as I am the son of my mother I shall drag home the carcass of the beast before sunrise, if you will help me."

After some hesitation, a dozen men volunteered, encouraged by the words of Mamood and the knowledge that he was a good shot.

"Good!" exclaimed Mamood, running his fingers along the gun-barrel, "I knew I could rely on you."

Then he and the men left.

"Believe me, daughter," said Fatima's mother, as she bolted the door after the men, "that boy Mamood is a wild tiger himself."

Fatima rose up from her mat and looked out of the narrow window. The moon cast a mellow radiance over everything it touched, and she could see the moon, broken like molten silver, through the rustling coconut fronds. Men moved about, calling out to one another in stifled, excited voices as they prepared for the hunt. Fatima stared sullenly at the men.

Then the men left until at last there was only the grey-garbed trees and the whisper of the fretful wind. Straining her ears she heard the faraway chuckle of the river.

Somewhere, she reflected, was the tiger about which she had wondered the whole evening. She hoped that it was far out of the men's reach.

"O Allah!" wailed her mother, pounding some areca-nut in a wooden vessel, "tonight is the night for death. Think of those men groping for a beast as cunning as a hundred foxes and which can measure its distance in the darkness. Sure enough there will be the cry of mourning before the night is over."

"They should have left the tiger alone," said Fatima, still looking out of the window.

"That's a crazy thing to say," said the woman. "Somebody has to kill the tiger before it kills us. That's sense."

"Perhaps it would have gone away of its own accord."

"A tiger which comes near a village does not go back until its purpose is accomplished," croaked the old woman. "They are generally killers which venture near a village."

"But this one didn't look like a killer," protested Fatima.

The old woman snorted contemptuously, but said nothing.

"The tiger was not more than twenty metres away from me and it could have sprung at me easily," said Fatima, "but it didn't. Why? Can you explain that, mother? It kept watching me, it's true, but then I was watching it too. At first its eyes glared at me, but later they were gentle and bored. There was nothing fierce or murderous about it. . . ."

"Now you are talking the crazy way your father used to," said her mother, fiercely pounding the areca-nut. "He used to say that the wind sang songs to him. Heaven forgive me that I should talk so of your dead father, but he was a crazy man sometimes."

Fatima scowled out of the window and listened. There was an unearthly silence over the village as though enveloped in a funeral shroud. Her hands, swollen and fleshy, were clenched tightly as she strained the silence for some revealing sound. The pound, pound of her heart kept pace with the jabs her mother made into the areca-nut vessel. Then a sharp pain shot through her. Her hands went over her stomach.

"What is it, Fatima?" said her mother, looking up.

"Nothing," answered Fatima between pressed lips.

"Come away from that draft and lie down," cautioned her mother.

Fatima stood by the window and felt the pain rise and fall. She closed her eyes and pictured the tiger crouching in the lalang, its eyes now red and glaring, now bored and gentle.

Then she heard the faraway crack of a rifle. Then another shot followed. Fatima quivered as if the shots had been aimed at her. Then came the roar of the tiger; not the mild growl she had heard that evening, but full of pain and defiance. For a few seconds the cry of the animal, long drawn-out in its agony, seemed to fill up her heart and ears. She wanted to re-echo the cry. Her face was tight with pain and her body glistened with sweat. A moan broke between her shut lips.

"*Allamah! Allamah!*"³ cried out the old woman. "You look ill. What is it? Come and lie down. Is it. . .?"

"I've got the pains, mother," gasped Fatima.

The old woman led the girl towards the mat and made her lie down.

"Oi, oi, it's a fine time to have a baby!" cried her mother, a little frightened. "You lie down here while I get you some hot water to drink. I'll have to wait till the men return before I go for the midwife. Ay, this is a fine night for a poor old woman!"

Fatima lay on the mat, her eyes shut tight, while her mother boiled the water and muttered.

"Listen," said the old woman, "the men are returning. I can hear their voices."

The air suddenly was filled with the excited voices of men and women outside.

The old lady opened the door cautiously and called out to someone.

"Hurrah for Mamood, auntie," cried a youth rushing in. "He's shot the tiger and they have dragged the beast home. It's a big animal. No wonder it put up a good fight before it was killed. After it was shot twice they had to spear it before it was really killed. And then what do you think happened?"

Fatima looked attentively at the youth. The old lady turned her tiny shrivelled head impatiently towards the youth.

"Well, what happened?"

"They said," explained the youth, lisping slightly, "that after they had killed the animal they heard noises. Then by the light of the hurricane lamps they saw three of the tiniest tiger-cubs. Their eyes were scarcely open and Mamood says that they could not be more than a few hours old. No wonder the beast fought like one possessed. Mamood says that he could sell the tiger-cubs for a good price."

Fatima moaned in pain. The sweat glistened like yellow pearls on her forehead.

"Mother!" she cried.

The old woman pushed the astonished youth towards the door. "Get the midwife, boy," she shouted. "Quick! Go! The midwife." The youth stared, gasped, and then ran for the midwife.

NOTES

[1]lalang grass: a coarse, tropical grass

[2]The betel nut is the seed of a tall palm, chewed with dried leaves and lime as a stimulant.

[3]*"Allamah"*: a Malay expression of concern or consternation

The Silent Traders

BY TSUSHIMA YUKO

TRANSLATED BY GERALDINE HARCOURT

TSUSHIMA Yuko (1947—   ) was only a year old when her father, the author Dazai Osamu, committed suicide. She published her first story in 1969, the same year she completed a university degree in English literature. She is considered by many critics as representative of the post-war generation of Japanese writers.

Tsushima's writing is characterized by imagery, loose structures, allusion to tradition and folklore, and keenly observed domestic details. Many of her stories explore the idea of human connectedness, especially the ties that bind family members.

"The Silent Traders" was awarded the Kawabata Yasunari Prize in 1983. Like the mother in the story, Tsushima herself raised two children alone, supporting the family with her writing. The story's title alludes to the silent trade of the "mountain men," nomads who were "invisible" to villagers because they were never recognized or mentioned.

There was a cat in the wood. Not such an odd thing, really: wildcats, pumas, and lions all come from the same family and even a tabby shouldn't be out of place. But the sight was unsettling. What was the creature doing there? When I say "wood," I'm talking about Rikugien[1], an Edo-period landscape garden in my neighbourhood. Perhaps "wood" isn't quite the right word, but the old park's trees—relics of the past amid the city's modern buildings—are so overgrown that the pathways skirting its walls are dark and forbidding even by day. It does give the impression of a wood; there's no other word for it. And the cat, I should explain, didn't look wild. It was just a kitten, two or three months old, white with black patches. It didn't look at all ferocious—in fact it was a dear little thing. There was nothing to fear. And yet I was taken aback, and I tensed as the kitten bristled and glared in my direction.

The kitten was hiding in a thicket beside the pond, where my ten-year-old daughter was the first to spot it. By the time I'd made out the elusive shape and exclaimed, "Oh, you're right!" she was off calling at the top of her voice: "There's another! And here's one over here!" My other child, a boy of five, was still hunting for the first kitten, and as his sister went on making one discovery after another he stamped his feet and wailed, "Where? Where is it?" His sister beckoned him to bend down and showed him triumphantly where to find the first cat. Several passersby, hearing my daughter's shouts, had also been drawn into the search. There were many strollers in the park that Sunday evening. The cats were everywhere, each concealed in its own clump of bushes. Their eyes followed people's feet on the gravelled walk, and at the slightest move toward a hiding place the cat would scamper away. Looking down from an adult's height it was hard enough to detect them at all, let alone keep count, and this gave the impression of great numbers.

I could hear my younger child crying. He had disappeared while my back was turned. As I looked wildly around, my daughter pointed him out with a chuckle: "See where he's got to!" There he was, huddled tearfully in the spot where the first kitten had been. He'd burst in eagerly, but succeeded only in driving away the kitten and trapping himself in the thicket.

"What do you think you're doing? It'll never let *you* catch it." Squatting down, my daughter was calling through the bushes. "Come on out, silly!"

His sister's tone of amusement was no help to the boy at all. He was terrified in his cobwebbed cage of low-hanging branches where no light penetrated.

"That's no use. You go in and fetch him out." I gave her shoulder a push.

"He got himself in," she grumbled, "so why can't he get out?" All the same, she set about searching for an opening. Crouching, I watched the boy through the thick foliage and waited for her to reach him.

"How'd he ever get in there? He's really stuck," she muttered as she circled the bushes uncertainly, but a moment later she'd broken through to him, forcing a way with both hands.

When they rejoined me, they had dead leaves and twigs snagged all over them.

After an attempt of her own to pick one up, my daughter understood that life in the park had made these tiny kittens quicker than ordinary strays and too wary to let anyone pet them. Explaining this to her brother, she looked to me for agreement. "They were born here, weren't they? They belong here, don't they? Then I wonder if their mother's here too?"

The children scanned the surrounding trees once again.

"She may be," I said, "but she'd stay out of sight, wouldn't she? Only the kittens wander about in the open. Their mother's got more sense. I'll bet she's up that tree or some place like that where nobody can get at her. She's probably watching us right now."

I cast an eye at the treetops as I spoke—and the thought of the unseen mother cat gave me an uncomfortable feeling. Whether these were alley cats that had moved into the park or discarded pets that had survived and bred, they could go on multiplying in the wood—which at night was empty of people—and be perfectly at home.

It is exactly twenty-five years since my mother came to live near Rikugien with her three children, of which I was the youngest at ten. She told us the park's history, and not long after our arrival we went inside to see the garden. In spite of its being on our doorstep we quickly lost interest, however, since the grounds were surrounded by a one-and-a-half-metre brick wall with a single gate on the far side from our house. A Japanese garden was not much fun for children anyway, and we never went again as a family. I was reminded that we lived near a park, though, because of the many birds—the blue magpies, Eastern turtledoves, and tits—that I would see on the rooftops and in trees. And in summer I'd hear the singing of evening cicadas. To a city child like me, evening cicadas and blue magpies were a novelty.

I visited Rikugien with several classmates when we were about to leave elementary school, and someone hit on the idea of making a kind of time capsule. We'd leave it buried for ten years—or was it twenty? I've also forgotten what we wrote on the piece of paper that we stuffed into a small bottle and buried at the foot of a pine on the highest ground in the garden. I expect it's still there as I haven't heard of it since, and now whenever I'm in Rikugien I keep an eye out for a landmark, but I'm only guessing. We were confident of knowing where to look in years to come, and if I can remember that so clearly it's puzzling that I can't recognize the tree. I'm not about to dig any holes to check, however—not with my own children watching. The friends who left this sentimental reminder were about to part, bound for different schools. Since then, of course, we've ceased to think of one another, and I'm not so sure now that the bottle episode ever happened.

The following February my brother (who was close to my own age) died quite suddenly of pneumonia. Then in April my sister went to college and, not wanting to be left out, I pursued her new interests myself: I listened to jazz, went to movies, and was friendly toward college and high school students of the opposite sex. An older girl introduced me to a boy from senior high and we made up a foursome for an outing to the park—the only time I got all dressed up for Rikugien. I was no beauty though, nor the popular type, and while the others were having fun I stayed stiff and awkward, and was bored. I would have liked to be as genuinely impressed as they were, viewing the landscape garden for the first time, but I couldn't work up an interest in seeing the trees over the brick wall every day. By that time we'd been in the district for three years, and the name "Rikugien" brought to mind not the tidy, sunlit lawns seen by visitors, but the dark tangles along the walls.

My desire for friends of the opposite sex was short-lived. Boys couldn't provide what I wanted, and what boys wanted had nothing to do with me.

While I was in high school, one day our ancient spitz died. The house remained without a dog for a while, until Mother was finally prompted to replace him when my sister's marriage, soon after her graduation, left just the two of us in an unprotected home. She found someone who let her have a terrier puppy. She bought a brush and comb and began rearing the pup with the best of care, explaining that it came from a clever hunting breed. As it grew, however, it failed to display the expected intelligence and still behaved like a puppy after six months; and besides, it was timid. What it did have was energy as, yapping shrilly, it frisked about the house all day long. It may have been useless but it was a funny little fellow. Its presence made all the difference to me in my intense boredom at home. After my brother's death, my mother (a widow since I was a baby) passed her days as if at a wake. We saw each other only at mealtimes, and then we seldom spoke. In high school a fondness for the movies was about the worst I could have been accused of, but Mother had no patience with such frivolity and would snap angrily at me from time to time. "I'm leaving home when I turn eighteen," I'd retort. I meant it, too.

It was at that time that we had the very sociable dog. I suppose I'd spoiled it as a puppy, for now it was always wanting to be let in, and when I slid open the glass door it would bounce like a rubber ball right into my arms and lick my face and hands ecstatically.

Mother, however, was dissatisfied. She'd had enough of the barking; it got on her nerves. Then came a day when the dog went missing. I thought it must have got out of the yard. Two or three days passed and it didn't return—it hadn't the wit to find the way home once it strayed. I wondered if I should contact the pound. Concern finally drove me to break our usual silence and ask Mother: "About the dog..." "Oh, the dog?" she replied. "I threw it over the wall of Rikugien the other day."

I was shocked—I'd never heard of disposing of a dog like that. I wasn't able to protest, though. I didn't rush out to comb the park, either. She could have had it destroyed, yet instead she'd taken it to the foot of the brick wall, lifted it in her arms, and heaved it over. It wasn't large, only about thirty centimetres long, and thus not too much of a handful even for Mother.

Finding itself tossed into the wood, the dog wouldn't have crept quietly into hiding. It must have raced through the area barking furiously, only to be caught at once by the caretaker. Would the next stop be the pound? But there seemed to me just a chance that it hadn't turned out that way. I could imagine the wood by daylight, more or less; there'd be a lot of birds and insects, and little else. The pond would be inhabited by a few carp, turtles, and catfish. But what transformations took place at night? As I didn't dare stay beyond closing time to see for myself, I wondered if anyone could tell of a night spent in the park till the gates opened in the morning. There might be goings-on unimaginable by day. Mightn't a dog entering that world live on, not as a tiny terrier, but as something else?

I had to be thankful that the dog's fate left that much to the imagination.

From then on I turned my back on Rikugien more firmly than ever. I was afraid of the deep wood, so out of keeping with the city: it was the domain of the dog abandoned by my mother.

In due course I left home, a little later than I'd promised. After a good many more years I moved back to Mother's neighbourhood—back to the vicinity of the park—with a little daughter and a baby. Like my own mother, I was one who couldn't give my children the experience of a father. That remained the one thing I regretted.

Living in a cramped apartment, I now appreciated the Rikugien wood for its greenery and open spaces. I began to take the children there occasionally. Several times, too, we released pet turtles or goldfish in the pond. Many nearby families who'd run out of room for aquarium creatures in their overcrowded apartments would slip them into the pond to spend the rest of their lives at liberty.

Rocks rose from the water here and there, and each was studded with turtles sunning themselves. They couldn't have bred naturally in such numbers. They must have been the tiny turtles sold at fairground stalls and pet shops, grown up without a care in the world. More of them lined the water's edge at one's feet. No doubt there were other animals on the increase—goldfish, loaches, and the like. Multistoreyed apartment buildings were going up around the wood in quick succession, and more living things were brought down from their rooms each year. Cats were one animal I'd overlooked, though. If tipping out turtles was common practice, there was no reason why cats shouldn't be dumped here, and dogs too. No type of pet could be ruled out. But to become established in any numbers they'd have to escape the caretaker's notice and hold their own against the wood's other hardy inhabitants. Thus there'd be a limit to survivors: cats and reptiles, I'd say.

Once I knew about the cat population, I remembered the dog my mother had thrown away, and I also remembered my old fear of the wood. I couldn't help wondering how the cats got along from day to day.

Perhaps they relied on food left behind by visitors—but all of the park's trash baskets were fitted with mesh covers to keep out the crows, whose numbers were also growing. For all their nimbleness, even cats would have trouble picking out the scraps. Lizards and mice were edible enough. But on the other side of the wall lay the city and its garbage. After dark, the cats would go out foraging on the streets.

Then, too, there was the row of apartment towers along one side of the wood, facing the main road. All had balconies that overlooked the park. The climb would be quick work for a cat, and if its favourite food were left outside a door it would soon come back regularly. Something told me there must be people who put out food: there'd be elderly tenants and women living alone. Even children. Children captivated by a secret friendship with a cat.

I don't find anything odd about such a relationship—perhaps because it occurs so often in fairy stories. But to make it worth their while the apartment children would have to receive something from the cat; otherwise they wouldn't keep it up. There are tales of mountain men and villagers who traded a year's haul of linden bark for five and a half litres of rice in hard cakes. No villager could deal openly with the lone mountain men; so great was their fear of each other, in fact, that they avoided coming face to face. Yet when a bargain was struck, it could not have been done more skilfully. The trading was over in a flash, before either man had time to catch sight of the other or hear his voice. I think everyone wishes privately that bargains could be made like that. Though there would always be the fear of attack, or discovery, by one's own side.

Supposing it were my own children: what could they be getting in return? They'd have no use for a year's stock of linden bark. Toys, then, or cakes. I'm sure they want all sorts of things, but not a means of support like linden bark. What, then? Something not readily available to them; something the cat has in abundance and to spare.

The children leave food on the balcony. And in return the cat provides them with a father. How's that for a bargain? Once a year, male cats procreate, in other words, they become fathers. They become fathers ad nauseam. But these fathers don't care how many children they have—they don't notice that they are fathers. Yet the existence of offspring makes them so. Fathers who don't know their own children. Among humans, it seems there's an understanding that a man only becomes a father when he recognizes the child as his own; but that's a very narrow view. Why do we allow the male to divide children arbitrarily into two kinds, recognized and unrecognized? Wouldn't it be enough for the child to choose a father when necessary from among suitable males? If the children decide that the tom that climbs up to their balcony is their father, it shouldn't cause him any inconvenience. A father looks in on two of his children from the balcony every night. The two human children faithfully leave out food to make it so. He comes late, when they are fast asleep, and they never see him or hear his cries. It's enough that they know in the morning that he's been. In their dreams, the children are hugged to their cat-father's breast.

We'd seen the children's human father six months earlier, and together we'd gone to a transport museum they wanted to visit. This came about only after many appeals from me. If the man who was their father was alive and well on this earth, I wanted the children to know what he looked like. To me, the man was unforgettable: I was once preoccupied with him, obsessed with the desire to be where he was; nothing had changed when I tried having a child, and I'd had the second with him cursing me. To the children, however, especially the younger one, he was a mere shadow in a photograph that never moved or spoke. As the younger child turned three, then four, I couldn't help being aware of that fact. This was the same state of affairs that I'd known myself, for my own father had died. If he were dead it couldn't be helped. But as long as he was alive I wanted them to have a memory of their father as a living, breathing person whose eyes moved, whose mouth moved and spoke.

On the day, he was an hour late for our appointment. The long wait in a coffee shop had made the children tired and cross, but when they saw the man a shy silence came over them. "Thanks for coming," I said with a smile. I couldn't think what to say next. He asked "Where to?" and stood to leave at once. He walked alone, while the children and I looked as though it was all the same to us whether he was there or not. On the train I still hadn't come up with anything to say. The children kept their distance from the man and stared nonchalantly out of the window. We got off the train like that, and again he walked ahead.

The transport museum had an actual bullet train car, steam locomotive, airplanes, and giant panoramic layouts. I remembered enjoying a class trip there while at school myself. My children, too, dashed excitedly around the exhibits without a moment's pause for breath. It was "Next I want to have a go on that train," "Now I want to work that model." They must have had a good two hours of fun. In the meantime we lost sight of the man. Wherever he'd been, he showed up again when we'd finished our tour and arrived back at the entrance. "What'll we do?" he asked, and I suggested giving the children a drink and sitting down somewhere. He nodded and went ahead to look for a place near the museum. The children were clinging to me as before. He entered a coffee shop that had a cake counter and I followed with them. We sat down, the three of us facing the man. Neither child showed the slightest inclination to sit beside him. They had orange drinks.

I was becoming desperate for something to say. And weren't there one or two things he'd like to ask me? Such as how the children had been lately. But to bring that up, unasked, might imply that I wanted him to watch with me as they grew. I'd only been able to ask for this meeting because I'd finally stopped feeling that way. Now it seemed we couldn't even exchange such polite remarks as "They've grown" or "I'm glad they're well" without arousing needless suspicions. It wasn't supposed to be like this, I thought in confusion, unable to say a word about the children. He was indeed their father, but not a father who watched over them. As far as he was concerned the only children he had were the two borne by his wife. Agreeing to see mine was simply a favour on his part, for which I could only be grateful.

If we couldn't discuss the children, there was literally nothing left to say. We didn't have the kind of memories we could reminisce over; I wished I could forget the things we'd done as if it had all been a dream, for it was a pain that we remembered. Inquiring after his family would be no better. His work seemed the safest subject, yet if I didn't want to stay in touch I had to think twice about this, too.

The man and I listened absently as the children entertained themselves.

On the way out the man bought a cake which he handed to the older child, and then he was gone. The children appeared relieved, and with the cake to look forward to they were eager to get home. Neither had held the man's hand or spoken to him. I wanted to tell them that there was still time to run after him and touch some part of his body, but of course they wouldn't have done it.

I don't know when there will be another opportunity for the children to see the man. They may never meet him again, or they may have a chance two or three years from now. I do know that the man and I will probably never be completely indifferent to each other. He's still on my mind in some obscure way. Yet there's no point in confirming this feelings in words. Silence is essential. As long as we maintain silence, and thus avoid trespassing, we leave open the possibility of resuming negotiations at any time.

I believe the system of bartering used by the mountain men and the villagers was called "silent trade." I am coming to understand that there was nothing extraordinary in striking such a silent bargain for survival. People trying to survive—myself, my mother, and my children, for example—can take some comfort in living beside a wood. We tip various things in there and tell ourselves that we haven't thrown them away, we've set them free in another world, and then we picture the unknown woodland to ourselves and shudder with fear or sigh fondly. Meanwhile the creatures multiplying there gaze stealthily at the human world outside; at least I've yet to hear of anything attacking from the wood.

Some sort of silent trade is taking place between the two sides. Perhaps my children really have begun dealings with a cat who lives in the wood.

NOTE

[1]Rikugien, a park on the outskirts of Tokyo, was constructed in 1702 during the Edo period (1615-1867). Edo-period gardens were characterized by meandering paths and picturesque views which the walker came upon unexpectedly.

The Invader

BY SACHAPORN SINGHAPALIN

TRANSLATED BY JENNIFER DRASKAU

Sachaporn SINGHAPALIN teaches at Thamasat University in Bangkok. Her stories often deal with the effects of economic and cultural change on the individual, and are noted for their sensitivity and compassion.

"The Invader" is set in rural Thailand around the middle of this century (perhaps during the national development program of the early 1960s) and deals with a familiar theme: the peasant dispossessed by progress.

The cluster of paddy fields round his hut seemed to stretch forever. Old Uncle Chui [*Chuy*] himself had never been beyond to find out. At any rate there were no tall trees or houses within two kilometres' walk in any direction. The paddy was cool to the eye in the green time of rain, golden in the cool season, baked brown, the earth cracked, in the hot season. On the far horizon, red roof tiles shimmered through rich foliage. The hut faced south towards the road. Occasionally there were cars, but cars played so small a part in his consciousness that he had never even wondered what sort of cars they were.

Mostly, he went only as far as the house of the village headman, the Pu Yai Ban, at the eastern edge of the paddy on the bank of the klong[1] where coconut palms paraded rank and file. His longest journey had been to the district office. Just across the way was the market, but he never went to market. He needed nothing.

It was good when the rain held off. Then, meditating became an occupation. He had a special attitude for it, hands behind his back, eyes ranging the landscape. He watched the round red ball of the sun slip down the sky, staining it orange that charred to dusk. A cool ghost of evening breeze rose from the ground itself as if the earth sighed.

The old man regarded the landscape unburdened by the philosophy or appreciation of a romanticist. He wove no fantasies from the changing shapes of the cumuli. For him, the countryside was lexicon and newspaper. He could read the patterns of natural phenomena as efficiently as a nurse reads a temperature. When the air lay heavy and the sunlight was bilious yellow, he watched the ants, lugging their eggs, marching in solemn legions, single file, toward the high and dry places. When the frogs opened their humble throats and sang their guttural praises over the land, he had begun to close the doors and shutters against the rains even before the final warning of the lowering storm clouds.

The view never changed but he looked at it all the same. There was nothing else to do until night. Then it was time to sleep. If anyone had told him that there were cinemas and theatres to fill the empty hours between work and sleep with sound and colour, he would have shaken his head in disbelief. Especially when he heard what the fools could be asked to pay for a ticket. He had never in his life paid for anything he couldn't see the immediate need for. The idea of paying for non-essentials scandalized him.

But he, too, had felt the tug of distraction. At evening, when the drums called from Wat Tong Lang[2] along the klong, he had to make himself ready. He could not stay at home. Getting ready meant tying the check *pakhaoma*[3] about his middle. Then he set off along the paddy dykes, towards the drums and the wat.

The wat fair was worth the walk. The compound was a seething feast of things to do, see, and smell—crisp noodles, sizzling chicken and rice, minute delicacies in banana leaves, fizzy sugar drinks. Through it all he walked, eyes awash with colour, ears buzzing with sound, but his money gripped tight. Wat fairs or no, it was a major indulgence for old Uncle Chui to treat himself to a dish of *guitiew*[4] [*gwitio*]. There was plenty to see without parting with hard-earned cash. *Likae*[5] folk plays, singing—nobody asked him to pay for watching those, that was the best part. He could move on to another entertainment if he wished to, without feeling he had to stay to the end to get his money's worth.

Eventually someone would call out to him:

"Oh, Uncle Chui! Fancy seeing you here!"

"Just arrived, Uncle?"

If he was feeling communicative he might say "Yes." Nobody minded. Uncle Chui talked when he felt like it, which was not often. Where had they all sprung from, these people, among the open paddy he had known since childhood, though now his hair was white? It seemed impossible that the paddy could have been hiding such a crowd. Of course, he reasoned, you could count on the fair to bring them out, no matter how far the walk. He had known the paddy forever, man and boy, and nothing had changed, except that each year he had forgotten that there were so many houses on the horizon, and had to recount. Somebody had put asphalt on the road, too, in the last year. The winds of change: perplexing, stirring times.

His gaze stopped when it netted Maak and Prim, walking side by side, grinning. Was it only two months ago—and that was in the sixth month— that he had helped grind chilies for the curry at their wedding feast?

"Been here long, Uncle?" Young Maak raised his hands in a *wai*[6]. Prim followed his example, eyes shyly lowered. The old man grunted.

"We just got here. Haven't seen anything yet."

The grunt was reinforced.

"Excuse us. Have to keep moving. She wants to see the *likae*."

He nodded and wandered away. The ointment seller shrieked entreaties at him, but he did not linger. Everyone was there this time. Klam was walking with strides as long as he dared, his wife left far behind and scolding. The headman's daughters followed their father's walking stick through the throng. There were youngsters he could not remember, young girls whose melodious names he could not unravel one from another. No matter. If they lived nearby, they would speak. It amused his eye to see how the fair brought out the dandy and the belle in all of them. Now was the time for smooth hair, rice powder on noses, new clothes in gay hues. It was the orchestration of colour, not the solo, he recalled. He could never remember what anyone had had on. He knew only that together the bright cloth formed a symphony that pleased him. No one could remember what colour his own pants and plaid had been. Now they were the colour of their elements, mud and sun. Two reasons only had ever made him wear a shirt. The chill winter season, and—in deference to vested authority—visits to the district office.

He wandered on. Hawkers tried in vain to enlist his attention. They had a hoarse time of it, the hawkers, competing with the generator, the shouts and laughter, the happy girlish squeals, the bursting of balloons, as well as the usual cross-fire of out-shouting duels amongst themselves. He was in a mood to find even the cacophony entertaining. In the relentless monotony of his similar days, noise made as welcome a break as colour and conversation. Even his worry was monotonous—the same spectre, day in and day out. Drought...

The work changed with the seasons. At the start of the rains they were ploughing the paddy and he planted the rice. At harvest time he could pick up as many fallen grains as he liked while he helped them bring in the rice in the late cool season. He spent the summer doing anything that was to hand; he dug ditches, cut grass, carried bricks or stones. There was always something to do. There was always something to watch, too. People walking, swings swooping and soaring in circles, floating balloons, the wonder of new bright fluorescent strip lighting, the flickering green gaslights of the shop vendors, set bright touches to his life. He never missed a wat fair. But the sight of the happy newlyweds, Maak and Prim, had stirred an uneasiness within him. Breaking the habit of a lifetime, he found his mind chewing on words. It was at their wedding feast that the Pu Yai Ban had spoken of strange things.

"Paddy's getting smaller," Chui had said to the Pu Yai Ban. "Look at those hedges, those roofs. People will be building right on the paddy next thing you know. They've been creeping up on us. Nearer every time you turn round."

"Don't tell me you didn't know, Uncle?" said the Pu Yai Ban, stirring curry into his rice. "Now they've finished the road, people will be building all over the place."

"Who made the road? The government?" someone asked.

"Not at all. The fellow who bought the land. He built it."

"Bought the land?" Uncle Chui stared. "But the land belongs to Mrs. Sai."

"It did, Uncle, it did. But she sold the lot of it, the whole plot."

"Where's she going to plant her rice?" said the old man, still struggling to grasp this amazing development. Someone laughed.

"Poor Chui, Mother Sai won't be planting any more rice. Selling land is a better business than planting rice—she got a big sum of cash for the land, enough to dance with—why should she go back to rice? Damned back-breaking, mister—she won't walk in the paddy all the rest of her life. And why should she?"

There was a note in his voice that Chui had not heard before. Chui went home after the feast but sleep would not come. There was a tiny thought that would not fit into the smooth pattern of his other thoughts. He could not put his finger on it, but it kept sleep at bay. He no longer plunged into sleep with the abandon of a drowning man, as when he was young, body exhausted by hours of sweating in the hot sun. He was old, he needed less of everything, even sleep. A bark from Dam, his black mongrel, was enough to frighten sleep away.

As time went by and the rains came, he forgot the Pu Yai Ban's words, and even the wat fair receded, in the excitement of the fish. He hardly waited for the squall to subside into the persistent seeping drizzle before seizing his pail and knife and setting off, stooping and searching in the flooded paddy. He kept his knife-arm raised and strike-ready for any pale movement in the water. If the fish were sharpest in the battle of speed, there would be an untidy flurry and splash and a grunted oath. Failure meant moving to fresh hunting grounds on the other side of the dike, to fish that were not yet on their guard. The villagers claimed the fish liked swimming in the rain. It might be true, he reasoned, for there were more of them after rain than at any other time. He did not wonder where they came from. They were there, from early morning, big fresh fish, asking to be caught. How could a man sleep, when food littered the fields? Once he had stocked his larder with fish, vegetables were a minor matter. A few of them grew all by themselves in the flooded paddy. The bamboo clusters near the hut were shooting out so fast you could almost watch them grow, and the young shoots were a delicacy to smack lips over. The tall kae tree grew hurriedly, too, and the nameless bush with the golden flowers at the water's edge. The only tree he had planted himself was the banana, but it had seeded and multiplied by itself until it threatened to smother the hut.

Replete with rice and fish, he was sitting empty-minded on the bench before the hut at dusk when an extraordinary thing happened. He was looking across the paddy at the road when suddenly it lit up. He snatched up his waist cloth and set off towards the lights, knotting the plaid as he went. As he drew near, the brightness made him close his eyes. It was the miracle of fluorescence, and in its wake, as is the way of miracles, there followed business. There were cars, and in the stillness of the night, the rumble of ten-wheeled trucks. Even after sundown, the cars passed. Someone said there was a trade fair on.

"Going to buy a ticket for the fair, Uncle?" they asked him.

"Pay to go in? I should think not! Damned foolishness!" said Uncle Chui.

These revolutions were tiresome but a man could always turn his thoughts elsewhere. But one day, as he tugged up rice stumps and cursed the sun, three men and a woman came walking across the field. He stopped to wipe the sweat out of his eyes to see who they were, but even through the glare he could tell they were strangers. City people, by their looks, not used to walking over the paddy dikes. Their clothes were bright and the woman shaded her face carefully under a large green umbrella. They stopped and looked this way and that, pointing. After a minute or two they went towards the street. They seemed in a hurry to leave the nakedness of the paddy. The old man went on tugging at the rice stumps.

It was summer, so there were only odd jobs to do. The harvest had been good. A good harvest was good for everyone, even for Chui who did not own a single field. Good for the Pu Yai Ban, who did. Chui decided to ask the headman for a couple of planks to fix the floor of his hut. The good rice harvest would have disposed him to be generous. He was pleased to see the headman walking through the paddy towards his hut. Now he would not have to go himself to ask for the wood.

"Good day, Chui. Have you eaten yet?" called the headman, by way of greeting.

"I've eaten," conceded Chui.

"Not so much doing this time of the year, eh?"

"That's right." He wondered how soon he could decently mention the planks. Not now, while the Pu Yai Ban was studying the banana trees so intently.

"Good banana crop, eh? Too many for one man to eat."

Chui chuckled. "Oh, don't worry. The kids will soon be round asking."

"Of course they will," said the headman thoughtfully. "How could a man living alone eat so many? Living alone has its advantages, though. No responsibility. No need to worry your head about your family, eh, old timer? Eat what there is to eat, however little, move on when you like...no problem..."

There was something odd about the way the words came out. Uncle Chui looked at the headman, hoping for a clue. As if he was afraid that his courage would not last but must immediately be harvested, the headman said:

"I've sold the paddy."

"Sold?" Chui lifted his wrinkled face, hoping to pull a more satisfactory answer from him by the power of his eyes.

But the Pu Yai Ban was not to be trapped so easily. His gaze floated innocently over Chui's head. When he spoke again his tone had hardened.

"Sold. They'll be here pretty soon to subdivide it into lots—split it into small plots—but I shan't be here to see it. I'm off out of this."

After the Pu Yai Ban left, Chui stood long looking into the darkness. He had neither hated nor loved the paddy. It was just there. But now he felt its presence threatened by a shadow like his own. "Subdivided..." he muttered. The word was a stone in his heart. From then on, every morning when he woke he at once inspected the landscape for changes that might have overtaken it under cover of darkness. But things went on as usual. The stumps still bristled on the parched fractured earth. He took heart as days went by and nothing happened, except that the heat was greater every day and the trees began to look dry.

The old man had long forgotten that he did not own that earth as it owned him. On paper it belonged to the headman, but everything that the headman's family did he was part of. If there were feasts, he helped in the kitchen and with clearing up afterwards. He straightened his back from weeding the patch near the hut and stood under the shade of the kae tree to consider his next operation. He had decided to cut two bunches of bananas to present to the Pu Yai Ban.

Then he heard it. He had grown used to the rushing cars by day, and, though it was harder, to the earthquaking trucks by night—but this latest shattering development was too much. He looked disapprovingly for the source of the racket on the road—and saw to his horror that the "thing" had left the road and was advancing towards him. It came relentlessly, horribly, with a slow clumsy creep like a giant lizard.

He stood frozen, the knife dangling from his hand, forgotten.

It came slowly, without hesitating, and its roar swelled deafeningly until he thought he would never get another sound into his ears again after that angry thunder. His ears would be so coarsened that they would never again hear the wind.

After a while his mystic terror of the "thing" began to evaporate. It was nothing but an overgrown yellow tractor after all, under the power of a human driver. The driver wore a broad-brimmed hat and crouched high on the "thing's" back like a mahout[7]. The machine had a great steel slab in front to move the earth aside out of the way of the things it wanted to build. The paddy wouldn't stand a chance against it. Anyone could see that.

Here and there in the paddy little red flags he had not noticed till that moment fluttered anxiously. The patient had been prepared for the surgeon's knife. The bulldozer made its first plunge. It was nowhere near his hut. Yet...

NOTES

[1]klong: canal

[2]A wat is a Buddhist temple.

[3]*pakhaoma*: a long strip of patterned cloth which can have many functions, such as a turban, loin cloth, sash, or towel

[4]*guitiew*: Chinese noodles

[5]*Likae*: musical folk drama

[6]*wai*: a Thai greeting where the palms are pressed together and lifted to the base of the nose, the forehead, etc., to show varying degrees of respect or reverence for the person addressed

[7]mahout: elephant driver

Dark Glasses

BY KHAMSING SRINAWK

TRANSLATED BY DOMNERN GARDEN

Khamsing SRINAWK grew up in a peasant village in Thailand, nine kilometres across rice paddies from the nearest town. He was one of the first in his family to learn to read and write, and as a boy read everything he could find while tending his family's water buffaloes. When he finished high school, his brother gave him a pair of shoes so that he could go to Bangkok, where he hoped to become a writer.

Srinawk writes about the life of peasants in the rural villages of Thailand, where most of the population still lives. His stories offer a great deal of social criticism, often focusing on the consequences of outside influences on a traditional village. He describes a world of poverty, perpetual need, and indebtedness that is a reality for many Thai peasants.

"Dark Glasses" is set in a typical Thai village; the story was originally published in 1969 under the pen name of Lao Khamhawm.

It was more familiar than an ordinary visitor, though known about rather than seen. It often walked on invisible legs into the mother's heart and left again, as featureless as before. It came and went but she did not know how. Sometimes it came after midnight; sometimes it intruded in the early morning and lingered until nightfall. It followed her into the rice fields and stayed with her as she gathered leaves and sticks for the fire. It didn't visit just anyone, only people well-known to it like herself, and the father.

A few days before, while she was busy preparing for the temple festival, it vanished and she could not recall exactly when it came back or where it came from. She had been stitching up a new sarong for Boonpeng, her youngest son, when from the wood a gong boomed. She put her work down and looked over the fields where no breeze, no clouds in the azure sky disturbed the soft afternoon sunlight. The gentle but sad reverberations saturated the landscape. She turned her eyes back to the blankness around her. Boonpeng's blanket was still heaped on the mattress on the porch where he slept; beyond it, the plaited bamboo partition of their room—hers and her husband's—and next to it was the solid room, properly walled with wooden boards, its door shut, empty. She stared at it for a long time. It was probably then that it welled into her heart again, this anguish.

Any living thing nearby would have dispelled the loneliness, a little lizard on the roof beam, a wasp on its regular flight past her head, but they were not there. The yellow sparrow that used to cling to the tree in front of the house was gone. Its absence reminded her of another bird she had ignored in a cage hanging from the eaves. The sight of it made her feel good and as she approached, the still creature fluffed its wings, stretched its neck, and cooed. Unaware of the warm tears in her eyes, the mother glanced over to the sealed door in deep shadow. The father often stood there motionless so long she wondered what was wrong, but never, until now, did she realize why.

It was hard to believe that three years had passed since the very day of this festival. Well, perhaps, not the very day. In fact, it all began several months before this season on a bright afternoon soon after the harvest. She and her husband returned early to find a car parked under the mango tree in front of their house, the same one that more than once had enveloped the mother in swarms of dust, not that she had seen it clearly through the clouds of billowing dirt. It was something new for the villagers of Dong Cam, and the mother knew like everyone else from gossip that it was the engineer's car. She did not know when those people had appeared, although from their conversation with her daughter, she thought it could not have been long before. The father had gone straight up into the house while the mother fussed with some mangoes and kept an eye on her daughter who was sitting at a loom weaving. The two men around her, both wearing caps and light blue long-sleeved shirts, were smiling conspiratorially at one another. Whether or not they were old the mother could not tell because of the dark glasses both had on.

"You were born a beauty, Camkham," the one leaning on the loom said.

"Born a real beauty, Camkham," the friend of the first echoed.

The mother couldn't make up her mind whether it was better to stay or to go up into the house.

Camkham, in whose dialect the word for beautiful merely meant a time of day, replied, "Oh no, I was born in the afternoon."

"Is that so? Well, still born beautiful."

"No, you don't understand." She rested the purple-threaded shuttle on the cloth, brushed her hair away, and looked at the dark glasses. "Why don't you listen to me? I was born in the afternoon."

The young men's eyes exchanged smiles and the young girl continued.

"My mother told me that when I was inside her, she began to have labour pains while she was harvesting rice in the fields and my father brought her back to the house and I was born in the afternoon. Isn't that right, mama?"

The woman was startled to be called as a witness by her daughter.

"That's right, Camkham," her mother's voice was unsteady, "Camkham was born in the afternoon, later than it is now."

As she spoke, she measured the height of the sun now touching the tips of the trees but before she could continue the father interrupted from up in the house.

"Idiots! Both of you, mother and daughter. They were just saying, in Thai, she's pretty."

The tone of the father's voice was short and not pleased. At supper, the mother saw her husband look at their daughter as if he wanted to tell her something but it never came out. There was no moon that night. The father sat alone at the end of the porch and did not go in to sleep until after midnight, and in the room with walls of proper boards the mother heard Camkham turn and twist restlessly until the same late hour.

The mother knew as did the rest of the village that the father treasured his daughter for deeper reasons than that she was the only one. Before the mother had moved into the village of Dong Cam, her husband had migrated from place to place so often that she became inured to it but when they reached Dong Cam, the father declared they would not move again and he set out to clear rice fields. Delighted when Camkham was born the following year, he named her himself, which he had never done before with the other children, and when the new-born child turned out to be a weakling, he blamed himself for working his wife too hard. So concerned was he to save Camkham from heavy work, that his neighbours and especially the country lads made fun of him. As their house stood isolated at the edge of the paddy fields, the father was meticulous in fencing it. One day the local boys, who would take delight in taunting him from outside the fence, called out, "Hey,

it's thorns that make a fence, uncle, not the smooth bamboo you used!"
Though not a man open to suggestions, the next day he went out into the
wood to dig up some spiked bamboo to add to the fence. The road that was
built penetrated not merely backwoods villages but the fences and doors of
the villagers' homes. The father fell victim to further adolescent teasing.
"Thorns may keep out water buffaloes and country boys, uncle, but not cars."

The father's uneasiness came with the passing of the rain clouds from
the sky. Dong Cam ceased to be a remote hamlet. The villagers excited with
the new road took to gathering under the eaves of the coffee shop and began
to go abroad more. The young people, the girls and boys, got kicks by
hitching rides in the construction trucks even as far as the district town. They
returned dressed in gaudy clothes from the market. But the father went more
often to the temple, and became more reserved. "I'd put it off, if possible." He
was speaking of the Merit-making Festival[1] held every year in the fourth
month. "If no one's interested any more, why should I worry?" But he was
wrong. Before long, the people got used to the new things, to the strangers
and then to traffic on the road, and turned their talk to the festival although it
was not quite the same. This time it began with green and red invitation cards
printed in the town and handed out to all the families and even to people
living outside the village. On the night of the festival, the temple which used
to be all rosy and warm in the light of torches and incense was now brashly lit
by electric light supplied by a portable generator and strident with people and
music. The pulpit that used to be so fresh in a mantle of banana leaves, sugar
cane, and wild flowers was now festooned with flashy multi-coloured cello-
phane. Cars, trucks, and buses were squeezed in the temple yard. The monk's
sermon, blasted forth by loudspeakers, could be heard in several surrounding
villages.

The mother's wandering mind returned to her sewing for a moment and
then again sought out the bird cage.

It had bright red little eyes. Each time the mother moved, it bobbled its
head and cooed. The big gong tolled again but though its voice was as soft as
before, the loneliness of the sound had vanished. She glanced from the bird
cage out across the rice fields to a cluster of figures moving out of the trees
beyond. The sound of the gong became more frequent and was punctuated by
periodic cheers from the procession. As it neared, she could see the old monk,
composed, on the palanquin in the front. There were two men clowning
around, with green and purple sashes, playing the part of the children of
Vessandara, the Buddha-to-be. Behind them were the villagers carrying the

gong at the rear of the file. She gazed after it until it turned and disappeared around the bend at the end of the village. A little later she heard the deep thrumming of the temple drum telling the world that the Buddha in a previous reincarnation had returned. After that it would be the time to decorate the pulpit with the flowers and leaves.

The mother could not remember when the little bird came to share their roof. She guessed it must have been when she was so upset she didn't know whether the moon was waxing or waning and her husband had withdrawn into stunned silence. When her grief had abated, she noticed him fooling with the bird cage but never felt like asking him about it. This was really the first day she had taken a close look at the bird, a pretty thing looking as if it were made of talcum powder. As she fell in love with the tiny bird, understanding of her husband and sorrow at thinking ill of him for his outward indifference to the disappearance of their daughter suffused her heart. After that festival three years before she did not think her husband would go again to the temple and she never thought she would again see such a fine procession as had just passed. The fields were still bright, the air cooling, and she knew that grief, in time and if life lasts, relents.

The father returned home before the sun had disappeared, and though weary, his face showed contentment after the merit-making ceremonies. He was holding a little box of saffron and hesitated a bit when he saw his wife standing next to the bird cage.

"It's a tame little thing," he said as if not knowing what better to say.

"It is."

"I didn't mean to keep it caged so long. You know I thought when its wings were strong enough, I'd let it go. Well, three years have already just slipped by. I've made it suffer enough. What a shame."

"Yes," was all the mother could say.

Early the following morning, after blowing saffron water on the bird for good luck, the father carried the cage to the temple and, at peace with himself, listened to the sermon. When the gong sounded the end of the chapters it was almost noon; he prostrated himself three times in the direction of the monk and then crept over to the cage placed at the foot of the pulpit. On seeing the man, the bird cooed softly to him; he smiled with joy; his neighbour tittered.

He turned to his wife: "Join me in letting the bird go?"

"You go ahead."

"Well, it's really my sin to have kept it locked up."

The father carried the cage from the temple, passed under the sacred Bo tree[2], and cut across the field to the end of the fence where he put the cage on the ground. A few children trailed after him to watch. "Let this be the end of our troubles," he intoned. He extended his hand to the door of the cage. "Back to the woods. Help your mate hatch your eggs. Feed your babies with grass seed. Go, go. Off there. Off as far as you can." The father tapped the cage gently but the bird held fast to the perch. In a moment, the pink-tinted downy little bird hobbled out of the cage, its legs crimson in the sunlight. The children closed in to see. It beat its wings but fell to the ground after a few metres. The children clapped their hands and chased it. It flew again, this time more than twenty metres. At the third try it made a bamboo branch and smoothed its feathers with its beak.

The father stayed on at the temple to help put away the pulpit and the other things until late in the afternoon; and reflected that even if his happiness were only as heavy as bits of gravel, he wouldn't have the strength to carry it all home that day. He felt he was floating in the air; the sky above was clear, the land around beautiful. The group of children tending the water buffalo were playing happily. He hardly noticed the distance to the house. Before he could climb the stairs, he was transfixed by Boonpeng's cry: "Pa, I was in luck today." He held up his trophy proudly to show his father. "It was fat and stupid. I beat it down with a stick."

The boy placed his good fortune in his father's hand and, turning to the fence, shouted, "Hey, sister, Cam, Cam!"

The father dully watched his returning daughter mince uncertainly down the path. The mother came down from the house and began to cry. He gazed stonily at the little bird in his hand, the saffron still showing under its wings.

NOTES

[1] The Merit-making Festival, which takes place at the end of the harvest season, is held to gain favour with the gods and to raise money for the local temple.

[2] Also known as the bodhi tree or peepul, the bo tree is considered sacred by Buddhists. Buddha was sitting under the bo tree (a type of fig tree) when he received enlightenment; hence, it is known as the "tree of wisdom."

Wings

BY PENG CAO

TRANSLATED BY HANNAH CHEUNG WITH D. E. POLLARD

PENG Cao [Ping Chao] (1946–   ) is the pen name of Feng Shuyan, who was born and educated in Hong Kong. After teaching for several years, she went to Paris in 1975 and studied at the Université de Sorbonne and at a translation school. She currently lives in Paris.

Peng's work is familiar to an international audience of Chinese readers. Although she is especially known for her stories and essays, she has also written film and television scripts.

"Wings" is set in a contemporary Hong Kong publishing office.

They mocked Ah Mu behind his back: Ah Mu was mad, they said. First of all, who was "Ah Mu"? And who were "they"?

Ah Mu was a man; his features were perfectly regular, but he was slightly bigger built than most people. When he was born, Ah Mu's parents probably foresaw that he would grow up to be bigger than others, like a tree, so, on the third day after his birth, they named him "Ah Mu"—"timber."

Back to Ah Mu. As a matter of fact, he was just a very ordinary person. He had the proper "human" qualities—modesty, kindness, gentleness. And in his conversation he was very discreet, he never let his tongue run away with itself. Usually such an ordinary man is not worth writing about. However, the aforementioned "human" qualities have for some time ceased to be valued and respected by the average person. Ah Mu was unfortunate because he had to live among these average people. These people were "they." They could not bear Ah Mu's being "a cut above the rest," so they mocked him behind his back and called him mad.

Every morning when Ah Mu woke up, he always softly kissed his wife, who was lying beside him, on the cheek. He did this out of immense respect and gratitude. He felt it inconceivable that such a beautiful and caring woman could actually be sleeping by his side. The two of them had been together for a long long time. Ah Mu said that feelings, especially love, should grow richer and deeper with every passing day. Of course, many people did not think like Ah Mu. Most of them had very complicated feelings, and loving a person would often turn out to be something painful. They felt that Ah Mu was too simple-minded, and they looked with pity on his innocence.

And the whole thing, that is, the fact that Ah Mu was happier than ordinary people, made them very resentful. Why was it that Ah Mu wore a smile on his face from morning till night? Once, some youngsters who enjoyed mischief-making saw Ah Mu approaching slowly from the other end of the long corridor. They deliberately rushed towards him at full speed, and bumped right into him. Big as he was, Ah Mu was knocked staggering for a few steps. However, not only did he not lose his temper, he even asked with an alarmed look, "Where are you off to in such a hurry? I hope nothing untoward has happened?" This reaction made the youngsters very angry. They thought Ah Mu was being deliberately sarcastic, so they viciously stamped on his toes before running away.

Ah Mu never let such things bother him. When he reached home, his wife saw his dirty shoes and asked him where he had been. Ah Mu had forgotten about being bumped into and stamped upon; he rolled his big bright eyes, thought for a while, and smiled at his wife apologetically: "Don't know!"

His wife was by now used to his "strange" character. She believed she was the only person in the world who could understand Ah Mu, and took upon herself the responsibility of protecting him. When Ah Mu sat cross-legged and bared to the waist on the sitting room floor, cast his eyes down, and "meditated" (this was Ah Mu's way of maintaining bodily and mental health), and did not move or speak for an hour, his wife would drape a garment round his shoulders. It was a good thing she did, otherwise Ah Mu was likely to catch a chill and fall sick.

But Ah Mu did not realize that even such seemingly uncontroversial matters as meditation would arouse resentment in others. He worked in a publishing company designing book covers and drawing illustrations, and even did some layout work when the editor was too busy. And if the old man who delivered articles got sick and failed to come, Ah Mu would chase off in his stead to the typesetter some four streets away. This seemed the most natural thing in the world, because Ah Mu never refused any work that others placed on him and never expected gratitude afterwards, so nobody felt it necessary to express gratitude towards him. All along, his colleagues might indeed have overlooked his presence—that is to say, apart from asking Ah Mu to do this and that for them, they would not have noticed his behaviour particularly.

Except one day, when they began talking about eating out. "A" thought that the "Spicy Chicken" at Tianxianglou [*Ti-en-siang-lou*] Restaurant was simply the tops, while "B" scoffed at the idea and at A for being no gourmet. Firstly, the "Spicy Chicken" dish used such strong seasonings that it was impossible to detect the taste of chicken. Besides, the "Spicy Chicken" at Tianxianglou had nothing special whatsoever about it, there must be some-thing wrong with A's taste buds. When A heard that, he flew into a rage and went on the attack. He told B he looked like a down-and-out: nobody would believe that a shabby character like him would be let into the Tianxianglou in the first place, so he could never have tried the "Spicy Chicken" there. The personal slanging match ranged back and forth.

Only too pleased to stir up trouble, the other colleagues divided themselves up into two factions and egged on the contestants. Feelings ran high: it seemed that a fight would break out at any moment. Ah Mu really could not imagine how "Spicy Chicken" could become a subject for argument. When he heard the various insulting, even disgusting, words flying about the office, he gradually turned pale and put down the pen in his hand. His colleagues cursing at each other then saw a strange sight—Ah Mu sat down on the floor of the office, crossed his legs, put his hands on his knees, closed his eyes, and began to meditate, as if to elevate himself to a higher plane. For a moment they were stupefied, then they looked at each other in consternation. Everyone returned to his own seat. A feeling of shame came upon them, followed by loathing towards Ah Mu—it was Ah Mu who made them ashamed of their own behaviour! This Ah Mu was really detestable! Besides, he was mad!

Ah Mu did not know that he had become a detestable figure among his colleagues. But if he had known, would he have minded? Ah Mu still did the extra work the others dumped on him with great enthusiasm; he still did not expect a word of thanks. He only wished to see an occasional friendly smile. That, more than the sunshine outside the window, would have made Ah Mu happy.

His colleagues finally thought of a way to play a trick on him. One day, when he had gone to the washroom, they put three sleeping pills in his tea. Ah Mu came back, raised his glass, and gulped down the tea together with the drug. His colleagues smiled to each other secretly, casting sideways glances at him. Very soon, Ah Mu's big body shifted slightly in his seat, the pen in his hand slipped onto the floor. Finally, he slumped over his desk and fell into a deep sound sleep. His cheek rested on a half-finished picture. In the picture, there was a bird about to take flight, but it was still missing one wing. His colleagues roared with laughter, and waited eagerly for the editor to come out of his office.

This trick had a consequence which may not have been what they intended. As they pointed out in their mutual justification and explanations afterwards, they bore Ah Mu no ill will, they just wanted to have a game with him. But when the editor walked past Ah Mu and yelled at him several times, and Ah Mu did not wake up, he flew into a furious rage. In fact, the editor's ill temper was mainly due to his family affairs. He did not get along well with his wife and often had quarrels at home. That morning they had just had a row, and naturally he was not in a good mood. He glared at Ah Mu sleeping soundly on the desk and cursed him up hill and down dale. He absolutely refused to stop and find out the reason why, and was determined not to take into consideration Ah Mu's customary diligence and hard work. He wrote a notice of dismissal on the spot, threw it in Ah Mu's face, and ordered one of the others to call Ah Mu's wife to take him home. His tone of voice left no room for argument. "He must go at once!" There was dead silence. Among those who played the nasty trick, there might have been some who felt regret and even wanted to explain the whole thing to the chief editor. But they did nothing. They reasoned that under the circumstances, there was nothing they could do.

Ah Mu's wife walked into the office. She was a beautiful and quiet woman. She looked at Ah Mu who was dozy with sleep, and then at the people sitting around with guilty looks. She understood everything at once. She did not need to ask anything. They were just a lot of cowards, and were not worthy of her hate. She called in the taxi driver, and together they helped Ah Mu into the taxi.

Afterwards, not one of Ah Mu's colleagues mentioned his name again. It was, after all, an awkward topic. But they heard by chance that Ah Mu and his wife had left the city. A streetsweeper who knew Ah Mu (because every morning when Ah Mu left his home, he would always smile and bid him good morning) insisted that he had seen Ah Mu and his wife: it was a bright and lovely spring day, and they each had a big knapsack on their back, and Ah Mu was pushing a wooden cart as well. There were books and pictures piled like a little hill on the cart. The streetsweeper said they walked away in this way. They were smiling "as if they were going to a distant and beautiful place!" When he said this, he couldn't help sighing softly, but that may not have had any special meaning.

About Ah Mu, there was one other minor detail. According to Sanjie [Sanji-eh], the cleaning woman at the publishing company, Ah Mu had been back to the office the morning after he was sacked. It was very quiet at that time; nobody was in the office as it was not yet time for work. Sanjie, who was outside the office, saw Ah Mu walk up to his desk, sit down, and add something to a picture. In fact, when Ah Mu had woken up, he had remembered the unfinished bird. So he came back and added its other wing, so that it could fly high in the sky. That was all he had come for.

China

Contemporary Chinese Short Stories. 1983. Beijing: Panda Books.

HSU, Vivian Ling, ed. 1988. *A Reader in Post-Cultural Revolution Chinese Literature.* Hong Kong: Chinese University Press.

LIU, Nienling, et al., trans. 1988. *The Rose Colored Dinner: New Works by Contemporary Chinese Women Writers.* Hong Kong: Joint Publishing (H.K.) Co. Ltd.

TAI, Jeanne, ed. and trans. 1989. *Spring Bamboo: A Collection of Contemporary Chinese Short Stories.* New York: Random House.

WANG, Anyi. 1989. *Baotown.* Translated by Martha Avery. New York: Norton.

Hong Kong

Xi Xi. 1986. *A Girl Like Me and Other Stories.* Edited by Rachel May et al. Hong Kong: The Research Centre for Translation, The Chinese University of Hong Kong.

Indonesia

AVELING, Harry, ed. and trans. 1976. *From Surabaya to Armageddon: Indonesian Short Stories.* Singapore: Heinemann Educational Books (Asia) Ltd.

TOER, Pramoedya Ananta. 1981. *This Earth of Mankind.* Translated by Max Lane. Ringwood, Australia: Penguin Books.

Japan

APOSTOLOU, John L., and Greenberg, Martin H., eds. 1987. *Murder in Japan: Japanese Stories of Crime and Detection.* New York: Dembner Books.

GESSEL, Van C., and Matsumoto, Tomone, eds. 1985. *The Showa Anthology: Modern Japanese Short Stories.* 2 vols. Tokyo: Kodansha International Ltd.

McKINNON, Richard N., ed. 1957. *The Heart is Alone: A Selection of 20th Century Japanese Short Stories.* Tokyo: The Hokuseido Press.

SHIGA, Naoya. 1987. *The Paper Door and Other Stories.* Translated by Lane Dunlop. San Francisco: North Point.

TSUSHIMA, Yuko. 1988. *The Shooting Gallery and Other Stories.* Edited by Geraldine Harcourt. London: The Women's Press.

Korea

HWANG, Sun-won. 1989. *The Book of Masks: Stories by Hwang Sun-won*. Edited by Martin Holman. London: Readers International.

OH, Yong-su (O Yongsu). 1985. *The Good People: Korean Stories*. Translated by Marshall R. Pihl. Hong Kong: Heinemann Educational Books (Asia) Ltd.

YUN, Heung-gil. 1989. *The House of Twilight*. Edited by Martin Holman. London: Readers International.

Malaysia

FERNANDO, Lloyd, ed. 1981. *Malaysian Short Stories*. Kuala Lumpur: Heinemann Educational Books (Asia) Ltd.

SHAHNON, Ahmad. 1980. *The Third Notch and Other Stories*. Translated by Harry Aveling. Singapore: Heinemann Educational Books (Asia) Ltd.

Philippines

FRUTO, Ligaya Victorio. 1969. *Yesterday and Other Stories*. Quezon City: Vibal Printing Company.

MOJARES, Resil B., ed. 1978. *The Writers of Cebu: An Anthology of Prize-winning Stories*. Manila: Filipinas Foundation, Inc.

Singapore

LIM, Shirley. 1982. *Another Country and Other Stories*. Singapore: Times Books International.

YEO, Robert, ed. 1978. *Singapore Short Stories*. 2 vols. Singapore: Heinemann Educational Books (Asia) Ltd.

Taiwan

ING, Nancy, ed. 1982. *Winter Plum: Contemporary Chinese Fiction*. Taipei: Taipei Chinese Center, International P.E.N.

PAI, Hsien-yung. 1982. *Wandering in the Garden, Waking from a Dream: Tales of Taipei Characters*. Translated by Pai Hsien-yung and Patia Yasin. Bloomington: Indiana University Press.

Thailand

DRASKAU, Jennifer, ed. 1975. *Taw & Other Thai Stories*. Hong Kong: Heinemann Educational Books (Asia) Ltd.

SRINAWK, Khamsing. 1973. *The Politician and Other Stories*. Translated by Domnern Garden. Kuala Lumpur: Oxford University Press.

ACKNOWLEDGEMENTS

Permission to reprint copyrighted material is gratefully acknowledged. Every reasonable effort to trace the copyright holders of materials appearing in this book has been made. Information that will enable the publishers to rectify any error or omission will be welcomed.

The Jade Pendant by Catherine Lim, from *Singapore Short Stories: Volume 1*, edited by Robert Yeo, © 1978 by Heinemann Educational Books (Asia) Ltd. Reprinted by permission of Octopus Publishing Asia Pte Ltd., Singapore.

A *Ge*-ware Incense Burner by Ni Kuang. Reprinted by permission from RENDITIONS, Nos. 29 & 30 (Spring and Autumn 1988), pp. 150–152. Hong Kong: The Research Centre for Translation, The Chinese University of Hong Kong.

Bus Ride from *Yesterday and Other Stories* by Ligaya Victorio Fruto, © 1969 by Ligaya Victorio Fruto, published by Vibal Printing Company, Quezon City.

Man with a Camera by Estrella D. Alfon, from *The Writers of Cebu*, edited by Resil B. Mojares, © 1978 by Filipinas Foundation, Inc., Manila. Reprinted by permission of Ayala Foundation, Inc. (formerly Filipinas Foundation).

One Good Turn by Pensri Kiengsiri, from *Taw & Other Thai Stories*, edited by Jennifer Draskau, published 1975 by Heinemann Educational Books (Asia) Ltd. Reprinted by permission of Octopus Publishing Asia Pte Ltd., Singapore.

Friends by Wang Anyi, from *The Rose Colored Dinner*, translated by Nienling Liu et al. Copyright © 1988 by Joint Publishing (H.K.) Co., Ltd. Reprinted by permission of the publisher.

Seibei's Gourds by Shiga Naoya, from *Modern Japanese Stories*, edited by Ivan Morris, copyright 1962 by Charles E. Tuttle Co., Inc.,Tokyo. Reprinted by permission of the publisher.

Forced Out by Hsiao Yeh, from *Winter Plum*, edited by Nancy C. Ing, published 1982 by The Taipei Chinese Center. Reprinted by permission of THE CHINESE PEN, Quarterly of The Taipei Chinese Center, International P.E.N., Chief Editor: Nancy C. Ing.

Begonia by Xi Xi. Reprinted by permission from RENDITIONS, Nos. 29 & 30 (Spring and Autumn 1988), pp. 114–117. Hong Kong: The Research Centre for Translation, The Chinese University of Hong Kong.

Inem by Pramoedya Ananta Toer, from *From Surabaya to Armageddon*, edited and translated by Harry Aveling, published 1976 by Heinemann Educational Books (Asia) Ltd. Reprinted by permission of Octopus Publishing Asia Pte Ltd., Singapore.

Flatcar by Akutagawa Ryûnosuke, from *The Heart is Alone*, edited by Richard N. McKinnon, published by The Hokuseido Press, Tokyo. Copyright 1957 by Richard N. McKinnon. Reprinted by permission of the editor.

The Ox Bell from *The Yellow River Flows East* by Li Zhun. Excerpt published in Autumn 1984 edition of *Chinese Literature* quarterly. Copyright © 1984 by Chinese Literature Press, 24 Baiwanzhuang Road, Beijing 37, China. Reprinted by permission.

A Row of Shop-houses in Our Village from *Blood and Tears* by Keris Mas, translated by Harry Aveling, copyright © 1984 by Oxford University Press, Singapore. Reprinted by permission of the publisher.

The Rainy Spell (Part 3) by Yun Heung-gil, from *The Rainy Spell and other Korean Stories*, translated by Suh Ji-moon, published 1983 by Onyx Press Ltd., London. English translation copyright Readers International, Inc. 1989. Reprinted by permission.

The Soldier by Nugroho Notosusanto, from *From Surabaya to Armageddon*, edited and translated by Harry Aveling, published 1976 by Heinemann Educational Books (Asia) Ltd. Reprinted by permission of Octopus Publishing Asia Pte Ltd., Singapore.

The Sky's Escape by Yuan Ch'iung-ch'iung, from *Winter Plum*, edited by Nancy C. Ing, published 1982 by The Taipei Chinese Center. Reprinted by permission of THE CHINESE PEN, Quarterly of The Taipei Chinese Center, International P.E.N., Chief Editor: Nancy C. Ing.

Cranes by Hwang Sunwon, from *Flowers of Fire*, edited by Peter H. Lee, © 1974, 1986 by University of Hawaii Press, Honolulu. Reprinted by permission of the publisher.

Our Corner by Jin Shui, from *Contemporary Chinese Stories*, copyright 1983 by Panda Books. Reprinted by permission of Chinese Literature Press, 24 Baiwanzhuang Road, Beijing 37, China. Reprinted by permission.

Another Country from *Another Country and Other Stories* by Shirley Lim, published 1982 by Times Books International, Singapore. Reprinted by permission of the publisher.

Three Years of Carefree Happiness by Hou Chen, from *Winter Plum*, edited by Nancy C. Ing, published 1982 by The Taipei Chinese Center. Reprinted by permission of THE CHINESE PEN, Quarterly of The Taipei Chinese Center, International P.E.N., Chief Editor: Nancy C. Ing.

Spring Storm by Mori Yoko, from *The Mother of Dreams*, edited by Makoto Ueda, © 1986 by Kodansha International Ltd., Tokyo. Reprinted by permission of the publisher.

The Tiger by S. Rajaratnam, from *Singapore Short Stories: Volume 1*, edited by Robert Yeo, © 1978 by Heinemann Educational Books (Asia) Ltd. Reprinted by permission of Octopus Publishing Asia Pte Ltd., Singapore.

The Silent Traders by Tsushima Yuko, from *The Showa Anthology: Volume 2*, edited by Van C. Gessel and Tomone Matsumoto, copyright © 1985 by Kodansha International Ltd., Tokyo. Reprinted by permission of the publisher.

The Invader by Sachaporn Singhapalin, from *Taw & Other Thai Stories*, edited by Jennifer Draskau, published 1975 by Heinemann Educational Books (Asia) Ltd. Reprinted by permission of Octopus Publishing Asia Pte Ltd., Singapore.

Dark Glasses from *The Politician and Other Stories*, translated by Domnern Garden and edited by Michael Smithies, © 1973 by Oxford University Press, Singapore. Reprinted by permission of the publisher.

Wings by Peng Cao. Reprinted by permission from RENDITIONS, Nos. 27 & 28 (Spring and Autumn 1987), pp. 123–126. Hong Kong: The Research Centre for Translation, The Chinese University of Hong Kong.

PHOTOGRAPHS

pp. 10–11   Canapress Photo Service/Tim Graham
p. 37   Canapress Photo Service/Anabelle
pp. 46–47   Canapress Photo Service/Charles Seiler
pp. 94–95   Canapress Photo Service
pp. 160–161   Sandra Mark
pp. 214–215   Canapress Photo Service/Freddie Mansfield

ILLUSTRATIONS

pp. 12, 224   Nancy Lam
pp. 21, 66, 142, 158   Joe Morse
pp. 88, 200   Scott Cameron
p. 52   Sue Gauthier
pp. 57, 96   Lorraine Tuson
p. 78   Nicolas Vitacco
p. 113   Y. David Chung
pp. 128, 185   Harvey Chan
p. 171   Suzanna Denti
p. 216   Thom Sevalrud
p. 240   Chris Van Es
p. 248   Tracy Walker